KU-796-798

WIDOWS'
REVENGE

Read it
TD.

Withdrawn from stock

Dublin Public Libraries

Lynda La Plante was born in Liverpool. She trained for the stage at RADA and worked with the National Theatre and RDC before becoming a television actress. She then turned to writing – and made her breakthrough with the phenomenally successful TV series *Widows*. Her novels have all been international bestsellers.

Her original script for the much acclaimed *Prime Suspect* won awards from BAFTA, Emmy, British Broadcasting and Royal Television Society as well as the 1993 Edgar Allan Poe Award. Lynda has written and produced over 170 hours of international television.

Lynda is one of only three screenwriters to have been made an honorary fellow of the British Film Institute and was awarded the BAFTA Dennis Potter Best Writer Award in 2000. In 2008, she was awarded a CBE in the Queen's Birthday Honours List for services to Literature, Drama and Charity.

If you would like to hear from Lynda, please sign up to her readers' club at www.lyndalaplante.com for further information. You can also follow Lynda on Facebook and Twitter @LaPlanteLynda.

Lynda La Plante

WIDOWS' REVENGE

ZAFFRE

First published in Great Britain in 2019 by
ZAFFRE
80–81 Wimpole St, London W1G 9RE
www.zaffrebooks.co.uk

Copyright © La Plante Global Limited, 2019

Author photograph © Monte Farber

All rights reserved.
No part of this publication may be reproduced,
stored or transmitted in any form by any means, electronic,
mechanical, photocopying or otherwise, without the
prior written permission of the publisher.

The right of Lynda La Plante to be identified as Author of this
work has been asserted by her in accordance with the
Copyright, Designs and Patents Act, 1988.

This is a work of fiction. Names, places, events and
incidents are either the products of the author's
imagination or used fictitiously. Any resemblance to
actual persons, living or dead, or actual
events is purely coincidental.

A CIP catalogue record for this book is
available from the British Library.

Hardback ISBN: 978–1–78576–828–6
Trade paperback ISBN: 978–1–78576–829–3

Also available as an ebook

1 3 5 7 9 10 8 6 4 2

Typeset by IDSUK (Data Connection) Ltd
Printed and bound in Great Britain by Clays Ltd, Elcograf S.p.A.

Zaffre Publishing is an imprint of
Bonnier Books UK
www.bonnierzaffre.co.uk
www.bonnierbooks.co.uk

THE STORY SO FAR

Following a failed attempt to rob a security van, and a horrific explosion, three charred bodies are identified as Joe Pirelli, Terry Miller and Harry Rawlins.

Dolly Rawlins, Harry's widow, is left bereft. She had doted on her husband for twenty years. He was a revered and highly respected criminal, and his death leaves her unable to face life without him.

Then Dolly discovers her husband's carefully laid out plans for another security van robbery. She and the other widows, Shirley and Linda, have little in common, apart from their grief, but she convinces them to join her as they begin preparations to carry out the robbery that Harry had planned.

Initially, the other widows think Dolly is out of her mind. But the lure of money encourages them to believe they are ready to go through with the plan. Dolly realises they need a fourth person to make it work – a getaway driver.

Amongst Harry's plans, Dolly finds an address for Jimmy Nunn and decides to pay him a visit. At his run-down flat she meets Trudie Nunn, who has a young baby. Dolly had always longed to be able to have a child with Harry, but she tragically suffered a series of miscarriages. Trudie is young and nervous, and Dolly is shocked to learn that her husband, Harry, is still alive. Devastatingly, she also discovers that Harry is the father of Trudie's child.

This terrible betrayal fuels Dolly's determination to proceed with her plans. This is now revenge. Bella O'Reilly comes on board as the getaway driver and the four women succeed in carrying out the dangerous robbery.

After the heist Dolly hides the bulk of the money in a nursery school locker room, dividing it up into substantial amounts to enable each girl to escape to Rio. Dolly has outwitted Harry

Rawlins, who cannot believe that his faithful and loving wife has proved herself to be an equally, if not more, masterful criminal than himself.

Widows' Revenge begins with the women living the high life in Rio, all waiting for the right time to collect their money.

But they are fearful that the 'dead' man, Harry Rawlins, is going to come after them.

Brainse Bhaile Thormod
Ballyfermot Library   Tel. 6269324/5

CHAPTER ONE

Bella had recommended Mr Jarrow to Dolly as one of the best men in London, and so Dolly had made an appointment. She was slightly taken aback to find five other women in the reception area also waiting to see him – it was more of a conveyor belt than she had imagined. But she enjoyed taking furtive glances over the top of her glossy magazine and trying to work out what each woman was having done. In some instances it was obvious: a nose needed shortening by a couple of centimetres; eye bags could be removed. But she did wonder what the two women sitting in the corner were in for. Why bother with a nose job if your face was completely hidden behind a black *niqab*? At least their husbands would see their faces when they took them off, she mused.

Husband. Every time Dolly thought of the word she felt a strange tightening in the pit of her stomach. It had been a long time since she had referred to her 'husband' . . .

'Mrs Rawlins?'

Dolly was jolted from her thoughts. The receptionist, who spoke with a slight French accent, had a face that had obviously never needed any kind of cosmetic surgery.

'Mr Jarrow will see you now.'

The consulting room itself was as immaculate as the waiting room, from the pale green carpet and the imposing desk to the perfectly placed antique carver chair for the patients. Mr Jarrow himself was very good looking, but he seemed a little too neat; perhaps he'd had a job done on his own face? He was very quiet, his voice soothing.

'I'd like a facelift,' Dolly said simply.

'I see,' he said. 'A complete facelift, Mrs Rawlins?'

Dolly nodded.

Leabharlanna Poiblí Chathair Baile Átha Cliath
Dublin City Public Libraries

He got up from his desk and came over to her. He held her head as he inspected her eyes and her neck, and his hands when he touched her face felt cool.

'With this form of surgery,' he explained in his soothing voice, 'the stitches will be placed behind the ears; your hairline will remain just as it is now. We will stitch here –' he indicated where the stitches for the eye socket would be – 'and here.' She felt his feather-light touch below her right eye.

He took a seat back behind his desk and began to sift through her file, looking at the photographs she had had taken earlier that day – front, side-view right, side-view left – looking at Dolly, then back to the photographs.

Finally, he closed the file. 'You were widowed six months ago?'

Dolly nodded. She had already supplied this information.

'And you have no relatives, no family?'

Dolly shook her head. Again she had told him this already.

Mr Jarrow tapped the desk with a very fine, thin, gold pencil. 'You do understand . . .' He paused. 'You do understand that no surgery can permanently prevent ageing?'

Dolly nodded. This too had been gone over before. 'But you can make me look younger, isn't that right, Mr Jarrow?'

He looked up and gave her a sweet, direct smile. 'You were married for twenty-five years?'

Dolly said, 'Yes.'

'The loss must have been . . . very great.'

'Yes,' said Dolly. 'It was.'

He gave a slight cough and opened her file again. 'Did you love your husband, Mrs Rawlins?' He flicked through the pages.

He'd taken her completely off guard.

'Why do you ask me that?' she said. And then, very quietly, rather shakily, she added, 'I loved him.' She barely recognised her own voice.

Mr Jarrow looked up and slightly tilted his head. 'I'm sorry?'

'I loved him.'

He nodded. His pale blue eyes seemed to stare right through her. 'Then his death must have been a very great loss to you.'

Dolly could feel her breath leaving her body. 'Yes,' she said. 'Yes, yes, it was. It was a very great loss to me.'

* * *

Harry Rawlins stepped out from the terminal into the sunlight of Rio. The glare of the sun bounced off his mirror-tinted glasses and he could feel the sweat trickling down the back of his neck and into his crumpled linen suit. He shifted his small holdall from one hand to the other and looked up and down the lines of parked cars.

* * *

Jimmy Glazier had a strange lump in the pit of his stomach. There he was, Harry Rawlins, back from the dead. Jimmy's pudgy, sweat-glistening face beamed, he waved, and he saw Rawlins stare towards him. Jimmy scuttled between the parked cars and reached Harry. He felt so childish, with all the emotion swelling inside him, and all he got out was, 'Good to see you, Harry. Welcome to Rio.'

Jimmy had always admired Harry Rawlins. He'd been one of the big ones, one of the good men, and even though he'd only worked for Rawlins once, he'd gone to him twice for help, and Rawlins had never turned him down. When Jimmy received the cable, he felt it was his chance to repay him. As they moved towards Jimmy's car – a beat-up old Buick, which he'd bought when he first came to Rio – Rawlins was strangely silent. First he moved round to the wrong side of the car and Jimmy had to say jovially, 'Ah, no, Harry, it's this way round,' before nervously opening the passenger door for him. Then he clumsily took Rawlins' holdall – fumbling as if

Rawlins was some sort of royal guest – and asked if there was any more luggage.

Rawlins shook his head. 'No, just the one bag, Jimmy.'

Jimmy placed it carefully in the boot, before jumping into the driving seat. Inside the car was boiling, and Rawlins immediately lowered the window, with Jimmy doing likewise, before leaning his arm along the back of the seat and looking at Harry.

'When I heard the news, I just couldn't believe it,' he said, shaking his head. 'You lost a good team, good men, Harry. Christ, I thought you'd gone down with them!'

Rawlins cut him off sharply. 'Can we get out of here, Jimmy? I'm sweating like a pig.'

The air-conditioning didn't work, and as the car eased into the traffic, the wind blowing through the open windows did little to cool them down. Jimmy couldn't read Rawlins' expression behind his mirrored sunglasses, but despite the boiling hot sun, he was happy. He had the big man, Mr Rawlins, in his car, coming to stay at his place, in Rio.

They drove down the hill from São Paolo and headed towards the centre of town, passing several elegant-looking villas, with shady patios and their own pools, half-hidden behind heavy fencing, palm trees and shrubberies. Jimmy pulled up by a pale pink villa with solid-looking wrought-iron gates, to let a mangy-looking dog cross the road, before moving on.

* * *

The driveway to the pink villa was lined with lush-looking palm trees. It went sweeping past a garage and round to the side of the house, where five sunloungers with umbrellas were arranged round the pool. The faint sound of the Tijuana Brass could be heard coming from a small transistor by one of the sunloungers, where a woman was stretched out, covered with suntan oil.

Linda Pirelli.

She picked up the radio and turned the dial to find a different station, but all she could get was a garble of voices in a language she didn't understand. She turned back the dial until she found the Tijuana Brass again, then hurled it into the pool, where it gurgled for a moment before sinking to the bottom.

Up on the balcony above the pool, Shirley yelled, 'Linda! Come up 'ere for a minute, will you? I saw that!' before stalking back into the bedroom. The twin beds were covered with neatly folded piles of clothes, ready to be placed into open suitcases. Shirley was all made up, hair done to perfection, and wearing a silk shirt, knickers, suspenders and stockings, and very high-heeled shoes. Carefully and methodically, she started filling the cases.

Linda stormed into the bedroom. 'Whaddya want?' She looked through the drawers. 'Oi, you bin going through my things!'

'I have not been going through your things,' Shirley retorted. 'I just want that blue shirt back that you borrowed yesterday. Where've you put it?'

Linda stomped over to the chest of drawers, rifled through a tangled mess of clothes and dragged out a crumpled shirt. ''Ere yer go.'

Shirley looked at it in disgust. 'Never mind, you can keep it!'

Linda flopped down on the bed and sullenly watched Shirley go back to packing her beautifully folded, crisp new clothes.

'Yer got enough bleedin' suitcases?' She snorted.

'Yes, they're nice, aren't they?' Shirley replied with a smile. 'They're all mock croc leather, you know.'

Linda picked one up. 'Well, they weigh a ton before yer even put a bleedin' Kleenex in. 'Ow much did they cost?'

Shirley squinted at her watch, the digits seeming to blur. She should have got the other one, the Cartier. 'Bella's going to miss me. I've got to go.'

'Well, 'ow yer gonna get to the airport?'

Shirley went back to her packing. 'I've got a taxi coming. But Bella said she'd be here to see me off.'

'Yeah, she also said she'd teach me to swim!' Linda threw herself back on the bed.

'Linda, move off!' Shirley chided. 'Go and sit over there!'

Scowling, Linda moved to a chair and stuck her feet up on the edge of the dressing table.

Shirley turned. 'By the way, that cistern overflowed again. When you gonna move that money? Bella's bought diamonds; why don't you buy diamonds? I mean, I got my money changed into dollars. What did Dolly say? Change that money as soon as possible. That money's traceable, Linda!'

Linda frowned. 'I'll do it tomorrow.' She then started unscrewing pots of cream from Shirley's already neatly packed vanity bag. She dabbed her finger in and began rubbing lotion into her face.

Shirley watched her disapprovingly. 'You don't put dollops of that on your face, Linda. That's Queen Bee jelly with vitamin E. You've only got to use a drop.'

Linda moved away from the dressing table. 'Sorry, sorry, sorry. Queen Bee jelly! Christ, Shirley, if they put gnat piss in a bottle you'd buy it if they said it was good for your face!'

Shirley squinted at her watch again. 'Wonder where Bella is?'

'Yeah, I've been waitin' by that pool for her all mornin'.'

Shirley looked at her. 'You're burning, you know. Look at your skin. It's awfully bad for it, Linda. I've told you, you shouldn't sit in the sun, you'll get cancer.'

'Bollocks.' Linda sat down on the bed. She watched Shirley finishing packing for a moment, then asked, rather plaintively, 'Why can't I come wiv yer, Shirl?'

Shirley turned. They'd been over this before. 'You are not coming with me and that is final. Dolly said separate, and that's what we're gonna do!'

Linda mimicked her. '*Dolly said sep-a-rate!* Dolly also said no taxis to the villa. Well, you've just blown that, 'aven't you? She said no taxis and no cars. Bella's bin in and out of 'ere like a dingbat in that Rolls-Royce . . .'

Right on cue they heard the crunch of gravel on the drive. Linda rushed to the balcony.

''Ere she comes. Gawd, what does she think she's come as – Shirley Bassey? Look at 'er!'

Linda watched as Bella stepped out of the white Rolls-Royce. She looked stunning. It was a strange thing with Bella – she might have been a tart, she might have come from the streets, but God she had taste. She knew what she wanted, and she always wanted – and got – the best.

Linda yelled down, 'Dolly said no taxis and no cars to the bleedin' villa! Well, you've come fucking incognito, I must say!'

Shirley had packed her suitcases and was now inspecting a jacket. 'You sat on this, Linda. Look at it, you've crumpled it.' She stepped into her skirt and zipped it up.

'I'll take a couple of yer cases down for yer.' Linda walked unsteadily down the stairs, staggering under the weight of two suitcases, and dumped them in front of the Rolls.

Bella looked at them quizzically. 'Hey,' she said, 'unbelievable! We've got the same suitcases – just different colours.'

Linda stomped back into the house, paying no attention, as Shirley appeared with suitcase number three. 'What's the matter with her?' Bella asked.

Shirley shrugged. 'I don't know, she's like a bear with a sore behind, sometimes.'

Bella jerked her head towards the chauffeur. 'It's all right, he doesn't understand English.'

Shirley nodded. 'Oh, well, thanks for coming.'

Bella handed her a small packet. 'This is for you, kiddo. You take care of yourself!'

Shirley unwrapped the tiny locket decorated with an 'S' in diamonds; very tasteful and no doubt very expensive.

'Thanks, Bella, it's lovely.' She beamed.

Bella grinned. 'Well, kiddo, you have a good time in LA. If you do everything I'm doing, you will!'

Shirley gripped her hand. 'I hope it works out for you, Bella. He's a super guy.'

Bella nodded. 'Yes, he is, Shirley. He's everything I've ever wanted. I've never been so happy in my whole life.'

Shirley's jacket suddenly flew down from the balcony and landed on the roof of the Roller.

Shirley whipped round. 'There was no need to do that, Linda!' She turned to Bella. 'She hasn't changed her money yet, you know! It's still in the cistern; made me soak my skirt.'

Bella shook her head, smiling. 'I'll have a word with her later.'

Linda appeared with suitcase number four. 'That's it!'

Shirley looked at Bella. 'Just waiting for the cab, then I'm off.'

At that moment the taxi appeared through the wrought-iron gates and came to a halt with a spray of gravel.

Linda was already shouting at the top of her voice: 'Four suitcases, amigo, to the airport, pronto!'

Shirley turned to her. 'There's no need to shout, Linda.'

The driver got out of the cab and started piling the suitcases into the boot. At the same time the chauffeur got out of the Roller and opened the rear passenger door for Bella.

She turned to Shirley with a grin before getting in. 'This is the life, eh, kiddo? This is the life.' The chauffeur shut the door, and the electric windows slowly glided down. 'Look after yourself, hon. See you back in London.'

The chauffeur slowly turned the Roller round and drove off, as Bella gave a last wave to Linda, which she pointedly ignored.

Shirley started checking that all the suitcases had been packed into the taxi, then suddenly remembered and shouted after the Roller as it disappeared through the gates, 'Thanks for the present!'

Linda gave her a bemused look. 'What present?'

'Oh, Bella gave me ever such a nice little thing. A farewell gift.'

Linda looked miffed: one, because she hadn't thought of it her-self, and two, because nobody ever told her anything. She started to get into the taxi but Shirley put a hand on her arm. 'Oh, come on, Linda, there's no need for you to come with me.'

Linda turned. 'I'm just comin' as far as the airport, OK? Come on, get in.' She flicked the driver on the back of the neck as Shirley settled in next to her. 'OK, amigo, move it, pronto!'

Both girls slammed into the back of the seat as the taxi whipped round in a U-turn and sped down the drive.

* * *

Harry Rawlins looked round Jimmy Glazier's small, untidy flat. It was crazy – it was as if they'd moved a tower block from Padding-ton smack into the centre of Rio. The building was certainly just as noisy, as the sound of stereos and transistors blaring, couples arguing and screaming kids drifted up from outside and through the shut-ters. The kitchen was separated from the dining room by stripped plastic curtains, from behind which he could see a woman furtively watching them.

'Maria!' Jimmy yelled. 'Come out and meet my friend!'

Maria stepped through the curtains. She was heavily pregnant and there was something very sensual about her, with her long, dark hair in one big braid down her back. She nodded to Harry, looked at Jimmy, then turned and went back into the kitchen.

Jimmy was sweating freely, and Rawlins could smell the reek of it filling the little room.

'Hey, don't pay any attention to her,' he said, popping open two cans of beer. 'She's a bit broody. She's expecting another kid. It's this heat. With no air-conditioning in here, it boils you up, yer know what I mean? Boils you up, Harry. Siddown!'

Harry pulled out one of the kitchen chairs and sat. 'What time do the banks open, Jimmy?'

Jimmy looked at his watch. 'It's siesta now, so give it about an hour. The bank's in the square.'

He pulled his chair closer and Harry was overpowered by the sickly sweet smell of Jimmy's body odour.

'Harry . . . I've got a little number lined up in England. It's a doddle, honest!'

Harry couldn't help but smile. How many times had Jimmy Glazier been put away because of his sure-fire doddles?

He patted him on the shoulder. 'Look, Jimmy, I'm over here to collect cash, and that's it. I'm out of the business now, OK?'

Jimmy nodded. 'Anything you say, Harry.' He guzzled down his beer and flipped open another one.

Harry stood up. 'I'm a bit whacked, Jimmy. Mind if I put my head down?'

Jimmy was on his feet. 'Anything you say, Harry. All you gotta do is ask. My place is your place, you know what I mean? You been good to me, Harry. This is my chance to repay you.' He continued to prattle on as he led Harry towards an even smaller room off the lounge. This was a child's bedroom, with a tiny cot bed and toys littering the floor. The shutters were closed, but the air was still hot. Jimmy kicked the toys out of the way and pulled back the grimy sheets.

''Ere you go, 'Arry. I'll give you a shout in a couple of hours, OK?'

Harry nodded. 'Thanks, Jimmy.'

Jimmy hovered by the door for a few moments, still beaming, before going back to the lounge. After a moment, Harry heard the sound of yet another beer can being ripped open, and the low murmuring of Jimmy and Maria, speaking in Portuguese. Obviously Maria didn't want Harry to stay, but by now he was too tired to even think about it. He lay on the bed, the clammy heat stifling him, and then he fell asleep.

* * *

Dolly looked at the sheet of instructions Mr Jarrow's over-polite Frenchified assistant had just handed her. She was supposed to bring night clothes and dark glasses. The operation was to be in two weeks, the only time Mr Jarrow had available. He was obviously a very, very busy man.

Dolly looked up at the assistant. 'Are the glasses compulsory?'

'No, Mrs Rawlins, just a suggestion. If you could be here at 3:30 on the day of the operation just to have a final check, we'll take you over to the clinic.'

Dolly smiled. She felt as if she was actually bursting with happiness, like a child who's just been told she's won a prize. She picked up her handbag, gave the assistant a brief nod, and walked out into the street. The sun was shining and she felt good; things were going just as she'd planned.

She walked across to the meter – it was always a good sign when you got a meter immediately, particularly in Harley Street – and got into her hired green Ford Fiesta.

Now, she thought, for stage two.

She'd found his name in the Yellow Pages. She soon discovered that most private detectives were connected to one large firm, so she'd kept on ringing numbers until she found one who seemed to work on his own. That was the kind of man she wanted. His name was Victor Morgan – Victor Morgan of the Victor Morgan Private Investigation Bureau.

* * *

Victor Morgan had had his offices in Kensington for about four years, in a sprawling old building off the Cromwell Road. That afternoon he was studying his newest acquisition, a word processor that had set him back five and a half grand. But he thought it was going to be worth it. In a few months he would have a filing system of floppy disks that would fit into one drawer. Yes, things were looking up.

He was busily checking over the computer's manual when he heard footsteps outside the door. He looked at his watch – Mrs Marsh was smack on time.

The door handle rattled and he yelled out, 'Push . . . push, Mrs Marsh!'

Dolly, from outside, turned the handle one more time, gave it an almighty shove and hurtled into the office.

'You OK?'

'Yes, I'm fine,' she said, patting herself down. 'Something wrong with your door?'

He smiled. 'Gotta get it fixed one day. It's a tricky lock, but it's all right when you get the hang of it. Do sit down.'

He shut the door behind her, and Dolly took stock of the man she'd chosen. He was big, well over six foot, and stocky with it. Not particularly good-looking, but there was a kind of warmth to him that didn't fit with the conventional image of a private investigator.

His bulk filled the chair as he sat back down at his desk and leant forward. 'Well, Mrs Marsh, what can I do for you?'

Dolly placed her handbag on the desk. 'I would like you to watch . . . er . . .' She broke off.

Here we go again, thought Victor: the hesitant wives too embarrassed to admit they wanted you to follow their husbands.

Dolly coughed. 'I'm here on behalf of my sister, actually.'

Why they had to lie, Victor never knew. He looked her in the eye. 'Your sister?'

'Yes. My sister believes her husband is having an affair with another woman, and we would like you to watch her house and find out a little about her. Do you do that kind of thing?'

He nodded. He did do that kind of thing. He didn't like it, but the truth of it was that it was his bread and butter.

'Yes,' he said. 'You'd like me to keep a woman under surveillance?'

'Yes, exactly.'

He got out a sheet of paper and began to make notes, in what seemed to Dolly a very professional manner.

'Right. Her name?'

Dolly hesitated for another moment. 'Trudie. Trudie Nunn.'

'OK.' He nodded. 'And the address?'

Dolly gave him Trudie Nunn's address in Islington.

'And how long would you like the surveillance on Mrs Nunn?'

Again Dolly hesitated. She'd had it all worked out in her mind before she came in but suddenly she was all of a dither.

'Well . . . we . . . my sister and I would like to know . . . what kind of work she's doing, and if . . . my sister's husband is visiting her and who she sees . . .'

'Absolutely,' he said. 'That's all part of the job. But how long do you want me to watch –' he looked at the page – 'Mrs Nunn? Or Miss Nunn?'

'Mrs Nunn. Mrs Trudie Nunn.'

'Right.'

Dolly thought for a moment. 'Well, how much do you charge, Mr Morgan?'

He leant back in his chair. 'Twelve-fifty per hour, plus expenses. Usually I don't do round the clock – I work from seven in the morning to seven at night, but if you want the night shift I can go from seven at night through to two in the morning.' He smiled. 'In my experience, if there is any hanky-panky going on, it will have happened before then, if it's going to happen at all.'

Dolly was not amused. 'I see. Well, I'd like you to do three or four days to begin with, and see how we go from there.'

'OK, four days of seven to seven, or on the seven to—'

'Day and night,' insisted Dolly. She'd already opened her bag and taken out her wallet.

Ah. He rubbed his hands. Now's my chance, he thought. He shifted his chair round towards his new toy and began tapping out numbers. Instantly a flashing sign appeared, saying: 'BOOT ERROR – BOOT ERROR – BOOT ERROR.'

Dolly looked up from her calculations. 'I'll pay you in advance for two days, is that all right? I make that £475.' She counted out the money and put it on his desk.

Morgan's computer was now flashing: '£35.02'. He shook his head sadly.

'I've not quite got the hang of this yet . . . But that's fine.' He tried to switch off the machine. 'Er . . . another thing, Mrs Marsh. Do you have a photograph of your sister's husband, or any particulars? His name, for a start.'

Dolly was taken aback. 'Yes, his name is John, er, *Jonathan* . . . Jarrow . . . J-A-R-R-O-W.' She spelt it out, then described Harry Rawlins while Morgan nodded, taking careful notes.

'Right you are. So you want me to watch this Trudie Nunn, and if this Mr Jarrow turns up you want me to make a note of it – how long he stays, et cetera. Is that it?'

Dolly nodded. 'Yes, yes, that's precisely it.' Despite the shenanigans with the computer, she reckoned Mr Morgan wasn't as dumb as he looked. She made a mental note not to make any slips in front of him.

Business done, she stood up. 'Is there anything else you want to know?'

'Well, I'd like to know where I can contact you.'

Dolly opened her bag, searching through her wallet for the card she'd picked up at the hotel desk that morning. Morgan went back to tapping out something on his word processor.

'You'll find me here, should you need me.'

Still tapping, he flicked a look at the card she'd placed on his desk and said, 'I don't know that one.'

'It's very quiet, just by Queen's Gate.'

'And that's where you'll be, Mrs Marsh?'

'Yes, you can contact me there . . . but I'll call in.'

He smiled. 'I'm sure you will, Mrs Marsh.'

He stood up and they shook hands. His grip was firm.

As he walked Dolly towards the door, Helen, the group secretary for a number of offices, entered with her arms full of papers. 'Oh, I'm terribly sorry, I didn't know you had—'

'That's all right,' said Dolly, 'I'm just leaving.'

As Dolly closed the door delicately behind her, Helen gave Morgan an enquiring look. 'Something juicy?'

'Not really.' Morgan crossed back to his desk. 'Oh my God,' he said, 'now what's happening?' The machine seemed to have taken on a life of its own, the printer churning out sheets and sheets of paper.

Helen rushed up behind him. 'You've got it on repeat!'

'God damn it, I set it to receipt! I wanted a receipt!'

Helen turned the machine off and looked at the receipt. 'Ooh,' she said, 'cash. That's unusual for you!'

He smiled. 'Yes. Look, there's some letters for you to do, and whatever you put in the machine yesterday, I'm afraid you're going to have to put back in today. I wiped it!'

She shook her head. He was reaching for his old camel hair coat, the one he always wore, whatever the time of year.

'OK,' she said. 'You know you're going to have to employ me full-time now you've got that machine.'

He turned with a grin. 'My darling girl, this is the age of technology. When I get that machine going I won't even need an office!'

'Chance would be a fine thing,' she retorted.

He went to open the door, giving it its usual tug, followed by its usual pull – but it remained firmly stuck.

'Forget about your fancy computer – why don't you get that door fixed?' Helen said.

He gave it one more tug and the door swung open. 'Just a matter of technique!' he said with a wink and breezed out.

Helen sighed. She'd been in love with Victor Morgan for almost two years, but he'd remained totally oblivious, showing no sign that he thought of her as anything more than just another piece of office equipment.

In fact, he didn't seem to care very much about anything – with the possible exception of his old car. Whatever the ups and downs of the business, he didn't seem to worry about money, and she wondered if he had private income from somewhere. She knew he'd been in the police for twenty years before retiring to open his own investigation bureau – mostly dealing with petty debt collecting, marriage troubles, divorce settlements, writs, warrants and, of course, the odd industrial espionage job, which paid a bit more. But there was an awful lot about Morgan that she didn't know, like the story of the boy in the photograph that was always tucked behind his bookcase. Good-looking boy; the image of his father. Once she'd asked about him, asked his name. Morgan had just shrugged. 'It doesn't really matter what his name is, Helen. He's been gone a long time.'

'Gone where? Abroad somewhere?' she'd asked.

'No, he was a heroin addict,' he'd replied. And that was all he'd ever said.

There had been a wife, she knew that much, and maybe a divorce. But Helen would have had to be a very good private investigator to find out anything more about Morgan's personal life.

As for her chances, she'd given up thinking anything would ever come of it. She'd once screwed up her courage to ask him to her place for dinner. He'd said yes, briefly kindling her hopes, and it had been a very pleasant evening. But that was as far as he'd ever let it go.

Helen sighed, then began to read the manual for his new word processor. If he was never going to get the hang of it, maybe she'd better.

* * *

Shirley squinted at her watch as the taxi pulled up at the airport. 'You know something, I can't tell the time on this. I wish to God I'd got the other watch. What do you think, Linda, d'you like it?'

Linda looked and said, 'Well, if you can't tell the bloody time by it, what's the point?'

Shirley looked at it again. 'Oh my God, I've got it on upside down. No wonder I couldn't tell the time!'

She reached to open the door, but Linda grabbed hold of her. 'You know I won't forgive you for not telling me. I think it's absolutely disgusting.'

'Linda, we've been over this all the way to the airport,' Shirley sighed. 'Bella and I didn't tell you because we knew you'd react like this.'

'Oh, so Bella knows, does she? Well, that's marvellous, that's bloody marvellous. Both of you know and you don't tell me!'

'We didn't tell you, Linda, because we knew this is what would happen. Dolly went back to England because she—'

'She wanted a face job, yes,' Linda interrupted. 'I hear you, I hear you, you told me that four times already. But do you really believe it?'

Shirley looked at her. 'Why shouldn't I believe it? She was going to go to Geneva, I know she was going to go to Geneva, but Bella suggested she go to London because there's this amazing guy there – all Bella's mates have been to him.'

'What, all the prostitutes? Come off it. Do you really think Dolly was going for a facelift? God almighty, you two are so stupid!'

Shirley was starting to get angry. 'Why are we stupid, Linda?'

'You never thought who else was in London, did you? Harry Rawlins, that's who. Dolly's husband. And that's where our money is, too.'

Shirley was getting to the end of her tether. 'What are you insinuating?' she demanded.

'I'm not insinuating anything, Shirley, love. I'm just saying, don't you think it's odd? Dolly Rawlins is in London, Harry Rawlins is in London, and our bloody money is in London!'

Shirley pushed the car door open. 'Well, as far as I'm concerned, that's just fine. Dolly'll keep an eye on it for us, and if you think that she's going to be doing anything else then you're mistaken, Linda!'

Linda followed Shirley out of the car and started shouting to the driver about getting a porter.

Shirley was rummaging in her bag for her passport and ticket. She whipped round and said, 'Linda, will you leave it out! I'm trying to find my—'

'You've got everything! You checked it four times in the bleedin' taxi!'

Shirley finally had them in her hands. 'Oh, yes. Right, Linda, I'm going now.'

'I'll come into the airport wiv yer.'

Shirley was still annoyed by Linda's suspicions about Dolly. 'It's not necessary, Linda.'

'Oh yes it is. Can't put a bleedin' sandwich down in this place without somebody nicking it. Come on, get a move on. You don't want them posh suitcases nicked, do yer?' Linda insisted, pushing Shirley into the airport.

* * *

Arriving back at the villa, Bella called out for Linda and decided she must still be at the airport. She went into her own room and lifted out the suitcases from their big paper packages. Identical to Shirley's, she had felt that the mulberry was a little more subtle than bright orange. Opening the wardrobe, she couldn't help but stand back in admiration. Each garment was so special, so beautifully made, such gorgeous material. She took out her Norma Kamali, with the shoulder pads, and held it against her. Worth every penny of the $280 she'd paid for it.

Bella folded the dress with exaggerated care, then took out a long, flowing, pure-silk gown. This hadn't cost $280 – more like $2523 – but then José had bought it for her. She'd modelled it for him, walking up and down as if she was on a catwalk, and he'd simply said, 'If you like it, darling, then you have it.' She got a warm feeling inside when she thought about it. It was funny, all the men she'd screwed, every single one, she couldn't remember a single face – but as soon as she saw José for the first time, she knew she wouldn't be able to forget him. She'd been shopping, walking along the main thoroughfare, and she noticed him walking towards her. He was with another woman, talking and laughing, and she'd been so busy staring at him she'd almost walked straight into him. He turned aside for her to pass, and then strolled on. She'd tried to distract herself with more shopping, but when she emerged from a shop an hour later, her arms full of clothes, there he was again. This time, alone. And this time Bella gave him her most seductive smile and said, 'Hello.' They started chatting, he offered her a lift, and she'd been with him ever since. José Camarana turned out to be older than the men she usually went for (he was in his late forties) but he was so sexy, and such a gentleman. In fact, he was everything she'd ever looked for in a man, and on top of it all, she reckoned he must be a multimillionaire.

Bella was still mooning over herself in the mirror when she heard the front door slam, and there was Linda, hands on hips, and a voice like thunder. 'Thank you very much!'

Bella turned. 'What?'

'Why didn't you tell me, you fuckers! Neither of you told me!'

'Told you what, Linda?'

'Dolly. Dolly's not gone to Geneva. She told me a bleedin' lie! Told me to my face, said she was gonna go to Geneva! She's only back in London!'

Bella continued to fold her clothes. 'So what?'

'Didn't you think?' Linda shouted. 'Dolly's in London, our money's in London, and Harry's in London.'

'Yeah, we thought about it. So what?'

Linda slumped down on the bed. 'I don't fucking believe it! Dolly Rawlins, Harry Rawlins, and our money!'

Bella stopped what she was doing. 'Don't be so damned stupid, Linda. Dolly's not going back to Harry. And she'd protect our money with her life!'

'Oh yeah? Well, we'll see, won't we?' Linda scowled. 'We'll just see about that!' She clocked the suitcases. 'What are you doin'?'

'Well, what does it look like – playing table tennis? I'm packing, aren't I?'

'Where you goin'? You goin' away?'

'Well, you could say that.'

'Where're you goin'? You never told me!'

'Linda, I don't have to tell you everything. But you know what we agreed – we would separate, all of us, and change our money. And your bloody money is still in the cistern!'

'I'm doin' it tomorrow, aren't I?' Linda pouted.

Bella shook her head. 'Everything's tomorrow with you, Linda. You better get off your arse and start moving!'

'I am moving, I am doing things . . . Hold on, what's that?'

Bella turned with a big grin and held out her left hand. 'Ta da!'

Linda's eyes went wide. 'Is that a bleedin' diamond ring?'

'Yeah, it's a diamond, Linda. But look where it is. Look what finger it's on.'

Linda's jaw dropped as it sank in. 'Yer goin' wiv 'im? Yer movin' in wiv 'im?'

Bella turned and grinned. 'Oh, baby, am I movin' in! Once I get a foot over that threshold, you'll have to get a crowbar to get me out!' She sat on the bed. 'Oh, Linda, what a place! He's got this ranch, with orchards, swimming pools . . . The size of it! He's got stables and—'

'Well, we've got a swimmin' pool 'ere,' Linda interrupted.

'Linda, he wants me to live with him.'

'Oh, so you're not gonna marry 'im?'

'Look, I don't know, maybe I'll marry him, Linda. But the point is, I love him.' Bella turned back to admiring herself in the mirror.

'Do me a favour!' Linda snorted. ''Ow d'yer think 'e's gonna react when 'e knows?'

Bella glanced at Linda in the mirror. 'What do you mean? Knows what?'

'You know what I mean – when 'e knows!'

Bella turned. 'You don't think I'm gonna tell him about the raid, do you?'

Linda rolled her eyes. 'I don't mean the raid, Bella. How d'yer think 'e's goin' ter feel when 'e finds out about you?'

'Well, who's gonna tell him about me, Linda?'

'Well . . . nobody . . . but I'm just sayin', what 'appens if 'e finds out somehow? He's in politics or somethin' over here, isn't 'e? I mean, you don't know anythin' about him. 'E's old!'

'Don't try changing the subject, Linda. Who's gonna tell him about me? Eh? If you open your mouth—'

'Look, don't be stupid, I wouldn't say anythin' . . .'

'You better not, Linda. This means everything to me, and I'm not gonna let it go, you understand me? He's the best thing that's ever happened in my life, and if you try and fuck it up, by Christ I'll smash your—'

'Try it!' Linda jumped up from the bed. 'What d'yer bleedin' think I am, Bella?'

'I don't know, Linda. All I do know is you've done nothing but moan since you got here and your money's still stuck in the toilet. This is your chance too, Linda. Why don't you get yourself together and do something like the rest of us?'

'I'm goin' to, I'm goin' to, all right? Just leave me alone. Everybody's pickin' on me!' Linda marched into the bathroom and slammed the door.

Bella snapped shut the cases with a sigh, then carried them over to the door. How did Linda always manage to turn it round like this? Now Bella was feeling bad. She went and stood in front of the bathroom door.

'Linda, you comin' out of there?'

'No!' came the sullen reply from inside.

'Look, Linda, we're going to the Coconut Grove tonight, you hear me?'

Silence.

'Linda, d'you wanna come out with us tonight – dinner, cabaret? It's a dress-up do.'

A childish little voice said, 'What time?'

'Ten o'clock. We'll pick you up. And Linda, lay off the booze, all right? Don't start drinking before we get there.' Bella picked up her suitcases and walked out.

Linda sat on the loo, wanting to cry. Why couldn't she get herself together? What was the matter with her? Everyone else seemed to know what they wanted, and how to get it. But she wasn't like the others. She had never had much interest in clothes and jewellery and all that. She had never had much interest in anything, really. Suddenly she felt all alone, as alone as she'd felt when she was four years old in a convent, and she'd asked one of the nuns, 'Is my mummy coming back?' And the nun had just looked down and said, 'No, Linda, Mummy's not coming back, but we're here, and we love you.' She'd patted Linda's head gently, but Linda knew it wasn't love. There'd been no arms round her, no hugs, no real affection, and every visiting hour she'd waited, and every visiting day she'd ask, 'Is my mummy coming to see me?' But her mummy never came.

And then there was Joe. She'd been in the arcade when Charlie limped over and said, 'Linda, come into the back for a minute.'

At first she'd laughed at him. 'I'm not goin' down the back wiv you, Charlie. What you want, a bit of a touch-up?'

He shook his head. 'Come on, Linda, don't mess about. Come into the back room.'

She knew then something was wrong. He'd taken her into the back room and shut the door, before reaching into his hip pocket and pulling out a new bottle of brandy. He was unscrewing the top. That's when she knew something terrible had happened.

'What is it, Charlie?'

He'd handed her the bottle. 'Have a drink, darlin'.'

'It's Joe!'

'I'm afraid they want you down the police station,' he said.

'Has there been an accident? What's 'appened, Charlie?' Already she was beginning to feel numb.

'He's dead, Linda. Joe's dead.'

And even then it still didn't feel real. She'd been to the morgue, she'd identified the terrible, charred remains of Joe. And then she'd gone home and she'd been just like that little girl in the convent, sitting, waiting and asking, 'Is Joe coming home?' And her own voice had answered her, saying, 'No, Linda, Joe's not coming home. He's never coming home ever again.'

And then Dolly had come along, taking charge of her life, bossing her round and telling her what to do. But even though she'd fought her corner and argued with her, she'd had a good time when she'd been with Dolly and the girls. She'd felt as though things were happening in her life. She had to admit it, she'd never known such excitement, such a buzz.

And now they'd all gone!

Bella didn't see the sad little face at the window, watching her as the Rolls-Royce slowly glided down the driveway and away from the villa. Nobody saw it, and nobody heard the sobbing from the girl sitting by herself in the bathroom – the girl who in some ways had everything going for her. Now she had money, she just had to decide what to do with her life. But the cash meant nothing to Linda, and the rest of her life stretched ahead like a long, empty road.

With the girls gone, she felt more alone than she'd ever felt in the whole of her life.

* * *

Jimmy opened the bedroom door and edged over to the bed, where Harry was still fast asleep. He nudged the bed with his knee. 'Oi, Harry! Harry, wake up!' Jimmy leant closer. 'Banks are open, if you wan' em. You've had a couple of hours.'

Harry opened his eyes and squinted against the sunlight coming through the shutters. 'What time is it?'

'Almost five.'

'All right. Thanks, Jimmy.'

'D'ye wanna drink?'

Harry shook his head, and Jimmy edged out of the room. 'If you want somethin' to eat I can get it on now.'

'No, no thanks, I'll just go to the bank.'

The door shut and Harry started to scratch his arm where the mosquitoes had bitten him. Christ, what a shithole! He sat up on the edge of the bed.

'Jimmy!'

He was there in a second, almost as if he'd been waiting outside the door. 'Yeah, Harry?'

'Could that . . . your woman . . . do something with my suit?'

'Sure, Harry!' Jimmy scuffled round and picked up the crumpled jacket and trousers. 'You got a clean shirt?'

Harry nodded, unzipping his holdall. 'Soon's you can, Jimmy. I wanna get this over and done with.'

'Right you are, Harry.' And he was gone again.

Harry took out a clean white T-shirt, crossed over to the small dressing table and looked at himself, pinching his waist. He'd put on a little weight, but he was still looking fit. Yeah, he didn't look bad at all, considering. He leant down closer to the mirror and rubbed his stubble. He needed a shave.

Harry could hear Jimmy and Maria going at it hammer and tongs in the kitchen. It sounded like she wasn't happy about valeting his suit.

He crossed to the shutters and pushed them open, the stench from the street filling the room. Poor old Jimmy – he'd got out of one shithole and straight into another one.

* * *

As they sat opposite each other in the restaurant, Dolly remembered why she had never liked Barry Sutcliffe. They always said if you want to get yourself a sharp lawyer, make sure he's Jewish – and if he's a little bit crooked with it, then you've got the best. Well, Barry Sutcliffe certainly ticked all of those boxes, but his pushy and uncouth manner had always grated on her. Now, with his pot belly pushing against the table, he cracked open the topping of his crème brûlée with his spoon and a couple of pieces shot across the table. Sutcliffe quickly scooped them up and shovelled them into his mouth, dribbling creamy custard down his shirt.

Dolly looked up from the papers she was checking. 'All right, are you, Barry?'

'Yeah,' he said, dabbing at his shirt with his napkin. 'I don't think it'll stain.'

Dolly went back to reading.

Sutcliffe jabbed at the custard with his spoon. 'You know, Dolly, you're outta your mind. Take those two betting shops – I coulda got another twenty grand for them, easy. It's the wrong time to sell, sweetheart, how many times do I have to tell you? There was no need to do it all in one go.'

'And how many times do I have to tell you, Barry,' Dolly shot back, 'this is what I want!'

'Harry'll turn in his grave,' he muttered. 'You know that, don't you?'

Dolly ignored him and carried on going through the papers – signing, checking, signing, reading the small print.

Barry began scraping his bowl. 'You've given away those betting shops, Dolly, when Harry—'

She looked up. 'Well, with all your business acumen, I'm surprised you didn't put a bid in for them yourself, Barry.'

He dropped his spoon. 'Come on, do me a favour, Doll, you know that's not my line. I'm just trying to guide you, darling, trying to help you do what your old man would've done.'

'I'm handling it now, Barry. Not Harry – me.'

'I know that, Dolly, I know that.'

She picked up one sheet of paper and began staring at it quizzically.

'You remember about the house?' he asked. 'You know, the Chinese are willing to pay outright cash, but you've gotta get any stuff you want out of there by noon tomorrow.'

She nodded. 'I know, I know. Don't worry, it'll be done.'

Sutcliffe tried to see what Dolly was reading. It looked like a bank statement. Even if she was giving it away, Dolly was still a very rich woman.

He waved a waiter over. 'Want a brandy, Dolly? Port?'

She shook her head.

'Gimme a Martell, large. You sure you don't want one, Dolly?'

Again, she shook her head.

Sutcliffe lit up a fat cigar, then leant across the table, blowing smoke into her face. 'I believe Harry had a couple of accounts in Rio. Don't know how much he had in 'em and I don't know much about them. He kept those to himself.'

Dolly signed one last paper and smiled. 'No, he didn't keep them entirely to himself, Barry. He told me all about them, in fact.' She passed the bundle of papers over the table, satisfied that she'd been through them with a fine-toothed comb. 'Anything else I should sign? Anything else I should read?'

'Nope. Just a couple of leases he had on lock-ups round the place, but you said you weren't interested in them.'

Dolly picked up her handbag. She caught the waiter's eye and made a sign in the air indicating she wanted the bill.

Sutcliffe looked at her. She was looking good, elegant as always. 'So, Dolly, you're a very rich woman now. Whatcha gonna do with your life?'

'I would say that's none of your business, Barry, wouldn't you?'

He couldn't help but smile. Beneath the smart exterior, she was tough as old boots, this one, but he admired her – liked her, even, despite the fact that she didn't like him. He watched the way she picked up the bill, looked through it carefully, then took out her wallet and counted out the notes, rubbing each one between her fingers just in case there were two stuck together.

She looked back to the waiter. 'Service included, is it?'

The waiter nodded.

Barry noticed she gave no extra, just folded the bill neatly on the plate and handed it back with the cash.

'Cheers, Dolly.'

'You're welcome, Barry.' She stood up. 'By the way, you shouldn't be doing that, darlin'.'

He looked puzzled.

'Smoking. Not good for you.' She turned on her heel, swinging her bag, and walked out.

Sutcliffe looked at the half-smoked cigar in his hand. Very odd. He was sure she used to chain-smoke. Well, maybe she'd given up. Come to think of it, maybe there were a lot of things about Dolly he didn't know.

* * *

Ex-detective George Resnick was sitting in a wheelchair in the conservatory of the convalescent home. Kathleen, his wife, was sitting in a chair beside him, dabbing at her eyes with a tissue. It was the second time she'd been in tears.

He turned to her with a sigh. 'Look, dear, if you want the house, have it. Take anything you want. You'll be doing me a favour.'

With a sob, the tears started up again. She wanted the house. It was her home and she didn't want to sell it. But somehow it would have been easier if he'd argued about it. It had taken all her courage to tell him that she wanted him out. She wanted the divorce finalised and everything settled. She'd handed him a cheque for £1500 – the money her father had left her – hoping it would be enough to put a deposit on a place of his own. And then he'd have his pension. But instead of arguing, he didn't seem to care, and that made it even worse – made her realise that they hadn't really had any love for each other the whole twenty-five years they'd been married.

The fact was, he was simply too tired. Talk about being in a convalescent home, he'd felt ill from the moment he'd been brought here. He'd known something was wrong with him, something inside, even before the symptoms started. Now he couldn't move his right arm properly, and he still had the terrible nagging pain in his groin, never stopping, day in, day out. They said he might have to have a prostate operation, but he hoped to God it wasn't true. If he could just get out of this place, and the sooner, the better. But what was going to be waiting for him when he did? Well, one thing was for sure, he didn't want it to be this shell of a woman he'd once loved, muttering on about how she wanted the house, she'd always loved the house, and he'd never loved her. He looked at her, tight-lipped and red-eyed. Maybe she was right.

'Kathy, take whatever you want, take it, and just go. Leave me alone.'

'Oh, George!' she wailed. 'Why are you being so difficult!'

Difficult! All he wanted was for her to go away and leave him alone.

He turned his head away from her and saw a young police constable sitting across the room with his wife – a nice chap, he'd been in the bed next to him. He'd been knocked down by a getaway vehicle for some job or other. Now George couldn't help watching the way they kissed, the way they touched, laughing and looking into each other's eyes. Christ, it'd been a long time. He turned back to Kathleen. She was blowing her nose, which was getting even redder. It had already been red from crying when she'd come in. She must have been sobbing for hours, wondering how she was going to tell him. And now it was done, she couldn't stop.

'Kathleen, get the divorce, do whatever you want. Just leave me in peace.'

She stood up and glared at him. 'Well, if that's the way you want it, George, that's the way you can have it.'

'It's the way we both want it.'

She sniffed. 'What about all your things at the house? What about your clothes?'

'Burn 'em, give 'em to the YMCA, do whatever you like with them. Leave me alone, woman. Get out of my life!'

'I don't think I've ever been in it, George.' She turned and walked away.

Resnick waited for a minute, then glanced over to the main doors to make sure she was gone. Hovering by the potted plants was Andrews. Why that young feller had ever thought of joining the police force Resnick would never know. He was just too sensitive, too tentative in everything he did.

Resnick waved him over, and he came and stood by the chair Kathleen had just vacated.

'Mind if I sit here?'

'Feel free.'

Andrews held a bunch of white grapes in his lap. They were already seeping through the paper bag and he didn't know quite what to do with them. 'You got a bowl, guv'nor?'

Resnick was still holding the cheque Kathleen had given him. 'Look at this. One thousand, five hundred pounds. Not bad for twenty-five years, eh?'

As Resnick folded the cheque, Andrews noticed his right hand was stiff and seemed to pain him a lot. There was an embarrassed pause as Andrews desperately thought of what to say, but Resnick came to his rescue.

'How's it going, son?'

Andrews shifted his weight in the chair. His hands were now sticky from the grapes. 'Oh, fine . . . er . . . I'm still in uniform. Looks like I'll be there for quite a while yet.'

Resnick nodded. There was another awkward pause, then both men spoke at once, Andrews starting to say how nice the conservatory was, then stopping to let Resnick continue.

'I hear Fuller's gone up a peg or two.'

Andrews nodded. Fuller had been made inspector.

'Always was a sharp little arse, wasn't he?'

Andrews nodded again. Fuller was certainly that, as well as being a two-faced bastard, but he had to admit he was very good at his job, and was going to rise to the top, whereas Andrews still wasn't sure whether he should stay in the police force at all.

Resnick patted him on the arm. 'Thanks for coming. I appreciate it.'

Andrews smiled. 'S'OK, sir.'

Resnick felt a pang. *Sir, guv'nor* – he was going to miss it, and he didn't know what the hell else he could possibly do.

'Any word on Rawlins? Anybody picked him up?' he asked.

Andrews shook his head. 'I'm not on that division any more. No idea what's going on. There's a thirty thousand pound reward for any information on the underpass raid, I do know that.'

Resnick nodded. 'Yeah, so I hear.'

'And you know Eddie Rawlins' cousin got five years, along with Bill Grant?'

Andrews wasn't sure Resnick heard him. He seemed miles away. Andrews could feel the grapes getting stickier and stickier through his fingers as he tried to think of something else to say. Then, to his relief, the bell went. He saw people beginning to shift themselves and got to his own feet.

'Well, better be off. Matron looks a bit of a dragon.'

Resnick nodded. He lifted his hand, but Andrews didn't want to cause him any pain by shaking it. Instead he patted Resnick on the shoulder.

'I'll come again soon, sir.'

Resnick nodded. 'I appreciate it, son, I appreciate it. None of those other fuckers have shown their faces.'

Andrews flushed with embarrassment and was already halfway to the doors before he realised he was still holding the grapes. He hesitated for a moment and then just kept going, leaving Resnick sitting like an old man in his wheelchair with a tartan rug tucked round his knees.

* * *

Maria opened the door without knocking, walked in and stood holding the white linen suit on a hanger. It looked as if she'd pressed it well, and Rawlins took it from her with a nod of thanks. She gave him a strange look. He knew she didn't like him, but there was definitely something sexual in it, and Rawlins was sure, even though she was six months pregnant, he could have her. She turned and left the room and Rawlins took the suit off the hanger and got dressed.

Jimmy looked up as Harry entered the lounge. Beer cans littered the table and he was holding a fresh one in his hand. He stood up and gestured for Harry to follow him. Jimmy quietly opened the door to an adjacent room and pointed to the double bed. There, lying curled up, fast asleep, was a little boy of about four or five. With his black curly hair and olive skin, he didn't look much like Jimmy, but Jimmy beamed and whispered, 'My kid.'

Harry watched Jimmy creep over to the bed and gently touch the child's head, before bending over and giving him a sloppy, wet kiss from his beer-soaked lips.

He looked up at Harry. 'Great little feller, isn't he?'

Harry nodded. It was the way Jimmy looked at him, as if to say, 'Here's something that you haven't got, Harry – a son,' that made it come out, and Harry heard himself saying, 'I've got a kid.'

Jimmy looked surprised. 'Yeah?'

'Yeah.' Harry walked out of the room.

'Oh.' Jimmy tucked the little boy in, gave him one last adoring look, and followed Harry out.

Again, Harry had the feeling that Maria was watching him from the kitchen through those wretched plastic strips. He checked his face in the small, cracked mirror by the front door.

'Where's the bank?'

'Can't miss it, Harry – right in the square. You want me to come with you?'

Harry shook his head. 'I'll find it.'

As he walked down the stairs he could hear Maria starting in again on Jimmy, shouting at him in Portuguese. No wonder the man was always drinking.

After a few minutes walking in the oppressive heat, it was a relief to walk into the bank, with the airy coolness of all the marble. Harry straightened his tie, checked his reflection in one of the cashiers' windows, and asked for a withdrawal form for one of the private banking accounts. The cashier handed him the sheet without even looking up, and Harry sat down and quickly filled it out, having done it many times before, and brought it back.

The cashier was tapping away at a calculator. He flicked a look in Harry's direction, muttering, *'Um momento, senhor,'* before resuming his work: *click, click, click.*

Harry slipped the paper underneath the railing in front of the cashier, who snatched it up with a grunt of annoyance and marched off before Rawlins could hand him his identification. He watched as the cashier started talking to a colleague, waving the form about in his hand. He then looked down at the form, glanced back at Harry and murmured something to the clerk. Then they turned their backs to him and murmured some more. Harry shifted his weight from one foot to the other, looked at his watch and waited. The clerk then took the form and walked towards him with an embarrassed look on his face.

'May I enquire if you are a relative of the deceased?' he asked in perfect English.

Harry didn't know what he was talking about. 'I'm sorry?'

The clerk repeated the question and Harry gave an uncertain nod, even though the question made no more sense the second time round.

'You have requested withdrawals from accounts 441880EJ and 4456880. That is correct?'

Harry nodded. 'Yes, but what's all this about being a relative of the deceased?'

Even in the cool of the bank, he could feel himself starting to sweat, the drops trickling down his neck and under his arms.

The clerk seemed to choose his next words very carefully. 'Mr Rawlins' widow, a Mrs Dorothy Rawlins, provided a Certificate of Probate.'

Rawlins swallowed hard. 'She's . . . she's been here?'

The clerk nodded. 'Mrs Rawlins withdrew all monies from her late husband's accounts.'

It took every ounce of Harry's willpower to control himself. He clenched and unclenched his fists, feeling the sweat in the palms of his hands, as a dapper little man in a black suit emerged from the manager's office and started walking purposefully towards them. Even from a distance, Harry could feel the man's eyes boring into him, and he was suddenly conscious of the sweat running down his forehead and soaking through his shirt.

The man in the suit stood beside the clerk and gave Harry a polite nod. 'How may I be of assistance?'

Harry nodded back, trying to keep his voice calm. 'I would . . . very much like to contact her . . . Mrs Rawlins. Do you have an address, by any chance?'

The clerk flicked a look at the manager and, after a moment's hesitation, got a nod in return. 'Yes, the Hilton Hotel.'

Harry swallowed. 'Thank you. '

The manager gave a little bow. 'It's the least we can do for a relative of Mr Rawlins.'

*   *   *

Jimmy knew something was wrong as soon as Harry walked in, slamming the door behind him. He grabbed hold of a beer can, ripped it open and drank most of it in one go.

'Er, everything all right?' Jimmy stammered.

Harry banged the can down on the table. 'She around? Where is she?'

Jimmy was starting to get flustered. 'You mean Maria?'

'Where is she?'

'She's gone out. I told her to get some food in. Is that OK, Harry? What do you want her for?'

Harry sat down heavily and put his head in his hands. 'I'm gonna need some help, Jimmy. I'm gonna need some help.'

Jimmy pulled out a chair and sat down. 'Sure, Harry, anything you want. Whatever I can do, you know. Has something happened?'

Harry slowly lifted his hands from his face. 'Yeah, you could say that. She's cleaned me out.' He laughed bitterly. 'The little bitch has cleaned me out.'

Jimmy still didn't understand. 'Who? Who're you talking about?'

Harry almost spat out her name. 'Dolly.'

Jimmy finally understood. 'You mean she thought you were dead?'

Harry nodded. 'Yeah.'

'So she's in Rio?'

Harry nodded again, and then said, very quietly, 'She's cleaned me out, Jimmy. Five hundred grand.'

Jimmy swallowed. 'Five hundred? Christ almighty!'

'Yeah, and now she's got it.'

'You know where she is?'

'Hilton Hotel.'

Then there was a pause. He looked at Jimmy.

'We're gonna have to find her. You know somebody who can help us?'

Jimmy gave him a puzzled look. 'Well, if she's at the Hilton, why don't you just go and find 'er?'

Harry shook his head. 'I'm a dead man, Jimmy. Understand me? I'm a dead man. I go walking into the Hilton Hotel, I start putting my face about, what the fuck do you think's gonna happen to me? It cost me a fortune to get a fake passport.'

'OK, Harry. OK, OK, I understand. OK, leave it to me, I'll find her.'

Harry gripped him by the arm. 'You bloody well better, Jimmy. You bloody well better.'

* * *

Morgan found Dolly's hotel in a back street just behind Queen's Gate. Only the discreet plaque on the wall was any indication that it was a hotel. She had class, this lady, you had to admit it.

He drove round until he found a meter, but he couldn't find any change, so he scribbled a note saying 'meter out of order' and stuck it on the windscreen.

Inside, the hotel was as tastefully understated as the outside. At the reception desk he asked for Mrs Marsh, and a prim-looking, elderly lady informed him in a posh voice that Mrs Marsh was taking breakfast in the dining room.

'Is she expecting you?'

'Yes,' he replied with a smile, and the receptionist led him through a thickly carpeted hall, lined with antique-looking oil paintings, to a pair of glass doors leading into the small dining room. He spotted Dolly sitting alone at the far end with her back towards him.

'Ah, I see her, thank you.'

As he threaded his way between the tables, there was no talking, only the soft clink of cutlery and the rustle of newspapers. The residents were mostly well into their seventies and eighties. One old gentleman, sitting with his eyes closed and mouth half-open, looked as if he was at death's door, and Morgan wondered if he was actually still breathing. He was so distracted, he almost bumped into the table as he sidled up to Dolly.

'Morning,' he said brightly.

Far from seeming surprised, Dolly turned round and nodded to the place opposite. As Morgan sat down, a pretty young waitress appeared with a cup and saucer, and enquired if he would like tea or coffee.

'Coffee's fine, thank you.' He lowered his voice. 'Very nice hotel, if I may say so.'

Dolly smiled. 'Yes.'

'Very quiet,' he whispered.

Dolly's plate of scrambled eggs, crispy bacon and thinly sliced toast looked very appetising, and Morgan found himself licking his lips.

'Er, mind if I take my coat off?'

'Please, make yourself comfortable,' Dolly replied.

Shrugging himself out of his coat, he almost slapped the elderly man at the table next to them with his sleeve – 'Sorry, sorry!' – but the old gentleman was buried so deeply in his *Telegraph* that he didn't seem to notice. Morgan finally managed to hang the coat over the back of the chair without further upsets, but Dolly held on to the table with both hands as he sat down just in case he overturned it.

The waitress appeared with the coffee pot and poured Morgan a cup. He heaped in the sugar and looked greedily at Dolly's plate.

'Mind if I have a piece of toast?'

Dolly passed him her side plate and clean knife, watching as he heaped on butter and marmalade and started chomping noisily. Dolly placed her knife and fork together, even though she'd hardly touched her breakfast. Her appetite seemed to have disappeared.

She waited patiently as Morgan finished his toast, wiped his mouth on a napkin, turned and fished a Woolworth's notepad out of his coat pocket, then started leafing through it.

'Right,' he said. 'Trudie Nunn. Works as a waitress cum hostess at the Golden Slipper, a tatty little drinking club in Soho. Maybe she should apply for a job here.' He looked round. 'Liven the place up a bit, eh?'

Dolly didn't smile.

'Oh, there's a kid. Did you know about him? A little boy.'

Dolly said nothing.

'This kid seems . . . He's left with a landlady most days, or a neighbour.'

Again he looked at Dolly. No reaction.

She pushed the toast towards him. 'Another slice, Mr Morgan?'

'Oh, ta.' As Morgan buttered the toast, he sensed a tension behind his client's composed demeanour. He took a bite, then consulted his notebook again. 'Er, it seems that Trudie, Mrs Nunn, had a live-in lover. Husband went missing about six, seven months back. This chap moved in, kept himself very much to himself . . . The law not looking for your sister's husband, are they?'

Dolly shook her head. 'Why do you ask?'

'Well, it was just that there seems to have been a bit of a rumpus one night. Cops came, broke down the door, searched the place, but whoever the feller was, he'd done a runner.'

'Did you find out his name?' Dolly asked.

Morgan laughed. 'I think he went by the name of Mr Smith. But then they all do, don't they, Mrs Marsh?'

Dolly opened her bag. 'I really wouldn't know, Mr Morgan.' She handed him an envelope. 'I'd like you to continue watching Mrs Nunn for at least another two days. And like I said, don't bother calling me. I'll be in touch.' She stood up and Morgan watched her curiously as she made her way out of the dining room.

Funny woman, he thought. Something not quite right there. He knew she was lying, but that was common with women looking for their husbands. He couldn't quite work out what she was lying about. Then he suddenly remembered something, got up from the table and caught up with her in the foyer as she was about to walk up the stairs.

'Mrs Marsh!'

Dolly turned with a startled expression.

'About the photograph. I did ask you for a photograph of your sister's husband.'

Dolly nodded. 'Y-yes, I-I'm sorry, I'd forgotten. I'll get one to you as soon as I can.' Then she hurried up the stairs.

Morgan was now certain his instincts were right. There's a lot more going on with Mrs Marsh than meets the eye, he thought to himself. And he was now actually looking forward to getting back on the job watching Trudie Nunn's house. He was curious to find out what sort of a man this Mr Jarrow, the husband, was.

* * *

Harry Rawlins watched Jimmy weave his way through the chequered tablecloths of the street cafe towards the little bar at the rear. He gestured towards the garden where Harry was sitting, talked briefly to the barman, grabbed another bottle of wine and brought it back. Harry realised that he hadn't seen Jimmy without a can of beer or a glass of something in his hand since he'd arrived, and his drinking only seemed to be getting worse. Jimmy slumped down at the table, still dressed in the same sweat-stained suit and T-shirt.

'Should be here any minute, Harry, no problem, and I'll tell you, if that wife of yours is in Rio, he'll find her. I've used him before, he knows what he's doing.' He gestured for Harry to pass his glass over but Harry shook his head. Jimmy swigged a mouthful of the wine and gritted his teeth. 'Christ almighty! This stuff's rotgut!' He looked up as a taxi drew up to the kerb. 'Here he is.'

Harry watched as the yellow cab pulled alongside three other taxis, their drivers dozing in the front as they waited for a fare. Tony Ramirez did seem to be a cut above the rest of the drivers; there was a sharpness to his clothes, and he also seemed to know everybody in the bar. He was laughing and patting a number of men on the shoulder as he looked round the tables. He nodded over to Jimmy and, seemingly in no hurry, walked across to their table.

Jimmy was already pouring a glass of wine for him. 'Tony, this is my friend I was telling you about – Harry Rawlins.'

Tony smiled, gold teeth glittering in his mouth. He picked up his wine and tapped the edge of Rawlins' empty glass. 'Nice to meet you.'

Despite a thick accent, Tony was obviously able to speak and understand English very well. He looked from one man to the other.

'So, you wanted to see me?' Although he directed the question to Jimmy, Harry felt he was really talking to him.

Jimmy nodded. 'Yeah, my friend here is looking for a woman. Need to ask a few questions round town, you know? She was staying at the Hilton Hotel. We didn't wanna put our faces in there, for reasons that we needn't go into right now, but we need to find her.'

Tony turned to Harry. 'You wanna find a woman, eh?'

Rawlins nodded. 'It's my wife.'

Tony laughed, drained the glass of the cheap wine and pushed it across the table. 'In Rio, most people try to lose their wives. This is very unusual, you understand, when a man wants to find his wife.' He threw his head back and started to laugh, but stopped short when he saw that neither Harry nor Jimmy were amused.

Harry took over. 'OK,' he said, 'her name's Dolly – Dorothy Rawlins. She booked in to the hotel last week. If she's still in Rio I want to find her, and as soon as you can.'

Tony nodded. 'She at the hotel now?'

Jimmy interrupted. 'Well, that's for you to find out. And if she's not, we want you to find out where the hell she's gone! We haven't got much time, Tony, so can you get a move on for us?'

Tony turned towards Harry. 'Why you can't find her yourself? She in some kinda trouble?'

Harry shook his head. 'No, she's in no trouble. I just wanna find her, OK?'

Tony shrugged. 'OK, I'll ask questions. You gonna be round here for a while?'

Jimmy nodded. 'Yeah, yeah, we'll be here.'

'You pay me in dollars, OK, Jimmy?' Tony said.

Jimmy looked to Harry and Harry nodded.

'Just get cracking, OK?' Harry said.

'What she look like?'

'She's blonde, about five-eight, mid-forties, well dressed,' Harry answered.

Tony smirked at Harry, as if to say, 'What you wanna find an old woman like that for?' He got up from the table. 'See you around, then.'

As Tony walked away, Jimmy picked up the bottle of wine and leant across the table. Harry again put his hand over his empty glass.

'No thanks, Jimmy, and why don't you try layin' off it for a while?'

Jimmy looked hurt. 'Come on, Harry, I can handle it. I know what I'm doing.'

Harry shrugged. He was watching Tony as he walked back to his taxi. He seemed in no hurry as he laughed and chatted with a couple of the other taxi drivers.

Harry turned to Jimmy. 'What the fuck does he think he's doing? We haven't got all night.'

'Hey, come on, cool it, Harry, just relax. If she's in Rio, he'll find her.'

Harry reached for the bottle of wine. He looked hard at Jimmy. 'I hope to God you're right.'

He poured himself a glass and tossed it back. It burnt the back of his throat. Jimmy was right – it was rotgut.

* * *

Linda looked at herself in the long mirror and wished that Shirley or Bella were still around. She still wasn't sure about the dress. It was Bella who had pushed her into buying it. She stood back. Maybe Bella was right: the bright red silk did set off her suntan a treat, but she still wished that Shirley had been there to do her hair or tell her what jewellery to wear. She put on some gold looped earrings, thought she looked a little too like Carmen Miranda, and decided instead to wear none. She was still wondering whether she should put her hair up or down when she heard the front doorbell go. She'd been so absorbed in getting dressed that she hadn't heard the Rolls-Royce coming up the drive. She quickly picked up her small evening bag, checked her keys and ran down the stairs.

José Camarana himself was at the door. The chauffeur stood by the Rolls with the passenger door open.

José smiled. 'I'm sorry, are we a little late?'

Linda had no idea what time it was, so she just shrugged and said, 'No, it's all right, it's fine.'

He stepped back to look at her. 'May I say you look absolutely beautiful.'

Unsure how to reply, Linda just grinned and said, 'Oh, thanks very much. Bella picked it.'

He guided her towards the car, and Linda bent to get in, bumping heads awkwardly with the chauffeur as he tried to help her into the car. Flustered, Linda scooted in and settled into the seat next to Bella. Bella eased over slightly, not wanting Linda to crush her dress.

Wow, thought Linda. Bella really did look stunning. She had on a pure white chiffon gown and a simple white wrap. It set off her black skin to perfection. She wore diamond studs in her ears, and, of course, the diamond on her hand. Linda also noticed that she now wore a diamond bracelet. She thought she'd sound silly if she told Bella how beautiful she looked, so she just sat in embarrassed silence, wondering if it would have been less awkward if they'd let José sit between them.

Oh, sod it, she thought, leaning back in the seat. 'Well, this is all very nice, isn't it?'

José got into the front passenger seat, nodded to the driver, and they drove slowly out of the villa. They travelled in silence for a moment, the only sounds the cultured purr of the engine, then José and Bella both started to speak at once. They looked at each other and did a kind of secret smile. Then José turned to Linda.

'Have you been to this club before?'

Linda shook her head.

'I think you will like it. The cabaret is –' again, that rather strange look between him and Bella – 'I think rather special. But I won't say anything more until we get there. I wouldn't want to spoil it. Are you comfortable?'

Linda nodded.

Again there was a silence. Bella looked at her watch.

'Shirley'll almost be in LA by now.'

José started talking about LA, how fond of it he was, and making general chit-chat, while Linda just sat there feeling like a gooseberry stuck between these two lovebirds, who obviously would have much preferred to be alone together.

Thankfully the journey didn't take very long, and soon they were entering the grounds of the club. Linda could see tennis courts and fountains; it was just like José said – a spectacular place. The car pulled up at the main entrance and the chauffeur opened the door. José offered his hand to Linda, who almost tripped over the hem of her dress as she stepped out, hitching it up just in time with a 'Thanks very much'. She hovered there, expecting Bella to follow, but Bella was sitting, calmly waiting, while the chauffeur went round to the other side of the car and helped her out. Taking the chauffeur's arm momentarily, she then came round and linked arms with José.

'Right, all set?'

Again they looked at each other; again that secret, intimate smile.

José offered his arm to Linda, she hooked hers through it, and the three walked up the entrance steps of the club.

The doorman jumped to attention when he saw them. 'Good evening, Mister José.'

Linda was impressed.

As they entered, the maître d' came up to them with a bow. 'Good evening, Mr Camarana. Good evening, madame,' he said to Bella. And finally a polite nod to Linda.

José turned to Bella. 'Would you want to go to the powder room?'

Bella walked off with a smile. He turned to Linda, as if expecting her to follow, but she didn't move.

After a moment's silence, Linda said, 'Funny, isn't it? She spends hours gettin' ready and as soon as we get here she's in the toilet!'

He nodded distractedly. Already he was smiling and waving to another group entering the club, and a beautifully dressed woman called out to him, then blew a kiss. Linda felt like a lump, then suddenly realised she was still clinging to José's arm. She released her hold and clutched her handbag instead. She was thinking that maybe she should go to the powder room after all when Bella reappeared, followed shortly by Filipe, the elegant head waiter, who stopped to greet them with the same deference as the maître d', paying particular attention to Bella, who inclined her head almost regally. Linda could have spat. She couldn't believe Bella was behaving as if she'd been brought up in a bloody place like this.

The next minute the three were walking towards the entrance of the main club room. The orchestra was playing something that

Linda didn't recognise as they were led towards a booth. Every-where were men in elegant evening suits and women in gorgeous gowns, dripping with diamonds.

So this is the rich set of Rio – *the* set, Linda thought.

And at every table they passed, José Camarana seemed to know either the woman or the man, stopping to introduce Bella and Linda. But despite his gracious manner, Linda couldn't help feeling like a well-dressed maid, brought along as part of the retinue.

They reached their booth and José seated himself between the two girls. He looked from one to the other and smiled. 'I'm a very lucky man! I am with the two most beautiful women in the room.' But Linda noticed that he only had eyes for Bella.

'Don't suppose you got any spare males hanging round 'ere that could come and join us? I feel like a bit of a gooseberry here!'

José smiled. 'But of course, if you would like someone to join us.'

Bella placed her hand over José's. 'I think we're fine as we are. This is our night, just the three of us – let's enjoy it.'

A waiter appeared with a bottle of Dom Perignon in a silver ice bucket, while another brought three fluted champagne glasses. He spoke in French to José, who replied fluently. Linda was beginning to feel seriously out of her depth.

The champagne poured, José lifted his glass and said, 'To my beautiful women – cheers.'

Linda drank the champagne back in one gulp and put her glass down on the table, only to realise that José and Bella had merely sipped delicately at theirs. She could have kicked herself, especially when the waiter instantly appeared and refilled her glass.

Ah well, what the hell, she thought. Might as well have a few drinks and try and relax a bit.

As she raised her glass to her lips, José leant forward and touched Linda's hand. For a moment she thought he was suggesting that she shouldn't drink any more, and was about to give him a piece of her mind, when he said, 'I think perhaps if we eat after the cabaret – would that suit you?'

Linda gulped her champagne and nodded.

'I think that would be fine,' Bella agreed.

The orchestra struck up a rousing Afro-beat music, and as the lights began to go down, the glass floor lit up. There were shouts and whoops as the stage was filled with women – twenty-four staggeringly beautiful girls in tiny, sequinned G-strings and bras, their lithe bodies oiled and shining. The women flowed across the stage, their feathered headdresses in brilliant peacock colours swaying to the beat.

Linda found herself getting caught up in the atmosphere. She grinned at Bella and Bella smiled back politely.

Oh, Christ, I wish she'd drop this Lady Muck act, Linda thought, but the women on stage were so mesmerising, so outrageous, so much larger than life, that she quickly forgot her annoyance.

She nudged José. 'Those women are amazing! They're all so tall!'

José leant in and whispered, 'They're all men.'

'What?'

He smiled. 'Yes, men.'

Linda's jaw dropped. 'Fuck me!' She felt a kick under the table from Bella. 'You havin' me on?'

He shook his head. 'This is one of the most famous cabarets in Rio. They are . . .' He turned to Bella, said something in French.

She leant over. 'Transvestites, Linda. They're transvestites.'

Linda's eyes were drawn back to the exotic creatures, leaping and gyrating round the stage. She'd never seen anything so spectacular and amazing in her life. She turned back to Bella and José. José raised his glass, and all three started to rock with laughter.

Maybe tonight wasn't going to be so bad after all.

* * *

Jimmy was now well pissed, the second bottle of vino empty on the table. Harry had checked his watch maybe ten, fifteen times, and he was about to do so again when Tony's cab finally pulled up. Again, he took his time to join them, stopping to chat to several people along the way, before casually sauntering up to Harry and Jimmy's table and sitting down.

'Well? You find out anything?' Jimmy asked eagerly.

Tony nodded. 'Yeah, yeah. You understand I've had to ask a lot of questions, I've had to – how d'you say it in English? – put out quite a few dollars.'

'You'll be paid back for whatever you've spent,' Harry snapped. 'Just tell us what you've found out.'

'Fifty dollars.'

Jimmy leant back in his chair. 'Oh, come on, do us a favour! Twenty-five.'

'Fifty. You don't get information for nothing in this town.'

Jimmy shook his head. 'You're having a laugh. How stupid do you think—'

Harry had had enough. 'Just pay the man what he fucking wants, Jimmy.'

Jimmy pouted. 'All right, twenty-five now and the rest if the information checks out. How about that?'

Tony shook his head. 'I already paid out this money, you understand?'

Harry tapped Tony on the arm. 'Don't worry about the money. Now, what did you find out?'

Tony took a crumpled piece of paper from his pocket. 'OK, I think I got the right woman. Does the name "Linda Pirelli" mean anything to you?'

Jimmy leant across to Harry. 'Joe Pirelli's old lady? I remember Joe Pirelli. Wasn't he part of your crew?'

Harry gave him a cold, hard look. 'Just go on, Tony, go on. Linda Pirelli and what?'

'There was a Linda Pirelli, a blonde woman – girl, not your wife – and a black girl, O'Reilly. They leave their passports with the hotel, you understand? That's how I have their names. O'Reilly,

Pirelli – they book a suite at the Hilton Hotel. Two women join them, a young blonde one, and an older woman, but they don't stay at the hotel, they spend maybe two, three hours there.'

Harry was fighting to control himself. 'Is she there? Did you find her?'

Tony leant back in his chair, letting Harry stew for a moment. He waved to a waiter, who brought another glass, then picked up the bottle and poured himself a glass of wine, clearly enjoying keeping the two men on tenterhooks.

'OK, this is where you understand I have to pay out the money. I have a friend on the desk ... Linda Pirelli, she go to the desk, she ask for villa rental information.' Tony sipped his wine and put down the glass slowly. It took all Rawlins' willpower not to take him by the scruff of the neck and shake the information out of him.

Eventually, Tony explained that Dolly Rawlins, Linda Pirelli, Shirley Miller and Bella O'Reilly had rented a villa on the outskirts of town for at least two months, paying in advance – in cash.

'You know where it is?' Harry asked.

'Sure,' Tony replied.

'And you can take us there?'

'That will be another fifty dollars, you understand?'

'OK, OK, a hundred dollars,' Harry agreed before Jimmy could start arguing. 'Can you take me there now?'

Tony nodded. All three got up, but Harry put a firm hand on Jimmy's arm. 'Not this time, Jimmy. I'll go by myself. This is my business, OK?'

Jimmy sat back down heavily. He looked hurt. 'You really don't want me along?'

Harry patted his arm. 'No thanks, Jimmy. You're pissed.'

Jimmy slumped back into his seat and watched them go. Harry could be a right bastard sometimes. He wasn't pissed, it was the heat. And if he did drink in this heat, he just sweated it out anyway.

Jimmy's hand was shaking as he reached for the bottle. He spilt a little of the wine over the rim of the glass. Perhaps Harry was right. He thought about Maria and what she would say to him when he got back to the flat. He pushed the glass away and looked round for the waiter.

A cup of good, strong coffee and I'll be fine, he told himself.

* * *

Linda was now clapping her hands and singing along with the cabaret, as the girls strutted round the stage for their final extravaganza, belting out, 'Oh-oh, vol-a-re, da-da-da-da . . .' She adored the fact that the girls sauntered up to the tables closest to the cabaret floor, flaunting their crotches and encouraging people to tuck money into their G-strings.

Bella watched her singing, laughing, clapping, and having an all-round good time, fuelled by the champagne that had been steadily flowing since the cabaret began.

She leant over and said, 'Not so loud, Linda.'

But Linda was too far gone to care. She kept asking loudly 'where they put it' and if they'd 'had it cut off'. A couple in a nearby booth turned and stared at them, just as Linda stood up a little unsteadily and started cheering: 'More! More!' as the girls finally made their way from the floor.

The orchestra struck up a dance, and Linda pulled José to his feet. 'Come on, let's dance!' she shouted, dragging him on to the floor. She glanced back at Bella, who just shrugged.

Bella watched the pair as Linda waltzed round the floor, pulling José with her. He was obviously embarrassed, but was trying not to show it, listening patiently as Linda started talking to him, whispering in his ear.

When they finally returned to the booth, Linda was flushed, beads of sweat standing out on her forehead. She grabbed the bottle of champagne and poured herself another glass before the waiter standing in attendance could pour it for her.

José turned to Bella. 'Linda's been telling me you used to be a dancer.'

Linda raised her glass, spilling the champagne. 'And a singer! Boy, can she sing! Tell him about the night we took over that club when we first came here . . .' And Linda was off on a rambling story about their first night in Rio. Then she started tapping the table with her hands. 'What was that song we sang? Go on, Bella, what was it?' She clapped her hands. 'I've got it!' And then she started at the top of her voice: 'Money, money, money, money, money, money . . .' over and over and over again, banging on the table with her hands.

Bella had had enough. She gripped Linda hard by the elbow and said, 'I think you'd better go to the ladies' room. Come on – out!'

Laughing, Linda grabbed José's arm. 'See? She's dragging me out! Won't let me have a good time!'

'You're drunk, Linda,' Bella insisted.

Linda nudged him. 'She thinks I'm drunk! I'm not drunk, I'm just having a good time, just like we used to have in the old days. Remember, Bella?'

José was unsure exactly what to do. Linda was obviously drunk, and Bella was getting very, very upset. 'Perhaps if I order coffee . . .'

'I don't want any coffee!' Linda snapped. 'I'm not drunk, all right!'

With that, Bella hauled her to her feet and marched her off towards the ladies' room, while José motioned the head waiter over and ordered a cup of coffee and the dinner menu.

Bella pushed Linda into the ladies' room. 'You're going back to the villa, and you're going back now!'

Linda was now a bit more subdued. 'Oh, come on, Bella, I didn't do anything!'

'Not yet, but you're building up to it. I just don't understand what gets into you, Linda. For Christ's sake, why're you saying those things? Huh? Why're you going on, nudge, nudge, wink, wink? You tryin' to break it up between us?'

Linda sat down, and suddenly the tears started.

Bella stood with her arms crossed. 'That's not gonna work, Linda. Every time you put your great big foot in it you start howling. Well, it's not gonna work, you're not gonna wreck this for me. You're going back to the villa and you're going now. I'll get the chauffeur to bring the Roller round.'

Linda caught her arm. 'No, Bella, don't, don't. I'll be all right – I'll have some coffee. I promise you I'll behave myself . . .'

Bella jerked her arm away. 'No, Linda, I'm through with you. I'm through with your moaning. That's all you've done since you've been here, moan, moan, moan. You've got everything going for you, and you haven't even changed your goddamn money. Well, you're not gonna wreck this, Linda, you hear me? You're not!' But as soon as she'd said it, she felt bad. She put her arm round Linda and spoke in a gentler voice. 'What is it, Linda? For God's sake, what's the matter with you?'

Linda shrugged. 'I dunno, Bella, I just dunno.'

Bella sighed. 'Maybe it would be best you go back, Linda. Go back to the villa.'

Linda grabbed her hand and held on tight. 'Come with me. Come back with me.'

Bella pulled her hand free. 'No, Linda, I'm never going back there. I'm with him, you understand me? I'm with him for good. He means something to me. He's the best thing that's ever hap-pened to me.'

Linda smirked. 'Oh, yeah? I'm sure he'll be the best thing when he finds out what you were!'

Bella's hand flew out, slapping Linda hard across the face, just as two women tottered in on six-inch heels, and then Linda was sobbing and Bella wished she hadn't done it. The women stopped in their tracks and started giggling with their hands over their mouths. Linda screamed at them to mind their own fuckin' business and they quickly scuttled into the toilet cubicles.

Bella handed Linda her little evening bag. 'Come on, Linda, let's get you in the car.'

But Linda shook her head. 'I'm stayin' here. I'm not going back to the villa. I don't wanna be there by myself!'

Bella's expression was hard, and her voice matched it, her old East End accent rising to the surface. 'You're goin' back, Linda, an' you better start realising you are on your own. An' you better start gettin' your act together an' all. I've got mine together, Shirley's got hers, Dolly—'

'Oh, yeah, Dolly, the lying, twisted bitch, doing whatever the fuck she's doing back in England . . .'

That was enough for Bella. She backed away. 'You make me sick, you know that? You make me fuckin' sick! You're twisted, Linda, you're all twisted up inside. You wanna smash things up between me an' José because you're jealous! You're jealous, aren't you? Why don't you admit it?'

Linda sat down on the floor, holding her head in her hands. 'Yeah, yeah. I am. How come you can get everything together and I'm just a fuck-up? I've always been a mess!'

Bella put her arms round her, trying to calm her down. 'I'll come round and see you tomorrow, OK? I'll go and get the Roller. Come on, Linda, go home.'

Bella walked out and Linda was left alone. Once again she had that sinking feeling in the pit of her stomach. What was the matter with her? Why was she like this? Why did she always feel this terrible need inside her, the need to have somebody with her? Then she remembered Joe, and instantly she was crying again. The two women came out of the cubicles and gave her a pitying look as they muttered to each other in Portuguese. Linda picked up a box of tissues and threw it at them.

'What you fuckin' lookin' at, you tarts?' Linda yanked open the door of the powder room and stormed out, flinging over her shoulder, 'Fucking foreigners!'

*   *   *

Harry had told Tony to park the car a little way up the street so they wouldn't be so conspicuous, but they had a good view of the villa. Harry sat staring at the main gates for a while. The villa was in darkness. After a few minutes they got out and walked down to it, through the iron gates and down the pathway to the main entrance. Tony looked up at the windows.

'Nobody seems to be at home.'

Harry tried the front door, then walked round to one of the ground-floor balconies. He climbed onto the balcony and found the French window open.

'I can wait.' He entered the villa.

Tony stood outside for a while, and then followed Harry in. Their footsteps echoed across the marble entrance hall.

Harry touched Tony's arm. 'I'm goin' upstairs, OK? See what you can find down here.'

'What am I looking for? Your wife?'

'Just see if she's still staying here. Look for a passport, suitcases, anything.' Then Harry was heading up the stairs.

Two of the bedrooms were empty. He opened the third bedroom door and walked in. The place was strewn with clothes, the bed unmade. He paused for a moment. He could hear Tony moving round below, doors opening and shutting. Harry started going through the drawers one by one, but apart from underwear and a few toiletries, they were empty.

Tony went through the kitchen and dining hall, into the lounge. The fridge was empty, apart from a few leftovers and a bottle of wine, and the place seemed deserted. He made his way upstairs, and found Harry on hands and knees, sifting through the contents of the bedside table.

He looked up. 'You find anything?'

Tony shrugged. 'There's nothing.'

Harry eyed him suspiciously. 'You find any money?'

Tony seemed to perk up. 'Money? You think there's money here? Believe me, if there's money, I'll find it.'

Harry smiled. 'Yeah, I bet you will.' He went into the bathroom. As Tony was pulling the mattress from the bed, he called out, 'Just make sure you put everything back where you found it!'

Harry opened the medicine cabinet above the washbasin. There were bottles of perfume, face cream and suntan lotion. Suddenly Tony shouted from the bedroom, and Harry knocked over a toothbrush glass in surprise. It smashed into the washbasin, cutting the back of his left hand as he tried to catch it. He lifted his bleeding hand to his lips, swore and sucked at the blood. It was only a small cut, but deep. A trickle splashed onto the white washbasin.

'We gotta go!' shouted Tony. 'There is a car!'

Harry went back into the bedroom and turned off the light. Tony was already at the door.

'Come on, Harry! We go!'

Swearing under his breath, Harry went to the balcony and pulled the curtain aside an inch or two so he could see out. Sure enough, the headlights of a car were sweeping down the drive.

The two men ran down the stairs in the dark, slipped through the French windows and jumped down from the balcony. They threw themselves into the shrubbery just as the Rolls-Royce pulled up at the front door.

Linda Pirelli stepped out of the Rolls, staggering slightly before regaining her balance. The chauffeur climbed out of the driving seat with a sigh and went round to help her. She shrugged him off and made her way to the front door. She stumbled, dropped her keys, and then fiddled with the lock for a minute, before finally the door opened and she practically fell inside. The chauffeur stood for a moment, arms folded, waiting until the door closed, then got back in the car, shaking his head, and drove away.

Linda turned on the lights, stood blinking for a moment, then made her way into the kitchen and opened the fridge. She reached for the wine and plonked it on the table. She was rummaging in the kitchen drawer for a corkscrew when she heard the sound of a car horn outside. She sat and listened for a moment, and the horn tooted again. She made her way through the kitchen and along the hall to the lounge balcony. She opened the window and looked out.

Tony was standing beside his taxi.

'Oi, what d'ya want?' she called out.

Tony smiled. 'You want the taxi?'

'No, you got the wrong house, nobody's called a taxi here.'

He looked disappointed. 'You sure you don't wanna taxi?'

'No, I don't wanna taxi!'

Tony moved towards the house. 'Maybe you gotta telephone I could use?'

Linda leant over the balcony. 'Don't you have a radio with you in your cab?'

'I'm sorry?'

'A radio. Haven't you got a radio in that taxi?'

He shrugged. 'It's broken. Please, I use your phone, I ring my office . . .'

Linda thought for a moment. She should probably tell him to get lost. Then she thought of being all alone in the big, empty house.

'Ah, well, why not?' She wandered through the lounge and opened the front door.

He was leaning against the doorframe. 'I thank you. I must have got confused with the address. I'm sorry to trouble you.' He smiled at her.

'You speak good English! Where'd you learn it?'

'I learn most of my English in bed,' he replied with a wink.

Instead of being offended, Linda roared with laughter. She waved him in and, still laughing, led the way to the telephone in the hallway. She leant against the side of the phone table as he picked up the phone.

'You wanna drink?'

'That would be very nice, thank you.'

Linda walked into the kitchen.

Tony picked up the phone and pretended to dial. Keeping an eye on the kitchen, he spoke rapidly in Portuguese, then replaced the receiver. He followed Linda into the kitchen. She was struggling to open the bottle of wine with a corkscrew.

'Would you please allow me?'

Tony took the wine from her and began to open the bottle, without taking his eyes off her. She stared back at him.

'So you're a taxi driver, are you?'

'Yeah, that's right.'

'What's your name then?'

'Tony.'

'All right, Tony, I'll get some glasses.'

He followed Linda into the lounge, carrying the bottle. She almost fell into the drinks cabinet, then bent down and brought out two wine glasses.

'Here you go!'

She could feel him close beside her, his body almost pressing against her as he poured the wine. She backed away slightly as she picked up her glass.

'Well, here's to you, Tony.' Linda swallowed a mouthful of the wine and instantly felt like she was going to vomit. She put down the wine glass as the room began to spin round.

'Ahh, excuse me for a minute, will you? Aw, Christ, I'm gonna chuck up!' She ran out of the lounge and began to drag herself up the staircase, holding on to the banister to stop herself from falling.

Tony followed her out of the lounge and stood leaning against the doorway, calmly sipping his wine and watching.

In her bedroom, Linda didn't even turn on the light, just tumbled into the bathroom. She fumbled for the cord and pulled it, and the light almost blinded her. When she was able to open her eyes again, the first thing she saw was a single drop of blood on the side of the washbasin. Then she saw the broken glass. Heart racing, Linda staggered to the cistern, lifted the lid, reached down into the water and pulled out the plastic bag.

Thank God, her money was safe. Clutching the dripping bag tightly, she went into the bedroom. Her nausea had disappeared, but it had been replaced by fear. She saw the drawers pulled out, the mattress half off the bed. Someone had been looking for something. What if they'd taken her money and just replaced the bag? She began ripping at the heavy black plastic and there, underneath it, in another see-through plastic bag, was her precious money. She opened it to make sure it was all there, sighing with relief as she walked out onto the landing. Tony was almost at the top of the stairs. He still had the wine glass in his hand.

'There you are, Leenda. Hey, what have you got there?'

She took two steps back, clutching the bag to her chest. 'What are you doing up here? Just get back down the stairs, you hear me? You go back down those stairs!'

He put on a hurt expression. 'Come on, Leenda, why don't you be nice to me, eh?'

Linda retreated towards the bedroom. She was holding the bag upside down and money began to spill out. She made a frantic grab for the tumbling notes, but then she saw Tony coming closer, with that creepy smile on his face, and rushed through the door, slamming it behind her and quickly locking it.

On the landing, Tony looked at all the money on the floor, wondering if Christmas had come early. He picked up a handful of notes, held them to his nose and breathed deeply. Yes, that was the smell of money. He knocked gently on the door.

'Leenda, open the door. Come on, Leenda . . .'

Inside the bedroom, Linda could hear his voice – soft and wheedling – and the sound of the doorknob turning round and round. 'Leenda, open the door for Tony. Come on, Leenda . . .'

The only way to escape was over the balcony. Linda pushed open the louvre doors and started to climb over, but hampered by her long evening dress and still clinging on to the money with one hand, she wasn't sure she was going to make it.

Below, Rawlins looked up. The crazy bitch was teetering on the edge of the balcony. He saw her hesitate for a moment, then there was a crash as Tony broke through the bedroom door, and she jumped.

Linda's breath was knocked out of her as she landed with a thud in the flower bed. Her head was throbbing and her shins felt as if someone had kicked them with hobnailed boots, but the pain was nothing compared with the desperate voice screaming inside her to run, run for her life. Kicking off her high heels and hiking up her dress with her free hand, she sprinted towards the shrubberies. At least there in the dark she could hide and maybe get her breath back.

Suddenly a figure loomed in front of her, his white shirt gleaming in the moonlight. She screeched in terror but managed to keep her footing, veering off to the right, towards the swimming pool.

Seeing Tony jump down from the balcony, Harry paused in his pursuit and called out, 'Turn the taxi round and wait by the gates, you hear me?'

Tony pointed at the figure in the red dress disappearing round the corner of the villa. 'Look, she has money, much money! Don't let her get away!'

Harry grabbed him and manhandled him over to the cab.

'You listen to me. Get in and start the fucking engine, all right? You wait for me!'

Tony pushed Harry away and Harry took off, following Linda towards the swimming pool. Tony got down on his knees and began picking up the money. So many fifty pound notes – it was crazy. He started stuffing it as fast as he could into his pockets, following the trail of money as it led towards the swimming pool.

At the edge of the pool, Linda turned. Harry was walking towards her.

'Stay where you are, Linda. Just stay where you are!'

She shook her head. 'No, leave me alone. Please don't hurt me, please don't hurt me!'

He held his hands out to calm her. 'Linda, I don't want to hurt you. I just want to know where she is. Where's Dolly?'

She heard him, but she was so panicked that his words made no sense. She backed away and tripped over one of the loungers. Whimpering in terror, she picked herself up and started edging along the side of the pool.

Harry kept on coming.

'I just wanna talk to you, Linda. Can you understand me? Linda?'

Linda started to run, but her dress, now torn and flapping round her ankles, got caught under her feet. She felt herself losing her balance. She flung an arm out to steady herself, dropping the almost empty money bag, then the world seemed to spin in front of her eyes, there was an almighty splash and she was underwater. Coughing and spluttering, she rose to the surface, her dress outspread around her. Thrashing the water desperately with her arms, she found the breath to scream: 'Stay away from me! Stay away from me!' before going under again.

Harry shoved the chair out of his way and knelt down at the edge of the pool.

Linda bobbed up again, gasping for air. 'I can't . . . swim . . . I . . . can't . . .' she spluttered in between heaving gasps.

'Give me your hand!' Harry shouted, but one hand was still holding on tightly to what was left of the money, while the other flailed desperately round in the water. 'Give me your hand, for Chrissake!'

Harry leant as far as he could over the pool, hand outstretched. She went under again, her dress weighing her down, and he made one last grab, catching hold of her hair. Now she was scratching at his wrist, screaming, screeching over and over again: 'No! No! Leave me alone!'

He pulled as hard as he could, her head crashing against the side of the pool, but her hair slipped out of his grip.

Linda went under again, a stream of blood from her nose clouding the water. She'd finally let go of the money, and Harry reached for her hand and managed to pull her towards him, then got hold of her hair again. Holding her head out of the water against the side of the pool, he leant down and put his mouth to her ear.

'Where's Dolly, Linda? Understand me? Where's Dolly?'

Linda couldn't hear, couldn't think. Her vision was blurred and her throat was raw.

'Listen to me, you stupid bitch: *where's Dolly*?'

Linda tried to say something but all that came out was a strangled croak.

Suddenly she felt him pressing her head down, under the water. Desperate for air, she tried to take a breath and water started filling her lungs. Her vision went black, she felt herself drifting away – and then her head was yanked out of the water again.

'Just tell me where the fuck Dolly is, you stupid bitch!' She felt her head crash against the concrete again.

Tony had seen enough. He scooped up a few last notes and got into the taxi. He started to do a U-turn, then saw the headlights of a car approaching the villa. He shouted out of the window to Harry, but there was so much screaming he doubted that he could hear. He glanced back down the drive as the headlights came closer.

* * *

In the back seat of the Rolls-Royce, José squeezed Bella's hand. 'She'll be all right.'

'I know, I'm sorry, but I worry about her, I always worry about her. She was drunk, and I shouldn't have let her go back by herself.'

He slipped his arm round her back. 'It's OK, it's OK, we'll make sure that she is all right.'

Bella looked into his face. 'Thank you.'

He pulled her closer and started to kiss her. Bella pulled free, touched the side of his face and whispered, 'I love you. You're the only man in my life I've ever loved.'

As he bent to kiss her again, the Rolls-Royce veered to the right with a screech of brakes, almost throwing them out of their seats. The taxicab screamed past them, engine roaring, as the Rolls-Royce came to a halt inches from the gatepost. Bella didn't wait for the chauffeur to open the door for her – she was out of the car in a flash and running up the driveway, her high heels in her hand.

She stopped short for a brief moment, gasping in shock as she came face to face with Harry Rawlins – and then he was gone, diving into the bushes.

José came up behind her. 'What in hell is going on?'

She grabbed his arm. 'For God's sake, get to the house, see if she's all right!'

Despite the encumbrance of her dress, Bella was running like a wild thing and got to the house first. Shouting over her shoulder for José to switch on the ground lights, she opened the door and ran up the stairs, into Linda's bedroom, all the while calling her name at the top of her lungs.

José found the light switch and instantly the grounds were flooded with pale green light.

Bella opened the windows on to the balcony and stepped out. 'Linda! Where are you?' She leant over the balcony to call down to

José when she saw her. It was the red dress, billowing round Linda as she floated in the pool.

Bella screamed, pointed frantically, and ran back into the house.

* * *

Mr Jarrow ushered Dolly out of his consulting room and signalled to his receptionist.

'Well, I look forward to seeing you next week, Mrs Rawlins.' He patted her arm reassuringly. 'Are you quite sure you're feeling all right?'

Dolly smiled. 'Not now, but I will be, after the operation.'

'I'm sure you will, Mrs Rawlins. Thank you for coming in. There are just a few final details my receptionist can deal with.' Dolly dismissed, he went back to his desk and opened another file, readying himself for his next patient.

The receptionist smiled at Dolly. 'Just one last thing, Mrs Rawlins: how will you be paying? Cheque? Banker's card?'

Dolly snapped her bag shut. 'Cash. I'll be paying in cash.'

She walked out on to Harley Street, got into her car and drove off. She arrived just ahead of the estate agent, checked her watch and looked at herself in the driving mirror. She pulled the skin a little tighter under her eyes and underneath her neck, and couldn't help but give herself a secret smile. She was still smiling when the estate agent tapped on the window.

'Mrs Marsh?'

Dolly almost jumped out of her skin. 'Yes?'

'Ah, I'm the estate agent. Sorry to keep you waiting.'

'Oh, that's all right.'

The flat had one bedroom, a kitchen, bathroom and lounge. It had the unmistakable smell of a rented place, a smell of carpet that had been washed very quickly after the last tenant had left. Dolly hated it. But it would serve its purpose.

The estate agent, in his shiny suit, carried in Dolly's last case with a grunt, obviously a little miffed at being asked to help with her luggage. He handed Dolly the keys and took out his folder with all the details. The phone, gas and electricity had all been connected.

He turned towards her with a smirk. 'Just a question of, um, the financial arrangements now, Mrs Marsh.'

Dolly loathed these weaselly little men. 'Would you just take the large case through to the bedroom for me, please?'

His smirk died. 'Yes, of course, Mrs Marsh.' Staggering under the weight of the large suitcase, he dragged it into the seedy bedroom. Dolly picked up the smaller case, placed it on the sofa and took out a set of keys. She checked that the estate agent was still busy with the case, then opened the lid. The money was still wrapped in the bank's plastic bags. She took one out, shut the case, locked it and put it back on the floor. Going to the table, she sat down and very slowly began counting out the money. The estate agent came out of the bedroom.

'As I was saying, Mrs Marsh—'

'Will there be any reduction if I give you cash?'

'Er ... er ... no, I'm afraid not,' he stuttered. 'It's a flat rate, Mrs Marsh. I, er, I have no bargaining power at all.'

'I see. Well, there's six months' rent in advance.'

He didn't know whether to sit and count it, glancing at his papers, then back at Dolly, and finally decided against it.

'I would like a receipt, if that's possible?' she said with a smile.

'Yes, of course, Mrs Marsh. I'll do that right away.'

'Thank you very much. You've been most helpful.'

'Oh, think nothing of it, Mrs Marsh.'

Dolly slipped a £10 note into his top pocket, and suddenly he couldn't do enough for her.

'If you have any problems whatsoever, Mrs Marsh, you just contact me. Ask for me personally – Mr Fish.'

'Yes, I will,' Dolly said, almost shutting the door in his face. And then she was alone. Alone in this awful flat.

She took a carton of milk, a jar of instant coffee and a packet of biscuits out of her shopping bag and into the kitchen. It had the same sparse, unloved feeling. She put the milk in the fridge, picked up the kettle, and then put it down again. She felt her hands – the handle of the kettle was greasy. Looking in the cupboard, the cups were chipped, and one of the saucers still had an old ring from the last occupant's tea.

Dolly ran the water in the sink. Even the bowl was grimy. She turned the tap off and stood for a moment. She thought of her home, her beautiful house, where everything had been so immaculate, so perfect.

She went back to her shopping bag and took out Fairy Liquid, Vim and a pair of rubber gloves. She brought them to the kitchen and turned the tap back on.

Well, if she was going to live here, she'd damned well make sure it was clean.

* * *

José had been the one to haul Linda's body out of the water. Bella had been worse than useless, weeping hysterically and asking Linda to forgive her. It was only José's calmness and quick thinking that had saved Linda's life. He turned her over, let the water empty out of her lungs, then gave her the kiss of life. It was José who carried her into the lounge, who somehow found the bandages and cleaned up her face. Knowing that the ambulance was on its way, he helped Bella undress Linda, wrapped a blanket round her and gave her brandy. As he fed her carefully with a teaspoon, her eyes opened and she stared into his face.

He smiled. 'You all right, Leenda? Everything's going to be OK, Leenda . . .'

It was the 'Leenda, Leenda . . .' that brought it all back, the taxi driver smiling as he walked towards her up the stairs. She started to scream.

José stepped away. 'She's in shock. You take care of her, Bella. I'll go and change.' As he was leaving the lounge, he turned back to Bella. 'Did you call the ambulance? The doctor?'

'Yes, yes, of course.'

'And the police? Are you going to call the police?'

Bella shook her head. 'No, no police. I don't want the police.'

'But you must call the police! The place has obviously been bur- gled. Leenda almost died!'

'I said no police.'

He was puzzled. He'd never heard her speak in that firm tone of voice before.

'We'll talk about it later,' he said and walked out.

Bella bent over Linda, held her hand and kissed her. 'Linda, it's Bella. You're all right. Linda, it's Bella!'

Linda was crying, without making a sound, just tears rolling down her cheeks.

'It's all right, baby, it's Bella.'

Linda slowly turned her head, opened her eyes and gripped Bella's hand hard. Bella could have wept herself – Linda's face was such a mess. She wasn't sure whether her nose was broken, but her eye was cut and bruised, her cheek and lips swollen. Bella just wanted to hold her, she seemed so fragile.

'Bella, oh God, Bella . . . it was him.'

Bella looked at the door. 'I know,' she whispered. 'I know. But it's all right.'

Linda turned away, closing her eyes again. 'He wanted Dolly,' she murmured, barely audible. 'He wanted Dolly.'

Bella gripped her hand tightly. 'Don't talk, Linda, don't talk. The doctor's coming, and everything's gonna be all right. Just lie quiet, please, baby.'

A shudder seemed to run through Linda's body and into Bella's. Her eyes jerked open and she clawed at Bella's arm.

'I told him, Bella,' she croaked, her eyes wide with terror. 'Oh, God help me, I told him.'

Bella couldn't make out what she was saying. She bent closer. 'What? What did you say?'

Linda choked, started to cough again, and Bella reached for the bowl, thinking she was going to vomit, but Linda shook her head.

'Bella, I've told him . . .'

A cold feeling moved up Bella's spine. 'Told him what? What have you said, Linda?'

'The money – I told him where it is, in England . . . the convent.'

Bella took a deep breath, trying to keep calm, but she could feel the panic rising. 'Did you tell him where Dolly was, Linda? Do you hear me, Linda? Did you tell him where Dolly was?'

Linda looked up into Bella's face. Bella had never seen an expression of such anguish. Time seemed to stretch out as she waited for Linda to speak. Then finally she managed a single word.

'*Yes.*'

CHAPTER TWO

José Camarana's ranch was just as Bella had described it: fantastic. Linda was in one of the guest bedrooms – very tasteful, with antique furniture – lying in a large double bed with a massive carved head-board, the drapes on the bed matching the curtains and the ice-blue carpet. Outside the window was the stable yard.

Sighing, she pushed away the large tray with the embroidered napkin and the lace-trimmed tray cloth. The perfectly scrambled eggs, toast and coffee turned her stomach. She picked up a hand mirror and stared at her face. She looked like a prizefighter after a particularly bruising bout. The stitches across her face were clean, but still crusted. Her right eye was all the colours of the rainbow, and her lips were still swollen. She put the mirror down and lay back.

Since she'd been at José's ranch, all she could think of was that she'd told Harry Rawlins where the money was. She'd betrayed them all. She wasn't that concerned about Dolly; it was just the fact that she had told him. She knew if she hadn't told him he'd have killed her, but that didn't make her feel any less guilty.

She'd *told* him.

She heard the clatter of horse's hooves outside. Slipping back the covers, she got out of bed and pulled the curtains aside. José Cama-rana, riding a black stallion, clattered into the yard. He wore a pale lemon cashmere sweater, riding jodhpurs and shiny brown boots. He really was one of the most handsome men Linda had ever seen and she couldn't help but stare at him. He got off the horse and flipped the reins to a boy already running from the stables. Then her heart jumped. Following behind him through the stable yard gates was a police car. A police officer with an awful lot of gold stripes on his uniform got out and started chatting with José in a friendly manner. They laughed together with their backs to Linda's window, then José turned, pointing in Linda's direction up to the window, and indicated that they should enter the house.

As Linda darted back from the window, Bella walked in.

'Look, I've got 'em, two tickets—'

Linda motioned for her to be quiet and come to the window. Bella looked down in to the yard.

'It's the police, Bella! What do you think they want?'

Bella shrugged. 'I don't know, Linda.' She went back to her bag that she'd left on the dressing table. 'I've got two open tickets – we can go as soon as you're fit.' Seeing the tray, she sighed. 'You've not touched your food again, Linda.'

Linda still stood at the window. 'I'm not hungry.' She was twisting her hands round each other.

Bella was beginning to get irritated. The last five days hadn't exactly been easy. Doctors had come and gone, and a nurse had been in attendance for two days, at José's insistence, but he couldn't understand why they wanted no police involvement. Their villa, after all, had been broken into, and Linda had very nearly been killed. But Bella had eventually convinced him that the best way to deal with the trauma was to try and forget all about it. Linda was in one piece, and that was all that mattered. They had collected all their belongings from the villa and returned to the ranch, and that was that.

'Do you think José's telling them something? I mean, what are we going to do, Bella?'

'What would he be telling them, Linda?'

Linda looked pensive. 'Well . . . he has been asking questions, Bella.'

Bella stiffened. 'What d'you mean? What sort of questions? Has he been asking about me?'

'No, nothing like that,' Linda said quickly. 'About the taxi driver . . . He wants to know what happened that night!'

Suddenly Bella seemed close to tears. 'I don't want to lose him, Linda. I've never met anybody like him, and I love him.'

Linda could feel her own tears welling up. 'I'm sorry. I'm sorry, Bella.' Then a thought suddenly occurred to her. 'Do you think Dolly's got the cable by now?'

Bella zipped up her bag. 'I don't know.'

'Did you send a cable to Shirley?'

'*Yes*, I sent a cable to Shirley.'

Bella just wanted to be out of the room now. Linda's nerves and constant questions – it was all getting too much.

As she opened the door, Linda said, 'Do you think Dolly would have been able to get to our money, Bella?'

'I don't know, Linda. You keep asking me and I keep telling you: I don't know. All I do know is I sent a cable to the clinic where I think Dolly may be.'

'But did you send one to the house as well?'

Bella was ready to blow her top. 'Linda, I don't know whether Dolly is at the house. She was going to sell the house. Which is why I sent a cable *to the clinic.* And before you ask, I've sent one to Shirley in Los Angeles at the hotel she was going to stay at, but *I don't know if they've got them!*'

Linda started to cry, the tears streaming down her face. 'Maybe we're . . . all right . . . Maybe Rawlins is . . . still in Rio.'

'And maybe he isn't. For gawd's sake, stop crying.'

Linda sniffed. 'I can't help it. It's all my fault. I told him the money's at the convent. I'm ruining everything!' She stopped suddenly in mid-flow. 'Do you think Dolly will be all right, Bella?'

'Well,' said Bella nastily, 'we just have to hope to God he hasn't got to her, don't we? If he did that to you, just think what he'd do to Dolly.'

A knock on the door, and they both froze.

'It's José,' came a voice from the corridor. 'May I come in?'

Bella picked up Linda's breakfast tray.

'Of course, it's open, José,' she called. She flicked a warning look to Linda as he entered. He smiled warmly and bowed towards Bella. Linda picked up some tissues and loudly blew her nose.

'How's our invalid today?' He looked at the tray. 'What's this? You don't like Anna's cooking?'

Linda muttered that it was fine, but she just wasn't hungry. That secret look flashed between José and Bella as José sat on the bed.

'I have some news for you.'

Bella smiled brightly. 'Oh, yes?'

'Yes,' said José. 'The taxi at your villa – my chauffeur was able to make out most of the number plate. The police are sure they will be able to trace the driver.'

Bella tensed up. 'I thought we'd agreed we didn't want to take it any further?'

José got up, touching her lightly on the shoulder. He caught sight of the two plane tickets on the dressing table and picked them up. 'What are these? *Two* tickets?'

'Oh, I just hadn't got round to telling you yet, darling,' Bella said lightly.

He placed the two tickets very carefully back on the dressing table. 'I see.' With a thoughtful incline of his head, he walked to the door. 'Excuse me.' His manners remained impeccable, but there was no disguising the iciness in his tone.

The door closed softly behind him.

'You'll have to tell him, Bella.'

Bella banged the breakfast tray down and turned furiously to Linda. 'Tell him what? We're running back to England because we're scared stiff Harry Rawlins is gonna nick our money?'

'I didn't mean that. You know I didn't mean that!'

'Then what did you mean?' Watching Linda squirming, tears in her eyes, Bella thought that sometimes she could really hate her. 'Well, come on, Linda. What? You want me to tell him about the raid?'

Linda shook her head.

'Oh, that's it. You want me to tell him about me. You want me to tell him what I was. He's asked me to marry him, Linda! You think he would have done that if he knew what I was? A tart?'

Linda began weeping. 'I didn't mean that. I . . .'

José had no intention of eavesdropping, but when he heard Bella's voice raised in anger, he couldn't help it. He stopped and listened. What he heard was the voice of a stranger – coarse and grating – not the Bella he'd come to know at all. As he listened it grew even louder.

'I'm telling you, Linda, he's not going to find out about me. I'm not gonna lose him, not for you, not for Dolly, not for anybody! I don't give a shit about the money. This is what I'm gonna do, Linda. *And stop crying for Chrissake!* I'm gonna tell him that we're gonna go back because you wanna see your mother.'

José moved closer to the door, straining to hear every word. Linda murmured something about not having a mother, then he stepped back sharply as Bella's voice screamed out, 'Well, you bloody got one now, you stupid bitch!'

As shocked as he was bewildered, José decided that he had heard enough and quickly walked back to his room. Pausing in the doorway, he saw Bella emerging from Linda's room, her face set in an ugly grimace. He closed the door.

* * *

Shirley Miller's mother, Audrey, had a new live-in lover – one Raymond Bates. Five foot six, Ray was a rotund little man with strange, dark tufted hair all over his chest and sticking up on top of his head. But despite his odd looks, Ray was her man and she loved him. Most importantly, he was straight – he had his own business, a garage – and that made Audrey happier than she'd been in years. Which was why she felt a little nervous when she saw the cable lying on the mat. Cables rarely meant good news. She opened it and walked into the kitchen.

'Our Shirley's comin' home.'

Ray looked up with a grin. 'All right, is she?'

Audrey sat down at the table. 'Well, that's my holiday up the spout. I've really been looking forward to it. "Come to Los Angeles," she said. I've only just gone out and got all that gear, all them summer clothes, and now . . .' Her mouth began to tremble. 'I'm not goin' now, am I?'

Ray reached over, gave her hand a squeeze and picked up the cable. 'What's she comin' home for? You think she knows about us?'

Audrey took out a crumpled bit of tissue and dabbed at her eyes. 'Oh, yes, I'm sure she's heard about us. Headlines in the *News of the World*, we are!' Her expression turned serious. 'Something's wrong, Ray, I know it. I mean, why did she call us up one minute and say, "Come out, have a holiday", say she's sending me money, then I get a cable next minute says she's comin' home?'

Ray put the cable down. 'Well, we're gonna find out, aren't we? What about you fryin' us up another slice of that bacon?'

Audrey blew her nose. 'Oh, Ray, love, you'll have to fry it up yourself. I'm gonna have to lie down, I don't feel too good!' Audrey didn't know what the matter was with her lately. She kept feeling sick all the time.

Ray went and picked up the frying pan. 'It's all right, darlin',' he said with a wink. 'I tell you what, one day I'll take you to Disneyland!'

Audrey gave him a sad smile and went to bed.

* * *

Dolly arrived at the clinic. The reception was all very tasteful – soft music playing, potted plants – but the soothing décor didn't make Dolly feel any less nervous as she walked up to the desk, carrying her overnight bag with everything in it, even the dark glasses. The receptionist smiled at her.

'It's . . . er . . . Mrs Rawlins. I'm, um, Mr Jarrow's patient.' Dolly could hardly speak.

The receptionist did her best to calm her. 'Ah, yes, we're expecting you. Good morning, Mrs Rawlins. Now, you're going to be in –' she turned the pages of her ledger – 'room 4E. I'll just call for a nurse to take you through. I'm sure you'll really love this room; it looks over the gardens. Oh, Mrs Rawlins . . .' She reached beneath the desk and brought out an envelope. 'This arrived for you two days ago.'

Dolly was taken aback. Mail? There shouldn't be any mail for her – nobody even knew she was here. Dolly's hand was shaking as she ripped open the envelope and read the cable inside. The receptionist was poised, pen in hand.

'I don't appear to have a forwarding address for you, Mrs Rawlins. Would you . . .' She stopped when she saw how shaken Dolly looked. 'Are you all right, Mrs Rawlins? Not bad news, I hope?'

Dolly hurriedly stuffed the cable in her pocket and picked up her bag. 'You've had this how long? This cable?'

'Two days, Mrs Rawlins. You see, we had no forwarding address.'

Dolly was already on her way to the exit.

'Please give Mr Jarrow my apologies, I'm afraid I have to . . . I'm so sorry.' And she was gone.

* * *

Harry was standing on the brow of a hill, looking down in to an orange grove. In a clearing he could see Tony leaning against his taxi, arguing with Jimmy, who was holding a handkerchief to his bleeding nose. The men were shouting at each other, but Harry couldn't hear what they were saying.

He watched Jimmy turn on his heel and walk up the hill towards him. 'He's a cocky son of a bitch,' Jimmy muttered as he reached Harry. 'He's only gone and butted me. Did you see 'im? He butted me one in the face!'

Harry's mouth tightened. 'Did you get the cash?'

Jimmy patted his bulging pockets. 'There's two grand. He said it's all that's left. He spent the rest. He's also panicking. The police have been round asking questions, and his girl—'

Harry cut him off. 'He tell them anything?'

Jimmy shrugged. He looked down at the taxi, then back to Harry. 'What do you want me to do?'

Harry put his hand out. 'Give me a coupla hundred.'

Jimmy fished a bundle of banknotes out of his pocket. Harry grabbed them and set off down the hill. Tony watched him approach, opened the door and got inside. Harry climbed in beside him.

'He got no right to do that to me – you owed me, you know?'

Harry gave him an ice-cold stare. 'I hear the police have been asking you questions. That right, Tony?'

'Yeah. They been to see my girl, too, and I don' like it!'

'Nor do I.' Harry smiled nastily. 'So I think you better take a trip, clear off for a few days.'

'What do you think I am?'

Harry moved fast, reaching over and gripping Tony's balls hard before he knew what was happening. Tony was in instant agony.

'You want to hang on to these, you better do as I say, all right?' Harry snarled.

Tony could only nod.

Harry let go. 'Here, enjoy yourself!' He tucked some notes into Tony's shirt pocket. As he got out of the car, he turned and leant in close. 'I don't wanna see you round for a while, all right?'.

Tony hunched over the steering wheel, his face a grimace of pain. Harry slammed the door and walked back up the hill. Jimmy met him on the path and they both watched as the taxi screeched off, raising a cloud of dust in its wake.

'You shouldn't have let him go, Harry.'

Harry shrugged. 'We got enough money to fix me a passport?'

Jimmy nodded. 'Yeah, I think so.' He dabbed at his nose, and Harry could smell blood alongside the usual reek of sweat.

'I need it quick. I'm leaving tonight.' Harry started down the hill.

Jimmy hurried after him. 'Maybe we could talk about that bit of business now? D'you wanna take a look at it?'

Harry just wanted to be rid of him. 'Yeah, yeah, I'll take a look at it for you.'

Jimmy was all over him. 'That's great!'

Harry snapped, 'Don't they sell deodorant round here, Jimmy? You stink!' He stalked off, leaving a crestfallen Jimmy literally stewing in his own juice.

* * *

Dolly drove to the convent and parked in the courtyard. Fortunately it was lunchtime, and she was able to get to the lockers, rip off the posters and remove the bags without being seen. They were so heavy, she had to take them to the car one at a time. Just as she closed the boot on the last one, the Mother Superior appeared at her side, as if out of nowhere.

She smiled. 'Mrs Rawlins . . .'

Startled, Dolly whipped round.

'How nice to have you back.' The Mother Superior smiled graciously. 'I hope you enjoyed your holiday.'

Dolly was desperate to get out. Suddenly she spotted a strap from one of the rucksacks sticking out of the boot. The Mother Superior watched as Dolly opened the boot and tucked it back in.

'I was, er, just collecting a few belongings from the lockers . . .' She desperately tried to think of an explanation. 'For the Brownies.'

'Oh, then you'll be seeing Mrs Gregory.'

Dolly stopped. 'I'm sorry, who?'

'Mrs Gregory – Brown Owl.'

'Oh . . . yes,' Dolly stammered. 'Yes, of course. I'm collecting these for Mrs Gregory. I-I really must go.'

The Mother Superior watched Dolly's little green Fiesta drive out of the main gates, then walked slowly back to the main door.

Strange woman, Mrs Rawlins, she thought to herself, always seeming to be in a rush. But a good woman, she was sure; a very good woman.

* * *

Jimmy's kitchen was littered with empty beer cans and dirty dishes as usual. Harry ripped the top off a beer can and took a deep pull while Jimmy leafed through an old copy of *Vogue* magazine Maria had brought back from the hotel where she worked as a cleaner. Harry wanted to get back to London as soon as possible, and the waiting was making him edgy.

Jimmy pushed the magazine over to Harry. 'Here, Harry, take a look at this.'

Harry looked at the centrefold spread in front of him. Photographed on black velvet were rows and rows of the most exquisite rubies, diamonds and emeralds – necklaces, earrings, tiaras, rings. As Jimmy leant over him, Harry again caught the stench of his BO.

'I talked it over with Micky Tesco while he was stayin' here. You know Micky, don't you, Harry?'

Harry lit a cigarette with a bored expression and shook his head. He looked at his watch.

'You sure this passport's on its way?'

'Yeah, the guy says he'll ring soon's it's ready.' Jimmy leant closer. 'Look at these babies, Harry. You know how much this lot's worth? Eight million. That's eight million quid's worth right there. Turn over the page.'

Harry looked at his watch again as he flipped the page.

'Look, Harry, I promise you, you'll be on the plane. But you just look at the blurb down the side of the picture, there. Look what it says.'

Harry read it. It was advertising a forthcoming charity fashion show being put on at Amanda's nightclub in three weeks' time, and all the jewellery on display was lent by Asprey, Garrard, Nijinsky – you name it.

Harry frowned. So what?

Jimmy rummaged through a drawer and came back with a stack of photographs. He grinned at Harry.

'Micky Tesco, he's a sharp one. You sure you never heard of him?'

Harry sighed. 'I told you, I don't know Micky Tesco.'

'He was on an embassy job. He's a clever lad.' Jimmy riffled through the photographs until he found the one he wanted, and placed it down proudly in front of Harry. It showed Jimmy with his arm round a tall, blond, handsome young man with a mean expression on his face.

Harry gave it a bored look.

'You see, you gotta have a crack team, Harry. For eight million, it'd be worth forking out a bit for the best.' He shoved the magazine under Harry's nose. 'All those little jewels will be on loan for the night. Look at 'em!' He picked up the photograph of Micky. 'He's a good-looking feller, isn't he? And he's sharp, he's very sharp, Harry.' He shrugged. 'But he's young. He needs the right man with him – someone with your experience, someone who knows the ropes.' Jimmy was still going on about it when the phone rang.

Harry jerked his head for Jimmy to answer.

As he picked up the phone, Jimmy was saying, 'I'd go over there myself, Harry, I'd pull it myself, but if I set one foot in London you know what's gonna happen to me.'

Harry knew only too well. Jimmy's past history was well known in the business. Jimmy'd always been a loser – he'd pulled that job at the airport, was picked up for it and did eight years. The stash he'd had from it he'd left with his wife, Myra – £22,000. But Myra's visits had soon stopped, and when poor old Jimmy got out of the nick there was no Myra, and no money. It turned out Myra had been having an affair with one of his closest mates. He had gone off to find him, his wife and his money. He never found his wife or his money, but he found the bloke, and he hit him a little bit too hard. He'd been on the run for two months when Harry had fronted him the money to get out of the country, and Jimmy had been in Rio ever since. Harry watched Jimmy talking on the phone and shook his head sadly. Poor Jimmy, always a loser, and now here he was, living in this shithole, still hustling, still after the big one.

'Passport's ready,' Jimmy announced, putting the phone down. 'You wanna come along with me and pick it up?'

Harry shook his head. 'I'll take a shower, get myself together.'

'OK by me, Harry. I'll be about half an hour.' Halfway out of the door he grinned, paused and pointed a finger at the magazine spread. 'Whaddya think, Harry? You could set it up, easy. It just needs somebody like you, Harry, to get things organised. It'll be like taking jam from a baby. Just look at them!'

Harry shook his head. 'It's not for me, Jimmy. Better shift yourself, I wanna get that plane.'

Jimmy's face fell. He opened his mouth as if he was going to say something, then just shrugged and walked out.

Harry lit a cigarette and pulled the magazine towards him. He looked at the picture of the gems for a moment, flicked through the rest of the magazine, then picked up the photograph of Micky Tesco. The blond, blue-eyed boy was tanned and fit, reminding him of himself when he was young. He threw the photograph down and went into the bathroom.

* * *

Dolly stood outside Mrs Gregory's house, carrying a large bouquet of daffodils. She rang the doorbell, stepped back and looked up. After a minute, she rang the bell again, and eventually a middle-aged woman opened the door.

Dolly smiled sweetly. 'Mrs Gregory? I'm from the convent. Mrs Rawlins. I don't believe we've met. Oh, these are for you.'

Dolly handed over the flowers and hovered on the doorstep, waiting to be asked in. 'I've got a few things from the convent in the car. I wondered would it be possible to have the drill hall keys?'

Mrs Gregory opened the door wide and gestured for Dolly to come in. In the lounge a very old lady was sitting by an electric fire, wrapped in blankets.

'Mummy, this is Mrs . . . I'm sorry, I didn't catch your name.'

'Mrs Rawlins, from the convent.' Dolly smiled.

'Mummy, this is Mrs Rawlins from the convent,' Mrs Gregory repeated in a slightly louder voice. She turned to Dolly. 'Do sit down – I won't be a moment.'

Sitting in the worn armchair, Dolly smiled at the little old lady, who didn't seem to be aware that anybody had entered the room, or that anything was going on around her at all. The room smelt of damp, polish and urine.

'It's a lovely day, isn't it?' Dolly said brightly.

No reaction whatsoever. When Mrs Gregory eventually came back she was carrying a large bunch of keys.

'I'm so sorry to keep you waiting. I will need these returned. Will you need them for very long?'

Dolly shook her head, smiling. 'I just want to store a few things and I'll bring them straight back to you.'

Mrs Gregory fiddled with the keys and removed two large ones from the ring. 'This one's for the main door of the drill hall and this one is for the inner door. The vicar had a separate set, but, um, I think he lost them some time ago, so these are the only keys now. I'd be most grateful if you'd return them as soon as possible.'

'Oh, I will,' said Dolly. 'I most definitely will.'

Mrs Gregory leant in closer to Dolly and whispered, 'My mother's totally senile now, I'm afraid. It's so sad – she really doesn't know what's what. Her only joy in life used to be the Brownies; it was the only time she could get out of the house. You know I'm the Brown Owl . . .'

'Yes, the Mother Superior said.'

'Would you have a cup of tea?'

Dolly was worried about leaving the rucksacks in the car. 'No, really . . . I ought be going as soon as I've put these bits and pieces in the drill hall. But thank you so much for your help.'

A look of real sadness spread over Mrs Gregory's face. Dolly realised how desperate for company she must be. The woman was probably her own age, and yet she seemed so old, so tired and worn.

After a moment, she said, 'Actually, a cup of tea would be very nice.'

* * *

José entered the bedroom and shut the door quietly. The bathroom door was open and he could see Bella's outline in the shower. She continued soaping herself, unaware of his presence. He turned away. Seeing the light on the side of the telephone was blinking, he picked it up as Bella stepped out of the shower and wrapped a towel round herself.

'I didn't hear you come in.'

'Oh, I am so sorry.' He gestured that he was on the phone, then spoke rapidly in Spanish, or was it Portuguese? Bella could never understand.

'*Sim, sim, não obrigado, sim.*'

Replacing the phone, he looked at Bella. She gave him a half smile and walked back to the bathroom. Following her, José leant against the bathroom door. The en suite bathroom was enormous, with a huge sunken bath, sauna, Jacuzzi, shower, and thick-piled carpet. Bella could feel his eyes on her as she studied her face in the mirror.

'Everything all right?'

He walked away from her into the bedroom. Bella knew something was wrong. She wrapped the towel tighter round her and followed him into the bedroom. He was slowly unbuttoning his shirt. He nodded towards the phone.

'That was my friend, from this morning, you remember? The police?'

Bella bit her lip.

'They found the taxi.'

She swallowed, trying to keep her voice normal. 'I'll tell Linda when she wakes up.'

José didn't take his eyes off her, and Bella knew he was watching her every move. She sat on the stool in front of the dressing table, picked up a brush and looked at him in the mirror.

Slowly, José continued to unbutton his shirt. 'Leenda is sleeping?'

'Yes.'

'They have the taxi, but not the driver. He appears to be missing.' He stared hard at Bella and she met his eyes in the mirror. 'But then, I don't think you wanted him found, am I right?'

Bella put down the hairbrush and turned to face him. 'It's not that. It's just that I think Linda's been through enough.' She stood up and moved sexily towards him, deciding to turn on the charm. 'I'd like her to stay, but she won't be persuaded. She wants to go back home, to see her mother.'

José knew she was lying. He sat down on the bed and kicked off one of his shoes. She touched his shoulder, but he shrugged her off.

'Are you all right?'

He kicked off the other shoe. 'I'm fine.' He stood up and pulled down the zip of his trousers.

Bella reached out a hand to touch him. He stepped back. Then he suddenly reached forward and pulled the towel away from her. She stood, naked, in front of him. He looked her up and down, examining every inch of her body with a cold expression. She put her hands over her breasts.

'Don't . . . don't do that . . .'

He flung the towel to the floor. 'I wasn't aware I was doing anything.' He stepped out of his trousers and folded them neatly, all the time watching her with that icy look in his eyes.

She bent to pick up the towel and wrapped it round herself again.

'Don't you like me looking at you?' he sneered.

Bella was starting to feel scared. Something was wrong, terribly wrong. She moved closer to him. 'You know I do. I love you, you know that.'

Still he stared at her; his face was hard, not the gentle, loving José she knew.

'Oh, you love me, do you? Because I'm rich?'

Bella gave a short laugh. 'No!'

He reached for her left hand, the one with the diamond ring. 'When are you coming back?'

Bella took that as a cue. She wrapped her arms round his neck and pulled him towards the bed. 'I don't want to go, and I don't want to leave you.'

He allowed himself to be pulled onto the bed, and she lay on top of him, kissed his chest, his neck. 'Mmm, I love you, I love every inch of you. I could eat you alive . . .'

He lay unmoving, not responding to her.

She leant on an elbow and stared into his face. 'I'm gonna make love to you, gonna give you something to remember me by while I'm gone.'

Then she kissed him again, licking round his ear, nibbling the lobe. Slowly she moved her hand down his body. Suddenly he pushed her, hard, and she fell to the floor. He stood up and walked into the bathroom. Bella remained in a heap on the floor, a trembling hand held to her mouth. He came back, wrapping a dressing gown round him, looking at her as if she was filth.

'Take your friend, your cases and get out tonight.'

She looked up at him with tears in her eyes. 'Has . . . Has Linda been talking about me?'

'Please, just leave, both of you – and for God's sake put something on.'

Bella slowly picked herself up and wrapped the towel round her.

'Is that all you're going to say? Just like that?' She went to take his arm, but he jerked it away, still looking at her as if she was a piece of dirt.

His voice was very quiet, and full of pain. 'I wanted you for my wife.' For a moment his expression softened, and he looked almost bewildered. Then as quickly as it had gone, the hardness returned. 'You . . . you don't belong here any more. I want you to go.'

'What did she tell you?' Bella almost screamed, her pain making her voice sound angry and spiteful. '*What did she tell you?*'

He said nothing, just looked at her with that stony gaze.

She spat out, 'I don't belong to *anyone!*'

He shrugged and walked into the bathroom. 'Then you won't mind leaving, will you?' he said over his shoulder, and closed the door in her face.

Bella banged on the door. 'Is that it? Is that all you've got to say?'

His answer was the loud click of the key turning in the lock.

*   *   *

Jimmy Glazier's bathroom was very different from José Camarana's – peeling paint, broken tiles, cracked loo seat, and a rusty shower with pink curtains half hanging off. Harry stood under the cold spray, having given up trying to get the water even a little warm. He swished the curtain back and it almost fell off its rail, as Jimmy banged on the door and pushed it open.

'Right, my old son, one-a passaporta, an-a one-a ticket. Get a move on if you wanna make that plane!'

Harry waved for him to pass a towel. Jimmy glanced admiringly at Harry's physique. He was still fit and muscular – very different from the flabby, paunchy Jimmy. He handed Harry the towel, then looked away, a bit embarrassed.

Harry wrapped the towel round his hips, picked up a razor and jerked his head towards the tub. 'Ever taken a shower, Jimmy? Maybe 'bout time you tried one.'

Jimmy laughed. 'Eh, do me a favour, they got nasty little thingies in the water here.'

Harry smiled and began to shave.

Jimmy walked into the scruffy kitchen. Maria was ironing Harry's suit with a sullen expression on her face. The magazine was gone. He went into Harry's bedroom and started poking round. He was just about to have a look in the holdall when Harry came in behind him.

'Where's that magazine?' Jimmy asked.

Harry smiled again. 'I'm gonna need something to read on the plane, aren't I?'

Jimmy beamed. 'So that means you're interested, then?'

Harry shrugged. 'Maybe. Tell you what, get hold of Tesco and tell him to pick me up at the airport. See if he can find me a place to stay an' all.'

Jimmy couldn't contain his excitement.

'Right away, Harry. Anything you say, Harry.'

'Good lad,' Harry said. 'And tell that wife of yours to get a move on with the suit.'

Jimmy scuttled off, almost bowing as he went. Maria was just putting the finishing touches to the suit when he went up behind her, put his arms round her and gave her a hug, singing, 'We're in the money, we're in the money . . .'

She turned round with a smile – the first Jimmy had seen in weeks – to put her arms around him and he squeezed her harder. This is more like it, he thought. Then he caught sight of the iron over her shoulder and smelt burning.

'Christ almighty, you stupid bitch! Now look what you've done!'

* * *

Dolly had to bend almost double to drag the rucksacks beneath the drill hall stage. The place was filthy with dust and grime, there were heaps of music stands, old curtains, bits of scenery, musical instruments, clowns' costumes – anything and everything had been stashed beneath the stage for what looked like the last two hundred years. Dolly was covered in dust, two nails broken. She had just managed to push the third rucksack to the very back, and was heaping boxes and old curtains round it, when she heard the sound of clumping feet – not just one set of feet, but a whole horde of them – thudding across the stage above her head.

She heard a voice say, 'Right, everybody, come along now, line up. Quietly, please!'

Oh, God, she thought. Now what?

The scoutmaster bellowed and screamed orders as more feet thudded across the stage, and as every little foot banged down, showers of dust fell on Dolly's head and all over her clothes, and she thought, Christ, how long am I going to have to stay here?

Then a whistle blew, followed by a strange bellowing and screeching, as if a load of farm animals had just been let out onto the stage, and she realised what she was in for – a band rehearsal. Dolly remained crouched uncomfortably in the darkness as the boys struck up a discordant rendering of 'When the Saints Go Marching In'.

*   *   *

Bella marched into Linda's room and banged the cases down. She ripped the bedclothes off and Linda shot up, a frightened look on her face.

'Well, you won, Linda. Don't know what you told him about me, but he's kicking us out. So get up – *now*!' She picked something up from the table. 'This your passport?'

'Wh-what's going on?' Linda was still dopey from sleep.

Bella started searching through the drawers. 'We're leaving now, so get moving!' Bella put Linda's passport in her own bag, along with the tickets, then flung open the fitted wardrobes, took out Linda's case and began throwing clothes into it.

Linda scrambled out of bed. 'What's happened, Bella?'

'The police think they've found him.'

Linda grabbed her arm. 'Rawlins? They've got Rawlins?'

Bella shrugged her off. 'No, you idiot, the taxi driver. *Now get dressed!* The plane leaves in three-quarters of an hour; we'll just make it if you bloody move yourself.'

Linda stumbled round the room, not sure where to start, what to do next.

Bella turned on her and grabbed her wrist viciously. 'I tell you, Linda, if Harry Rawlins has laid so much as a finger on my money, I'll kill 'im, so help me God I'll kill 'im!'

Linda whimpered. She'd never seen Bella so angry, her face contorted with rage. Bella let go of Linda's wrist, picked up her two suitcases and kicked her way out of the door. As she bumped her way awkwardly down the stairs, José emerged from his room, dressed formally in an elegant suit.

He leant over the banister. 'I've arranged for the car.'

Bella didn't even turn. 'That won't be necessary, I'll call a taxi.'

As she reached the bottom of the stairs, José's chauffeur opened the front door, and at a nod from José, picked up Bella's cases. She turned and began to walk back up the stairs. Midway she stopped, twisting the diamond ring off her finger.

Without looking at José, she said, 'I almost forgot, you'll want this back.'

He walked down to meet her. 'Keep it,' he said quietly.

'Fair enough. I'm usually paid cash, but this will do nicely.' She brushed past him without meeting his eyes.

Linda stood on the landing, clutching a beach bag bulging with clothes, along with a suitcase. Bella grabbed the case from her and started back down the stairs. Shaking, Linda held on to the banister. Linda gave José a weak smile, and he gave her his arm to help her down the stairs. When they reached the bottom, Bella yanked Linda roughly out of his grasp.

'We can manage, thank you!'

Bella marched to the front door, with Linda in tow. Linda tried to speak to José over her shoulder.

'Thank you for everything, you've been—'

Bella turned and gave her an almighty shove from behind. 'Just get out, Linda.'

She pushed Linda on to the porch, then paused. She could feel José behind her, the force of his gaze. All of a sudden the anger seemed to drain out of her. She turned, tears in her eyes, wanting more than anything for him just to hold her one more time. For a moment she thought he would. He took a step forward. Bella moved towards him. And then he closed the door in her face.

* * *

Dolly Rawlins glanced at her watch as she paced up and down the pavement. She had left several messages on Vic Morgan's answering machine, asking him to be at the office by nine o'clock. It was now nine twenty. She could feel her blood pressure rising.

A car pulled up outside his office building and Morgan got out.

'You're late, Mr Morgan.'

Morgan knew better than to reply, just walked ahead of her into the building and up the stairs. He could feel her fuming behind him as he fiddled with the lock on the door. Finally he opened it, and she marched past him into his office. Determined not to be intimidated, he paused to fiddle with the handle and push in the loose screw, before following her.

Dolly placed a briefcase on his desk. 'I want you to go to Australia House and get a visa for Trudie Nunn, and a baby. Make it out to be a big emergency. I've got two first class plane tickets, so she can have her kid next to her, and I want her on the first plane out of here. There's ten thousand in cash and she is to go to the Hilton Hotel in Sydney. Are you listening, Mr Morgan, I want that woman in Australia.'

Morgan hung his coat on a peg. It promptly fell to the floor. He picked it up and replaced it carefully. 'I'm listening, Mrs Marsh, go to Australia House and take that case to Mrs Nunn . . .'

He looked her up and down. 'You know you've got dust all down your back?'

Dolly brushed at her coat and realised that her hands were still grimy from the drill hall.

'I need you to do it straight away. I don't have much time.' She watched Morgan walk round his desk, pick up his unopened mail and sit down. He seemed in no hurry whatsoever. 'Mr Morgan, I want that woman on that plane.'

He looked at her. 'Why don't you just slow down a minute, Mrs Marsh?'

'I don't have the time, Mr Morgan,' Dolly snapped. 'And I'm paying you by the hour, in case you've forgotten.'

Morgan began to rip open his letters. 'I haven't forgotten, Mrs Marsh.' He eased his chair over to the computer, turned it on and began to type out a set of figures. 'May I enquire what's in the case?' he asked, without looking up from his typing.

Dolly didn't answer.

He looked up at her. 'You have a smudge here.' He pointed to his cheek.

Dolly took out a handkerchief, spat on it and rubbed her cheek.

Morgan continued to type for a moment. 'Are you paying Mrs Nunn off? Is that it?'

Again Dolly ignored his question. She opened her handbag. 'You'll want another advance, I suppose?'

Morgan pressed a key and waited. As the paper chugged out of the printer, he tore off a sheet and handed it to her. 'If you could just pay me what I'm due?'

Dolly glanced at the figures. 'Fine. Now look, I want you to check her passport's in order and take her to the airport. Just make sure that she gets on that plane. I'll settle this when I—'

'Now, if you don't mind,' he said with a firmness she hadn't heard in his voice before. 'And that's the last work I'll be doing for you, Mrs Marsh.'

Dolly looked at him in surprise. He seemed deadly serious. Then slowly she started to smile. 'Oh, I see. That's how it is. How much do you want?'

'It's nothing to do with the money, Mrs Marsh. I just don't like being ordered about.'

He looked serious, but Dolly was sure he was just using the fact that the clock was ticking to get a bigger fee.

'All right, I'll pay you fifteen pounds an hour.'

He said nothing.

Dolly tapped her fingers on the desk. 'Twenty. Twenty pounds per hour, but that's my final offer.'

Morgan stood up, walked round the desk and picked up the briefcase.

'No, thank you, Mrs Marsh. And if you haven't got the cash to pay me now, you can send it on. And don't forget these.' He handed her the plane tickets. 'Good morning, Mrs Marsh.' He gestured towards the door.

Dolly remained seated. She really didn't know what to do now.

'Is that your final word?'

'Like I say, Mrs Marsh, I don't mind doing the work, but I object to being treated like your skivvy.'

Dolly picked up the case, walked to the door, and then turned back to him. 'Is it because I'm a woman?'

He shook his head. 'That is immaterial, Mrs Marsh. Now, if you'll excuse me . . .'

Dolly realised she'd misjudged him. Trying to bully him or offering more money wasn't going to work. She need to change tack – and quickly.

She dropped the case with a sob. 'I'm sorry, Mr Morgan. I didn't mean to be rude. It's just that I'm . . .' Another sob, louder this time. '. . . desperate.'

He sighed. 'You really want this Trudie girl out of your way, don't you?'

Quietly, almost in a whisper, Dolly said, 'Yes, I do.'

'You must be very fond of your sister.'

A look passed between them that said they both knew it was a lie, but Dolly pretended it hadn't happened. She said simply, 'My sister loves her husband, and I'm asking you to help me.'

She was hoping underneath it all, Morgan really was a soft touch. She waited for what seemed like an age while he scrutinised her, seemingly making up his mind. Finally he picked up the briefcase.

'All right, Mrs Marsh, you win. My fee stands at the usual rate, all right?'

'Oh, thank you, thank you,' she gushed, quickly exiting the office before he could change his mind.

Morgan sat at his desk and shook his head with a wry smile. 'Women!'

* * *

Audrey's hair was still done up in rollers, but apart from that she was dressed up to the nines. Tea was laid out on the small coffee table, the cushions neatly arranged, a nice bowl of flowers on the sideboard. Ray stood uneasily in front of the mantelpiece, hands stuffed in his pockets, afraid to sit down in case he got a yell from Audrey and had to fluff up the cushions again. For the last half hour she hadn't been able to sit still, flitting in and out of the lounge like a mad thing while she got herself ready.

The doorbell rang, and Audrey started pulling the Carmen rollers from her hair, shouting, 'That's her. Ray, Ray . . .'

'Let her in, shall I?' he asked.

Audrey bustled back into the lounge. 'You just sit down there. No, not on the cushions, over there, on the edge of the sofa.' She ran her fingers through her hair and checked herself in the mirror one last time. 'Right, I'll let her in, then.'

'Good idea,' Ray said calmly. 'But bear in mind she might think she's come to the wrong house.'

Audrey started to the door, then turned back to him with a schoolmistress-like tone. 'Now, you let me do the talking, Ray.'

He smiled and nodded.

As Audrey went to the door, Ray patted his pockets for cigarettes. He was starting to get a bit edgy now. Damn. He opened a cigarette box on the mantelpiece and tinny music started tinkling, while a little ballerina turned round and round, but the box was empty. He could hear Audrey in the hall, shouting and whooping with joy, and another, lower voice laughing along with her. Shirley entered the room first, carrying a vanity case, and clutching several packages under her arm. She saw Ray and stopped in her tracks.

Audrey nudged her further into the room. 'Go in, go in.'

Shirley and Ray stood looking at each other.

'Ray, this is Shirley. Shirley, this is Ray, Raymond Bates.'

'I've heard a lot about you, Shirley, love.' Ray smiled.

Shirley didn't say anything. She obviously hadn't heard a word about Ray.

'I'll put the kettle on; you must be gasping for a cuppa,' he said, trying to ease the tension.

'Come on, love, sit down, sit down,' Audrey said as he left the room. 'Ooh, you look lovely. I wanna hear all about your trip.'

Shirley remained standing. 'Has Dolly Rawlins called?'

Audrey shrugged. 'Why would she? I thought she was on holiday with you.'

She was starting to worry that something was wrong, but still couldn't help eyeing the pile of presents. Shirley finally sat down and handed them over. Audrey started ripping off the tissue paper with a lot of oohs and aahs – her favourite perfume, a couple of boxes of chocolates, and then she took out the beautiful silk nightdress.

Ray came back in. 'Kettle's on.' Then he looked at Shirley and back to Audrey.

'Photos don't do her justice, Aud.'

Shirley said nothing. Audrey held up the nightdress, trying to cover the embarrassment. 'Oh Ray, look, it's silk, isn't it, Shirley?'

'You got your fags down 'ere, gel?' he asked.

Audrey began undoing her second parcel. 'A dressing gown. Oh, Shirley, you shouldn't . . . Look at this!' She took out a necklace. It was all bananas and cherries in bright plastic. 'Oh, this is lovely, really lovely. You get this in Los Angeles, did you? Ohh, it's beautiful!'

Shirley jerked her head towards the door. 'He seems to be making himself at home. Permanent fixture, is he, Mum?'

Audrey dropped the necklace. 'Now don't you start, you only just got 'ere.'

They could hear Ray whistling in the kitchen. He popped his head round the door. 'I can't find the fags, Aud.'

Audrey gave him a look. 'Come and sit down, Ray, and talk to Shirley.'

Ray remained standing in the doorway. 'Better not sit down,' he said with an awkward grin, nodding at the cushions. 'She'll have a fit if I put a dent in them. '

Shirley took a carton of cigarettes out of her vanity case. She didn't look at Ray as she started unwrapping them. 'So, you're living with my mother, are you?'

* * *

Vic Morgan sat in a rickety chair in Trudie Nunn's scruffy lounge and listened to the baby's cries coming from the bedroom. The smell of baby sick hung over the room. Toys lay on the floor, dirty crockery on the table. He wondered what on earth Mrs Marsh's so-called sister's husband was doing getting himself involved in this situation.

The baby carried on crying. How long was she going to be in there? He drummed his foot on the floor. It had taken him a while to get her confidence. At first she didn't want to let him in at all.

But then he said that he'd got something for her. He handed her the briefcase and the note, and the plane tickets, and she'd taken them into the bedroom.

He got up and tapped on the bedroom door. 'Mrs Nunn, if you wanna get your passport sorted out we really should make a move. Mrs Nunn?'

There was no reply.

He wandered round the room again. He stared at the photograph of a young, smiling boy on the mantelshelf. He wondered if that was her husband. There must be a Mr Nunn somewhere round the place.

Trudie Nunn sat in the bedroom, the open briefcase in front of her. She kept touching the money, not quite believing her eyes. Then she picked up the single sheet of notepaper. It said simply, *Trudie, get over to Australia. Sydney. Hilton Hotel. I am waiting. Ask the messenger no questions, just be on that plane. Harry.*

Again Trudie touched the money. It was almost as if he was in the room with her.

She whispered over and over to herself, 'Harry, I'm coming ... I'm coming, Harry.'

He hadn't let her down after all. He'd said he would send for her, and now he had, and nothing was going to stop Trudie from joining him.

* * *

Shirley could hear Audrey shouting 'Ta-ra' to Ray from the hallway. The front door slammed. The remains of the tea was still on the coffee table. Audrey came back into the room, blabbing on about Shirley's lovely suitcases in the hall, how she always loved matching suitcases, that it was the height of fashion to have everything matching, that one day she'd always have everything matching – shoes, handbag, luggage, the lot – it showed good taste. On and on she prattled. Shirley waited for her to run out of steam.

Eventually Audrey came out with it. 'Well, what d'ye think of him? Good-looking, isn't he?'

Shirley snorted.

'Well, he might not be your type . . .' Audrey said in a hurt voice.

Shirley sighed. 'No, he isn't, and you know why? He's got "small-time villain" stamped right across his forehead, Mum, just like all the others you've dragged back 'ere. When will you ever learn?'

'What about your Terry?' Audrey snapped back. 'He wasn't exactly Prince Charles, was 'e?'

Shirley ignored her. ''E's married, isn't 'e? You don't have to tell me – you've gone an' done it again, 'aven't you?'

Audrey stood up with an angry expression on her face. 'You watch your mouth, my girl!'

Neither of them said anything for a minute. Audrey busied herself clearing the tea table. Then Shirley picked up the large parcel on the sofa.

'Can you give this to Greg?' It was a tracksuit she'd got her brother in Los Angeles.

Audrey didn't look up. 'You can give it to Greg yourself – he's living at your place.'

'My place? Greg's living at my place?'

With the cutlery still in her hand, Audrey turned to face her daughter. 'I don't know what's come over you. You've changed, you know that? You've changed.'

Shirley picked up her vanity bag and walked out, pausing at the door to say, 'Well, I'm glad one of us has, Mum.'

She slammed the door behind her.

* * *

After a moment's trouble with the sticky door handle, Morgan entered his office and played back the messages on his answering machine. The first call was the mechanic from the garage, regretfully informing him his beloved old Rover needed a lot of work if it was going to pass its MOT. The second call, at 8:30, was from Mrs Marsh, asking if Trudie Nunn had made the plane. The third call was also from Mrs Marsh, with the same question only in a slightly tenser tone of voice. Morgan was just about to see if the rest of his messages were from Mrs Marsh, when he heard the doorknob rattling.

'Push, Mrs Marsh!' he called out.

The door opened and Dolly walked in. 'How did you know it was me?'

'She's on the plane, Mrs Marsh, with the kid. I have a couple of receipts for you – and a dry-cleaning bill. The little nipper was sick down me twice.'

Dolly smiled. 'I'm sure that never happened to Humphrey Bogart.'

Morgan laughed. 'No, and I don't come when people whistle, either.' He looked at her. 'So you just wanted to make sure I'd done my job?'

'No, not just that.' She handed him a photograph. 'This is my sister's husband. I'm sorry it's taken me so long to bring it to you, but now I want you to keep watching Trudie Nunn's house to see if he turns up, and, if he does, to follow him and find out where he goes.'

'Ha-ha!' said Morgan. He looked at the photograph, then at Dolly. 'So now you've paid off the girlfriend, you think lover-boy will want to find out where she's gone?'

Dolly nodded.

'How long do you want me to watch Mrs Nunn's place? Couple of days?'

Dolly shrugged.

'I see, until he shows, right?'

Dolly nodded. 'I have to go. No, please, don't get up, I'll practise with the door myself.' She wiggled the doorknob once, opened it with a click, and left.

Morgan leant back in his chair and began whistling between his teeth. He swivelled round and played back the rest of the messages on the answering machine. Nothing important, one Mrs Windsor wondering if he would call her at his convenience. Then the bleep, bleep of someone hanging up, then another call from Mrs Marsh, again enquiring if Trudie had made it to the airport. She was certainly very persistent, and determined to get that woman out of England and as far away as possible in Australia. He looked hard at the photograph Mrs Marsh had given him, then turned the answering machine off.

He tapped the photograph with his finger. Where had he seen this face before? When he suddenly remembered, he shot forward in his chair. Of course, Harry Rawlins.

Morgan picked up the phone, dialled and waited.

'Detective Inspector Resnick there?'

The reply came back that Resnick was retired.

'I see. D'you know where I can find him?'

* * *

Shirley just about hit the roof when she saw the state of her house. It looked as though it had been used as a Salvation Army doss-house for six months. Every room was a mess, especially the one where there were two rolled-up sleeping bags. Greg had shuffled and sniffed, and said all he was doing was looking after the place. He was going to get it all tidy, he just didn't know when she was coming home, that's all.

Shirley had made herself hoarse screaming at him as she marched from room to room, each one more of a tip than the last. 'I can't tell you how disgusted I am. You and your lousy friends are nothing but layabouts, lazy, no-good—'

'All right, all right.' Greg went and got a duster and some spray polish and started cleaning up in a half-hearted manner.

Shirley opened the fridge. She couldn't believe the stench – rotting bags of carrots, onions, cabbage, food that must have been left for weeks. She put on a pair of rubber gloves and began chucking them into a black plastic bin bag. She opened the crisper at the bottom of the fridge, which was packed tightly with videotapes. She took a handful out and looked at the labels. *Big Boobies and Suspenders, Flesh and Sex of a Superman, Supergirl and Supersex.*

Shirley stormed into the hall. 'Greg, what are these doing in the fridge?' she yelled. 'They're *pornographic!*'

Greg shrugged and carried on polishing. 'Nah, they're educational!'

'Oh, sure, *Big Boobies and Suspenders*! I'm gonna burn these!'

Greg put his duster down. 'Aw, leave it out, Shirl, they're Ray's.'

Shirley looked at him. 'Ray? Ray who?'

Greg shrugged. 'You know, Mum's boyfriend. They're his.'

'Oh, they're Ray's, are they? Right, I'm going round there.'

* * *

Linda and Bella's flight from Rio had been an excruciating experience. Bella had refused to speak for most of the journey, and when she did, it was only to bite Linda's head off. So Linda had tried watching a film, and mercifully had eventually fallen asleep.

Now she was sitting miserably by the luggage turntable, while Bella went off to get a trolley.

Linda's head was throbbing, her eye hurt, she was feeling nauseous all the time. She watched the suitcases going round and round, then spotted Bella lugging the cases off the turntable. Linda looked round the baggage section – and then gasped. Heading almost directly towards her was Harry Rawlins, carrying a small holdall. He was wearing a creamy linen suit, and had dark glasses on, but Linda was sure it was him. She was frozen with terror, unable to move as he walked within ten feet of her – and straight past, looking neither left nor right, towards the 'Nothing to Declare' channel. As he reached it he removed his dark glasses and slipped them into his top pocket. He looked round him, and for a moment Linda was sure he had seen her. She needed to warn Bella.

At that moment, Bella appeared with the trolley, laden with all their cases. Linda jumped up.

'Bella! Don't look round, but Harry Rawlins is here – he's going through Customs!'

'You're imagining things, Linda.' Bella turned and stood with her hands on her hips, scanning the passengers going through Customs. 'Must have been someone who looks like him. Come on, grab your case and let's get out of here.'

It was late at night, and on the other side, there were only a handful of people waiting at the arrivals barrier. Leaning casually against the barrier, one man in particular stood out. Blond and handsome, his muscular physique bulging under his fashionable Italian suit, Micky Tesco glanced at the arrivals board, and the flashing light told him that Flight 432 from Rio had landed.

He checked his watch and looked slowly round the terminal. A good-looking red-headed airline stewardess caught his eye and he gave her the once-over, from the top of her head down to the heels of her shoes. She turned towards him, as if she'd felt him looking at her, and smiled. She was fit, all right, and he knew he could pull her, easy. But he turned back to the arrivals gate without returning her smile. He had other fish to fry.

Harry came down the walkway in a scruffy suit and in need of a shave. Micky Tesco did a double-take. No way that tramp could be the man he was waiting to meet – *the* man, Mr Harry Rawlins. He looked over towards the lounge, wondering where the redhead had gone to.

At the same time, Harry spotted Micky and made his way over. He sidled up behind him while he was looking the other way and quietly said one word: 'Tesco'.

Micky jumped round, startled. Rawlins nudged him forward. 'Keep moving to the end of the barrier. Any minute now, two women, one white and one black, will be coming through Customs. I want you to stay on their arses, find out where they're staying.'

They spoke for a few more seconds, and then Tesco handed Harry a set of keys, and Harry quickly made his way out of the building.

Tesco walked back to the arrivals gate, just in time to see Linda and Bella emerge from the Customs Hall. Linda was leaning heavily on the trolley. Very pale, she looked as if she might pass out, while Bella just stared dead-eyed, her lips pursed. It was very easy for Tesco to slip quietly behind them and follow them to the exit and out to the taxi rank, neither paying any attention to the blond man sauntering along behind them.

* * *

If Dolly Rawlins' rented flat was threadbare and seedy, it was luxurious in comparison to the flat Micky Tesco had rented for Harry. But at least it had a phone, and the first thing Harry did when he arrived was put in a call to Gordon Murphy.

Gordon Murphy was an old-timer. Quiet, a bit of a loner, he'd spent most of his life in and out of prison, though right now he was living with his mother. He'd worked for Harry for years and Harry knew he could trust him. Gordon had a great respect for Harry and, even if the man called from the grave, Gordon Murphy wasn't going to ask any questions.

As Harry replaced the receiver, Micky Tesco let himself in. Harry hadn't realised he had his own set of keys.

'You could have knocked first,' he said irritably. 'How d'you make out, then?'

Micky dropped the keys with a shrug and sat down, putting his feet up on the rickety coffee table, showing off his shiny cowboy boots. Harry didn't like his manner. A bit too self-assured; a bit too cocky.

Micky took a piece of paper from his jacket pocket and looked at what he'd written: *The white chick got dropped off at a basement flat in Kensington. The black girl went on to a place up west, Phoenix House, behind the theatre.*

Rawlins put his hand out for the scrap of paper. 'This place is a dosshouse. I need groceries, booze, soap – there's a list on the table there. I also need a motor. You got one lined up for me?'

Tesco replied sullenly, 'Yeah, picking one up tomorrow.'

'What time?'

''Bout ten.'

'Right, see what you can get now, and bring the rest tomorrow.'

Tesco took that as his cue to get up and leave. He made sure Harry could see he was in no hurry. As he got to the door, he said, 'I'll be right back then, Harry.'

Harry was already dialling a number. He didn't look up. 'Mister Rawlins to you, son.'

Tesco thought he was joking and laughed. But when Harry turned to look at him, he knew he was serious. Tesco nodded and walked out.

*　*　*

Bella had rented her little one-room flat to Carla, a black girl she'd once worked with in a show. They'd become good friends, but Carla wasn't exactly pleased to see her when Bella arrived. She'd expected to have the flat for at least three months, and now she was going to have to find somewhere else.

'Sorry, darling,' Bella said, 'but that's just the way life goes.' Once she saw what a mess the flat was in, however, she eased up a bit. Carla would need some time to clean up. 'Tell you what, I'll book into a hotel tonight, but tomorrow . . . sorry.'

Carla walked Bella to the door and put her arms round her. 'That's OK. Things didn't work out, eh?'

For a moment Bella looked as though she was going to cry. Then she just shrugged. 'No, no, they didn't. See you tomorrow then, kid. I'm sorry about this.'

Carla shut the door, leaning on it for a moment. Ohhh, shit. Now what am I gonna do? she thought. She went and picked up an old suitcase and started throwing her clothes into it.

* * *

Harry liked the fact that Gordon Murphy didn't question his miraculous reappearance. Harry was alive, and that's all that seemed to matter. Murphy was a big man, six foot two, and well-built but still slim-looking. He wore tinted, rimless glasses, which gave him a slightly chilling look. He had brought Harry a bottle of vodka, wrapped in tissue paper.

As he handed it over, he said, 'I remembered your tipple, Harry. Vodka, that's right, isn't it?'

Harry smiled, slapping him on the back. He put the bottle on the coffee table, while Murphy went into the kitchen and found some glasses. Harry poured two large measures, and the two men clinked glasses and took a good belt.

'Good to see you, Harry.'

Harry patted his arm. 'I don't want anyone to know I'm around, yeah?'

'Sure, Harry.'

Harry knew his secret was safe with Murphy. He refilled their glasses and they both had another drink. Murphy put his glass down.

'So, you need me to do something for you, Harry?'

'Yeah, Gordon, I do.' Harry proceeded to tell Murphy as much as he needed to.

Murphy listened in silence, then said, 'If these girls know where Dolly is, then I'll find her.'

Harry smiled. 'I knew I could rely on you, Gordon.' He looked embarrassed for a moment. 'Look, I'm a bit strapped for cash at the moment, but I'll see you all right in a couple of days.'

Murphy looked into Rawlins' face, very serious, and said, 'Have this one on me – for old times' sake, Harry.'

'Cheers, Gordon.'

Gordon stood up, and Harry helped him into his coat, noticing how carefully he did up each button before he walked to the door.

'How's your mother?' Harry asked.

Murphy sighed. 'Not too good. Housebound now, but she's still a game old bird.'

'I'll bet she is.' Harry smiled.

At the door, Murphy said, 'I'll find her for you, Harry, you just leave it with me.'

Harry nodded. He knew that if anybody in London could find his wife, Gordon Murphy would – and no one would ever know about it.

* * *

Linda couldn't get warm. She switched on the electric fire in the lounge, then the one in the bedroom, and she put on the electric blanket before getting into bed, but she still couldn't get warm. She felt cold and lost, the flat so full of memories of Joe. She got out of bed and went down to the kitchen. The fridge contained half a bottle of rotten, stinking milk. She shut the fridge door and walked out of the basement and up the steps, wearing her dressing gown and fluffy slippers. She pressed the buzzer on the main door for Mrs Johnson upstairs. The old lady took her time, and Linda had to ring again. Eventually a feeble little voice asked who it was.

Linda put her mouth close to the intercom. 'It's Linda, from downstairs. Can I borrow some milk?'

The buzzer went and Linda slipped into the house, just as Gordon Murphy appeared. He took a quick look at the house, then headed down the basement steps. He rang the bell and waited, pressed again and waited some more. He peered through the window, rang the bell again, then flipped open the letterbox. He stood back and looked the door over – not too hard to break in, he reckoned.

He'd just check the other girl first.

Linda was opening the main door of the house just as Murphy came back up the basement steps. She stepped back sharply, pulling the door almost closed and watching him through the crack. When he was out of sight she scurried down the stairs and in through her own door, her hands shaking so much she could hardly open it. She wanted to call somebody, anybody, but she couldn't think of anyone, so she made sure the front door was locked and got into bed. She could see her reflection in the mirror. Her face was white, her eye still bruised, and the line from nose to cheek brought back an overpowering memory of how close she had come to being killed.

She lay back on the pillow and the tears came. After a long time, she cried herself to sleep.

*   *   *

Carla had almost finished packing. She had called up all her friends to see if anyone would let her crash the next couple of weeks, but it was always the same – no room at the inn. Everybody knew Carla; she was always looking for a place to stay. Her transistor radio was playing Diana Ross, and Carla hummed along. The doorbell rang.

She yelled, 'It's open!'

There was no answer.

'It's open!'

She thought maybe it was Bella coming to check up on her. She began folding a dress before placing it in the suitcase.

The door slowly opened, and Gordon Murphy stood there. His voice was very quiet.

'Just unpacking? Have a good trip, did you?'

Carla almost jumped out of her skin. 'Who the hell are you?'

Murphy stepped into the flat. 'I just want to ask you a few questions, darlin'. Tell me what I want to know and you won't get hurt.'

She just stared at him, terror in her eyes.

'Where's Dolly Rawlins?'

'I . . . er . . . who?' she stammered.

'Come on, don't mess me about – Dolly Rawlins,' he repeated, moving closer.

Carla started backing away. 'I dunno what you're talkin' about.'

Murphy removed his tinted, rimless glasses, putting them very carefully into his jacket pocket.

'I don't wanna hurt you, Bella, but I'm not gonna ask you again. Where's Dolly?'

Carla wanted to tell him that she wasn't Bella, that she'd never heard of Dolly Rawlins, but she was so scared she couldn't speak. Murphy picked up a pillow and moved towards her, while Diana Ross kept on singing in the background.

Murphy was a pro. That was one of the things Harry liked about him. Carla didn't even have time to cry out.

* * *

Audrey was sitting in the kitchen in her dressing gown. She felt the way she looked, pale and drawn, and the last thing she wanted to do was have an argument with Shirley, who was standing there with a paper carrier bag full of pornographic videos. Shirley dumped them noisily onto the table.

'They're porn, Mum, and they were in my fridge!'

Audrey giggled nervously. 'How d'you know? Watch them, did you?'

'Not funny, Mum. Did you have any idea what Greg has been up to in my house? As far as I can see, he's been running a porn movie rental service. And who do you think gave them to Greg in the first place? None other than your new, oh-so-straight, oh-so-honest, live-in lover-boy, Ray!'

Audrey suddenly came over all dizzy.

Shirley looked at her. 'You all right, Mum?'

Audrey rubbed her tummy. 'Yeah, just a bit of wind.'

As if on cue, Ray Bates breezed into the kitchen. 'Hello, Aud, me old darlin'! Shirley . . .' He turned and opened the kitchen door further. 'Come on in, Micky!'

Micky Tesco followed Ray in. Ray made a great show of introducing Micky to Audrey, and then to Shirley. Micky came out with the usual smooth banter.

'Oh, you don't look old enough – daughter? Where they been keepin' you hidden, then?'

Shirley wasn't amused and didn't reply. Audrey filled Micky in about her daughter being in Los Angeles as she got up, put the kettle on and opened the biscuit tin. Tesco was still giving Shirley the once-over.

'What kind of work d'you do, then?'

Audrey answered for Shirley again. 'Model. She's a model. That's why she's been in Los Angeles, modelling.'

Ray gave Audrey a pat on the bum. 'Any chance of a butty, Aud? Fancy a cup of tea, Micky?'

Micky looked at his watch. 'Another time, Ray. If you just get that log book, I'll be on my way.'

Ray whispered to Audrey that Micky'd just bought his Jag. 'Nice bit o' business.'

Tesco pulled a chair from under the kitchen table and sat down. 'So what kinda business you in?' Shirley asked him.

Tesco examined his cowboy boot. 'Property.'

Shirley wasn't really listening. She picked up her handbag. 'So you'll have a word with Greg about the videos, Mum?'

Ray came back into the kitchen with the log book.

'Oh, how's that little skiver, then?' Not waiting for an answer, he gave Tesco the log book.

Shirley gave Ray another of her cool looks. 'Greg's fine. He's moving back 'ere – if that's all right with you, Ray?' she added in a sarcastic tone.

Ray gave Audrey a look, then glanced back at Shirley. It was awkward that she didn't like him, but right now he didn't really care. He'd just done a very nice little bit of business. The motor trade wasn't doin' all that well, and to get that Jag off his hands was very satisfying.

Tesco carefully went over the log book, then reached in his jacket pocket and handed Ray an envelope. The two men shook hands and Tesco turned to Shirley.

'You wanna lift anywhere?'

Shirley shook her head. 'I've got my own car, thanks.'

Tesco shrugged and opened the kitchen door for her. Shirley gave a little wave to her mum, completely ignoring Ray, and walked out. Tesco gave Ray a wink and followed her.

As the door closed behind him, Audrey put the teapot on the table. 'You know, Ray, you should try and fix that boy up with Shirley. He seems very nice, and ever so handsome!'

Ray nodded distractedly. He was too busy counting the money.

*   *   *

Harry didn't think much of the Jag. He walked round it, kicked the wheels, then got behind the wheel and revved up the engine.

'How much you lay out for this heap of shit?'

That was the last straw for Tesco. He was still steaming about the list Harry had just handed him, with strict instructions to bring it all back to the flat by three o'clock. The list included shirts from Turnbull & Asser, suits, shoes, socks, underpants – Tesco couldn't believe it.

'What the friggin' hell d'ye think I am? Cash and carry?'

Harry was still revving the engine, watching the blue smoke coming out of the exhaust.

'Jimmy never said nothin' about me toggin' you out!'

Harry switched off the engine. 'How much have you got to play with, then?' he asked without even looking at Tesco.

Micky puffed himself up. 'I got plenty! Nearly eight grand.'

Harry laughed. 'Eight! You got eight grand? I said to Jimmy, "No cutting corners on this caper".' He was fiddling with the dashboard, still not looking at Tesco. 'You couldn't organise a raid on a sweet shop for that.'

Tesco snapped. 'I don't see you dippin' your hand into your pocket, Mister Rawlins. You matched my eight grand yet? How many men we got in yet? Zero! There's nobody. You an' me, that's all there is, an' all I'm doin' is schleppin' round buyin' you gear!'

Harry finally turned to him. 'Your eight grand, son, is a piss in the ocean. I'm gonna have to cover you twenty times over. Now, you just get the shoppin', darlin', and do what I tell you.' Harry switched the engine back on and put the car in gear.

Tesco hung on to the window. 'Hey, just a second, how am I gonna get about? I left my car up at Ray's . . .' He almost fell into the street as Harry drove off. 'Son of a bitch!' He screwed up Harry's list and threw it after the car as it disappeared down the road.

* * *

When Bella let herself in to her flat, the first thing she noticed was the radio, lying on its side in the hallway, as if it'd been thrown against the wall. It was still playing. She picked it up and turned it off.

'Carla?' she called out. Bella pushed open the bedroom door. The room was a shambles – chairs broken, stuff strewn all over the floor, the whole place smashed up. The bed was piled with sheets, blankets, clothes and suitcases.

At first, Bella didn't see Carla, just heard a soft mewing, almost like a kitten, and then she realised it was coming from underneath all the debris on the bed. Bella began pulling everything away and found Carla curled up like a baby. She was whimpering. Bella got down on her knees.

'Baby, oh baby . . . What happened to you?'

Slowly, Carla turned her face towards Bella. It was black and blue, her lips split open, one eye closed. Her nose was caked with blood that still dripped down her face. As Bella pulled the sheets back, she saw the state of Carla's body – bruises covered almost every inch of her. But all Carla could whimper was, 'My face, my face . . .'

Bella stood in shock for a moment, then went to pick up the phone. It had been torn from the wall. She went back to the bed.

'Just lie still, baby, I'll get an ambulance. Please don't move, darling.'

Carla struggled to talk. 'Thought I was you . . . said he wanted . . .'

Bella was down on her knees again. 'What?' What, darlin'?'

All she could get out was the word 'Dolly'.

Bella leant in closer. 'What about Dolly?'

But all she heard Carla mutter from between her puffy, bruised lips was, 'My face, my face . . .'

As Bella stood to go for an ambulance, she caught sight of herself in the broken mirror, and knew that that bruised and beaten face could so easily have been her own.

* * *

Harry used his key to enter Trudie Nunn's flat. And the first thing he noticed was how clean and tidy it was. In the kitchen everything was spotless. When he pushed open the bedroom door, he could see that the bed was stripped. He walked round the flat again to make sure, then kicked over a chair in frustration.

Trudie was gone.

On the floor by the chair he saw a tiny teddy bear. He recognised it as the one his baby had clung to from birth and in a sudden flash he saw the boy, sucking at the toy. He bent to pick it up. It was small enough to fit in the palm of his hand.

The front door suddenly opened and a big, blowsy woman marched in. 'Flat's gone, went this morning.'

Harry didn't turn. 'Where's Trudie? And the kid?'

'Little bitch did a moonlight, didn't she, with some bloke. Owed rent, milk bill . . . You a friend of hers? She owes me rent, you know!'

He pushed past her to the door. She followed him, and then stopped.

'Hey, you, just a minute – how d'you get in?' But Rawlins was already running down the stairs. The landlady looked over the banisters. 'Dirty, filthy little slut,' she muttered to herself.

* * *

Dolly poured a cup of tea and took it to Bella. They were all at Linda's flat – Dolly, Linda, Bella and Shirley. Bella was in a terrible state, almost hysterical.

Dolly quietly asked her again. 'You sure? You're sure it was Harry?'

Bella knocked the cup of tea out of Dolly's hand. 'How many bastards are lookin' for you, Dolly? He said your name – it was you he was asking for, over and over as he hit her, he kept on asking for *you*!'

'Did he think Carla was you?' Linda asked in a frightened voice.

Bella turned on her. 'Course he bloody did! I'm black, she's black – we all look alike in the dark, you stupid bitch!' Bella leant forward to slap her, but Dolly caught her hand.

'Now just take it easy, Bella. Pull yourself together!'

Bella jerked her hand away. 'What's she asking me stupid questions for, Dolly? It was Harry, I'm telling you. *It was Harry Rawlins!*'

Shirley was on her knees, mopping up the spilt tea. Dolly picked up the cup and the broken saucer.

'Well, we know one thing: the money's safe.'

There was no reaction. No whoops of joy.

'But we still can't exchange it yet,' Dolly explained. 'We've got to find someone we trust to handle it.' She glanced at Shirley, who was still mopping up the tea. Her skirt was badly stained. 'You all right, darlin'?' Dolly asked.

'Yeah.' Shirley turned to Bella. 'That was stupid!'

Dolly went into the kitchen. She could hear the two of them arguing. It was all so stupid, all their bickering, but she knew it was because they were frightened. She sighed and went back in.

'I think it would be for the best if we all stayed together from now on. Shirley, your place is big enough. Maybe we should all stay there.'

Shirley frowned. 'Why my place?'

Suddenly, Bella screamed. Dolly almost jumped out of her skin. They all stared at Bella.

'My diamonds, the earring – I've lost it!'

'What does it look like?' Linda asked.

'Like the other one, you stupid bitch!' Then she turned to Shirley. 'If we're all gonna be stayin' with you, darlin', you better keep her outta my sight!'

Shirley looked at Dolly pleadingly. 'I've only just got rid of me brother, Dolly. I was looking forward to some peace and quiet.'

*   *   *

Sister Teresa stood on top of a ladder, filling the lockers with hymn books. As she worked, the Mother Superior entered the room.

'Did Mrs Rawlins leave anything behind when she took her rucksacks, Sister?'

'No, Mother Superior. I checked and they were all empty.' Sister Teresa looked down. She gasped when she saw a man standing by the door. Harry waited patiently.

The Mother Superior turned to the man, smiling sweetly. 'I'm sorry, Mr Smith, I'm afraid you must have been mistaken. The lockers, as you just heard, were empty.'

*   *   *

Harry parked outside his old home. The 'For Sale' sign had 'Sold' stamped across it. The doors were shuttered and the windows barred. Harry walked up the garden path, wondering how many times he'd done it over the years. He also wondered why he was walking up the path now. He stood at the front door, but didn't get out his key, knowing the locks would have been changed months before.

A shiny BMW pulled up near the gate and he could see his lawyer, Sutcliffe, behind the wheel, staring at him as if he'd just seen some kind of apparition. Harry walked round the car, opened the passenger door and got in.

All Sutcliffe could say was, 'Christ almighty, Harry . . .' He gazed at him, shaking his head.

Eventually, Harry said, 'Look, it's me, Barry, all right? Take a good look. Wanna touch me?'

Sutcliffe's mouth went dry. He kept licking his lips. He didn't know where or how to begin.

Harry decided he'd better get on with it. 'She sell the house?'

Sutcliffe nodded, loosening his tie. Harry kept staring towards the house. He was miles away, thinking about other times, long gone.

'It's not the only thing she sold, Harry.' Sutcliffe shook his head in exasperation. 'You should have told me, Harry. Dear God, why didn't you call me, let me know what the hell was going on? I thought you were dead, Harry. You should have let me know!'

Harry didn't reply. He couldn't drag his eyes away from the house. When he finally spoke, his voice seemed strange, strained. 'Got a cigarette, Barry?'

Sutcliffe rummaged round in his pockets, then opened the glove compartment and brought out a packet of cigarettes. His hand was shaking. Harry took one, and Sutcliffe searched his pockets again for his lighter. He flicked it and flicked it, but it wouldn't light, his fingers were trembling so much. Harry took it from him, lit his cigarette and took a deep drag.

'Right, Barry, you'd better give it to me straight. What's been going on?'

Barry told him everything, leaving nothing out, but he wasn't sure if Harry was really listening. He made no reaction, just continued to smoke, flicking the ash into the ashtray. Sutcliffe continued, blow after blow after blow. It was like a judge giving a death sentence, and still Harry said nothing. Finally he stubbed the cigarette out slowly in the ashtray.

'I'm sorry, Harry, but there was nothing I could do. You were dead, she had a Certificate of Probate, she had a right . . .'

Harry turned and studied him, and to Sutcliffe it was almost as if Harry was freezing him with his eyes.

'Is there anything left?'

Sutcliffe could feel his left leg shaking; he couldn't stop it jigging up and down.

'I'm sorry, Harry, there's nothing, absolutely nothing.' He reached for his briefcase and took out some documents. 'Just a couple of leaseholds on those warehouses down by the station – you know, the lock-ups – but you've only got a couple of months to go on the leases.' For a moment he thought he saw the flicker of a smile cross Harry's face.

Harry took the leases, not bothering to look at them, and stuffed them into his coat pocket.

Sutcliffe heard himself saying, 'I'm sorry, I'm sorry, Harry, but you should have told me. If only you'd let me know.'

Harry opened the car door. 'Yeah, my own fault, Barry. Thanks for coming anyway.'

Sutcliffe let out a long breath. He'd thought that maybe Harry would kill him, rough him up a bit at least, but he'd taken it all so calmly. His wife had cleaned him out. She'd taken over every single bank account, every single property. She'd sold – lock, stock and barrel – the little empire that Harry had taken twenty years to build up, and all he had said was: 'Thanks for coming'. Sutcliffe waited for the other shoe to drop, for something else to happen, but it didn't. Harry stepped out of the car, slammed the door behind him and pulled up the collar of his coat. It started to rain. Sutcliffe watched Harry getting into an old, beat-up Jag. In a strange way, he felt sorry for him.

Sutcliffe started the car, but thought he'd better wait for Harry to go first, just in case. You never knew, with that kind of man, when they might turn. He might feel sorry for him, but that didn't mean he trusted him. The Jag coughed into life, the engine sounding as if it needed a good tune. Harry gave a brief nod in his direction and drove off.

Time to take a holiday, Sutcliffe decided. Get away from it all. As he started thinking about where he would go, he didn't notice the Rover pulling out and starting to follow the Jaguar.

* * *

Vic Morgan clocked the number of the BMW, jotting it down with his left hand as he steered with his right. He wondered what was going on. First he'd followed Rawlins to Trudie Nunn's flat, then to a convent, and now to an empty house in Totteridge. He kept his distance, making sure he wasn't spotted, but Rawlins seemed in no hurry. He drove slowly all the way back to Elgin Mansions.

Morgan passed Rawlins as he parked his Jaguar, driving two hundred yards further before he stopped. He got out of the car, keeping his back towards Rawlins, but still able to watch him in the wing mirror. He saw Rawlins enter the mansion block, and gave it a few moments before hurrying after him and pushing open the double doors. The old stone staircase was reasonably clean, but the place had a run-down feel to it. He could hear Rawlins' footsteps above him as he followed him up the stairs, trying to stay at least one floor below. Eventually he spotted him through the banister railings, letting himself in to one of the flats, then shutting the door behind him.

Morgan jogged up the stairs to the flat, number 44. The name on the doorbell was 'A. D. Judd'.

Now he had the name and address, Morgan decided he'd done enough work for the day. The question was, how much of this was he going to tell Mrs Marsh?

*   *   *

The following day, in Morgan's office, Dolly was twisting the strap of her handbag round and round her hand anxiously.

'So he's living at Elgin Mansions, then?'

Morgan shrugged and repeated what he'd seen.

'I can have the bloke in the BMW checked out. A friend of mine at the Yard, he can—'

Dolly stood up. 'That won't be necessary. I know who that was – my ... er ... sister's husband's lawyer.' She seemed very nervous. She opened her bag and handed him yet another brown envelope. 'That's everything I owe you to date, plus a bonus. Thank you for everything.'

Morgan held the brown envelope between his fingers. 'I'm off the job now, am I?'

Dolly was suddenly desperate to get out. 'Yes, I think you've done everything that ... Well ... I now know where my sister's husband is, so thank you very much.'

She put out her hand. He could see it was trembling, and there were also red marks from the handbag strap. He shook her hand.

'Oh, there is just one thing, Mr Morgan – the photograph.'

Morgan leant back in his chair. 'Oh, I'm sorry, Mrs Marsh, I've left it in the car. I'm afraid it's at the garage. If you like—'

'It doesn't matter,' she said. 'I'll, er, call in for it some time. Thanks again for everything.'

Morgan waited until she was gone, lifted a copy of the *Guardian* off the desk and stared down at the face of Harry Rawlins. He picked up the photograph, opened his wallet and put it inside.

* * *

The bedroom at 44 Elgin Mansions was as seedy as the rest of the apartment. The threadbare curtains were drawn, a couple of hooks hanging loose. No lights.

Harry lay face down on the bed. His coat and crumpled jacket were in a heap on the floor where he'd thrown them. The little teddy bear was peeking out of one of the jacket pockets.

His head buried in the pillow, Harry murmured over and over to himself, *'Bitch, bitch, bitch . . .'* He turned over and punched the pillow viciously. His teeth were clenched as he said the word yet again. *'Bitch.'* And then he lay, stretched across the bed, arms spread wide, and found tears were streaming down his face. He couldn't remember the last time he'd cried, and he didn't want to be doing it now. He tried to stop, but the tears just kept on coming, and eventually he gave in and let the wave of sadness wash over him.

* * *

The women were all sitting in Shirley's lounge, watching her thumb through the phone directory.

'Here it is, A. D. Judd, 44 Elgin . . .'

Bella leant back against the sofa and sniffed, looking at the three of them all staring at the phone book as if it was the Holy Grail.

'So now what? We know where he is, an' that he's got a phone, so what's the next move? Phone him up for a chat?'

Shirley stubbed out her cigarette, took another one out of the packet and offered it to Dolly.

Dolly's eyes were already smarting from all the smoke. 'No, thanks.'

Shirley shrugged and lit up, then blew out a thin stream of smoke, looking thoughtful.

'We could hire a hitman, have him bumped off,' Linda suggested.

Bella kicked her and told her to shut up. 'Why don't we hire Batman and Robin while we're at it?'

Linda pouted. 'It's not such a stupid idea. I even know someone who'd do it for a grand.'

Dolly massaged her temples. Her head was throbbing, and the arguing was only making it worse.

Shirley took another deep drag of her cigarette. For a non-smoker she was certainly making up for lost time. She blew the smoke out and Dolly wafted it away.

'Dolly, what if we told the police where he was? D'you think they'd come after us? Dolly?'

Dolly didn't bother to reply. Sometimes she felt as if she was back at the convent with the kids.

Shirley nudged her.

'Yes,' Dolly said, sounding as if she was lecturing a bunch of ten-year-olds. 'If we tell the police where he is and they pick him up, then he's going to tell them he had nothing to do with the raid, and even if they don't believe him, they're going to have to follow through and pull us in.'

Bella stood up, hands on hips. She hated the way Dolly talked down to them.

'OK, so what do we do?'

Linda looked at Dolly. 'Why can't we just pay him off, get him to leave us alone?'

Dolly gave Linda a look, as if that was too stupid for comment.

'Hold on, why not?' Bella said. 'Unless you've got a better idea.'

'It's got to be worth thinking about,' Shirley agreed.

Bella leant over Dolly. 'What if we each chip in fifteen grand? That would give Harry sixty thousand. He might go for that.'

Dolly looked at their expectant faces, not believing what she was hearing.

'You wanna know what he'll say?' she said angrily, almost spitting the words out. 'Sixty grand? *Out of seven hundred and fifty?* Oh, yes, please!'

Bella's temper was heating up. She jabbed a finger at Dolly, almost poking her. 'Give us a bit more credit, can't you? We wouldn't just fuckin' hand it over. As soon as he's got the cash in his hot little hands, we'd tip off the law. They pick up a supposedly dead man, with sixty grand's worth of stolen money from the underpass raid—'

'You think they'd believe he wasn't in on it himself?' Shirley chipped in. 'It would work, Dolly. We could get him put away and out of our hair.'

Dolly felt the pain shooting across her eyes. It was all she could do not to start screaming at them. She clenched her fists and looked each one in the eye.

'You wanna make a deal with Harry, then you go right ahead. But count me out, you understand? I warn you, he'll come after you, each one of you – he'll never let you go.' Dolly walked stiffly to the door and yanked it open. She was icy calm now, her voice clear and strong. 'Don't play games with Harry, I warn you. If you do, you'll lose.'

The girls braced themselves for the slam of the door, but Dolly closed it quietly. They heard her walking into Shirley's kitchen. *Then* the bang came, as she slammed the kitchen door almost off its hinges.

* * *

Micky Tesco had so many boxes and packages, he almost dropped the lot as he fiddled with the key to Harry's flat. Inside, he dumped them on the sofa, before pushing open the door to the kitchen.

'Harry?'

Tesco looked round. Something was wrong. The place was dark, an empty bottle of vodka lying on its side on the coffee table. He turned the handle of the bedroom door, then thought better and tapped lightly. He waited, then slowly opened the door and looked into the room. A strange muffled sound came from the bed. He closed the door again.

'Christ, now what?' he muttered to himself.

Unsure what else to do, Tesco began unwrapping the tissue paper from a stack of shirts, every now and then turning a worried look towards the bedroom. At least that awful sound had stopped now.

* * *

Dolly sat in the kitchen with her handkerchief over her mouth so the girls wouldn't hear her crying. Her face was puffy, her eyes red-rimmed. Linda walked in and Dolly looked away. She didn't want to be caught crying, not in front of them. Linda sat down, pulling the kitchen chair close so their knees were touching. She was going to pat Dolly's hand, but instead suddenly put her arms round her and held her tight. At first Dolly stiffened, trying to resist, but then she gave way and held on to Linda too. They stayed like that for only a moment, but it was as if there was now a real bond between them.

Linda broke away first, looking into Dolly's face. She looked old and worn out, and Linda felt her heart go out to her; sometimes they all forgot that Dolly wasn't as young as the rest of them.

She touched her cheek. 'Your eyes are all puffy.'

Dolly managed a wobbly smile and blew her nose, then said something about having to cancel her operation. Her eyes filled with tears again.

'Nothing worked out, Linda – not the way I thought it would.'

Linda could feel herself wanting to cry with Dolly, but she managed to hold herself back. Instead she hugged her again, and told her not to cry any more.

'Nobody means to go against you. No one wants to argue. We're all frightened, Dolly. Bella too. She comes on heavy, but she's scared. We need you now. We need you more than ever.'

Bella leant against the kitchen door. She looked hard at Dolly, then at Linda. 'We've decided to put in a call to Harry.'

Linda, holding on to Dolly's hand, felt her withdraw.

* * *

Harry was in the bathroom when the shrill tone of the old black telephone rang out.

Micky Tesco walked out of the kitchen, eating a piece of toast, and picked it up.

* * *

Shirley was shaking, and her mouth felt dry. Bella and Linda stood behind her, looking equally nervous. Dolly stood well back at the open door, with her arms folded.

'He's coming to the phone,' Shirley whispered. Suddenly she couldn't carry it through. She held out the receiver to Dolly, but Dolly shrank away, refusing to come within a foot of the phone. Bella snatched it out of Shirley's hand.

* * *

Tesco looked towards the bathroom, wiping his mouth with the back of his hand. The bathroom door opened.

'It's for you, Harry – said it's your wife.'

Shaved and showered, immaculate in a new suit and shirt, with his tie hanging round the collar, Harry felt like a new man. His face seemed to have changed; that beaten-down look had gone. Now he looked confident, even arrogant, and couldn't help a glimmer of a smile as he put out his hand for the phone.

Tesco was taken aback. You never knew where the hell you were with this man. He was like a bloody chameleon.

Harry's outstretched hand was steady, his voice cold. 'OK, you can get out.'

Tesco didn't argue. He felt Harry's eyes boring into him as he picked up his coat and searched round for his car keys. As he reached the front door he was about to say 'see you later', but Harry had turned his back on him.

Close to the phone was an old gilt-framed mirror. As the door closed behind Tesco, Harry looked at his reflection, smoothed a stray bit of hair behind his ear, then held the phone close to his mouth. He spoke softly, huskily.

'Hello, Doll, that you?'

*   *   *

Bella felt herself go cold. That voice, calling her 'Doll'. Now she knew why Dolly always hated anyone calling her that; it was his name for her, like a pet name.

She swallowed. 'This isn't Dolly, this is Bella. She's here, but . . . Look, we got a proposition for you. We want to make a deal.'

Behind her, Linda and Shirley, faces tight with worry, almost took a step back, as if they were trying to put more distance between themselves and Harry, while Dolly just stood, clenching and unclenching her hands, her palms slick with sweat.

*   *   *

At the other end of the phone, Harry was smiling and nodding, his voice relaxed and friendly. He said it was a deal. He would do whatever they wanted.

He was about to replace the phone when, as an afterthought, he said, 'Give Doll my love, won't you? I'll wait to hear from her.'

Harry put the phone down and turned back to his reflection in the mirror. His eyes were laughing, his mouth twisted into a strange smile. He began to knot his new silk tie. He was humming a tune and stopped to wonder where he had heard it. Must have been on the radio. 'We will meet again,' he sang tunelessly. 'We will meet again . . .' He started to laugh. He was looking forward to it.

CHAPTER THREE

Dolly arrived at the car park on Hampstead Heath early, knowing the girls would not be there for at least another ten or fifteen minutes. It was seven in the morning, and she wanted to look over the area by herself. She parked her car dead centre of the car park and sat. In front of her was the pond, and she turned round to look up to the hills and trees and the narrow pathways. Through the trees lining the car park she could see the row of elegant houses opposite. She sighed. Even at this hour of the morning the nearby roads were crammed with parked cars.

She got out of the Fiesta and slammed the door shut. In the middle of the car park were two large oak trees. You could either drive between the trees or to a small area to the left. Dolly walked across and looked down. A ditch ran around the car park, and a small wire fence. She began pacing carefully round the park, checking, double-checking, and all the time a voice inside her head kept saying, It won't work, it can't work – not here, it's too open, it's too vulnerable.

She heard a car pull up. Shirley was driving with Bella and Linda in the back. Bella got out, very businesslike, with a small notebook. Dolly glanced at her watch; she didn't bother to mention that the girls were late.

Linda started wandering off towards the pond, and Bella barked at her like a bossy headmistress to 'stop messing about!' It was clear Bella had taken over things.

'Right,' she said, 'everybody pay attention.'

They all stood in silence as Bella looked at her little notebook.

'OK, this is the way it goes down.' Bella went over the plans. Bella would be the co-ordinator and the lookout. She would position herself at the bottom of Pond Street by the cinema, close to a telephone booth. Shirley would park her car facing towards the car park, with a good view to the right and left. Linda would park her car midway between Shirley and Bella. When the girls were in position and saw that all was clear, and there was no sign of anyone else in the area . . .

At this point Dolly made a sweeping gesture, indicating the hundreds of residents' cars.

'Look, come on, Dolly, just let me get through it,' Bella said sharply. 'I know there's gonna be a lot of parked cars, but not in the car park, all right? We're gonna leave it till two, three o'clock in the morning, and it'll be empty. There won't be anybody round. And if it turns out there is, then we don't go through with it!'

Dolly nodded her head. 'OK, go on, I'm listening.'

'Right. When everybody's in position, we check out the area. If there's anybody around, or anybody sitting in cars, we call it off. It's crucial that the actual car park area is deserted, all right?'

All three nodded their heads in agreement.

'OK, so this is how it goes down. Dolly . . .'

Dolly kept hearing Bella saying, 'This is how it goes down, this is how it goes down . . .' She wondered if they would be going down along with it.

When Bella, Shirley and Linda had checked the area and it was safe, they would wait. Dolly would have to pass Bella to be given the 'OK' signal to go ahead. She would then continue along Heath Street and park her car exactly across the exit gate of the car park. By this time, if all went to plan, Harry, having been given instructions to come alone, would have parked his car dead centre of the car park with the interior lights on and his hands held up. This way they could see if he was alone and unarmed. When Dolly saw Harry and got the OK from the girls, she would get out of her car with the briefcase with £60,000 of stolen money from the raid. She would hand the briefcase over to Harry once she'd got his assurance that it would be the pay-off, and that he would leave the girls alone.

Dolly would then return to her car and be the first to leave the heath. She would be backed up by Shirley, who would drive off behind her. Linda would flash her lights to Bella, who would then put in a call to the police. The call would simply say that Harry Rawlins was alive, that he was at the location in a dark blue Jaguar with this registration number – information they already had from Vic Morgan – and he was believed to be carrying stolen money from the underpass raid.

Bella looked round at the watching faces. 'Well? What d'ya think? It's gotta work, Dolly. It'll work, I know it.'

Dolly stared back. She didn't think it would work at all. 'How long d'you reckon the police will take to get here?' she asked.

'Well, we're gonna test it out. I'll put in a call from the phone booth and we'll just see. The police station's only just up the road, Dolly.'

Dolly sighed. 'This area is so open, we're so vulnerable – he could have any amount of people here.'

Bella looked exasperated. 'Dolly, we're gonna check out the area before you even drive up!'

Dolly went back to her car. Over her shoulder, she snapped, 'You just make sure the police can be here in time to pick him up. I don't want him to follow me, because if he does, I'll lead him straight back to us and straight back to the rest of the money – and you know it.'

Bella marched after Dolly. 'Look, I keep on telling you, it'll work, Dolly, I know it!'

Dolly gave her an icy stare. 'Fine. So they pick Harry up with the stolen money. What happens if he talks?'

'What if he does?' said Shirley. 'There's nothing to link us back to that raid!'

Dolly opened the driver's door. 'But they may start asking questions, Shirley. So I'd better get to that cash now, hadn't I, 'cos we're gonna have to move fast. You said it, Bella – we've got to cover ourselves three times over.'

Dolly slammed the door shut and the three girls watched in silence as she drove away.

* * *

Harry stared at his face in the mirror. He was unrecognisable, unshaven and wearing a filthy boiler suit, a workman's cap and a scarf pulled round his neck. He turned to Tesco, who was sitting on the sofa, similarly dressed.

'Less they see of our faces the better.'

Tesco picked up his cap and jammed it on his head. He grinned. 'Sixty grand, eh? You think she's gonna try something, Harry?'

Harry didn't answer, just pointed to the gold watch on Tesco's wrist.

'Take that off.'

Swearing under his breath, Tesco took the watch off and slipped it into his pocket.

'What d'you think she's gonna do, Harry?'

Harry ignored him as he opened the plans of the nightclub. These were architectural blueprints, each area mapped out. Harry pointed at it.

'We need to know how many work the kitchens, and what the access is like from the back of the club. That's all we're gonna do today.' He walked to the door. 'You got the crates set up?'

'Yeah, and the truck's standing by. We've got it for the whole morning. Come on, Harry – what do you think Dolly's gonna do?'

Harry picked up a pair of gloves, said, 'Don't forget yours,' and walked out.

As Tesco followed, he noticed that the phone had been left off the hook.

* * *

Audrey entered the kitchen through the back door. The place was a shambles. Greg was standing at the door eating a piece of toast, butter dribbling down his chin.

'Don't you ever clear up?'

Greg shrugged. 'Gotta go to the JobCentre, then I got to sign on.'

Ray came into the kitchen and gave Greg a friendly clip round the earhole. 'Don't forget, you've got to be down at the garage by twelve o'clock.' He grinned at Audrey. 'I've hired Greg to clean motors for me.'

Audrey began to take her coat off. 'Fine. But no more videos, right, Greg?'

Greg grinned. 'Come on, you enjoyed them really, didn't you, Mum?'

Audrey chucked a dirty dishcloth at him. Greg dodged it and darted out of the back door.

She was in no mood for jokes. She picked up the cloth and threw it into the sink, which was piled high with dirty dishes. She sighed, muttering under her breath. Ray came up behind her and slipped his arms round her.

'You get out o' the wrong side of the bed, did you, darlin'?'

Audrey pushed him away. 'You're gonna wish I had!'

Ray collected the rest of the dirty dishes from the table and took them to the sink. 'I'll wash up, Aud.' He turned the tap on.

Audrey sat down, twisting her hands in her lap. Without looking at Ray, she said, 'I bin to the doctor. I'm up the spout.'

Ray couldn't hear her properly over the sound of the sink filling up. 'What's that? What you got?'

He looked at her over his shoulder and could tell from her miserable expression that it was something serious. He came and put his arm round her. 'What's up? Somethin' serious, is it, darlin'?'

Audrey still couldn't look at him. 'You could say that. I'm pregnant, Ray.' Audrey's eyes filled with tears. She finally managed to look Ray in the eye. 'Doctor reckons I'm about two months gone.' She managed a teary smile. 'So it wasn't indigestion after all. I never thought . . . Well, I did, I thought it was the change, didn't I? Gawd almighty, some change!'

Ray was rooted to the spot, staring, open-mouthed.

'Well, say somethin', like "I'm packin' me bags!" or . . .' Audrey fished in her pocket for a tissue and blew her nose. 'I'm sorry, Ray.'

Ray got down on his knees. 'Sorry, bollocks! From now on I'm takin' care of the two of you. There'll be no more market for you, my girl, eh?' Ray was almost crying himself.

They held each other close, and the water spilt over the side of the sink and onto the floor.

* * *

Vic Morgan walked down the hospital corridor, tapped on the sister's open door and popped his head in. She was standing at a filing cabinet, looking through the files.

'Sorry to bother you, Sister, but I was wondering if there's a George Resnick on the ward – Detective Inspector Resnick.'

She gave him a quick, appraising look, then nodded, before carrying two files over to her desk.

Morgan still stood at the door. 'Er, I wonder if I could see him for a few minutes?'

She sat down, then opened a drawer in the desk and took out a biro. 'Are you a relative?' she asked without looking up from the files.

Morgan grinned. 'Brother-in-law. I know it's not visiting hours but I would appreciate it if I could just have a couple of minutes with him.'

He could tell from her expression that she knew he was lying. 'I'm afraid Mr Resnick is rather poorly.'

Morgan stepped into the room. 'Is he going to have another operation?'

Sister shook her head. 'No.'

'Oh good – no need to cancel next Saturday's football match, then!'

The sister showed no reaction to his joke.

Morgan moved a little closer to the desk. 'Is he . . . er, having chemotherapy, then?'

She looked at him properly for the first time. 'You know what a melanoma is? I would be grateful if you would stick to visiting hours in future. You'll see them on the board outside the ward. But since you're here, I'll let it go today. You can see Mr Resnick for a few moments.' A sad expression crossed her face. 'He has so few visitors.'

Morgan walked out of the office and closed the door quietly behind him. It was as if somebody had slapped him in the face. Melanoma ... Morgan pinched his nose and closed his eyes. Disconnected pictures, like a jigsaw puzzle, flashed across his eyes, and he saw his wife's face, smiling at him, holding his hand – then the doctor telling them that she only had a little time to live. He couldn't believe how little time. He remembered his wife clinging to his hand, knowing she was going to die, but what she was worried about was their son, Mark.

'Take care of him, Vic,' she'd said.

He tried to joke with her, told her that Mark could take care of himself, all they were worried about was her, they wanted to take care of her. And she smiled a sweet, gentle, dying smile, and said, 'It's too late, Vic. It's too late.'

She died the following morning. He hadn't been able to get to the hospital because of his work. They'd all been very kind down at the station, given him a couple of weeks' leave, but it had happened so fast, so brutally fast. He didn't take the leave they'd offered him but continued to work, and four weeks later his son Mark had died from an overdose. He took the two weeks' leave then, and never returned.

Later, he'd opened his own investigation bureau. It seemed that he'd been alone for a long time now. Eight years. And one word had brought it all back in one flashing moment.

He breathed in, like an actor about to go on stage, put a smile on his face and pushed through the swing doors into the ward.

* * *

Micky Tesco drove the Warrington's delivery truck slowly through the gates marked 'In' at Amanda's nightclub and round the small car park at the front, with Harry in the passenger seat beside him. The 'Out' gates were on their right as they continued down a dip at the side of the club, and down a narrow alley that led into the large, open rear space of the club. There was building work going on, a couple of extensions in progress, as well as trees, garages and a fire escape. The only exit was the way they'd come in.

Harry swore under his breath. 'This is a bitch, you know that.'

They parked the truck outside the kitchen exit and Harry hauled a beer crate out of the back of the truck, all the time carefully taking in the whole area. He looked at the fire escape, the trees, the row of garages. He saw a number of parked cars, presumably belonging to the kitchen staff.

Again, he turned to Tesco. 'Christ almighty, a bitch and a half.'

Tesco began lugging a crate down. 'Reckon we'll need three or four blokes just to take the kitchens.'

Harry was already on his way to the kitchen entrance, down a flight of stairs in the basement of the building. As he got to the top of the steps, he paused.

'You do the talking, and leave the rest to me.'

* * *

George Resnick looked much more like his old self than Morgan had anticipated. He was very pale and most of his hair was gone, but at least he was sitting up, and Morgan was grateful for that. As he walked along the row of beds, he passed what looked like several terminal cases. The smell of the ward kept bringing back painful memories and the effort of pushing them away made him hold the bag of grapes too tightly – he could feel the juice squeezing out between his fingers. As he reached Resnick's bed, a wisp of smoke curled up.

'I'll have to ask you to put that out, Mr Resnick.'

George Resnick was startled for a moment, then grinned. 'Hello, you old so-and-so. You nearly gave me heart failure. How're you doing?'

There was something of the old Resnick there, but the spark had definitely dimmed. Morgan found he couldn't meet his eyes. He looked round Resnick's bedside table.

'You got something I can put these grapes in, George?'

Resnick leant over to open the cabinet. 'So what brings you here, Vic?'

Morgan managed a weak grin. 'Heard you were running short of grapes.' He pulled up a chair and placed it close to the bed.

Resnick was bent over, pulling a bowl out of the cabinet, when he winced with pain. He lay back on the bed, his face drawn, teeth clenched, and snorted as if the pain was coming through his nose.

Morgan looked round the bed and saw the tubes. 'You all right, George?'

Resnick lay back, exhausted, and let out his breath. 'I'm OK now. I'm OK.'

He didn't look OK, and Morgan decided to cut out all the chit-chat and get right down to it before the sister threw him out. He took out his wallet and held up the photograph.

'This is Harry Rawlins, isn't it?'

Resnick reached for the photo with his bad hand. Morgan could see how little movement he had in the fingers. Resnick nodded.

'And Rawlins' wife, she'd be blonde, about five-six, medium build, good taste in clothes?'

'Yeah, that sounds like her.'

Morgan moved closer to the bed. 'I've got her. She's looking for him, which is why she came to me. Gave me a cock and bull story about a sister with a cheating husband.'

A little gleam came back into Resnick's eyes. 'Who else knows about this?'

'Just you and me. Maybe we could do a deal, the pair of us. I'll trade you for what you know, and get a slice of that reward for any information on the underpass security raid.'

Resnick was now much perkier. 'You're on!' he said with a grin.

Morgan smiled. 'OK! You can start by telling me everything you know about Dolly Rawlins.'

*   *   *

The basement kitchens of Amanda's nightclub were a warren of little rooms. In one, there were two chefs, carving up some veal. In another, there were two washers-up, cleaning dishes and glasses.

Micky Tesco was going to town, chatting away with one of the chefs, saying that it wasn't worth his job to let these crates go in without being signed for; he had to have a docket filled in. So where was the manager?

'Too early. He's not here. You better come back later,' the chef told him.

Rawlins admired how Tesco worked on the chef, nattering on, picking up bits of food, acting as if he had all the time in the world.

Eventually the chef paused in his carving. 'Look, mate, if you want to try and find him, feel free to go on into the club, but I'm telling you he's not there.'

Tesco shot Harry a look and moved off.

Now it was Harry's turn. He asked the chef how many men worked in the kitchens, when they came on, what time they left, all the time keeping up the chat as if it was just one working stiff to another. In between chopping meat and barking orders at his second-in-command, the chef revealed that at least fourteen people worked in the kitchens at night when the club was in full swing.

He suddenly turned to Harry. 'What company did you say you were from again?'

'Warrington's,' Harry replied without a flicker. The chef grunted and carried on what he was doing.

Tesco reappeared in the kitchen with a grin. 'After all that, turns out we're in the wrong club!' He looked at Harry. 'We'd better get going.'

They picked up their crates and with a friendly nod to the chef, they walked out of the door and up the basement steps.

Tesco threw the crates in the back of the truck, then walked round and got into the driving seat. He turned to Harry.

'So what do you think?'

'What do I think? Like I said, Micky, the place is a bitch.'

*   *   *

As Shirley came downstairs, she could hear the TV blaring. She walked into the lounge and there was Linda, curled up nice and comfy amid the cushions, gawping at the screen. Shirley swore she was so fed up with having Linda and Bella living in her house – particularly Linda – she'd prefer to have Greg back. She stood in the doorway with her arms folded.

'Any chance of you cleaning the bath after yourself?' she asked in a sarcastic tone.

'Sure,' Linda replied distractedly. She pointed at the TV. 'What a load of old rubbish. Gawd almighty. I mean, I know it's a kids' programme, but it's completely ridiculous.'

Shirley looked round the room. There were dirty coffee cups on every surface. 'And maybe when you've finished with the bath, you could do some washing up? If you get a minute, of course, Linda. Linda? *Linda*, are you listening?'

Linda seemed totally absorbed in the TV programme.

Shirley rolled her eyes. 'Right, I'm going to see me mum.'

'Oh, in that case,' Linda said, without taking her eyes off the screen, 'would you pick up some coffee, tea, butter, eggs, milk . . .'

Shirley put her hands on her hips. 'Oh, fine, I said I was goin' to me mum's, but I'll take the trolley with me!'

'Great. Oh, and don't forget some soap, and cornflakes . . .' Linda was still adding items to the shopping list as Shirley walked out of the room.

After a while she got up to change the channel. She saw the video machine under the TV had a film in it. She pressed the button and went back to sit on the sofa. It couldn't be any worse than what's on TV, she thought. She just hoped it was something for adults.

A minute later, her jaw hanging open, she found that it was.

* * *

Ray Bates had spent most of the morning at Mothercare. He felt a strange thrill, walking up and down the shop, looking at all the gear he could buy. He'd come back with a pair of tiny blue bootees and he had them in his hand, smiling stupidly at them, when Micky Tesco arrived.

He looked at Ray and the boots. 'New line, is it?'

Ray beamed and told him the whole story. 'I'm gonna be a father, at my age! Isn't that fantastic?'

Tesco couldn't quite take it in. 'You mean Audrey?'

'Yeah,' said Ray.' A worried look suddenly came over his face. 'Tell you what, though, I hope to God business picks up!'

Tesco grinned and sat down. 'You've obviously been keepin' your end up!'

One of the bootees was flung at his head. Micky held it in his hand and plucked at the wool.

'Shirley working, is she? Doin' any modelling?'

'Why? Gonna offer her a job, are you?'

Micky tossed the little shoe back. 'Why not? Friend of mine runs a model agency. I think I could do something for her.'

Ray shook his head with a grin. 'I bet you could, Micky, I bet you could!'

* * *

The video was still playing when Linda ushered Dolly into the room. She picked up the remote control and began to play the film back to catch up on the bits she'd missed. Dolly put her bag down and began dusting off her coat. She'd been at the damned drill hall again, and it was still filthy, absolutely disgusting – you'd think with kids round they'd clean the place. Then she looked at the screen and her mouth dropped open.

'What in God's name is this?'

Linda grinned. 'I found it in the machine. Tell you what, that Shirley's a bit of a dark horse. Let me rewind a bit. There's a bloke – no word of a lie – who's got one down to just below his knees.'

Dolly was disgusted. 'Turn it off!'

The front door slammed and Dolly called out sharply, 'Who's that?'

Bella pushed open the door. 'Only me.' She rubbed her hands together. 'How does this sound – cops were down in the car park in under a minute. Rang them, said I'd seen a flasher, and . . . Bloody hell, what's this?'

'One of Shirley's videos,' Dolly told her.

Bella roared with laughter. '*Shirley's?*' She got closer to the screen. 'Oh my gawd – how did those two get into that position?'

'I think there's three of them,' Dolly said, shaking her head.

'Oh yeah?' Bella screeched. 'You seen it before, have you, Doll?'

Furious, Dolly went and ripped the plug from the wall. 'If that's all you two have got to think about then I'm sorry for you!' She looked at Linda. 'You get a case for the money?'

'Me and Bella talked it over,' Linda said, 'and thought a briefcase was a bit too obvious. So we decided to use one of Shirley's old shopping bags.'

Dolly thought for a moment. 'Fair enough.'

'What time are we going to call Harry?' Linda asked. She had to repeat the question three times as Dolly was just sat, staring into space.

Eventually, sounding distant, as if she was talking to herself, Dolly answered. 'Not until way after midnight. The later the better. We still have to work out exactly how long it's going to take us all to get there. Shirley will need at least three hours, knowing her driving.'

She opened the holdall to look at the money she'd taken from the drill hall, then leant back on the sofa and closed her eyes, muttering, 'This is crazy, it's crazy!'

'You think Harry's gonna try something?' Bella asked.

Dolly opened her eyes and tipped all the money out of the bag. Her voice was chillingly cold. 'I don't think, I know it. Now, where's Shirley?'

Linda picked up some of the money and began counting it. 'Shopping.'

'What time did she say she'd be back?'

Linda shrugged. 'Dunno. She said something about seeing her mother.'

Bella picked up some of the money. 'It'll work, Dolly. Sixty thousand pounds is a lot of cash!'

This was the moment when Dolly could have told them just how much she'd cleaned out Harry for. But she didn't. She just sat there and watched the two girls carefully counting out Harry's pay-off.

* * *

Shirley couldn't believe her ears.

'Yeah, two months!' Audrey repeated, a bit sheepishly.

Shirley almost had to hold on to the kitchen table to stop herself falling down. 'But you can't be! You're too old!'

'Oh, thanks a lot!'

Shirley picked up her shopping bag and put it on the table. 'You're not gonna have it, are you?'

Audrey laughed. 'Of course I'm gonna have it.' Then she looked at Shirley and added, 'Ray's over the moon about it.'

'Oh, I'll bet,' Shirley shot back. 'Gonna have a white wedding, are you, Mum? He gonna marry you, is he? Oh, come on, don't be stupid. You can't have it!'

Audrey put the teapot on the table and looked at her daughter.

'I mean, what's everybody gonna say, Mum?' Shirley continued. 'You can't have a baby at your age. It'll be a mongol!'

Audrey gasped. 'That's a terrible thing to say. Don't say things like that, you hear me?'

Shirley took a cake out of its box and put it on a plate. 'Does Greg know? How's he gonna take it?'

Audrey got some plates from a cupboard. 'I really don't care what he thinks. It's my baby – mine and Ray's.'

Shirley went to the cutlery drawer and took out a cake knife. 'Well, he's gonna go off the deep end, I reckon.' She shook her head. 'I dunno – never mind about having another kid, you can't even handle the ones you've got!'

Audrey took the knife from Shirley. 'Well, if Ursula Andress can do it . . .'

Shirley looked puzzled.

'The blonde movie actress – you know!'

Shirley rolled her eyes and Audrey started cutting the cake. Shirley put a hand on her arm. 'You know you needn't bother coming to me for a handout when Ray hops it – because that's what he's going to do. That's what Greg's so-called father did, what mine did. I haven't seen my big brother Mike for years. And when he does come home you get into a right old state because of our dad leaving to live on the military base in Germany. It's no wonder Mike wanted to go there and be with him instead of living here in this Shithole. Every man you've ever had has only hung round long enough to get what they wanted and then pissed off!'

Audrey's hand shot out and slapped Shirley hard across the face.

There was a strange moment as the two women looked at each other. In all the years and all the troubles they'd been through, Audrey had never slapped her daughter before.

Shirley picked up her bag. 'You're making a big mistake, Mum. You know you could still—'

'Get out!' Audrey yelled. She sat at the kitchen table, looking at the cake. She picked up a piece, then let it drop. Gently she rubbed her hand over her tummy.

'You just don't understand, Shirley,' she said to herself. 'It's gonna be different this time.' She wiped a tear from her eye. 'Yeah, this time everything's gonna be all right.'

A wave of guilt washed over her as Shirley opened her car door. For a moment she thought of going back and apologising, but something stopped her.

She was just about to get into the car when she felt a slap on her behind. She turned round in a fury, expecting to see Greg, but it was Micky Tesco, standing there with a big grin on his face.

'I can't stand people who do that!' she snapped.

He held the door open for her, still smiling. Shirley could smell his cologne.

'You been to see our mum-to-be, eh, darlin'?' he asked with a smirk.

Shirley could have hit him. She got into the car, but he still held on to the door.

'You been doing any modelling lately?'

She opened her handbag and searched for her keys, wishing he'd shut up and go away.

He stuck his head in the car. 'Friend of mine runs a modelling agency. I was talking about you.'

Shirley just laughed. 'Oh, yeah?' She couldn't find her car keys.

'Straight up! She wants to meet you. Marion Gordon.'

For a moment she stopped searching for her keys. Marion Gordon . . . she knew that name.

Micky straightened up. 'You must have heard of her. I can fix you up an interview, no problem. You're just the kind of girl she likes – you know, fresh, natural-looking.' He paused, as if he was thinking. 'What're you doing right now?'

She looked at him, and he knew he'd got her, hook, line and sinker.

Shirley bit her lip. 'What, meet her now? I'd have to change.'

He reached over and took the keys out of Shirley's hand, then helped her out of the car.

'Don't forget your handbag, sweetheart.' He reached into the car and handed her the bag.

Shirley knew he was manipulating her, but what rather disturbed her was that she didn't seem to mind. She watched him shut the car door and lock it, before handing her back the keys. Then he gripped her elbow and led her across the street to his E-type Jaguar. He opened the passenger door, helped her in, shut the door – the perfect gentleman – and he was whistling when he got in next to her.

'Well! Let's go and see if I can get you a modelling job, yeah?'

'What's in it for you?' Shirley asked, even though she knew the answer.

He smiled. 'Well, one good turn deserves another, doesn't it? So maybe you'll have dinner with me one night. What do you say?'

Shirley didn't reply, but he seemed to take that as a 'yes'. He revved the engine and they sped off.

'Put your safety belt on, sweetheart. Don't wanna lose you.'

Shirley did as he asked, but noticed he wasn't wearing his. She glanced sidelong at him as he drove, and noticed a few other things.

She liked the way he dressed: clean and sharp. And that cologne was rather nice. With his blond hair, piercing ice-blue eyes and perfect, even white teeth, she had to admit he was very striking. She settled back in her seat, liking the way he drove: fast, but always seeming to be in control.

'Have you ever done any modelling?' she asked after a while.

He threw his head back and laughed. 'Yeah, once. I did a knitting pattern for Marion. That's how I know her.'

'So what happened?'

'I couldn't stand all the woofters about.'

'So what do you do now?'

'I'm in property, sweetheart. Buying and selling.'

Well, he must be doing all right, Shirley thought to herself. These cars aren't cheap.

Micky accelerated expertly through the gears.

Got her, he told himself. I've got her . . .

*　*　*

Dolly had been washing up in the kitchen, and now she turned her attention to the stove, which was covered in grease after one of Linda's fry-ups. She'd been back and forth to the various rooms in the house collecting dirty cups and saucers, including a saucer full of cigarette ends. Just the smell of it made her glad she didn't smoke any more. She missed having something to do with her hands, but that was a small price to pay, especially now that she was watching her weight.

Dolly was miles away when Linda came in, carrying a few more cups and saucers. She took them to the sink and picked up a dishcloth.

'D'you want me to give you a hand, Dolly?'

'If you like, love.'

Dolly had noticed a change in Linda of late. She was still nervous and jumpy, but instead of running off at the mouth, she was usually quiet. Often when they were together, she'd look over to see Linda just staring into space.

They washed and dried the dishes together for a minute in companionable silence, and then Dolly saw that Linda was crying, silent tears running down her face.

'Has Bella been having a go at you again?'

Linda nodded. Dolly usually kept her emotions to herself, and she didn't give her affections lightly. But she felt drawn to Linda now, almost like a daughter. She carried on scrubbing at a plate.

'Harry knocked the stuffing out of you, didn't he, sweetheart?'

Linda was quiet for a moment. 'I was so scared, Dolly. I thought I was dying. It was the water, I've always been terrified of water, ever since I was a kid.'

Seeing that Linda's nose was running, Dolly held her hands up in their rubber gloves. 'Here, there's a tissue in my apron pocket.'

Linda pulled out the tissue and blew her nose. She started to tell Dolly a story about when she was at the orphanage. It was strange, really: these women had spent so much time together – had been through so much together – and yet they didn't really know each other, what each of them was feeling deep down. Dolly was moved by Linda's description of life at the orphanage; how she remembered her mother taking her there when she was three, three and a half. She remembered her smell, but she could no longer visualise her face. What she did remember was those endless days waiting for the mother who never came. And then the final realisation that she never would.

'Were you ever happy there?' Dolly asked, as she carried on washing up. 'Were they kind to you?'

'Yeah, they were kind, but it could never make up for not having a mum. D'you know what I mean, Dolly?' Linda's drying up slowed to a stop with a plate still in her hand. 'The only real home I ever had was the one with Joe. I'm not saying it was perfect, but he was always there for me.'

Dolly felt Linda's hand on her arm.

'When this is all over, when the money's sorted and everything, will you . . .?'

Linda was finding it difficult to tell Dolly what she felt, what she wanted. But eventually it all burst out.

'I'm no good on my own; I never was. I mean, I should be, 'cos that's all I've ever been, really, on me own, apart from Joe. But Dolly, will you stay with me? I don't know what to do with the money – I need help. I'll even give you my share to look after!'

To cover her own emotions, Dolly turned the hot water on. 'Oh, come on, you don't want an old woman like me hanging round you!'

'You're not old, Dolly! You're so strong – you never seem to worry about anything.'

Dolly laughed, shaking her head as she turned the water off. 'Never worry? Oh, Linda, if only you knew!'

Linda suddenly felt protective. She slipped her arm round Dolly. 'I'm gonna take care of you, Dolly. After tonight, it's all going to be over. An' then, well, we'll be together, you an' me. Is that a deal?'

Dolly hugged her. She realised that for all these months she'd had no real human contact – no hugs, no kisses – and she held on tight, not wanting to let go.

'It's a deal, darling,' she said eventually, and Linda beamed at her, bright as a button.

'Be like 'aving a mum!'

Bella's voice cut through the air like a knife. 'This a private conversation or can anyone join in?'

Linda and Dolly broke apart, a little embarrassed. Dolly picked up the dishcloth and chucked it to Linda. 'Come on, get cracking!'

Bella hovered at the doorway for a moment, then said to Linda, 'There's some cups out by the telephone you could wash up.'

Linda meekly walked out of the kitchen to pick up the dirty crockery. Dolly continued to wash, placing each bit of crockery carefully on the draining board. Without looking at Bella, she said, 'You lay off her, Bella, you hear me?'

Bella picked up the dishcloth and started drying. 'Me? What have I done?'

Dolly scrubbed at a cup furiously. 'She swears she never told that feller of yours anything, so just let it drop!'

Bella dropped one of the plates she'd been drying with a crash. 'Oh, shit! That's one of Shirley's best.'

Dolly took off the rubber gloves and started to pick up the pieces.

Bella watched her. 'I don't mean half the things I say to Linda, I don't, it's just . . . I don't know what gets into me, Dolly. But she's changed – you don't realise how much.'

'Maybe she has changed, Bella. Maybe we all have in some way. Now go on, go and give her a hand.'

Bella gave her a little smile and went out. Dolly opened the bin. It was full of broken cups and saucers.

* * *

By the time Micky led her into Marion Gordon's outer office, Shirley's confidence was sky-high. He seemed to know the secretary very well, chatting easily with her, and then asked for the ladies' room so that Shirley could go and freshen up. It was this thoughtfulness that Shirley liked, and all the time he kept encouraging her, telling her not to be nervous, that she was beautiful and there was no way Marion Gordon was going to turn her down. This was going to be her big break. He even took her to the ladies' himself, opened the door and found the light switch for her.

'Just put a comb through your hair, darlin'. Don't put any make-up on – you look lovely as you are. And Shirley, smile! Come on, give us a smile!'

Shirley smiled back at him, then took a brush and comb out of her handbag and looked at herself in the mirror.

Micky stood at Suzy, the secretary's, desk, his manner subtly different. 'I'll go on in, then.'

Suzy leant back in her chair. 'You are naughty, you know, Micky. She's very busy.'

Micky leant over the desk and stroked her cheek. 'So am I, my darlin', so am I.'

He strode into Marion's office without knocking. There wasn't even time for Suzy to bleep her boss and warn her that he was coming in.

Marion sat behind her desk. The whole office seemed to gleam: white carpet, a white canvas director's chair, white walls that were covered with photos of models, from magazines and commercials.

Micky leant casually on the door, while Marion flicked the switch on the intercom and told her secretary to hold all her calls.

She was in her mid-forties and still looked good. She was a beautiful woman, but a face-job had probably helped.

She pushed her tortoiseshell glasses back on her head and frowned. 'What do you want, Micky?'

He sauntered across the white carpet and sat in the director's chair. He seemed harder, sharper, than when he'd been with Shirley.

'I haven't got much time, Micky. I'm a busy woman.'

'It wasn't always like that, was it, Marion? Once upon a time you had plenty of time for me.'

'Times have changed, Micky. What do you want?'

*   *   *

Shirley came out of the ladies' room and Suzy looked her up and down. Quite nice, she thought. Natural. But she seemed nervous.

Shirley looked round for Micky.

'He's with Marion. Would you like a coffee?'

'Yes, thank you very much.'

From the small kitchen, Suzy watched Shirley walk round the office, looking at the photographs. She was really raw, this one. She wondered where Micky had found her.

*   *   *

In Marion's inner sanctum, the atmosphere was getting heated. Marion stood up from behind her desk.

'You heard what I said: no. I'm a good agent, darlin', but I can't just take anybody on, especially with no experience. What d'you take me for?'

Micky just smiled. 'Legit now, are you? Straight?' The old Cockney accent was creeping back in. He got up and walked round to her. 'Nice office, sweetheart, but who're you kiddin'? You think the Sundays wouldn't relish a nice tip-off, eh? How many girls have you got on the game nowadays?'

Marion turned to him. 'Give me a break, Micky. That's all in the past. I'm a legit models' agent now – I'm not into anything else. Why don't you leave me alone?'

'I'm only askin', Marion, darlin'. She's a lovely girl – why don't you just look 'er over?'

Marion resisted the urge to slap him. She went back to her desk and opened a large leather-bound diary. 'All right, Micky, I'll see 'er. But I'm not agreeing to take her on. Knowing your taste in women, she's probably a right little scrubber.' She turned a page in the diary, but Micky snapped it shut, catching her long, red fingernails. She withdrew her hand quickly. 'All right, Micky, I'll see her next week.'

'No, darlin', you'll see her now. And what's more, you'll take her on.'

Marion sat back. Micky Tesco frightened her, but then he always had. She watched him walking casually round her office as if he owned it. God, how she hated him. He peered at the photographs of the models, looking them up and down, then came back to her.

'You'll take her on, Marion, and then I want her doing the charity show on the fifteenth, at Amanda's club. Be a grand in it for you.'

Marion laughed and shook her head. 'You joking? Amanda's nightclub? No way, baby. Look, I've already got a crack team going in on that; they want the best girls I've got. I can't take on a rank amateur. What d'you think I am?'

Micky moved fast. He grabbed hold of Marion's wrist, making her wince. 'I know what you are, and I want her on that job, you understand?'

She pulled her hand free. 'I can't do it, Micky.'

He pulled her to her feet and gripped her tight by the arms. 'Yes, you can, Marion. You can do anything I want. We go back a long way, remember?'

'You never let me forget it, Micky, do you?'

She felt his hands gripping her tighter. He was like a snake, squeezing the life out of her. Then suddenly he eased off, and his voice was gentler.

'This is the last time, Marion. I swear, on my life, it'll be the last favour I ever ask you. Just get that little girl on that job at Amanda's.' Then he pulled her head back and kissed her, a hard, vicious kiss, and however much she hated him, Marion could feel a surge of heat inside her. Even now he could still do it to her, just like he had when he was a kid of sixteen. She'd been a fool to pick him up, but then she'd always liked pretty, sixteen-year-old boys, and Micky Tesco was a classic. He'd grown up now, though, wasn't a pretty little boy any more. He was more like a monster, and that feeling in the pit of her stomach made her ashamed.

She pushed him away, but he wouldn't let her go. He wasn't finished with her yet. He pulled her head towards him again and she felt herself responding. And then it was just like it had always been. With one hand, Micky cleared all the diaries and notebooks from the desk. He lifted her up and laid her across the desk.

'Well, Marion, here's one for old times' sake . . .'

* * *

Shirley had finished her coffee and smoked a second cigarette. Suzy was getting a little edgy, continually looking towards the door, then back to Shirley. Eventually the door opened and Micky stood there, smiling.

He grinned over at Shirley. 'Won't be a moment, sweetheart.' Then he shut the door again.

Marion was sprawled on the desk with her jeans round her ankles and her silk shirt unbuttoned. Micky looked at her with disgust.

'Tidy yourself up. Come on, pull your trousers up, for Christ's sake!'

Marion hastily hitched up her jeans and buttoned her shirt. She had to search round for her glasses.

'Smile, sweetheart.' Micky held his hands together like a camera. 'That's a good girl.'

He opened the door wide, beckoning Shirley over, and Marion just had time to sit back down at her desk, trying to hold back the tears.

'Marion, I'd like you to meet Shirley.' Micky ushered Shirley in and closed the door behind her.

Marion's hands were shaking as she motioned for Shirley to sit down in the director's chair. She looked at the pretty, innocent-looking girl before her and wondered if she had any idea what sort of a man Micky Tesco was.

'So,' she said, with a deep sigh. 'You want to be a model, do you?'

* * *

Bella was standing at the window, waiting. They'd already called Shirley's mother, only to be told, in a rather abrupt tone, that Shirley had left hours ago. Bella closed the curtain again and turned back to Linda.

'Where the hell is she?'

Linda was sitting on the sofa. 'You remember that little gun?'

Bella switched on the TV. 'What film is this?'

Linda got up and switched the TV off again. 'Listen to me. At the lock-up. Dolly had a gun.'

'What about it?'

Linda chose her words very carefully. 'Well, if something was to go wrong, I'd feel a lot safer if I had it.'

Dolly walked into the lounge. 'Had what?'

'Your gun,' said Bella. 'Linda was saying she'd feel a lot safer if she had it.'

'No. No guns,' Dolly said.

Linda appealed to her. 'Look, I just thought . . . for protection, you know – if something goes wrong.'

Dolly turned on her sharply. 'Didn't you hear what I said? No guns!' She sat on the sofa. 'Right, I've been working out exactly what we'll say . . .' She looked at the sofa. 'What in God's name is that?'

It was the most extraordinary Guy Fawkes dummy: a pair of ratty jeans stuffed with old tights and bits of newspaper, a bulging sweater – and now Linda was stuffing the seat of a pair of tights with bits of old magazines.

She held the dummy up. 'It's great, isn't it? When I'm parked, for cover, I'm going to put his arms round me like this. And then, you see, we'll look as if we're snogging. I mean, if Harry drives past and sees me sitting in the car, he might think it looks suspicious, right? But if he sees a couple snogging, he won't pay any attention, right?'

Bella was sarcastic. 'Brilliant. What sort of a feller has a head the size of a peanut, with a pair of knickers on top?'

Linda giggled. 'It's not finished yet. He hasn't got his hat on.'

Dolly shook her head, watching the two girls. 'You're like a couple of kids!'

Linda was now dancing round the room with the ridiculous dummy, a pair of shoes dangling from the legs of its jeans.

'For Christ's sake,' said Dolly. 'Can't you two concentrate on anything for more than two seconds? Didn't you hear what I said? I've worked out what we say to Harry.'

Linda put the dummy down. 'Sorry, Dolly. Which one of us is gonna make the call then?'

Dolly looked up. 'Who the hell do you think?'

* * *

In a cosy corner in a little pub in Mayfair, Micky poured Shirley another glass of champagne, and she drained half of it in one go. She couldn't believe her luck. The meeting with Marion Gordon had gone just the way she'd always dreamt it would. Marion had looked her up and down, asked her to walk the length of the room, and then sat back. She'd seemed a little bit edgy, but maybe they were always like that, these high-powered model agents. Quick as a flash, she'd said she'd fix up a photographic session, and might even have a job lined up for her.

Shirley was brimming over with happiness, and the words were tumbling out over each other.

'Oh, Micky, the girls she's got, they do *Vogue, Elle, Tatler,* all the really top jobs. I'll never be able to thank you properly!'

Micky smiled and filled her glass again. 'Oh, I'll think of a way, darlin'.' He took a quick look at his watch. 'I'm afraid I'm gonna have to make a move.'

Shirley looked at her own watch and gasped when she realised the time. She stood up. 'Oh, my God, I'd no idea it was so late!'

Micky picked up her bag. 'I'll drop you back at your car. Here you go, don't forget your handbag.'

'Oh, thanks, Micky.'

Micky stood close, but he didn't reach out to touch her, he just smiled down into her eyes. 'That's all right, Shirley. Come on, let's go.'

For a moment Shirley had thought he was going to kiss her, and even though part of her wanted him to, she was pleased he didn't. It made her like him even more.

He opened the door and guided her towards the E-type. Still the perfect gentleman, he helped her in, then bent over the seat belt. This time she really wanted him to kiss her. She was intensely aware of his hands, his body, the smell of his cologne. Shirley was tall, at least five-eight, and Terry, her husband, had only been about five foot six. She'd never minded, never really thought about it, but suddenly it was nice to be with somebody so tall, so strong-looking.

As the car moved off, she seemed to be in a dream. Micky was looking at her.

'What are you thinking about?'

'I can't believe I'm gonna be a professional model now. It's what I've always wanted.'

He smiled. He had a lovely smile, thought Shirley.

But Tesco was thinking: Shit, I'm gonna be late for Rawlins. He'll hit the fucking roof.

* * *

Harry entered the lock-up and put down the cases he was carrying. Gordon Murphy had already made coffee and was sitting on one of the orange boxes, studying the layout of Amanda's nightclub.

'Not exactly a piece of cake, is it, Harry?' he said.

Harry helped himself to coffee and sat down with a wry smile. 'Never said it was, did I?'

Murphy grunted. 'Well, the man we need to look over the place is Colin Soal. D'you know him? You'll have to pay through the nose, but he'll do a good job. He'll scope out every inch of the place, down to the toilet paper. We've gotta have a good man inside there, Harry. There's so many entrances and exits, and that kitchen's a bastard.'

Harry didn't answer. Eventually Murphy looked at him. 'What d'you reckon about Colin Soal?'

Harry seemed tetchy, looking at his watch. 'Yeah, I remember him. He was ... A bit long in the tooth now, isn't he? Where the hell is Micky?'

Murphy nodded at the suitcases. 'You on the move?'

Harry smiled. 'Well, if the wife can find me, so can half of London.'

'D'you think Dolly's going to try and pull something tonight?' Murphy asked. 'You got any idea where she's gonna hand over the cash?'

Harry's mouth tightened. He didn't like all these questions. 'No idea.'

Harry got to his feet and started pacing up and down. His fists clenched and unclenched as he worked himself up into a temper. It was coming back to this place, he thought, this stinking lock-up. He hated it, but it was one of the few things he'd got left; she'd taken everything else, the bitch.

Harry went to the telephone, which was in a small annexe.

'Don't worry, Harry, the phone's on. I got that sorted,' Murphy called to him. Harry made Murphy nervous when he was like this, prowling round like a caged animal.

Harry went back to his pacing. Then he stopped, facing the dividing wall with the adjoining lock-up.

'You check out the place next door?'

'Yeah, couple of kids bought the lease, and the next one along. Printers or something. They're a bunch of wallies. What's the matter, you hear something?'

Harry was still facing the wall, listening.

'Oh, it'll be the rats,' Murphy said. 'The place next door's crawling with them.'

Harry slammed his fist into the wall. 'Where is that stupid git?' He turned sharply as Tesco breezed in.

'Someone mention my name? Hey, you should keep that door locked, you know. Anyone could come in.'

Harry just stared at him. 'You're late.'

Micky sat down next to Murphy and picked up a coffee mug. 'This hot, is it? Good.' He turned to Harry, trying to keep up the chat, telling him everything he'd done, before Harry could tear him off a strip. 'I been fixing up that girl I told you about, the model for the nightclub. You said, "Get a girl on the inside." Well, I've got one.'

Harry came and stood over Micky. 'When I tell you to be some-where at a certain time, I want you there.' He gave him a cold stare for a few seconds. 'How much does she know?'

Micky shrugged. Harry really did frighten him at times, but he was determined not to show it.

'Nothin', I told her nothin'. She's straight, just a dumb chick. What is this? Why the third degree?'

Harry sat down next to him. 'You gotta new place for me to stay?'

Micky could feel his own temper rising. He hated being pushed all the time. He also hated being stared at by Gordon Murphy.

'Yeah, I got a pad for a couple o' weeks. I bin doin' what you told me, Harry – I can't be in four bleeding places at once!'

All Harry said was, 'I don't care about that. You were late.'

'All right! I was bleedin' late!' Micky snapped.

'Why don't you drop it, Harry?' Murphy said quietly.

Harry gave him a look. 'Fill 'im in. We'll meet up here later.' He turned and walked out.

Once he was gone, Micky stood up and kicked over the orange box. 'Who the friggin' hell does he think he is? I'm not takin' that, not from him, not from anybody!'

Murphy smiled and put the orange box back. 'You just did, son.'

*   *   *

'Where the bloody hell have you been?' Dolly shouted, her eyes blazing with anger.

Shirley stood in the centre of the lounge with a hangdog expression. 'I . . . I went out for a job.'

Dolly lifted her hands in despair. 'A job? You went for a bloody *job*? I don't believe it.'

'She's been drinking too. You can smell it on her!' Linda chipped in.

Dolly whipped round with a furious look and just managed to stop herself from slapping her. 'Shut up, Linda!'

Linda was hurt. 'Well, she has been,' she protested. 'My God, if it was me . . .'

'Well, it isn't, so that makes a change!' Dolly snapped.

Seeing them bicker gave Shirley her courage back. 'It's not as if I'd done something terrible. You told us to act like normal – and that's what I've been doin'. I've always wanted to be a model . . . And, I mean, you're not even goin' to make the call till after midnight!'

Dolly couldn't believe this girl. 'Didn't it ever occur to you that we might have been worried?'

Shirley did feel bad about that, but she wasn't going to back down. 'I wasn't gonna give up my chance, Dolly; not for you, not for anybody! I don't care about my share – you can have it!'

'Just you hold your temper, my girl,' Dolly said.

'Why the hell should I?' Shirley shouted. 'This is *my house*! You're shouting at me and it's *my house!*'

Bella snorted. 'Two weeks in LA and she thinks she's a bleedin' movie star!'

Dolly turned to Linda and Bella. 'Right, get into the kitchen, the pair of you, and make us something to eat. Go on, now! And you, Shirley, *sit down*.'

Shirley stomped over to the sofa and plonked herself down. 'All right, Dolly, I'm sorry, OK?'

Dolly ignored her while she fetched her notebook from her handbag, then joined her on the sofa. Shirley took out her cigarettes and lit one. Dolly wafted the smoke away from her face.

'Right, fine, now this is what you've got to focus on. I've worked it out. This is your route, Shirley. You head towards Hampstead, coming up Haverstock Hill here . . .' She pointed with a pencil. 'You turn right into Pond Street, here. You pass Bella, standing on the corner by the phone booth outside the cinema.'

'Me mum's pregnant,' said Shirley.

Dolly looked as if someone had just hit her on the head with a brick. She did a very slow turn towards Shirley. 'What?'

'I know, it's disgusting, isn't it?'

Dolly threw down her pencil. 'I don't believe it, I just don't believe it.'

'Well, nor could I!' said Shirley. 'I mean, she's forty-four, same age as Ursula Andress, but . . .'

Dolly could feel the fury building up inside her, but she knew she had to control herself. Between gritted teeth, she said, 'Shirley, just pay attention, all right? Let's go over your route again.'

In the kitchen, Linda was frying up bacon and eggs. Not used to an electric cooker, she had the heat on too high and the bacon was burning, grease spitting everywhere.

'It's all sticking to the pan!' she called out.

Bella was hacking her way through a loaf. 'It can't be, Linda. It's a non-stick pan. Why don't you put some butter in?'

The smell of burning brought Dolly into the kitchen. She was about to ask Linda what the hell she was doing when there was a scream. The three women froze.

Shirley burst into the kitchen, clutching Linda's dummy. She was hysterical, her voice shaking.

'Is this supposed to be funny?' She threw the doll on the floor. She was almost in tears.

Dolly sighed and turned to Linda. 'Where did you put it?'

Linda was like a naughty schoolgirl, head down, blushing. 'I sat it on the toilet. It was a joke . . .'

'Well, it bloody backfired, didn't it? Just take it away.'

Linda picked it up from the floor.

Shirley was taking deep breaths, getting herself under control. 'I thought it was him . . .'

Dolly looked at each of them in turn. 'You want out? Well, so do I. The sooner I see the back of the lot of you, the better.' She walked out of the kitchen, slamming the door behind her.

For a moment they just looked at each other, then Shirley suggested that someone should take the pan off the cooker before they burnt the house down. She followed Dolly out, giving Linda one last, filthy look before she went.

Linda stood there, still clutching the dummy. 'I didn't mean any harm . . .'

Bella took the pan off the stove and turned it off. 'It showed us one thing, didn't it? We're all scared of him.' Her face was tight. 'I hate him.' She thought for a moment. 'You leave first, don't you, Linda? D'you remember where it is? In the boot of the second or third car, just by the door.'

Linda looked confused. 'What d'ya mean? What're you talkin' about?'

Bella looked at her. 'When we leave tonight, you go first, you go to the lock-up, and you get that gun.'

'But . . . But Dolly said no guns, Bella.' Linda hugged the dummy.

Bella's voice was harsh. 'Yeah, she said a lot of things. But I want bloody protection. If that bastard Rawlins tries anything, I'm gonna kill 'im – so help me God, I'll kill 'im! Now will you get the gun, Linda?'

Linda swallowed. 'OK.' Like a child, she put her hand out for Bella to shake. 'Friends?'

Bella walked out of the kitchen.

Linda started to feel that old, clammy fear, the one at the orphanage, when Mummy didn't come – when nobody came – and she knew she was all alone yet again.

* * *

Rawlins sat at the small table by the telephone, drumming his fingers impatiently while he waited for it to ring. Next to the phone was an A-Z and a notepad. Rawlins checked the time on his watch. He wondered if he'd been wrong; perhaps Dolly wasn't going to call. But then he relaxed in the chair. No, he knew his Dolly; he knew she'd call.

* * *

The girls were all sitting in the lounge, eyes on the clock. Bella gave Linda a slight nod.

Linda got to her feet. 'Right, it's best if I go now, Dolly, so I can check out the area.'

Dolly looked at her watch, as if she didn't trust the clock. 'All right, Linda, off you go. But remember, if you see anything, anything at all—'

'I know.' Linda nodded. 'I'll call it off. But don't worry, if I get a move on, I can give that place a really good once-over.' She marched to the door, then came back with a sheepish grin and picked up her dummy. 'Good luck, everyone – see you all there!'

At the door she changed her mind, went over to Dolly and kissed her on the cheek. 'Take care, Dolly.' Then she went to Shirley and gave her a kiss. 'Take care,' she said. She turned hopefully to Bella, but Bella gave her one of her looks, then, as Linda bent down, she whispered, 'Just get the gun.'

* * *

Micky Tesco was wearing black leathers and a motorbike helmet, the visor raised. He looked over at Murphy, who was sitting calmly, reading a trashy women's magazine.

'I can't take much more of this hanging round. If I'd known we were goin' to be this long, I'd have brought me bleedin' camp bed! I'm not waiting all fuckin' night!'

Murphy didn't look up from the magazine. 'For sixty grand, you'll wait, Micky.'

* * *

Dolly tried to keep her hand from shaking as she dialled. Bella and Shirley stood over her, watching the phone as if it were a live thing.

Dolly's back suddenly went rigid. 'It's ringing!'

Bella whispered, 'I'm with you. Go on, do it, girl . . .'

The phone was picked up.

'Harry? This is Dolly . . .'

That was the signal. Shirley and Bella nodded to Dolly, gave her a last thumbs-up, and left her to make the deal with Harry.

* * *

Linda drove towards the lock-up, the dummy propped up on the passenger seat. She drove fast, concentrating hard on not making any mistakes, and she could feel herself beginning to sweat. She turned the radio on and fiddled with the tuner until she found Radio Luxembourg. There was a ballad playing, a heartbroken girl singing, 'We will meet again, when the night is over, we will meet again . . .' It sent chills up Linda's spine, so she turned it off and drove on towards the lock-up in silence.

* * *

'Fifteen minutes? You must be joking!' Harry protested. 'I'll never make it! All right, all right. Now, you wanna go over the details one more time, Doll?'

While he spoke, Harry was carefully tracing a route with a red felt-tipped pen across the map. 'OK now, this car park, Dolly . . .' He ringed it with his pen. 'I don't know any car parks on Hampstead Heath, Doll . . . All right, OK, just take it easy, I'll find it.' He traced the roads surrounding the car park. 'OK, yup, I'll find it, but it might take more than fifteen minutes, all right?'

Dolly's voice at the other end of the phone was tense. 'Fifteen minutes is all you've got. And I want the headlights off, interior lights on. If I see any sign of anyone, anything suspicious, I'll drive straight on by.' She found her mouth had gone dry. 'I want you to step out of the car. We meet out in the open.' Up to this point she'd managed to stay calm, but now suddenly she could feel her voice cracking, tears welling up. She wanted more than anything not to cry, and she gritted her teeth, trying to keep her emotions under control. 'Harry, if you try anything – if you come after me, if you try and follow me – I'll talk. I'm prepared to lose everything, you understand me, Harry? Everything. You've got to leave us alone, all of us.'

Harry was on his feet now, the book and maps bundled together in his pocket. 'It's a deal. You've got my word. I'll see you in fifteen minutes, then, Doll? You there, Doll?'

But Dolly had already hung up. Harry slammed the phone in its cradle, then quickly picked it up and began dialling.

* * *

Linda let herself into the lock-up and looked round at all the half-wrecked cars. Then she saw the light coming from an open door and heard the muffled voices. She looked round in panic, dropped her car keys, and bent to pick them up just as Micky Tesco ran past her, his visor over his face. He fired up his motorbike, which was parked near the main doors. He was followed by Gordon Murphy.

Linda crawled behind one of the cars, trying to make herself invisible. She peeked out to see Gordon Murphy walking towards the main doors. As he started opening them, he yelled, 'Just you make sure you get the money!'

Micky was revving up the bike. 'I hear you!' he shouted back. Then the bike sped away.

The place went dark as Murphy closed the doors. Linda stood up and began to search frantically round the floor for her keys.

* * *

The car park was dark, silent and deserted.

Shirley dropped Bella by the phone booth next to the cinema. Bella looked round the empty streets towards the car park. 'It looks pretty quiet, but have a good check round and come back.'

Shirley drove off.

Bella checked that the phone was still working. She stepped out of the booth and stood in the cinema entrance. Hidden from the street, she watched.

* * *

Eventually Linda found her car keys and started searching the boots of the old cars. She found the small velvet bag in the third one, just where Bella had told her it would be. She felt inside and there was the gun.

She was scared that Murphy had put a chain on the door, but her luck was in. The door opened and she slipped out.

* * *

Harry had a quick look round the flat, seemingly in no hurry, before shutting the door behind him. He calmly crossed the road to his Jaguar and drove away.

* * *

Dolly checked her watch for the fifteenth time and picked up the bag containing the £60,000. She turned off all the lights in the house and went out to her car.

* * *

As Shirley pulled up, Bella stepped from her hiding place in the cinema entrance and hurried to the car.

'Linda's not in position!' Shirley exclaimed.

Bella was calmer. 'Have you checked out all the parked cars?'

Shirley nodded. 'I've looked in every last one. It's like a grave-yard up there. But where's Linda? What should I do?'

Bella looked back up Pond Street. It was empty. She turned back to Shirley. 'Look, go and get into position. Park right on the comer. Anything goes wrong, just give me the signal, flash your lights.'

'Yeah, I know what to do, but what about Linda?'

Bella decided to tell her. 'It's OK, she's gone for a gun.'

* * *

Riding the bike hard, Micky Tesco came up East Heath Road and on past the ponds, ignoring the car park to his right. He continued towards the Vale of Health, then veered across the road, up onto the pavement and cut the headlights. He moved onto a narrow pathway on the heath itself, then switched the engine off and pushed the bike towards the top of the hill. It took time; the bike was heavy and he needed all of his strength to do it. He heaved it into a position where he had a perfect view of the car park below him. The place was still deserted. He was in good time. Looking up the hill from the car park, Tesco, in black leathers and helmet, on the black bike, would be practically invisible.

* * *

Gordon Murphy headed in the opposite direction, coming down East Heath Road towards the car park. He passed a block of exclusive flats overlooking the heath, passed the car park and the ponds on his left, then turned right on to Downshire Hill, making a quick U-turn so he could park facing the car park. His instructions were to keep out of Harry and Micky's way. His job was to follow Dolly and find out where she was staying. That was all he had to do. He switched off his lights and sat, waiting.

* * *

Shirley was unaware that while she had been talking to Bella on the corner, Tesco and Murphy had taken up their positions. As she returned and parked her car, the heath seemed as still and silent as before. She was now in position, facing the car park, waiting. Linda had still not shown up.

* * *

Linda had reached Englands Lane. She knew she was late, still more than five minutes from the car park, and the dummy lurched sideways in the seat beside her as she screeched round the corner.

* * *

Bella watched Harry Rawlins' Jag pass the cinema, heading towards the car park. She looked towards Shirley's parked car. There was no warning flash, so all must be well. But where the hell was Linda? She looked up Pond Street again, towards Haverstock Hill, hoping to see her appearing.

* * *

Harry arrived at the car park, drove up past the big oak tree and did a slow U-turn, ending up dead centre of the car park, as Dolly had instructed him. He turned his lights off, and for a moment he was in total darkness. He glanced up towards the hill, hoping Micky Tesco was in position. Then he turned and looked across East Heath Road to where Murphy should be parked. He flicked on the interior light and opened the doors.

* * *

It was frightening. There he was, sitting in the car just as they had planned, clear as daylight. For the first time, Shirley had a really good look at Harry Rawlins.

* * *

As Bella was staring up Pond Street, desperate for a sight of Linda, Dolly drove past, heading towards the heath. With no warning signal from Bella, she drove on.

Shirley saw Dolly in the green Ford heading towards the car park and inched herself up in the seat. As arranged, Dolly parked her car exactly across the exit. Now Harry couldn't get out. So far, everything was going according to plan. The one missing link was Linda . . .

* * *

Micky Tesco tensed when he saw Dolly's car pulling up.

* * *

Gordon Murphy had the key already in the ignition, poised, ready to follow Dolly as soon as she started to move.

* * *

Dolly stared. She could see him now. She watched as he got out of the Jaguar and stood there. He was smiling. He lifted his hands above his head, then shook his arms in a comical gesture to indicate that he had nothing up his sleeve, nothing in his pockets. He turned round, as if he was making a joke of the whole thing. Seeing him there, actually seeing him, just two hundred yards away, made Dolly suddenly unsure whether she could go through with it. His presence totally unnerved her. She clenched her fists hard, her nails almost cutting into her palms, in an effort to pull herself together.

Right, here we go, she thought. She reached over the back of the seat and picked up the shopping bag full of money.

* * *

Linda veered right on to Pond Street, her tyres squealing – and straight into the path of a car accelerating up the hill. Blinded by her lights, the other driver swerved out of her way and crashed into the wall surrounding the church. Linda pulled up and stared in panic behind her. The driver and a female passenger got out, shouting and screaming at her. The windscreen had shattered, and the front end was badly dented, but they were both on their feet and she couldn't see any blood, so Linda turned and drove on towards the heath.

Seconds later, the badly shocked driver saw a patrol car passing on Rosslyn Hill and ran towards it to flag it down. Linda was so focused on catching up with Bella she didn't see it turning down Pond Street behind her, its lights flashing. As she accelerated down the hill, the patrol car was already radioing in for backup: 'Red Ford Capri heading down Pond Street towards the heath, registration RKT 23X, repeat . . .'

At the bottom of the hill, Linda already had the passenger door open as Bella ran from the cinema. She was hysterical, shouting, 'Give me the gun!'

As she drove on towards the car park, Linda tried to fill Bella in on what had happened at the lock-up. 'There was a motorbike! Harry's not . . . It's the motorbike, the motorbike!'

Bella leant across Linda and hit the horn as hard as she could, trying to warn Dolly not to hand over the money.

* * *

Dolly and Harry were only yards apart. He held his hand out for the shopping bag as he approached her.

Linda and Bella, car horn blaring, screeched up.

Dolly turned; Harry turned.

Bella was out of the car, running like a crazy thing towards Dolly, screaming: *'Dolly, run! Don't give him the money! Run! Run, Dolly!'*

As soon as Tesco saw the bag about to be handed over, he kicked the bike into life and raced down the hill without lights, wheels lifting off the ground at one point, bumping fast across the pathway. When he hit the car park, he headed straight across the gravel towards Dolly.

Bella was still running towards Dolly, the gun held out stiffly in front of her, Linda trailing behind. Dolly clutched the shopping bag to her chest as she backed towards them. Harry took it all in, saw Tesco coming towards them on his bike, and turned back towards the Jaguar.

From his position, Murphy couldn't make out what the hell was going on. There seemed to be people running in every direction, car horns blaring, people shouting, lights flashing. He strained forward for a better view, turned the engine on, and then his headlights – still it was chaos. Gravel churned as Tesco hurtled towards Dolly.

Linda screamed at her to get away. 'It's the bike – the bloke on the bike's going to take the money. *Run, Dolly!'*

Harry started the Jag. Bella was running towards him, shouting something, pointing a gun.

Dolly was dazed, trying to work out who was shouting what. As Shirley jumped from her car and ran for the car park, Tesco tried to grab the shopping bag out of Dolly's hands. He got a good grip on it, but Dolly wouldn't let go. As he tried to accelerate away, she was pulled off her feet and, still holding on to the money, was dragged across the gravel behind the bike. With a snarl, Tesco kicked out at her, his foot connecting with her arm, and she lost her hold on the bag. Then he was gone, almost doing a wheelie as he screeched round the tree, out of the car park and down the road towards the cinema.

Harry was also on the move, aiming the car at the gap between the tree and the ditch. Bella was running alongside, trying to open the driver's door, while keeping the gun aimed at Harry. The car bounced over a dip and Bella stumbled, let go of the car and dropped the gun.

Murphy still sat, watching to see where Harry was going and trying to decide what to do.

Shirley had now joined the other women, and the four of them made a circle round the still-moving Jaguar. Harry was heading towards the tree where Dolly was standing, her face picked out by the headlamps. She held her hand over her eyes, blinded by the glare. Linda was the one who realised what would happen. She ran up behind Dolly and, screaming at the top of her lungs, pushed her out of the way of the car as it lurched past.

As Dolly picked herself up, they all heard the siren as the patrol car hurtled up the road from the cinema towards the car park. That was enough for Murphy, who quickly left his parking spot and drove away in the same direction as Tesco.

Still surrounded by the running women, Harry manoeuvred the car backwards and forwards, tyres spinning on the gravel, and then crashed straight through the barrier on to the road and away, the patrol car flashing past him in the other direction.

Shirley screamed a warning to Dolly.

'Police! Police!'

Dolly didn't need telling twice. 'Get out! All of you back to your cars! Move!'

Dolly and Bella made for the green Fiesta.

'Where's Linda?' Dolly asked, her breath heaving. They could see the red Capri, the doors still open.

'She's there,' Bella yelled. 'Now come on, let's go!'

The three cars all hurtled out of the car park just as the police approached the entrance. They sped off into the night, leaving the patrol car uncertain who to follow.

Dolly watched anxiously over her shoulder as Bella drove. 'Linda . . . Has Linda made it?'

'It's all right, I saw her in the car,' Bella told her. 'The money, Dolly. Did you get the money?'

Dolly's face was set, her mouth rigid. 'Just drive, Bella. Just get us home.'

* * *

Murphy couldn't get any sense out of Micky Tesco. He was so proud of his motorcycle antics, he kept looking at the money, saying, 'We did it, by God we did it! You see that wheelie I did, over the ditch? Eddie Kidd, eat your heart out!' Then he suddenly looked at Murphy. 'Murphy, you shouldn't be back 'ere. What you doin' back 'ere?'

Harry entered the lock-up silently. 'I'd like to know that, Murphy. What are you doin' back here?'

Murphy looked at Harry, then at Micky. He knew he'd blown it. 'It was the Old Bill, Harry.'

Harry nodded. 'The Old Bill.'

'They were there in a flash, Harry. Somebody must have tipped them off.'

'Doesn't mean you've gotta piss off! What a bloody cock-up!' Harry shouted furiously.

Micky grinned, pointing at the money. 'Come on, Harry. Does that look like it's a cock-up?'

Harry glared at him. He felt like slapping his face. He jabbed his finger at Murphy.

'I told you to stay on her, follow her. That's all you had to do. She must have driven straight past you, and you blew it!'

Micky didn't understand why he was so angry. 'But we got the money, Harry!'

This time Harry did slap him, a quick, vicious swipe. Micky reeled back, and Harry looked at the money spilt across the floor.

'That is a frigging piss in a frigging, fucking ocean.'

'Better than a kick in the arse, though, isn't it?' Micky said sullenly, rubbing his cheek.

Murphy could see Harry was on the point of really losing it. 'I panicked, Harry,' he said, holding his hands up defensively. 'It won't happen again, honest.'

Harry looked at him almost in disgust. '*Again?* You think you've got the bottle for the jewel caper, do you?' Again Harry prodded him. 'Do you? You make me sick, the pair of you. Fuckin' amateurs!' Harry walked out, throwing instructions over his shoulder. 'Lock the place up and stash the cash . . .'

Micky picked up Harry's two suitcases and jogged after him. 'I've got a great pad for you, Harry. Just you wait and see . . .'

Left on his own, Murphy looked at the bundles of banknotes spread over the floor. He got down on his hands and knees and started to pick them up.

* * *

'You told her to get this?' Dolly held out the gun, deliberately pointing it almost at Bella's face.

'It was for you. To protect you,' Bella said sullenly.

'Well, you certainly made a bloody mess of that, didn't you?' Dolly snapped.

She began pacing up and down the room, hands on hips. 'I'll give her hell when she gets here!' Dolly looked down at the scrunched-up sheets of newspaper and old tights – stuffing for the dummy – scattered on the sofa. It suddenly dawned on her. 'Oh God, it was the dummy!'

Bella looked puzzled.

'You didn't see Linda in her car – it was the dummy.'

Shirley and Bella looked at each other, dumbstruck, then back to Dolly. She was rubbing her head, trying to piece it all together.

'Which one of you pushed me?'

They just stared at her.

'Out of the way of . . . his car.' She couldn't bring herself to say his name. 'Come on, which one of you was it?'

Bella and Shirley both shook their heads.

Dolly picked up the gun and slipped it into her coat pocket.

'Where are you going?' asked Bella.

'I think we'd better get back up there. Shirley, you stay here in case she comes back.'

Shirley looked nervous. 'But what shall I tell her? I mean, what should I do?'

'Tell her she's for it. Tell Linda she's really for it this time.'

* * *

Micky was showing Harry round the flat he'd rented for a couple of weeks – well, not rented, *borrowed*. It was certainly much more Harry's style, all very plush, with gold dolphin taps in the bathroom. Micky pointed to the bidet and picked up a bottle of Badedas.

'You never know who you'll meet . . .' he drawled in a TV ad voice.

Sometimes Micky really got up his nose, but Harry couldn't help smiling. He walked out of the bathroom and into the stunning lounge, with the brown-tinted mirrored walls and thick-pile carpets.

'How long we got this place for?'

'Few weeks. Friend of . . . a friend had a slight run-in with Her Majesty's . . .'

Micky didn't mention that it belonged to a coke dealer who'd been done for dealing and was serving six months. Flashy so-and-so, Italian feller. Micky knew Harry would really go for a flash place like this. Yeah, he thought to himself, he was beginning to suss Harry out.

'Fancy a drop of chilled Chablis, Harry?'

Harry smiled, patting Micky on the shoulder. 'I shouldn't have sounded off like I did, Micky. You did a good job, and like you said, sixty grand is better than a kick in the arse.'

Micky grinned from ear to ear. Suddenly, him and Harry were friends.

* * *

The area round the oak tree in the car park had been sealed off with blue and white tape. There were two police cars in attendance, an ambulance and four other cars standing by. Already, great arc-lamps had been erected to illuminate the ditch and the surrounding area.

Linda's car was also surrounded by red tape. Local residents in dressing gowns huddled outside the tape, watching the goings-on. A man with a coat over his pyjamas wandered over.

'It was a woman, but they wouldn't let anyone look. Nobody can get close,' he told them.

Two police officers were standing ankle-deep in the muddy ditch, pulling the body of a woman out of the filthy water. An ambulance crew were waiting with a stretcher at the edge of the ditch, and the police officers carefully passed the body over. It looked like a muddy, discarded rag doll.

Dolly and Bella stood with the group of watchers, frozen to the spot.

Dolly made a move towards the body on the stretcher, but Bella held her back. 'Don't, Dolly.'

Hanging on to each other, they watched as the ambulance crew covered the body with a red blanket.

'She's dead.' Dolly's voice was empty, expressionless.

More uniformed and plain-clothed officers clustered round the shape under the red blanket. It seemed so small and still in comparison with the milling bodies.

Bella couldn't believe it. She kept staring at that little figure under the blanket, willing it to get up, sit up and say something – something

silly, something funny, that this wasn't true, this was just a nightmare, and she was going to wake up any minute.

Dolly had left the scene and was walking briskly up the street.
Bella ran after her.

'Dolly, Dolly, you can't just walk away.'

Dolly kept going, her face white. Bella tried to stop her, pulling
her back, but Dolly shook her off, walking stiffly as if under remote
control, just saying, 'Go back and tell Shirley.'

Bella stopped and saw them lifting the stretcher into the back of
the ambulance. She started to cry. She looked to Dolly for help, but
Dolly kept on walking.

Bella leant against a tree and wept.

* * *

Over and over in Dolly's mind, a voice was saying: 'Be like 'aving a
mum . . . Don't leave me, Dolly . . . I want to stay with you, Dolly . . .
Be like 'avin' a mum . . . a mum . . .'

Her rage was like a train in a long, black tunnel. Then suddenly
it burst out into the light and Dolly screamed, 'You bastard, Harry!
You *bastard*!'

Some of the little group of bystanders turned when they heard
it, but they couldn't make out what the woman was saying, and
instead their attention was caught by Bella, who still stood weeping
against the tree.

Then somebody said that they were bringing something out of
the red Ford Capri. They all turned as the policeman held up Linda's
dummy, its feet dangling, its head nodding, still with its cap on.

* * *

It was 6:30 in the morning when Vic Morgan pulled up outside 44
Elgin Mansions to begin his round-the-clock watch on Harry Rawlins' place. He poured himself a cup of coffee from a Thermos, and

was settling in for a long, uneventful wait, when he saw someone walking up the road towards him, and almost dropped the coffee in his lap.

Dolly Rawlins. She seemed different, an odd, haunted look on her face, and she seemed to be walking in a daze. She stopped outside the entrance and just stood, staring up for a long time. Then, as if snapping out of a dream, she pushed through the swing doors and into the block. Morgan got out of the car and followed.

Dolly's feet were like lead as she trudged up the staircase. She felt the gun in her pocket. The metal was icy cold.

Morgan moved soundlessly up the stairs behind her until she reached the door of number 44. He watched through the banister rails and heard the bell ringing through the empty flat. Dolly's left hand was held to her side and that was when Morgan saw the gun.

She rang the bell again, and as it dawned on her that nobody was there, she seemed to deflate, leaning her head wearily against the door.

He moved quietly behind her. Very gently, he said, 'Mrs Rawlins, you all right, love?'

She didn't seem surprised, just turned her face away, muttering, 'No . . . no . . .' under her breath.

She let him take the gun, let him hold her for a moment, then guide her down the stairs, and all the time he was talking to her, as if he was talking to a child. 'That's it, that's a good girl, you lean on me, that's a good girl. Now mind the stairs, easy does it, good girl. You all right now?'

Dolly rested her head against his shoulder, the fear and the anger all drained out of her, and for the first time since she could remember, she felt safe. Safe and at peace.

* * *

The chalk squeaked down the blackboard as the mortuary attendant wrote the name 'Linda Pirelli', checking the spelling against the file in his hand. He then walked past the rows of drawers until he found the one that had been pulled open and there she was – naked, her head and shoulders covered with terrible bruising.

He checked that the name tag was still attached to her right toe, and could feel that she was not yet cold. He slowly pushed the drawer back in.

He flipped a page, noting that this one was due for post mortem the following day. There were already brief notes from the doctor, who'd done the first examination, stating that the girl had not died from the injuries inflicted by some kind of vehicle but from drowning. She had been found face down in four inches of muddy water.

The attendant put the report on the desk. Another day, another body. He picked up the morning newspaper, turned to the back page with the sports headlines, and began to read.

CHAPTER FOUR

Bella had kept vigil all night, and was still sitting by the window in Shirley's lounge when dawn broke. She was no longer looking out, no longer waiting for Dolly, she was just sitting, and thinking. Several times she got up to make herself a cup of tea, then left it undrunk.

Shirley had been in bed when Bella had come back and told her that they had found Linda, that she didn't think Linda would be coming back. Shirley couldn't take it in to begin with. She made Bella repeat everything she had seen. Bella broke down and cried when she described the figure on the stretcher, with the red blanket over her face . . .

All the memories now flooded back into Bella's mind, making her cry again. In Rio, during the robbery, when they'd first met. In the back of her mind was a tiny, fragile hope that they'd been wrong, that perhaps she was still alive. But deep down in her heart she knew that Linda was dead, and she would never see her again.

Shirley had been shocked at first, then she'd cried, then she'd got calm again. She asked Bella if she was sure, and then she started to cry again, and Bella had left her crying herself to sleep, while she went to sit by the window, waiting for Dolly.

She kept asking herself questions, but she couldn't find any answers, so she just sat and waited, and during the waiting time the memories flooded back in waves, drifting in and out, behind them all a terrible feeling of guilt.

She couldn't stop thinking about how she'd turned away from that last kiss. And how Linda had then put her hand out to her, asked if they were still friends, and Bella hadn't shaken.

She could hear Shirley moving round and looked at the clock on the mantelshelf. It was after nine. She heard the toilet flush, and then Shirley came into the lounge.

Bella couldn't quite believe what she was seeing. Shirley was dressed, made up; she looked very smart.

'Are you going out?'

Shirley sounded uneasy. 'Yes, I . . . I've got an appointment.' She joined Bella at the window. 'Still no sign of Dolly? Where do you think she's gone?'

Bella shrugged. Shirley picked up a tray with the cups of tea Bella had made in the night.

'Just leave them,' Bella told her.

Shirley put the tray down again. 'We don't know, not for certain,' she said suddenly.

Bella shook her head. 'I saw her. I saw them put the blanket over her face. She's dead, Shirley.'

Shirley's mouth quivered as she tried to hold back the tears.

Bella got up, just wanting to get out, to get away from her. 'Don't smudge your make-up,' she said with a brittle smile. 'If you've got an appointment, you'd better keep it!'

'Oh, Bella,' Shirley whispered, reaching for her hand, and Bella clasped it tight.

'I'm sorry,' Bella said. 'Look, you go ahead, do what you have to do. I'll wait here for Dolly.'

Bella watched as Shirley walked down the path. She turned at the gate and gave a little wave. Bella didn't wave back. The anger had gone, but she still couldn't quite believe that Shirley had something so important to do that she could walk out of the house now, with Linda dead and Dolly who knows where, and everything in pieces.

She wished Dolly would come. Dolly would know what to do. Dolly always knew what to do.

* * *

Dolly woke with a splitting headache, as if someone had clamped a band round her head and was pulling it tight. She opened her eyes and everything was hazy. For a moment she didn't know where she was. The furniture was heavy, Victorian, masculine. There was a big dressing table, and Dolly saw her handbag on top of it. Then she saw the chair, with her torn stockings, her skirt and blouse, all neatly laid out, with her mud-spattered shoes on the floor underneath. She looked at the pillow next to her, the half-full brandy glass on the bedside table and felt a momentary panic.

There was a tap on the door and Dolly reached for the sheet to cover herself. Vic Morgan walked in with a smile, carrying a cup of coffee.

'How are you feeling?'

Dolly just wrapped the sheet tighter round her.

He put the coffee down and picked up the brandy glass. 'Do you feel like something to eat?'

Dolly was still desperately trying to remember what had happened the night before. It was all a blank. How did she get here? And, more importantly, what had she told this man? How much did he know?

Morgan carried the glass to the door and took the dressing gown that was hanging there off the hook.

'Would you like this? If you want a bath or something, it's first on the left.'

Dolly managed to say, 'Thank you,' then added, 'Do you have an aspirin?'

He opened a small drawer in the dressing table, took out a bottle of aspirin and handed it to Dolly. 'Your gun's in there as well, by the way,' he said casually.

As she took the bottle, she felt the sheet slipping away from her breasts, and Morgan could sense her discomfort. 'I slept on the sofa,' he said gently. 'You got yourself undressed, I just laid them out.' He turned to leave.

Dolly could feel herself flushing with embarrassment. 'Thank you, Mr Morgan.'

'That's all right . . . Mrs Rawlins.'

A bolt of lightning hit Dolly. Did he just call her 'Mrs Rawlins'? Then he *knew*.

'Er . . . what time is it, Mr Morgan?' she asked, trying to keep her voice relaxed and casual.

He turned to her with a smile. 'Almost 9:30, Mrs Rawlins.'

* * *

Detective Inspector Alex Fuller also had a headache that morning. He was washing his hands in the cloakroom, wondering why he'd had so many lately. Probably something to do with his sinuses. He took out a nose spray and gave himself a squirt, hoping that would help matters. He wiped his nose and then washed his hands again. He examined his clean, short-cut nails and dried his hands, before looking at his watch. Perfect. Just time to nip up to the canteen for a cup of coffee before sifting through all those reports.

Detective Constable John Reynolds was assigned to Fuller. At that moment, Reynolds was sitting behind his desk in the annexe, carefully typing Fuller's diary reports and silently cursing his boss. Fuller was a stickler for accuracy, and everything had to be by the book, while on a personal level he could be stiff and unfriendly. But at least, Reynolds thought to himself, as Detective Inspector Eric Frinton banged through the double doors, Fuller was a professional.

Frinton was carrying a coffee and eating a bacon sandwich as he strolled over to Reynolds' desk and perched himself on the corner.

'Got you going, has he? Bit of a slave-driver, our Detective Inspector.'

Reynolds stopped typing with a frown. 'Something I can do for you?'

Frinton took a slurp of his coffee, almost spilling it over Reynolds' neatly typed papers. 'Your guv'nor about? Might have somethin' of interest for him.' He took a big bite of his bacon sandwich and began chewing noisily.

'Like what?' Reynolds asked, pushing his typewriter to one side.

Frinton swallowed his mouthful and wiped his mouth on his sleeve. 'Your guv'nor was working on the Rawlins caper, wasn't he? With Resnick? You gotta fag?'

Reynolds shook his head. 'I don't smoke.'

DI Fuller appeared through the swing doors, carrying a coffee cup in a saucer. He gave Frinton a cool nod.

Frinton pushed himself off the desk. 'I was just telling Mabel Privet, here, I might have something that'll interest you.' He shrugged. 'On the other hand, it might not. Christ, I'm gasping for a fag,' he added hopefully.

Fuller looked at him with distaste. 'Come on, out with it, Frinton. I've got work to do.'

Frinton coughed. 'Yeah, right. We had a stiff on Hampstead Heath last night, a girl – Linda Pirelli.'

For a moment Fuller looked blank. 'Pirelli?'

'Yeah, Joe Pirelli's old lady. He got fried on that underpass raid, remember?'

'And she's dead?' Fuller was now very alert.

Frinton grinned. 'Yeah, as a doornail. Could be suspicious. My lads are looking into it.'

'Suspicious how?' Fuller asked.

'Well, the body was twenty yards from a car, in a ditch. Hit and run, by the look of it.'

'Another vehicle?'

'Well, I don't suppose she ran over herself. '

Fuller looked thoughtful. 'How come you're involved?'

'Couple of my boys were just drivin' past – seems the Pirelli girl had a smash at the top of the road, they followed her down and found her in the ditch.'

Fuller looked bemused. 'So what the hell happened?'

Frinton shrugged. 'Look, you want any details, come over to my place. I'm on the way home now, but my lads'll give you anything you want. But just remember you owe me, right?'

Fuller nodded. 'Right.'

Frinton gave him a wink, took another bite of his sandwich and lurched away, spilling coffee as he went.

Fuller turned to Reynolds. 'Let's get a car organised and go over to his office. Nothing else on, is there?'

Reynolds shook his head. 'Very quiet at the moment, guv.'

'Right, and while you're at it, get out that file on . . . Tell you what, go and see if you can pick up all of Resnick's old files on Harry Rawlins, all right?'

Fuller picked up his cup and took a sip of his coffee, deep in thought. He didn't seem to notice that it had gone cold.

* * *

Dolly sat at Vic Morgan's elegant dining table and thought what an extraordinary jumble the whole place was, with antique furniture rubbing up against modern lamps, typewriters and other gadgets. It had the uncared-for feel of a bachelor pad, but somewhere along the line it could have been his mother's. She looked at the photograph of a woman and a young boy on the mantelshelf.

Morgan stood at the door. 'They've got her in the mortuary. I'm sorry.'

Dolly knew Linda was dead, but hearing him say it was still a shock, somehow.

'D'you want some more coffee?'

Dolly shook her head. 'She pushed me out of the way. It should have been me.'

Morgan poured himself another cup. Dolly was ripping up a piece of tissue paper, pulling it apart, piece by piece.

'They're doing a post mortem this morning.'

He wasn't sure she heard him.

'Why in God's name didn't you go to the police in the first place?'

She didn't answer.

'You must have known he'd come after you. You took everything he had – plus you sent his girlfriend and baby to Australia!'

Dolly stood up and walked across the room to a wastepaper basket, dropping the torn-up tissue in. 'I was frightened. I told you, I just wanted to pay him off, to be left alone.'

Morgan spooned sugar into his coffee. 'Didn't look that way to me.'

'Well, it's the truth,' said Dolly.

Morgan took a sip, frowned, and added some more sugar. 'When I found you last night, what were you going to do?'

Dolly sat down at the table again. 'I was going to kill him.'

'Well, that wouldn't have been very clever, would it?'

Dolly gave a short, sharp laugh. 'Obviously not; he wasn't there.'

Morgan shook his head. 'What I meant was, there are other ways of getting rid of someone. Did he get any money from you?' He leant across the table. 'You said you were going to pay him off. Did he get the money?'

She hesitated for a moment, then shook her head and picked up her handbag. 'No.'

Morgan chose his words carefully. 'You see, there's a friend of mine who wouldn't mind getting his hands on your husband.'

Dolly shrugged. 'Well, you won't find him in that flat. He'll have moved on by now.'

Morgan persisted. 'There's a big reward up for grabs, for any information on the cash missing from the underpass raid – thirty thousand.'

Dolly snapped her bag closed. 'I see.' She stood and picked up her coat. 'That what all the questions are for? Reward money?'

He watched her put on her coat.

'You're all the same, whichever side you're on. It's all he ever wanted, all my husband ever cared for – money. Well, you can chase after it all you like, but don't try using me to get it.'

She walked out. He didn't try to stop her, but he was angry with himself for the way he'd mishandled things. At least he had a lot more information now, even though he knew for certain that Dolly Rawlins was holding something back, something big.

He took another sip of his coffee, thinking what a strange, fascinating woman she was. He'd held her half the night, held her tenderly as she'd sobbed her heart out for Linda Pirelli. Yet in the morning she behaved like a total stranger. It was going to take time before she truly trusted him.

* * *

Ray Bates was sorting through a pile of bills, tapping his pencil on the desk, when Micky Tesco arrived at the garage.

Micky leant against the door. 'Come on, what d'ya say? I just need a couple of motors, two Transit vans, maybe a spot of driving?'

Ray scratched his head. 'I dunno. I been straight for a long time, Micky. I don't want to get into anything heavy.'

Micky picked up a handful of bills. 'Business doesn't look too good to me. Reckon you could do with a few readies.'

Too right, Ray thought. His business was going down the drain – and at the worst possible time, with Audrey pregnant.

'Who's running the show?'

Micky shook his head. 'Can't tell you the name – but a big man, well known. And the money's big, too. But if you're not interested –' he shrugged – 'there's plenty of people who will be.'

He turned away, knowing Ray was hooked like a big, fat salmon. 'I'm in, Micky. I'll do it.'

Micky smiled. 'Good boy! OK, first off I want you to sort that Jag out for me, get a replacement . . .'

* * *

When Dolly finally reappeared at Shirley's, her relief was short-lived, because Bella couldn't stop crying. Dolly calmed her down and put the kettle on, thinking how odd it was the way everybody always offered cups of tea, not wanting to actually talk about what had happened. Eventually Bella calmed down enough for Dolly to ask her how Shirley had taken it.

Bella sniffed. 'Yeah, she cried, you know, but I don't think it's really hit her yet. I think it's the same for me. I still can't believe Linda isn't going to walk through the door.'

Dolly watched the kettle. 'She isn't coming back, Bella, and we're just going to have to carry on without her.'

Bella badly needed someone to hold her, but Dolly made no move towards her.

'What are we gonna do, Dolly?'

Dolly just shrugged. 'I don't know. I don't know . . .'

It was the last thing Bella expected Dolly to say and it shook her. Dolly suddenly seemed just as vulnerable and lost as she felt herself. But without a leader, someone to organise the three of them, what were they going to do?

* * *

Shirley's brother, Greg, was in one of the garages washing the Jag with an old, white T-shirt when Ray slid the doors open. Greg got up off his knees and held out the shirt.

'See these stains, Ray? I think this is blood.' He pointed at the front of the car. 'It's all along the mudguard. I think he must've hit a dog.'

Ray turned on him sharply. 'Just do as you're told, son, and keep it buttoned. You understand? Keep your mouth shut.'

Greg nodded.

'Just get it cleaned up and then take it to the paint shop for a respray. Got it?'

The garage door clanged shut behind him. Greg dipped the cloth in the bucket and went back to washing the car, trying not to think too hard about what had really happened.

* * *

Suddenly everything that had happened the night before was forgotten. Shirley was perched on a high stool in front of a blue 174 backdrop in the photographer's studio. She only had her underslip on, which had been Sellotaped to her nipples, giving her a very low cleavage. At first it had embarrassed her, having Sellotape stuck round her, having her body touched and painted, but gradually she relaxed and even began to enjoy it. The girl who had done her make-up was very chatty, helping her to feel at home, and the outrageously camp hairdresser, who spent hours putting a blonde rinse in her hair, was hilarious. He used a can of gold spray, then back-combed, teased, pulled, pushed, and now her hair was like a lion's mane. The make-up girl had matched the hair, using glistening, golden tones and heavy black eyelashes. She'd plucked away at Shirley's eyebrows, giving her a very high arch, moulded her cheeks, and instead of lipstick she'd used a silky gloss. Shirley looked in the mirror and hardly recognised herself.

The photographer was obviously well into his forties, but didn't behave like it – he was like an old hippie. He spent hours in the make-up room, looking at her, checking her out before photographing her. He'd decided that they should lower the slip even more, but there was nothing sexual in it – just professional. He wanted to do all the shots cut low, just neck and shoulders. The make-up girl told Shirley that he was one of the best.

'Cost a fortune, he does. You from Marion Gordon?'

Shirley had nodded, feeling like a million dollars. This was what she had always dreamt about . . .

And then she remembered Linda.

'You all right?' the make-up girl asked.

Shirley took a breath. 'Yes, I'm fine.'

Then the photographer had come in. 'We're ready to roll in a minute, darling. I want you up on this stool.'

Shirley's blondeness against the deep blue backdrop looked fantastic. Shirley went hot and cold as the lights went on, then off, and then they started work.

The photographer rapped out instructions: 'Turn your head right, left, just relax, chin up, now chin down, look at me, now right to the camera, left to the camera, flick your head back, come on, back, back, open your lips slightly . . .'

Shirley felt self-conscious and slightly foolish, especially when he said, 'OK, now I want you to look really angry – come on, come on, give me an angry look!'

Then Shirley let herself go and just did whatever he asked her to.

'Run your fingers through your hair, that's it. Hairdresser! *Hairdresser!*' And there was the hairdresser teasing her hair, giving her a wink, and the make-up girl redoing her lips.

'That's a lovely girl. Hold that, Shirley, hold that.'

Shirley lost track of time as they went through roll after roll of film, and all the while he was telling her how beautiful she was, how perfect. Then he changed tack.

'Now give me something a bit different, different mood, lips parted slightly, that's it. Now think of something sad, something really sad – yes! That's it. Just hold it like that.' And all of a sudden it was as if Shirley was frozen. She'd thought of Linda, and as the photographer kept snapping away, telling her how brilliant she was, how beautiful, the tears started to slide down her cheeks.

The camera kept clicking, and then he called for a rest.

He nodded enthusiastically to Shirley. 'That was a good session, darling. I've got some really good stuff.'

Shirley slid off the stool and ran to the make-up room.

He turned to the hairdresser. 'What do you reckon?'

The hairdresser pursed his lips thoughtfully. 'I think she's special. She could really do something.'

'She's a bit neurotic, though – all that bursting into tears,' the make-up girl chipped in.

The photographer began packing away the lights. 'Well, darling, all the really good ones are – they're all neurotic. I mean, if all you've got is a face, wouldn't you be?'

The hairdresser was quite surprised the photographer hadn't made a pass at Shirley. Rumour had it he'd been through most of the beautiful faces in London.

Then he saw Micky Tesco walk into the studio and instantly knew why.

Micky gave a brief nod to the photographer, then turned to the hairdresser.

'How'd it go?'

'Fine, Micky. New girlfriend, is it?'

Micky smiled his charming, lopsided smile. 'You might be right; there again, you might be wrong.'

The hairdresser packed up his tools and his scissors in his neat little bag. He'd never liked Micky, ever since they worked on a shoot together, finding him big-headed and pushy. And he'd heard plenty more about him since. Like he was a nasty piece of work, and even that he'd been put away for five years.

'How's Marion? You still seeing Marion Gordon?' he asked with a wry smile.

'Don't know what you're talking about,' Micky replied, giving him a cool stare.

The hairdresser zipped up his bag, tucked it under his arm and left the studio.

The make-up girl was chatting away to Shirley, trying to cheer her up, when Micky tapped on the door and walked in. He took one look and couldn't keep the surprise from his face. She looked fantastic.

She was also half-naked.

Shirley put her hands across her breasts shyly, and Micky said, 'Sorry, I'll wait outside.'

The make-up girl gave Shirley a nudge. 'That your feller? He's lovely looking, isn't he?'

Shirley just smiled.

'Is he your feller, or not? If he isn't, give me a chance. I'll move in on that!'

Shirley didn't answer. She began to pull the Sellotape off her breasts. She looked in the mirror and she could see why Micky had been so impressed. And then Linda's face floated in front of her again. Shirley reached for a dressing gown, tears swelling up.

The make-up girl sighed. Not again! What an odd girl. Oh well, you meet all sorts in this business. She began filling her make-up box with all her bottles and tubes. You had to admit, though, neurotic as she was, she'd certainly landed a good-looking bloke.

*　　*　　*

Sonny Chizzel's antique shop was almost as neat and elegant as he was, with his tailored suit and cravat, his pink, clean-shaven face and his coiffured white hair. He'd never seen the woman before. She seemed nervous, well-spoken but rather shabbily dressed. The little ormolu clock she'd brought in was a very nice piece, though, and he reckoned he could get at least two grand for it.

He took his eyeglass out and put the clock down as the doorbell pinged. He hadn't seen Gordon Murphy for at least five years, but he wasn't the sort of man you forget. He gave Murphy a curt nod and turned back to examining the clock.

Murphy put down his briefcase, looking round the shop. Sonny hadn't changed; he was still into this fancy Louis Quatorze stuff. He inspected an ornate dresser, tracing the inlaid wood. It was so highly polished that he could see Sonny and the woman as if he was looking in a mirror. The woman saw him observing her and pulled her headscarf round her face.

Murphy watched Sonny at work. He was a crafty old bastard, always had been. Sonny removed the eyeglass, put it down carefully, then gave a little shake of his head.

'Mmmm, the timer's gone, inlay missing, see . . . here . . . here . . . To be honest, I don't know if I can take it . . . I could give you one-fifty – best I can do.'

Again the woman looked at Murphy, then turned back to the counter.

Sonny put his eyeglass in again, held the clock up, then put it down. 'As I said, one-fifty. It's up to you, love. Take it or leave it.'

Murphy listened to the woman trying to argue, and felt sorry for her.

'It was my mother's. I'm sure it's worth more than that – it's good, a good clock . . .'

Sonny shrugged. 'Yes, well, it doesn't work, sweetheart. Look, I tell you what, and this is my last offer – one-sixty. Now, I can't go any higher than that. As I said, your timer's gone, there's inlay missing, it's gonna take a lot of work. I'm gonna have to take this down to the workshop anyway. I mean, it's not original, darling, it's a copy.'

The woman nodded. 'Yes, all right.'

Sonny picked up the clock, wrapped it in its newspaper and shoved it under the counter, then disappeared into the back of the shop, the inner sanctum.

Murphy was now opening a roll-top desk, touching the beautiful carving with his fingers. The woman was definitely edgy. Murphy wondered if the clock had been nicked. But she didn't look like a regular or anybody he recognised. Mind you, nowadays, everybody was dealing in hot stuff. That was the way life was. He saw Sonny come out of the back room and hand over the cash. The woman pocketed it fast, fast enough to convince Murphy that the clock was more than likely hot. If Sonny Chizzel had taken a bit more time, he'd have realised it too, but he was acutely aware that Murphy wanted something. And Murphy was not a man to keep waiting.

As soon as the woman left the shop, Gordon Murphy went to the door. Sonny watched him turn the key, turn the OPEN notice to CLOSED and pull the blind down.

'What do you want?' Sonny asked nervously.

Murphy picked up the case. 'Business. We talk in the back?'

Sonny hesitated for a moment. He looked at the briefcase in Murphy's hand, then gestured for Murphy to follow him out back.

* * *

Shirley looked round her mother's kitchen. It was a tip: the ironing board up, with a basket of ironing waiting to be done, the washing machine going, breakfast things still on the kitchen table – even the back door stood half-open.

'Mum!' she called out, but there was no reply. Then she heard what sounded like a radio playing in the bedroom. She put her bags down on the kitchen table and went through. Her mother's bed-room was in the same state as the kitchen. She paused outside her own bedroom door.

'Lift your right leg. Now hold . . . straighten . . . and lower. Lift your left leg and hold . . . straighten . . . and lower. Now, lift both legs together . . . lift . . . hold. Don't strain, whatever you do, ladies, don't strain . . . lift . . . and hold . . . and down . . .' Shirley opened the door. It was a jumble of ladders, pots of paint, sheets thrown over her bed. Audrey was sitting on a chair, smoking a cigarette, her feet up on a box. She was reading a copy of *Woman's Own*, as the radio cassette player on the floor beside her continued, '. . . and relax. Now lift both legs again, hold . . . straighten . . .'

Audrey turned and gave Shirley a grin. 'Hello, love, didn't hear you come in.'

Audrey surveyed the room. 'What's all this, then?'

'It's the nursery,' said Audrey, stubbing out her cigarette. Audrey showed Shirley the fabrics she'd chosen, and where she was going to put the cot. Then she lifted a sheet from a crib.

'Greg gave me this.'

Shirley crossed her arms. 'Yeah, I'll bet 'e did. Nicked it from Mothercare, did 'e?'

Audrey frowned. Shirley really had been getting on her nerves lately. 'Look, love, Greg's giving me housekeeping now. I'm getting things organised here.'

'So I can see, Mum,' Shirley replied with a shake of her head.

Audrey waddled back to the chair and sat down. 'Look, if you've only come over to pick on me, you can leave. A woman in my condition don't need any aggravation.' She plonked her feet back on the box and picked up the magazine. 'You seeing Micky, then, are you?'

Shirley didn't reply.

'I 'ope you are. I think your problem is you're not getting it. Everyone knows it makes you ratty.'

'Well, the whole world can see you're getting yours, and look where it's got you,' Shirley retorted, sitting down on the bed.

The two women looked at each other as the tape played on: '. . . repeat the exercise on your left side, lift the right leg up . . .'

'Oh, shut up!' Audrey flipped it off.

Shirley looked round the room again. She'd spent her childhood in this room, but it was a long time since she'd lived here. She was glad, in some ways, that it was all going to be done up.

Audrey caught her looking at her. Slightly embarrassed, she held her tummy. She was now showing very clearly.

'Did you want something, darlin'?'

Shirley shrugged. 'I just came over to see you, that's all. D'you wanna cup o' tea or anythin'?'

'No thanks, love, I just 'ad one. I'm watchin' me liquids. You go an' 'ave one if you like. I'm just trying to decide on the wallpaper.'

Shirley felt as if she wasn't wanted, wasn't needed.

'I'm sure it's going to look very nice, Mum.'

Audrey held up a picture in the magazine. 'I'm doin' it just like this. I'm thinking of callin' 'im 'Arry if 'e's a boy, after the prince. Be nice, that, don't you think? Harry Bates?'

'Is he gonna marry you then, Mum?'

Audrey flicked through the pages. 'When 'e gets 'is divorce, yes 'e is.'

Shirley shook her head. 'That's what they all say, isn't it, Mum?'

Audrey was sharp this time. 'Why don't you just get out? Go on, go!'

Shirley picked her way through the mess and into the kitchen. She looked round distastefully, then picked up her handbag – but she didn't want to go home. She didn't want to face Dolly. She didn't want to face Bella.

She wondered why she hadn't told Micky about Linda, but then, he'd seemed so proud of her, of the way she'd looked, she hadn't wanted to ruin the moment.

She sighed. Time to face the music.

*   *   *

Vic Morgan was worried about Resnick. He seemed to be deteriorating fast. He needed to get a move on with things.

Morgan leant forward. 'I checked out Dolly . . . Mrs Rawlins' story. Linda Pirelli was found last night, exactly where she said. Seemed she'd pushed Dolly out of the way. He was trying to kill her; Rawlins was trying to kill his wife.'

Resnick lay back on the pillows and sighed. 'And the girl's dead? Linda Pirelli's dead?'

Morgan passed Resnick the post mortem report. As he flipped through it, Morgan noticed again how little movement he had in his right hand.

Resnick handed the report back. 'Could mean a murder investigation. We're gonna have to move sharpish if we're going to find

Rawlins.' He grimaced with pain. 'You think his wife's on the level, do you, eh?'

'I dunno,' said Morgan with a shrug.

'Come on, you do, don't you? You think she's on the level?'

'All right, yes, I do.'

Resnick then rolled up a piece of newspaper and swatted at something on the bed Morgan couldn't see.

Morgan hoped to God Resnick wasn't beginning to lose his mind.

Resnick took another swipe. 'Can't you see these little buggers? Bloody flies everywhere.' Then he seemed to come back to reality. 'You think Mrs Rawlins is on the level, huh? Stayed at your place, did she? State of shock, I'll bet. Don't let that bitch wind you round her fingers, 'cos she's all we've got, Vic, and if Rawlins wants her, then we'll get to him through Dolly.' He swatted Morgan's elbow. 'Can't you see it? They're everywhere.'

Morgan put a hand on his arm. 'George . . .'

Resnick focused again. 'I reckon if you stay on her tail, we'll get him. We'll also get thirty grand's worth of reward money. And you know something? I reckon with that money behind us, you and I could open up an agency. Whaddya say?'

Morgan nodded uncertainly. Then he saw one of the tiny fruit flies land on Resnick's pillow. So he wasn't losing his marbles after all. He breathed a sigh of relief.

'Just you keep a watch on her,' Resnick repeated. 'Watch her round the clock. Because he'll find her, wherever she is, you'll see.' He lay back and closed his eyes.

Morgan turned round to find DI Fuller standing at the bedside.

Morgan stood up and gave Fuller a nod. 'I'm afraid he's not too good.' He patted Resnick's arm.

'Be seeing you, mate.' He walked off down the ward.

Fuller stood awkwardly for a moment, unsure if Resnick was awake. Eventually his old boss opened his eyes and coughed, before grimacing in pain. Fuller sat down in the vacant chair.

'I'm sorry to hear . . . I . . . thought you'd be up and about by now.'

Resnick pulled himself up. 'Why don't you cut the bullshit, Fuller? What do you want? You're not here to enquire about my health. If you were, you would 'ave been 'ere weeks ago. So what is it?'

Fuller took a deep breath, then told Resnick all about Linda Pirelli.

Resnick stared at him. 'Who?'

Fuller thought he knew what Resnick was doing. He'd done it to him often enough in the office. He thought he was being funny. 'Look, George, I've been over all your old files. You know there's thirty grand for any information on the raid?'

'What raid?' asked Resnick.

'The second raid.'

'Ah, yes . . . Well, nobody'd really be interested in the first raid, would they? I mean, they all died, didn't they? Yes, they all . . . Joe Pirelli, of course! Terry Miller . . . Harry Rawlins . . . They all bought it on that raid.'

Fuller had had enough. 'Come on, George, don't mess me about! Rawlins isn't dead. You know that as well as I do.'

Resnick just looked at him. He couldn't stand the little prick.

'Come on, George, you saw him.'

Resnick shrugged. 'I must've been mistaken. I'd taken a hell of a beating, remember? Must've been seeing things.'

Fuller tried another angle. 'What about his wife?'

Resnick smiled and nodded. 'Oh, she's a lovely lady.'

Fuller had had enough. 'All right, George, have it your own way.' He shook his head. 'You always were a stubborn bastard.' He carefully pushed the chair back against the bedside cabinet, then leant against the bed. 'Rawlins is alive, and I'm gonna damned well find him – with or without your help.'

He waited for some witty retort from Resnick, but it didn't come. 'You hear me, George? Rawlins is alive, and I'm gonna get him.'

Resnick nodded. 'Well, I hope I live long enough to see it, sonny.'

He watched Fuller turn and walk stiffly off towards the doors. God, how he loathed him. He saw Fuller stop to charm the matron, saw her get all fluttery, before ushering Fuller out. He hadn't wasted any time; by God, he'd risen fast. Detective Inspector – and he must be, what, thirty-three? Thirty-four? Smooth bastard.

Matron was steaming down the ward towards the bed.

'Mr Resnick, as you well know, visiting hours are between two-thirty and four. Please, in future, do not entertain during rounds. It isn't fair to me, the doctors, or the other patients. We've already had a complaint.'

Resnick frowned. 'And I've got a complaint, too. There's damned flies everywhere in this bloody ward!'

She opened Resnick's bedside cabinet and brought out a bowl of mouldy grapes. She turned and smiled sweetly at Resnick. 'Are you intending to eat any of this rotten fruit?'

Resnick was about to give her a smart reply, when he buckled up in agony, gritting his teeth, his breath hissing.

Matron moved quickly to his side, then looked round the ward and beckoned for a nurse to join her. Leaning over Resnick, she said, 'It's all right, Mr Resnick, just lie back. Everything's going to be all right.'

He looked up into her face. Even gripped with pain, he managed to grin. 'Is it, you reckon . . . ? All gonna be all right?'

That was the moment when she realised, despite his bravado, just how scared Resnick was. Something had happened. He'd somehow lost a fight, way back, and he was afraid to get into the ring again for this final bout. She took his hand, feeling an unexpected surge of emotion. To her surprise, after all her years on the ward, this loud, blustering, rude and lonely man had got to her.

*   *   *

She didn't really know why, but Shirley had expected Dolly or Bella to be sitting in the lounge, waiting for her, when she got back. But Bella was in the kitchen cooking, and when Shirley asked her where Dolly was, all she said was, 'Upstairs.'

In the spare room, Dolly had a suitcase open on Linda's bed and was filling it with clothes.

Shirley touched the case. 'Are these all her things?'

'I thought it was best to clear them away,' Dolly answered. She held up a bright blue silk dress. 'You don't want this, do you? Knowing Linda, it's probably yours anyway.' She stopped, bit her lip and threw the dress into the case, then grabbed a whole bunch of clothes from the wardrobe, coat hangers and all, threw them in on top.

Shirley went to the door.

'Where are you going?'

Shirley felt close to tears. 'I don't want to talk about it. I can't talk about it.'

Dolly spoke to her firmly. 'We're gonna have to, love. Linda's dead and we're all gonna have to talk about it. '

Shirley twisted her hands together. 'I know. I know.' Then the tears started.

Bella suddenly barged into the room.

'Put the kettle on, will you?' Dolly asked her quickly. 'We'll be down in a minute.'

'That's all I ever seem to be doing,' Bella complained. 'Putting the kettle on, taking the bleedin' thing off!'

Dolly gave Bella a hard look and jerked her head. She was starting to get a little bit too pushy, that one.

Shirley was sitting on the bed, still twisting her hands. Dolly didn't quite know how to begin. She went back to packing, aware of Shirley watching her.

'So you got yourself a job, did you?' She tried to keep her voice light.

Shirley told Dolly all about her day and about everything that had happened at the studio – that there'd been times when she'd been able to forget, and then it would all come rushing back to her.

Dolly sat next to her on the bed and took hold of her hand.

'Oh, what are we going to do, Dolly?' Shirley asked in her little girl's voice.

Bella reappeared at the door, then picked up a brush from the dressing table and began brushing her hair. 'Well, first we've got to change the money.'

Shirley stood up. 'I hate the money! I hate it, I hate it. I don't want anything to do with it!'

Bella threw the brush down. 'Is that right? Well, we've still got to change it.' She turned to Dolly. 'You got it worked out, then, Dolly? What we're gonna do about the money?'

Dolly moved away from the bed and took another of Linda's dresses from the wardrobe. She began folding it. She couldn't look at Bella.

'I can't find the book,' she almost whispered.

Bella just looked at her. 'What?'

'I said I can't find the book.'

'What book?' Shirley asked.

'The book with the list of names. The little black book. I put all the names down, the fences. I copied them down from Harry's ledgers.'

'What d'you mean you can't find it?' said Bella.

'Well, I've lost it, that's what!' Dolly sat down on the bed, going over everything in her mind. She'd burnt the ledgers, and when she'd come back from Rio she'd burnt all the other paperwork in the bonfire at the house, just before she'd sold it. Maybe she'd burnt the book then.

'I might have . . . burnt it.'

Bella shook her head in amazement. 'You burnt it? Is that what you're tryin' to tell us? You *burnt the book*? I don't believe it, Dolly. You *knew* we'd need it.'

Dolly rubbed her head. 'I'm trying to remember when I last had it.'

Shirley looked as if she didn't understand. 'But you *always* had it, Dolly!'

'But I haven't got it *now*!' Dolly snapped. She began walking up and down the bedroom, and then started miming putting a coat on, taking it off. She stopped abruptly and snapped her fingers. 'It's in the pocket of my raincoat!'

'OK, Dolly,' Bella began in a coaxing voice, as if talking to a five-year-old. 'Where do you think the raincoat is? Can you remember?'

Dolly's face brightened. 'It's behind the door.'

'What door?'

'At . . . the lock-up,' Dolly said slowly. 'It's hanging behind the door at the lock-up.'

* * *

Murphy was strolling through Alfie's Antique Market in Paddington, scanning the stalls. He was looking for stall 54A, Sonny Chizzel's extra little bit of business – the stall he used to get rid of the smaller items, the little knick-knacks he acquired. Murphy had always loved the place, and he took his time wandering among the stalls, picking things up and checking them over. He liked to buy the odd little thing for his mother. She liked antiques, especially pictures. Eventually he arrived at stall 54A, only to find it bolted up. The woman on the next stall dealt in Art Deco masks. They were quite nice, and he wondered if maybe his mother would like one.

He pointed to a mask. 'How much is that one?'

'Well, it's a Goldscheider,' the woman replied in a posh voice, smiling sweetly. 'It's about two hundred and eighty, the little one, and four hundred and fifty the big one.'

Murphy had to hold on to the edge of the stall. 'Right . . . er, I'm looking for Sonny, Sonny Chizzel. He has the place next door.'

The woman rolled her eyes, realising he wasn't a customer. 'Oh, 'e's in the coffee bar, love.'

Oh yeah, the coffee bar, Murphy thought to himself.

Sonny Chizzel was already on his second cup of coffee. He hated to be kept waiting, and he also hated to be carrying this amount of money.

He spotted Murphy coming his way, wandering casually through the market, picking up bits and pieces. Anyone who saw him for the first time would think he was harmless – just a typical punter. But Sonny knew better. He was a strange one, all right. He still lived with his mother – the only person he had ever seemed to care about. It was a well-known fact that Murphy wrote to her every single day when he was in prison, but his mother never wrote letters back; she used to send him tape recordings instead, and Murphy would sit in his cell and play them over and over. He said it was as if his mother was in the prison with him.

Sonny shuddered as Murphy approached the coffee bar. He quickly picked up his newspaper and from behind it watched him go to the counter and look down the menu.

'I'll have a coffee, milk and three sugars, and a toasted ham and cheese sandwich.' Murphy scanned the people at the small tables. Then he took out his wallet and handed one pound to the boy at the counter. 'Keep the change, son.'

'Er . . . it's ninety-nine pence, sir.'

Murphy gave him such an icy glare that the boy went white.

He came over to Sonny's table. 'You mind if I sit 'ere?'

'Help yourself.' Sonny tried to look casual as he carefully folded the newspaper. The tables behind him were empty. He leant towards Murphy.

'Thirty grand, used notes, best I could do. Case under the table.'

The boy appeared at Murphy's elbow with the coffee. 'Sandwich'll be two minutes, sir.'

Murphy slurped a mouthful of coffee. 'That's a very good price, Sonny, very good. My guv'nor'll be well pleased with that.'

Sonny felt the briefcase with the £30,000 between his feet and pushed it towards Murphy. 'You got it?'

Murphy made no effort to reach down. He spooned more sugar into the coffee, stirred, took another mouthful, heaped in yet more sugar.

Sonny got to his feet and busied himself putting on his jacket. He put a pound coin on the table. 'I'm not doin' any more business, understand me? Not that hot, anyway. You wanna see me, leave a message here, don't come to the shop. I've given you a very good deal, Murphy.'

Murphy stared straight ahead, sipping his coffee as if Sonny didn't exist. The boy brought the sandwich to the table. Murphy picked up the pound coin and put it in his hand.

'Thanks very much, son.'

* * *

Shirley slid back in the bath and could feel the hot, soapy water relaxing her. Her little transistor radio was playing quiet, soothing music. It was so lovely, she could have gone to sleep. In fact, she was almost drifting off . . .

Dolly popped her head round the door. 'We're just off.'

Shirley jerked awake, sending water splashing over the side.

'Oh, sorry, did I make you jump?'

'No, it's all right,' Shirley said, taking a breath. 'You don't mind me not coming, do you, Dolly?'

'It doesn't take three of us to pick up a book, love. See you later.' She gave her a private smile. 'Have a nice time, darlin'.'

Shirley sunk low down into the suds again and closed her eyes. She waited to hear the front door shut, so she could finally be alone. She was sick and tired of the house.

The front door slammed and Shirley's whole body relaxed.

She opened her eyes again. Linda was always here, though. Even though she was dead.

She tried to conjure up Micky Tesco's face in her mind, some of his expressions. Funny, the soapsuds smelt like him; he smelt so clean, like a bar of Camay soap. She laughed at the thought of Micky Tesco sitting in the bath, washing himself with pink Camay. Then she saw Linda's toothbrush. Only Linda would have a Mickey Mouse toothbrush. She saw a vision of her brushing her teeth with the silly thing, and all thoughts of Micky vanished.

* * *

Arnie Fisher was having a helluva day. He'd schlepped all the way to the prison to see his brother, but once he got there he'd had nothing but complaints from him about not having any visitors. Arnie had spoken to the governor; he suspected that Tony was having some kind of nervous breakdown. Life on the inside was tough.

But life was getting tough on the outside, too. The club was really going downhill, and business was lousy. Arnie was going to have the place done over, completely redecorated; try and get a better class of punter in. All these things were flashing through Arnie's mind, so he didn't catch the nervous looks between the waiters.

'Oi,' Arnie shouted, 'any of you seen that ape, Murphy?'

He felt a looming presence behind him, and turned to see Murphy pushing his rimless glasses up his nose.

'I'm right here, guv'nor.'

'Well, I'm bloody glad you are,' Arnie said quickly, recovering himself. 'You're supposed to be on the door. That's what I'm payin' you for. That's what I'm payin' all these useless idiots for. I just walked through the club an' I could 'ave been anybody – any Tom, Dick or Harry! We're not open yet, right? I don't like people comin' in an' out!' Arnie carried yattering on as he climbed the stairs. He undid his overcoat and tossed it over his shoulder to Murphy, who was following behind.

Arnie opened a door and bellowed into the room: 'Gloria!' He turned to Murphy. 'You see what happens? I'm not here one half of a day, and what happens? The whole place falls apart!' He opened the door to his office. 'You see what I mean, Murphy?' Then he froze.

Seated at his desk, lounging back in his chair, was Harry Rawlins. Arnie's stomach churned and he thought he was going to be sick. He took a deep breath. Please not on the new carpets.

Standing close to Rawlins was a kid he'd never seen before. Good-looking boy, but Arnie still didn't like the look of him.

Arnie took a step back and felt Gordon Murphy behind him. He turned, and Murphy pushed his glasses back up on the bridge of his nose with a crooked smile. The double-crossing bastard!

He watched the blond boy almost skip round the desk, gesturing for him to sit in one of his own chairs.

Rawlins leant on his elbows. He nodded to the blond boy. 'Get him a drink. The man looks as if he's seen a ghost.'

Arnie began sweating. He watched the blond boy go to the drinks cabinet.

'I'm taking over the club,' Rawlins said, deadpan.

Arnie's mouth gaped open, his eyes wide, and Rawlins laughed. 'Just for one night, Arnie! Just for one night!'

Arnie saw the boy filling a glass with his best brandy as if it was cheap whisky. Christ almighty! Then he realised it was just what he needed, and reached out to take the glass. Arnie's hand was shaking as he swallowed half the brandy in one go, feeling the hot liquid burn its way down. He put the glass back on the desk, pleased to see his hand was steadier. But he didn't feel any less anxious.

'We're throwing a little party, Arnie. You wanna come?' Rawlins said without smiling.

He got up and came round the desk. For a moment, Arnie thought he was going to smash him in the face, but instead Rawlins put out his hand and said, 'Is that a deal, Arnie? Let me take over the club for a night?'

Arnie swallowed and nodded, trying to make light of it. 'I guess I don't have much choice, do I?'

Rawlins leant back against the desk. 'No, Arnie, you don't.'

* * *

Bella was uncharacteristically subdued as Dolly drove to the lock-up, just staring out of the window. Eventually Dolly broke the silence.

'So who's this bloke Shirley's going out with?'

Bella shrugged. 'Some friend of Shirley's mother.'

'You know she's pregnant,' said Dolly.

Bella whipped round. 'What, Shirley? She never told me!'

Dolly shook her head. 'No, her mother.'

'Oh, right. That's all Shirley really wants, deep down – getting married, having kids. I mean, she likes the money, the flash clothes, but basically she's not like you and me, Dolly.'

Dolly wondered if she and Bella were as alike as she thought.

'Don't you want marriage and kids?'

Bella shook her head. 'Me? Kids? Nah, that's not for me.' She was silent for a while, then quietly she said, 'I reckon I lost my chance.'

Dolly knew she was talking about the man in Rio. Gently, she said, 'Maybe you can go back to Rio and patch things up?'

She felt Bella tense.

'It's over, Dolly. Finished. But he was a good man, decent. Guess he just couldn't really handle my kind.'

Dolly didn't pick up on 'my kind', just let it drop. They pulled in alongside the lock-up. Both of them looked at the old place, and it was Bella who said, 'Well, I never thought I'd come back here.'

'You and me both,' said Dolly.

They got out of the car, and Dolly searched in her handbag for the keys. From where they were standing it was obvious that there had been some changes in the row of lock-ups. One, in particular, had been done up, with freshly painted doors and a large sign saying Mercury Stationery Depot. The lock-up sandwiched between this and Harry's place looked defunct, but scrawled across its doors in white paint were the words, 'Property of Mercury Depot'.

Dolly unlocked the door and they walked into Harry's lock-up. For a moment they just stood and looked round. Nothing seemed to have changed; it was still cavernous, dark and dank, with water dripping from the ceiling. They heard a train rumbling overhead. They made their way to the annexe at the back, and Dolly removed the padlock and slid the door aside. As soon as they were inside the familiar space, it all started flashing through their minds: the raid, all the time they had spent working here, respraying the van. It was all a long time ago, but it felt like yesterday.

Dolly suddenly wanted to find her coat and get out as fast as she could. She went to the small kitchenette and checked behind the door. No coat.

'You find it, Dolly?'

'No.'

Bella started searching round, lifting up boxes. Dolly went further into the kitchenette. She remembered how they'd first come here, just after she'd been told that Harry was dead. Her stomach churned, and she remembered how she'd clung on to the kitchen sink to stop herself falling, trying not to weep. Now the memory just made her angry. She hated Harry even more, hated him for what he'd done to her.

She began searching the kitchen. There were the coffee mugs they'd used. She picked up a packet of biscuits. There was something wrong: the biscuits were fresh. She picked up a coffee mug. The dregs were still warm.

'Bella,' Dolly said quickly, 'we'd better get out. Somebody's using this lock-up.'

*　*　*

Shirley put on her underslip and sat at the dressing table. She brushed her hair, then plugged in the Carmen rollers and studied her face. She got out all her pots of make-up, then looked at her watch. Micky wasn't due for more than an hour. Plenty of time to make herself look wonderful for him. She got up and switched on the radio. The disc jockey was saying, 'Now, ladies and gentlemen, climbing up the charts we have the new single, "Widows' Tears".'

Shirley hummed along for a while. She looked at herself again in the dressing table mirror. It was true: widows' tears didn't last for ever. There was a warm feeling in the pit of her stomach.

'Micky, oh Micky . . .' she whispered.

* * *

With Arnie Fisher onside and the venue set up, Harry's next task was sorting out the guests. Back at his new pad, he began making a list.

Tesco remembered his date with Shirley and looked at his watch. 'You still want me round, Harry?'

Harry nodded. 'I'm gonna give you this list of names, and I want you to personally invite each of them. No mention of me; just say there might be a little bit of business going on, right?'

'OK.' Tesco cursed silently, went to the bedroom, shut the door and picked up the phone.

Harry was trying to remember everybody he'd ever worked with. He swore under his breath. If only he had the ledgers, it would make things a lot easier. All the names were in there. Now he sat back and tried to recall every job, all the faces and the names. Who would be the best men to use on the robbery, he wondered? He made careful notes, wondering what the hell Micky was doing in the bedroom. He poured himself a glass of wine from a bottle chilling in the fridge and gulped it down. He was beginning to feel good again, feeling like his old self. He went into the bathroom, turned the taps on, saw the Badedas and smiled. He squirted some into the water. Why not? he thought.

In the lounge, he picked up his list. Micky was standing there, looking anxious.

'Those the men you want?'

'Yeah, just check 'em over for me.'

Micky sighed. 'What're you gonna do, Harry?'

Harry was walking towards the bedroom. 'I'm gonna take a bath – if that's all right with you, Micky?'

Micky shrugged. Harry went into the bedroom and Micky checked the time. He was going to be late for Shirley. In fact, he was beginning to wonder if he would make the date at all.

* * *

Dolly had searched every corner of the lock-up, and still no raincoat. Bella was rummaging in the old filing cabinet.

'You sure it's here, Dolly?'

Dolly shook her head. 'I dunno where it is. Maybe I never left it here. It's just that I could have sworn I did. You remember the way I used to hang it behind the door?'

Bella was now on her knees, searching the bottom drawer of the filing cabinet.

'I think we should go, Bella. Somebody's using this place and if they come in now we're trapped back here.'

Another train rumbled overhead and Dolly shivered.

Bella held up a notebook. It was red. 'Is this it, Dolly?'

'No, it's a black book, a little black book.' She turned away. The drip, drip of the water, the damp and the cold were getting to her. 'Bella, I want to get out of here, I can't stand this place.'

Bella straightened up. She had a sheaf of papers in her hand. She spread them out on the orange boxes.

'Dolly, look at this lot!' She unfolded a large sheet – architect's drawings.

'For Christ's sake, Bella!' Dolly walked out of the annexe – and suddenly caught sight of what looked like the sleeve of her raincoat poking out from under one of the trucks.

'There it is, Bella, look! There's the coat! Somebody must have chucked it under here.' She pulled it out and searched in the pockets. 'Got it! I've got the notebook!'

Bella was still poring over the papers, opening one after the other. 'I think you'd better take a look at these, Dolly. What d'you think all this is?'

Dolly looked over Bella's shoulder, holding on tightly to the notebook. Then she picked up a sheet of paper. 'This is Harry's writing.' She studied the plans. 'Do you know what this is? Vans, motorbikes . . . Good God, it's a route! Security vans! Bella, he's planning another raid!'

* * *

Micky could hear Harry whistling in the bedroom when the doorbell rang. About bloody time!

The blonde standing at the door wasn't bad, but she was a bit older than he'd expected.

'You Micky?' she asked. 'Micky Tesco?'

'Yeah, that's right, darlin'. Come in.' He shut the door. 'I want you to be very nice to a friend of mine.'

She smiled. 'Oh, I can be very nice. You know what I charge, don't you?'

'Yeah, yeah, there's no problem. He's a very important man, so you make sure he has a good night, you understand me? What did you say your name was?'

'Sharon,' said the blonde.

'Right, Sharon, let's wheel you in, then, shall we?'

He guided the girl towards the bedroom door, tapped and pushed it open. Harry was in his dressing gown, combing his hair in front of the mirror.

'What d'ya want?'

'Got a little present for you, Harry.' Micky grinned. 'Something you might enjoy.'

Harry turned with a puzzled look and saw Sharon standing behind Micky. The blonde hair, the over-made-up face, the seductive smile. He turned back to the mirror.

'Get her out of here.'

'Hey, come on, Harry! She only wants to be nice to you! You wanna be nice to him, don't you, Sharon?'

'Get her out, Micky, just get her out!'

Micky hesitated for a moment, unsure what to do next. Sharon gave him a wink, and then went over and put her hands on Harry's shoulders.

'It's up to you, darlin'.' She slid her fingers gently down his back. 'You want me to go, I'll go.'

Harry heard the door close. He turned towards her and she took a step back, let him look at her.

'Take your coat off.'

Sharon obliged. She had a good figure, nice legs. Maybe she'd do, after all. Besides, he was a bit tense. It'd been quite a while.

'You want me to stay then, do you?'

Harry smiled. 'Yeah . . . Yeah, I guess you can stay.'

Sharon turned her back to him and wriggled her shoulders as an invitation for him to unzip her dress. He touched her hair and ran his finger down her neck.

'What's your name again, darlin'?'

'Sharon.' She reached round and began to unzip her dress herself. 'What's your name, then?'

He didn't answer, just pulled her roughly towards the bed.

*　*　*

Trudie was occupying quite a luxurious suite at the Hilton Hotel in Sydney. It had taken her a while to get over the jet lag, and the baby had been fretful on the lengthy flight. The experience of first class travel and the flow of free champagne had made her very unsteady when the plane had landed. She still blamed the jet lag for her being so tired, and not the minibar, which was kept replenished by the attentive hotel staff. She was constantly drinking and ordering room service. She had, by now, become agitated that after numerous calls to hotel reception asking if a Mr Rawlins had left a message, there was still no contact. She was even concerned about leaving the hotel in case he tried to reach her. She was disappointed when she went out for some cigarettes and formula for the baby and returned to the hotel hoping to see the blinking light on her telephone alerting her to a new message. There never was.

* * *

Shirley was beginning to think that she'd been stood up. She felt a fool, dressed to kill, sitting with the wine chilling in the ice bucket, two glasses, candles lit – and no date. She took a gulp of wine and looked at the clock again. Micky was three-quarters of an hour late. She was just pouring herself another when the doorbell rang. She'd been ready for nearly an hour, but now he was here she ran round the room in a panic, straightening the cushions, checking her face in the mirror.

When she opened the door, Micky's arms were full of roses.

'Wow, you look beautiful!' he said.

She didn't know what to say. Part of her was angry with him; part of her thrilled he was finally here.

She began stuttering like a stupid schoolgirl. 'You'd ... You'd better come in, then ...'

'Sorry I'm late, darlin'.' He handed her the roses.

'D'you want to come through into the lounge? I've got some wine. D'you drink wine?'

Micky followed her in. His eyes flitted round the room. It was quite nice, quite tasteful. There was more to this girl than he'd thought.

'No, thanks, darlin', I don't drink. Nice place you've got here, Shirley.'

She smiled. 'Thank you.' She was holding the roses awkwardly in front of her.

'Look, sorry about this, about bein' late, but I had a bit of bother. Couple of property deals fallen through at the last minute. I don't know how to say this, Shirley, but I'm not going to be able to stay. I wondered if . . . maybe we could do it another time?'

Shirley thought about all the trouble she'd gone to: the dress, make-up, hair, the wine. She bit her lip and said nothing.

Micky sat on the edge of the sofa. 'So, you gonna tell me how it all went with Marion Gordon? The photographic session? Come on, come on, I wanna hear more!'

'Well, you know, it went really well,' she said in a quiet voice. She couldn't believe he wasn't going to stay.

'And what about this job? I hear she's got a big job lined up for you.'

She moved closer to him. 'I was going to talk to you about that, Micky,' she began nervously. 'You see, it's quite an important job she thinks I could do. It's this big charity show at Amanda's nightclub. Well, all the other girls are professional and, well, I'm gonna take some classes, but I wondered whether I wasn't moving too fast.'

Micky took her hand. 'What? How d'you mean?'

'Well, I don't want to blow it, you know what I mean? I think maybe I should take things slower. It wouldn't be good if I blew it on my first job.'

Micky pulled her towards him. 'Darlin', you're not gonna blow it. Marion's a real pro – if she thinks you can do it, you can do it. What you gettin' all jumpy for?'

'Well, I just . . . I just don't want to run before I can walk.'

'Come on, Shirley . . .' He tilted her head and kissed her neck. 'You're gonna be a star!'

'Well, if you think I can do it . . .'

'I don't think, darlin', I know it.' He pulled her closer and kissed her mouth, very softly. He could feel her softening, moving towards him. He took the roses out of her hand and chucked them onto the sofa, then put his arms round her. He looked into her eyes. 'You can do anything you want, Shirley. It's been a long time since I've turned up at a girl's door, arms full of roses like a big kid. It's you, Shirley . . .'

Shirley could feel herself melting. He made her feel like a real woman, the way he touched her; he seemed to know exactly what to do. There was no fumbling, no schoolboyishness with Micky. She felt him slowly unzip her dress, felt it slip down to her waist. He kissed her shoulder very softly, and again she smelt that lovely cologne on him. Shirley bent and kissed his neck. She wanted him badly. She hadn't felt like this for years, not even with Terry. She wanted him there and then, on the carpet. It excited her, almost frightened her.

What she didn't see was Micky taking a swift look at his watch, wondering if he had the time to give her a quick one before he went and rounded up all those fellers that Harry wanted. The truth was, she was getting him excited, too.

Turns out she's a right little goer. Just shows you, he thought, you never know what girls are like. He pulled away from her and smiled.

'Who's a naughty girl, then?'

Shirley laughed, then took Micky's hand and led him up the stairs to her bedroom. She could hardly believe that she was doing this.

Micky quickly glanced at his wristwatch again. Yeah, he could still do it, if it was quick.

* * *

Dolly and Bella made sure they returned the plans to the drawer exactly as they had found them, and then double-checked that everything in the lock-up was exactly as it had been. Dolly's heart was thudding inside her chest as she turned off the lights, terrified that Harry was about to walk in and find them. She was first out, running towards the car.

Dolly waited while Bella finished locking up, drumming her fingers on the steering wheel. Then suddenly Bella veered off towards the Mercury depot.

'Bella, come on!' Dolly called out, but Bella just shook her head and gave her a wave. Dolly watched her knock on the small door within the big double doors and go inside. Dolly gave the steering wheel a bang with her fist, then got out of the car and followed her.

Unlike the lock-up, the depot was almost too bright, with strip lights hanging low on chains. Shelves lining the white walls were stacked with cartons of paper. Two printing machines hummed, while somewhere in the background they could hear the sound of Annie Lennox. Two young guys – one wearing a vivid sweater with a sheep bounding across the back, and the other in a torn T-shirt and jeans – were bent over a table, deep in conversation . . .

Bella was slightly taken aback by their public school accents.

She coughed. 'You own the place next door?'

The boy with the sheep sweater looked up, nodded his head, then turned back to the table. For a moment Bella thought she'd lost her touch. Then the guy in the T-shirt turned and started giving her the once-over.

'Are you using it?' she asked, with her most seductive smile. 'I'm from a film company. Maybe we could use it for a shoot, if it's empty?'

Dolly stood in the doorway, wondering what Bella was up to.

'What company?' asked the sweater guy.

'Feminist. You wouldn't have heard of us.' She jerked her thumb towards Dolly. 'My assistant.'

The two men looked at each other. The T-shirt guy fiddled with the cassette player, putting on the other side of the Annie Lennox album.

Bella was starting to get frustrated with their laid-back attitude. She turned and looked at Dolly, who just shrugged, flummoxed by the whole procedure.

'How long would you want it for?' the sweater guy said eventually.

Bella pretended to show interest in the sheets of paper coming out of the printer.'Oh, just a couple of weeks. Depends . . .'

Dolly moved quickly to Bella's side and gave her a slight push. They moved a little way off.

'What the hell are you doing?' Dolly whispered. Behind them the T-shirt guy searched in a drawer, then brought over a set of keys.

'It's in a pretty bad state. We've only just finished renovating this one. We haven't had a chance to do it up yet.' He gave Bella a smirk. 'I can show you round if you like.'

*   *   *

At that moment Harry drew up outside in the metallic gold Jag he was driving while the old one was being repaired. In the passenger seat was a tall man wearing a navy coat with a velvet collar. Colin Soal was a snappy dresser, but he needed to be in his line of business. He was basically a conman, someone who lived on his wits, and men like Harry Rawlins often used him when they needed a smooth-talking front man. It was Soal's job to sort out a place; with his chat he could get in anywhere, mix with anyone, and with his photographic memory, he could have a building analysed in minutes: entrances, exits, locks, windows, alarms, how many men would be required for a job – everything.

Soal's heyday was in the past, however. Once upon a time he'd been the best in the business, but on closer inspection there was a certain seediness about him now, his shirt-sleeves slightly frayed, a touch of dandruff on his collar. Soal was hurting for cash and Harry smelt it the moment they met up. Even before Harry started telling him about the job, he knew he'd do it. He just hoped he still had what it takes.

The two men entered Harry's lock-up.

*   *   *

Bella was negotiating with the print-shop boys. They had at first asked for two-fifty a week. Bella had laughed and offered a hundred, and they'd met in the middle: two weeks for one-fifty a week, cash up front.

Dolly got more and more tight-lipped as she listened to the bargaining, eventually stepping forward and telling the boys in a sarcastic tone that she'd like a word with her producer.

'Just give me the money,' Bella told her, holding her hand out.

Dolly counted it out while the guys watched, then turned and walked towards the door.

Bella slowly counted out the money into sweater guy's palm. He smiled, maybe even coming on to her a tiny bit. Perhaps he'd realised she wasn't just another of the hookers hanging round the area. Maybe she really did work for a film company. The older woman certainly seemed straight.

'Sure you don't want me to show you round?'

Bella smiled. 'Thanks, but we'll check it out ourselves.'

He handed over the keys with a shrug. Their hands touched, and she looked him in the eye. She ran a finger down his chest.

'Nice.'

He looked confused for a moment, then reached for her hand. She pulled it away before he could grab her.

'The sweater – very nice.'

He watched Bella saunter out, then turned to his pal and they both grinned. The woman might be a tease, but a hundred and fifty a week! Cash! And the boss would never know.

Bella was confronted with a furious Dolly, still wanting to know what Bella thought she was doing. Three hundred quid, for what? And why? They were arguing so intently, neither noticed the Jag – and the red E-type now parked behind the gold Jag.

'He's plannin' a raid, right?' Bella said as the door to the next-door lock-up creaked open. 'You're not the only one with ideas, Dolly. Come on.'

The hinges were rusty, and the door was hard to close behind them. Inside, the place was even danker and darker than Harry's lock-up, with pools of stinking water and duckboards squelching under their feet as the water rose over them.

Dolly looked down at her suede shoes and sighed. Bella picked her way round the wrecked cars, most without engines or wheels, their windscreens shattered. A train passing overhead seemed to shake the place to its foundations, and Dolly was afraid the roof was going to fall in. She stopped, with one soaked shoe caught between the boards.

'I'm not going any further, Bella. Bella?'

Dolly could hear her moving about. She inched forward in the darkness, squinting. She could make out Bella's silhouette as she lifted an orange box.

Then Bella's voice, a hoarse whisper, 'Dolly! Up here, come up here.'

Bella was now standing on the box, face pressed to the wall. The cement and bricks had been chipped away, and there was a chink of light coming through from Harry's lock-up next door.

'Somebody's next door, listen!'

She helped Dolly up onto the box. Dolly leant forward and peered through the crack.

Bella heard a scratching, rustling noise. She looked down – two rats nosed their way out of the box, which had obviously been their nesting place.

'Oh my God, rats,' she hissed, reaching out for Dolly.

Dolly swiped her hand away, hard, and pressed her face closer to the wall. Bella watched her, afraid to move.

Dolly could see him, almost directly in front of her. She could hardly believe it: Harry, smiling and drinking, just feet away. Her heart was pounding, and she felt like running, but she couldn't look away.

A young blond man sat on an orange crate, with his back to the wall. An older man in a blue coat was taking plans from his briefcase and laying them out carefully on another crate. He stood back.

Harry nodded to the man in the coat, then pulled up another box and sat down. 'The layout, gentlemen.'

* * *

DI Fuller stretched, yawned and looked at his watch. It had been a long and tedious afternoon, and now it was almost evening.

Reynolds put the last of the files in the 'Out' tray. They were all done; all up to date. The phone rang just as Fuller was about to reach for it to call his wife. He'd forgotten to let her know he'd be late, something he'd been guilty of several times recently, and she'd begun a campaign of silence in retaliation. He'd come home to find his dinner left on the table, cold, the place neatly laid for one. She'd have retired to bed early to watch their small colour TV, giving him a frosty look and shrugging away from him when he attempted to apologise. She could make it last, too. They'd sit in bed and silently watch some trite late-night American series, and as soon as it was over she'd turn on her side, switch off the bedside lamp and shut her eyes. Fuller would lie there and sigh, feeling the tension build, knowing he wouldn't sleep despite being dog-tired. What was she getting so bloody ratty about, just because he was late? It wasn't as if they had kids and he was neglecting his parenting duties.

Night after night, when he had finally dropped off, it was into a fitful sleep, which left him with a headache in the morning. And then it was his turn not to speak, getting his own breakfast and slamming out of the house.

Fuller decided he wouldn't pick up and reached for his overcoat instead.

Reynolds answered the phone and Fuller waited, dreading the familiar: 'It's your wife.'

Instead, Reynolds walked round the desk, his hand over the mouthpiece.

'It's that bloke again, wanting Resnick. Third time today.'

Fuller relaxed, relieved he didn't have to go through the nagging with Reynolds listening.

'What's he want?'

Reynolds shrugged, and Fuller jerked the phone out of his hand. Reynolds could be annoyingly indecisive at times.

'Yes? You want Resnick? Well, he's retired, no longer here, you understand?' Fuller listened, tapping his fingers on the desk. 'My name? Detective Inspector Fuller . . . yes, *Fuller.*'

Fuller made to put the phone down, then suddenly clamped it to his ear and started scrambling for a pad and pen with his other hand.

'What time? I'll be there. Hang on, this friend of yours, does he have a name? Hello, hello?'

He slowly replaced the receiver and looked at what he'd written. Then he looked at Reynolds and grinned. 'I told you that thirty thousand reward would bring somethin' in, didn't I? Well, it just did. Our friend –' Fuller tapped the phone – 'our friend thinks somebody just tried to palm him some of the money from the underpass raid.'

Reynolds felt a surge of adrenaline. 'Did he give a name?'

Fuller shook his head. 'Just a meet. But that's all we need.'

'You think Resnick would know who he is?'

'Resnick's not going to help us with anything.' Fuller picked up his umbrella with a tight smile. 'Well, screw him, then.' And with that, he pushed through the swing doors and left.

* * *

Colin Soal spoke softly, his accent meandering from Old Etonian to Cockney. He spoke with authority, though, and Harry and Micky listened intently.

'This is a tricky one, all right. You got no access from either of the toilets or the ground-floor windows – they're all barred – so you got to come in through the kitchens, and they're like a bleedin' rabbit warren, lots of small rooms, very dodgy. Then your front entrance – again, two corridors, plus a cloakroom. Fire exits lead out of the building on three levels; that's fine, get a man in on each level, move in from there, it's the only way. Come in front, kitchens and fire escapes, doors are a baby's turn, just need a jemmy, but I reckon you'll be coping with at least six or seven security guards, two at the front, one at the back, two on the ballroom doors and two with the jewels.'

Soal dropped his gold pen, leant back and looked at Harry, then at Micky. 'Need at least seven men to do it right, or forget it.'

Harry had heard enough; how many men were required was his business. The meeting was over. With a nod to Micky to begin packing up the plans, he reached for his coat.

'You're invited to the do, of course, Colin.'

*   *   *

Dolly was stiff from trying not to move or make any noise, and Bella took over her position. After a few seconds she turned to Dolly and showed her four fingers for four men: another man had been sitting, unseen by Dolly, to one side. Then Bella pressed her face against the wall again.

*   *   *

Murphy helped Colin Soal into his overcoat. Harry caught Murphy's eye and beckoned him over with a jerk of his head. Harry put his arm round Murphy's shoulder and turned him round, so they had their backs to Colin and Micky.

'Any problems with the money? Decent exchange?'

Murphy was happy Harry was being matey with him again; it made him feel the cock-up on the heath had been forgotten.

'Yeah, it all went without a hitch. I used Sonny Chizzel.'

Rawlins breathed in sharply. 'Keep an eye on him, he's a bit . . . I wouldn't trust him further than I could throw him.' He gave Murphy a friendly pat on the shoulder, then turned back to Micky and Colin.

'Nice job, very impressive,' Micky was saying. 'So how you gonna come and go on the day?'

Colin dusted the dandruff from his collar, then reached down for his briefcase. He didn't like this blond boy; he was too young, too pushy, and far too good-looking. He never trusted the good-looking ones; they were usually the ones that shat in their pants when things got heavy.

Micky realised that Colin didn't think he was worth talking to. He wasn't about to let himself be humiliated in front of Harry. 'Come on, Colin. How you gonna do it?'

Without looking up, Colin Soal used his poshest, smoothest voice. 'Press photographer. I've snapped them all, all the top models, don't you know?'

Micky raised his eyebrows. 'You got cameras, all the gear, then?'

Colin Soal looked at Harry, just a flick of his eyebrows, but it said 'get this kid off my back' as clearly as if he'd said it out loud.

'Good night, Micky,' Harry said, and again Micky felt the brush-off.

One of these days he'd have it out with Harry, put the man straight. No more 'do this, fetch me that'. They were partners. Yeah, one of these days, Harry would find out what Micky was really all about.

He walked out, giving Colin a wink on the way.

Murphy picked up his faded coat and, with the air of a good butler, folded it over his arm, nodded in turn to Harry and Colin, then followed Micky out.

Colin jerked his head after the disappearing Murphy. 'He's not changed, has he? Doesn't look any older. I'd watch that kid, though; pushy little sod.'

Harry didn't reply, just opened the briefcase from Sonny Chizzel and took out £2000, closing it quickly, so Colin couldn't see how much was in it. Good as Colin was, he wouldn't trust him any more than Sonny Chizzel.

'You still not interested in coming in on the action, Colin? Fifty G each, man, and that's just for starters; there could be even more.'

Harry saw Colin thinking it over, then shake his head. Colin might be short of cash – but he wasn't that short. Still, plenty of time to work on him, Harry thought, and he was definitely tempted.

Harry handed him the cash, and with no show of embarrassment Colin counted it, then tucked it into his wallet.

'I'm gettin' a bit long in the tooth to be wielding the old shooters, Harry, but I'll complete the layout as agreed, get it all sewn up for you. There won't be a door in that place you don't know about – that and the tip-off. But I want to be clean away before the aggro starts, agreed?'

'Sure, Colin.'

'To be honest, Harry, I don't fancy your chances of pulling it off. You're gonna need the best there is on this one.' Colin hesitated, and Harry frowned. What was he hedging about?

Colin picked up his briefcase, then put it down again. 'Word is out on you, Harry. Plenty of people won't touch you; they reckon you ditched those men, let them burn alive. Joe Pirelli and Terry Miller were good blokes, well liked.'

Harry just wanted Colin out now. Stupid prick with his fancy voice and holes in his shoes.

'There's a new DI,' Colin continued, oblivious. 'Took over from that old bloke Resnick. Name's Fuller, and I hear he's a right bastard, pulls in anyone just to feel the material on their suits. He's straight, and he's got the finger on everyone. You gotta be careful, Harry.'

Harry guided Colin to the door, resisting the urge to give him a kick in the arse to send him on his way. 'You know what, Colin?

There's never been a copper, sitting behind a fancy desk or walking the beat, that couldn't be bought. All you need is the right amount of cash.'

* * *

Bella didn't move a muscle until the lights went out and she heard the door clang shut behind Harry, then she let out a deep breath. She looked at Dolly, standing hugging herself, her knuckles white.

'We've got him this time, Dolly. My God, we know enough to pull it ourselves.'

Dolly didn't answer, just walked back to the door, sloshing through the water without noticing it now.

Bella hurried to catch her up. 'Come on, it was a joke! Just a joke, Dolly.'

Still Dolly kept walking. When they reached the door she fumbled for the keys.

'But we can get him this time, Dolly. We can really set him up this time.'

Dolly shivered, her teeth chattering. She felt frozen to the bone. All she wanted to do was get out, get away from this place, away from Bella. The vision of Harry's smiling face wouldn't go away. What had really scared her, made her sick to her stomach, was that even after all this time, she wanted to cry out to him, call his name. Those twenty years couldn't be blanked out; twenty years she had loved him and no one else. Even now she clung to a pitiful dream that Harry was really only waiting for her to contact him, and then they would be together again, just as it had always been. But it was a dream; the house had gone, the home they had built up, all gone. She had all the money, but it didn't mean anything to her, not without him, and it was this she couldn't face – that everything was gone, ruined, destroyed, except her love. Even now Dolly couldn't stop herself loving him, a man who was not worth—

'*Dolly!* Dolly, you all right?'

She came to as if out of a drugged sleep. For a moment she didn't know who she was, then it swept over her, like a dark cloud blocking out the sky. There was no way out for her, she just had to keep going – but to what end?

* * *

Trudie had been presented with an invoice from the hotel that scared her as she'd had no concept of the cost of her room, or of how much the constant supply of room service would be.

There had still been no contact from Harry, and she began to worry that the money would run out. Harry had only sent her a one-way flight and she had no way of discovering whether or not he was coming to join her, or where he was as he hadn't left her any contact details.

She rang her sister Vera and, in typical Trudie fashion, had not thought about the time difference. Vera was woken in the middle of the night in her home in Devon by Trudie asking if anyone had called for her. Vera hadn't heard from Trudie for months.

'Why would anyone call here for you?' Vera said sleepily.

'Are you sure there's been nobody asking where I am?' Trudie had to make sure she didn't make any reference to Harry Rawlins, as she knew he was wanted by the police.

'Do you know what time it is? Where on earth are you?'

'I can't tell you.' Trudie could feel the panic rising as she said that she would call again and asked if it would be possible for her to stay in Devon. She also asked that if someone should call for her, just to say that she was still at the hotel.

* * *

Micky was driving fast, and Murphy hated fast drivers. His mother had almost been killed by an idiot like Micky. He glanced at the speedo: eighty-five. Eighty-five miles an hour down the bleeding Euston Road. He looked at Micky.

'You in a hurry to get some place? Take it a bit slower, son.'

In answer, Micky put his foot down and they hit ninety through the underpass, shooting the lights at Marylebone Road.

Murphy grabbed Micky's arm. 'If you don't slow down, I'm going to put the bleedin' handbrake on.'

Micky grinned, taking his foot off the gas a little. 'Can't take it, Murphy?'

'I'll take anything you want to dish out, any time, any place, son,' Murphy assured him. 'But getting picked up for speeding just before a blag is fuckin' idiotic.'

Micky slowed to forty and drove on in silence for a while. Then he started to tell Murphy about the whore he'd given Harry for a present, something to loosen up the tension.

Murphy looked out of the window; he hated tarts.

Micky prattled on, gave Murphy a sideways look and chuckled. 'Next morning, she was sitting there waiting for me in her rabbit fur coat, in a right old state.'

Murphy pricked up his ears, interested now.

'I paid her off, and then she says I should get my friend some vitamins or something – turns out Harry couldn't get it up. It wasn't for want of trying, neither; said she'd tried every trick in the book, but nothing doing.'

Micky was laughing as they pulled up outside Murphy's council house. He was about to open the door when Murphy put a hand on his arm.

'You need to get a few things straight, son,' he said in a quiet voice. 'First off: loyalty. I don't like hearing filthy gossip, you understand? You're lucky enough to be working with one of the best, so you treat him with the respect he's due. If that filthy slag is puttin' round stories about the guv'nor, then you better give me her name.' Murphy pushed his tinted glasses up his nose. 'She'll never be able to open her legs again, and the same goes for your mouth if you're not careful. So learn to keep it shut.'

Then Murphy was out of the car, the door slamming behind him.

Micky slammed the steering wheel. 'Prick.'

Murphy had made him feel like a ten-year-old kid. He thought about going round to see Shirley, then thought better of it. He'd given her a right old seeing-to; she might not even be up and walking yet. He roared off down the road, grinning.

* * *

Murphy opened his front door and closed it quietly behind him. He took off his shoes and crept into his mother's room. Her bedside lamp was still on but she was fast asleep, her mouth open and her teeth in a glass by the bed. He tucked the bedclothes in, checked the electric blanket was off and took away the teapot and cup to wash. He left the light on, in case she woke up in the night.

In the kitchen, he made sure everything was spotless and in the right place, his breakfast dishes laid out ready for the morning. He had never got out of the habit of leaving his cup face down on the saucer, spoon at the side. In prison, some things you never forget.

* * *

Bella watched Dolly drive off. She hadn't spoken a word since they'd left the lock-up, and the drive back to the house had been made in uncomfortable silence.

Sometimes Dolly unnerved Bella, the way you couldn't tell what she was thinking, what was going on in her head. Not like Shirley – or Linda. Bella bit her lip. Linda . . . poor Linda. She wasn't coming home again, not now, not ever. And they'd let her be buried without so much as a single flower. Dolly had given them strict orders: no one was to contact the mortuary or the Pirelli family. Linda would be laid to rest with Joe. Well, that was one thing, at least: the Pirelli family might have hated Linda, but in the end they had to let her be buried with him.

Bella slipped into the house. The hall light was on. She popped her head into the lounge and saw Shirley's dress on the sofa. She turned the lights off and went quietly up the stairs. The landing was dark, and Bella pushed open Shirley's bedroom door. She could see a vase of roses on each side of the bed, and Shirley sprawled out between them, with just a sheet over her, deeply asleep. Bella closed the door. It was strange, Shirley didn't seem to have been affected by Linda's death; she'd cried at first, but just as quickly it was over.

Bella undressed, tossing her clothes onto the spare bed – Linda's old bed. She pulled back the covers and climbed in, not bothering to wash or clean her teeth.

Sleep wouldn't come. She lay there, staring at the empty bed beside her, going over what had happened that night: the lock-up, Harry, the plans. Then she turned and whispered to the empty bed: 'We'll get him this time, Linda. This time we will.'

*　*　*

Dolly was exhausted. All she wanted was sleep, but like Bella, everything that had happened was churning over in her mind. Her feet were like lead as she turned the bend in the stairs up to her flat and saw Vic Morgan.

Her face fell. This was all she needed.

She opened her bag, not meeting his eyes, and searched for the keys. Morgan was holding a bunch of wilting flowers. He gave her a grin.

'I'd just about given up on you.'

Dolly dropped the keys and he bent down to pick them up, glancing at her filthy shoes. It hadn't been raining, and he wondered where she'd been. He fitted the key into the lock and opened the door.

'Please leave me alone, Mr Morgan. I'm very tired.'

Morgan tried to hand her the flowers but she wouldn't take them. She just stood there, holding the door, frowning.

'I wondered if we could have dinner one evening . . . or lunch? OK, cup of tea then? I'm not fussy.'

'Oh, just take your flowers and get out, will you?' she snapped angrily, turning to close the door.

He put his foot inside, not too forcefully, but she couldn't shut the door.

'D'you want me to start screaming the place down?'

Morgan knew she meant it. Her expression was cold and hard. She was hardly recognisable as the woman who had spent the night at his place. He slowly removed his foot and looked down at the flowers still in his hand.

'Blimey, these look about as wilted as I am. I'll get some fresh ones next time.' He made no move to go.

'All right, I'll meet you for lunch,' Dolly said, just wanting him to go away. 'Next Saturday.' It was far enough off that she didn't have to think about it.

He grinned. 'OK, good. Saturday. Lunch it is.'

The door slammed shut.

'I'll just leave these on the mat . . . if you want them,' he called through the door. He laid the flowers down gently and started down the stairs. Halfway he stopped, hearing her door open. He crept back up to see Dolly reach down and pick up the flowers. She held them close to her, almost burying her face in the wilting heads, then she shut the door.

As Morgan turned back down the stairs, he could hear her sobbing.

* * *

The rain was pelting down and Fuller was in one of his moods as the patrol car turned through the gates of Regent's Park. He'd had yet another silent breakfast, and now he had indigestion. He popped a tablet out of the packet in his pocket and put it in his mouth.

They were cruising slowly down the lane towards the cricket pavilion. 'How close do you want, guv'nor?' the driver asked.

Fuller tapped the driver's shoulder. 'Here will do.' He turned to Reynolds. 'You see him?'

Reynolds leant forward and they both scanned the park, squinting to see through the rain.

'There he is, sir.'

Sonny Chizzel was standing under a large golfing umbrella, facing the boating pond, throwing soggy bread to the ducks.

Fuller watched for a few moments, then hitched up his collar and got out. 'Shit.' He'd forgotten his umbrella. He began to walk briskly towards the boat house.

Reynolds leant back, watching. 'Right old mood he's in this morning, isn't 'e? Trouble at home, I reckon.'

The driver turned round, holding out a packet of cigarettes. Reynolds shook his head.

'You're probably right. He does his nut if he smells smoke in the car – starts spraying deodoriser all over the place.' The driver put the cigarettes back in his pocket without lighting up.

They could see Fuller talking to the man with the umbrella, but both men were still facing away from them, towards the water. Fuller was gesticulating animatedly, shaking his head. Reynolds laughed as a goose went up behind Fuller and started nipping at his trousers. Fuller turned and shooed the bird away, then continued his discussion. Eventually the man with the umbrella moved off, and Fuller, with shoulders hunched, walked to a nearby bin and started rummaging through the refuse before he found what looked like an old Mother's Pride wrapper. He jogged back to the patrol car and yanked open the door.

As Fuller dried himself off with his handkerchief, Reynolds opened the bag and found a slip of paper inside.

'This is it?' It was just a list of numbers.

'I bloody well hope so. Should be serial numbers.'

Reynolds nodded. 'Who was it?'

'The Jewish Chronicle himself, Sonny Chizzel. Says a bloke wants to launder some cash, and it might tally with the missing dough from the underpass raid. He's very cagey. We got something on him?'

Reynolds nodded and looked down the list of scrawled numbers. It should be easy enough to check them with the security firm.

Fuller prodded the driver's shoulder. 'Let's get bloody going. I'm soaked to the skin.' He took the list of serial numbers from Reynolds. 'Sixty thousand quid. Reckon he's been tapped, and he thinks he'll make more from the reward. If these numbers are notes from the underpass raid, we'll haul the little prick in.'

'Did you offer him a deal?' Reynolds asked.

'Look, I could have offered him the Crown jewels – doesn't necessarily mean I'm gonna come across. And definitely not with a bastard who won't even let me under his brolly.' Fuller blew his nose loudly. 'First thing we do back at the office, we take another look at all those files Resnick hoarded and see if Mr Chizzel's in there somewhere . . .'

As they drove on towards the station, a radio message came though confirming that Sonny's tail was in position.

Fuller rubbed his hands. 'Good. I told them to make it obvious. Let him know we mean business.'

* * *

Bella opened up the door. She'd had a rotten night's sleep, only finally getting into a nice dream just before the doorbell had woken her up, and there was Dolly, fresh as a daisy, giving her a ticking off for keeping her waiting for the whole world to see. Bella picked up the milk from the doorstep, peeled off the gold top and drank.

'Don't do that, it's a filthy habit.'

Inside the kitchen, Dolly put her shopping bag on the table, then picked it up again and went to the sink for a wet cloth to wipe the table down.

'Where's Shirley?'

Bella, still drinking from the milk bottle, took the note that had been stuck to the fridge and handed it to her. Dolly read: '. . . dance class . . . modelling class.' She ripped it up and dropped the pieces in the bin. 'What did she say – about last night?'

Bella dropped a slice of bread in the toaster and pressed the switch down. 'I haven't had a chance to tell her. She was dead to the world when I came in. And by the look on her face I'd say she got her rocks off well and good.'

Dolly made a sour face.

'You get out of bed on the wrong side, huh?'

Dolly turned on her. 'I came back here to work out how we're going to exchange the money, now that we've found the book, but Shirley's not even bloody here – she's off dancing or modelling or Christ knows what, while we're sat here twiddling our thumbs.'

Bella's toast began to burn, and she fished it out of the toaster with a fork, then opened the fridge for butter.

'Well, as soon as Sleepin' Beauty gets back, we'll sort it.'

Dolly sat down. 'D'you have to treat everything as a joke?'

Bella slammed the butter dish down and let fly. 'A joke? Do I think it's a joke Linda's dead? Do I think it's a joke that I've lost the only decent thing I ever had in my life back in Rio? No, Dolly, I don't think it's a fucking joke.' She glared at her and went back to furiously buttering her toast.

Dolly sighed, seeming to sag in her chair. 'I'm sorry, Bella. It's just I haven't been able to sleep, thinking about whether it's really going to work, watching the lock-up and then tipping off the law about the job, without Harry getting on to us. I just don't know . . .'

Bella jabbed the air with her knife. 'Don't you worry about us, and don't you treat us like idiots. It's *you* he's after, and you think we don't know why? You wiped him out, Dolly – sent his girlfriend off to Australia. It's *you* he's after, not me, not Shirley . . . but it was Linda he killed.'

Dolly swallowed, then got up and put the kettle on. She leant against the sink.

'I underestimated you.'

Bella laughed. 'If things had been different, you wouldn't have given me the time of day, would you? Turnin' tricks for a living's not your style, is it, Mrs Rawlins?'

Dolly blushed and turned away.

'I got a tough hide, Dolly. And little Shirley's not as sweet as she seems, neither. Next thing we do, we do it together, the three of us. No more ordering us about. What I want is Harry caught, and put away. Linda deserves that at least. And we can do it. We just have to hold our bloody nerve.'

* * *

Sonny Chizzel stood behind the door of his shop and peeked through the blind. The patrol car was still there. Bastards. What had they put a bleeding car on him for? Sonny shook out his wet raincoat and put his umbrella in the holder. The whole world and his mother would know something was going up, sitting directly outside like that, the sons of bitches.

Sonny went through into the back and put the kettle on, picked up his accounts and began checking the figures. Business was bad; the bottom seemed to have fallen out of the Louis Quatorze period and he hadn't shifted half the stuff he'd been buying of late. Bloody fads, he thought, they come and they go, and he was left with a shop full of legit pieces that he couldn't shift. It was then that he remembered the small ormolu clock under the counter. Sonny bustled back into the shop. There was thunder now, booming right over his head. He bent down to unwrap the clock, and the doorbell pinged. A customer. He scuttled to the door and opened it, but it was just some student, wanting to know if the magazine shop next door opened on Saturday. Sonny told him to piss off, and again he saw the police car sitting like a squat frog opposite. He was going to have to tread very carefully. If the cash Murphy had brought round was from the underpass raid he'd make a nice bundle, thirty grand. He could put the finger on Murphy, and that would get him off his back. The last thing he wanted was bastards like Murphy coming round with more cash and coming on heavy to make him change it. He was through with that; it wasn't worth the risk any more. And besides, his wife Sadie had made him promise to go on the straight and narrow.

Sonny decided to give her a call and tell her what he fancied for dinner. The phone rang for a long time before it was answered.

'Oh, it's you. Hold on, I'm covered in flour. Let me get cleaned up.'

He waited for a minute, then she started speaking again, but her voice was muffled by the sound of running water. He just managed to catch the end of what she was saying. '... put on weight. I'm going to have to get your suit let out.'

'What? What are you talking about, woman?'

'Arnie Fisher's club, I'm telling you. There's a big do on – everyone's invited. He said DJ so I'm going to need a new dress ...'

'Who said? A do at Arnie Fisher's club? Why the hell would he invite us? I can't stand the man, and he knows it. Ever since he tried to knock me down on that desk—'

'Sonny, listen to what I'm saying,' his wife interrupted. 'It was a Mr Murphy that rang, said his guv'nor wanted to meet you, and that you'd understand. Now, if I wear the red ...'

Sonny put the phone down without hearing any more. Why was Murphy ringing up, and at his home? He didn't like that. 'His guv'nor' – did he mean Arnie? Sonny paced up and down, his brain ticking over, trying to make sense of it.

* * *

Shirley was exhausted. She'd had a two-hour dance class, then worked out at Lucy Clayton's, and on top of it practically killing her, it had cost her an arm and a leg. Still, the photos had turned out well, not that Marion deigned to see her when she'd turned up at the office; in fact, the girl on reception had seemed a little bit frosty.

'You listenin'?'

Shirley snapped out of her reverie as Bella gave her a prod.

'Yeah, of course I am.'

'OK, we're gonna go through each name in turn, see who offers us the best deal, right?'

Shirley thought they'd already agreed on it. Bella kept going on and on about all three agreeing, all three working together. Shirley wondered what the hell she thought they'd been doing up to now. Bella spoke to Shirley as if she was a retard.

'The one that offers us the best deal we'll go with, OK?'

Shirley sighed. Well, they wouldn't go with the one that offered them the worst deal, for God's sake. Surely all you had to do was ring the numbers and get on with it.

The phone rang and Dolly and Bella jumped. What are they so edgy about? Shirley wondered as she picked up the phone.

She put her hand over the receiver and mouthed 'my mum', then listened while Audrey told her all about her visit to the clinic, how she'd had a scan, then had a test done, and the baby was normal, and it was a he – she was going to have a baby boy.

Shirley listened, rolling her eyes, while Dolly and Bella paced up and down, glaring at her.

'Look, Mum, I've got to go.' Then the pips started, but Audrey shouted that she had another ten pence, if she could just hold on . . .

'Sorry, Mum.' Shirley put the phone down.

* * *

Audrey sat with the coin in her hand, listening to the dialling tone at the other end of the phone. She sighed and put the receiver back in its cradle.

At the bus stop, she recognised a girl who'd been at the clinic.

She patted her stomach and smiled. 'Well, I've had the test, and it looks like everything's all right.'

The young girl just looked at her, then looked away.

'And guess what? I'm going to have a boy,' Audrey continued. 'How about you?'

The girl scowled. 'Me?'

She wanted to tell Audrey that, yes, her test had been positive, but that she'd been told she'd have to wait another three or four weeks for an abortion, and that was going to be shit because now she'd have to go through all the lies and the dramas and the British Pregnancy Advisory Service, the concerned faces asking if she was sure, sure she didn't want it, on and on.

But she didn't say any of that. Instead she just turned her face away.

When the bus pulled up, the conductor shouted that there was only room for one.

The bus moved off, and the girl was left standing alone at the bus stop.

* * *

Sonny didn't recognise the voice of the woman on the other end of the phone. She seemed nervous, asking twice if she was speaking to Sonny, Sonny Chizzel. He had a lot like her, usually flogging something they shouldn't be.

'Yes, this is Sonny. Now what can I do for you? I didn't catch the name, darlin'?'

He listened while she told him what she was proposing.

'Rawlins . . . You're calling on behalf of Harry Rawlins?'

His hand was clammy as he put the phone down. His mind started racing. What if – dear God, pray that it wasn't – but what if Murphy's guv'nor turned out to be none other than Harry Rawlins? Sonny paced up and down. Rumour had it that he was alive. What if he was, and what if it had been *his* sixty grand? Sonny got more and more agitated. If Rawlins was behind the sixty grand that Murphy had brought to him, then he had just grassed him up.

Sonny went to the door and checked the police car was still there, his brain working overtime. Think, Sonny! Think! OK, it was still possible he could wriggle out of it. He'd never said a name, all they had were some of the serial numbers. He could feel his lunch coming up. Never a good idea to get involved with the likes of Rawlins. He had done once before and Harry had squeezed him dry. Now if Harry knew he'd grassed him up, then he was in real danger – or Sadie, or his—

Sonny had to run to the sink. He stood there retching, then wiped his mouth on his sleeve. The thought of anyone harming a hair of his daughter's head, his lovely Dinah, was too awful even to think about. He had to get home, get away from that damned patrol car, get away and think, and work out what to do.

* * *

Fuller ran to the patrol car, with Reynolds trailing behind. Reynolds had never seen him so hyped up. The serial numbers Sonny Chizzel had given them matched some from the £60,000 stolen in the underpass raid. At last they had a solid link. Sonny Chizzel would be in line for the thirty grand reward money – but he'd have to cough up a lot more than a list of numbers before that.

As soon as they arrived at the shop, Fuller's patrol car pulled in alongside the surveillance vehicle. Reynolds jumped out and ran to the shop door. The lights were on and Sonny's raincoat and brolly were hanging on a coat-stand. Reynolds hammered on the door.

'Round the back!' shouted Fuller, jumping into the car.

His driver put the car in gear and screeched off round the corner. Reynolds took a couple of steps back, then put his shoulder into the door with a crash.

Sonny slipped out the back door without bothering to lock it and scuttled down the back alley, coming to a sudden halt when the patrol car appeared, blocking his exit. Fuller let the door swing open.

'Hello, Sonny. In a hurry to get somewhere?'

Sonny turned to run back into the shop. Then he saw Reynolds walking calmly towards him. Too late. It was all too late. He held out his hands to indicate that he wasn't going to make any more trouble, then walked to the patrol car and got in the back. Fuller moved over to make room for him.

'Numbers match, Sonny,' he said with a broad smile. 'That money's definitely from the underpass raid.'

Sonny's head was pounding and he felt sick again. The passenger door slammed shut and Reynolds got into the front seat. Sonny tried to hide the fact that he was shaking.

'Look, there's n-n-no deal,' he stammered. 'The guy . . . he never called back.'

Fuller's mouth tightened. He tapped the driver on the shoulder. 'Let's go.'

As the car moved off, Fuller wound down his window. He could smell Sonny's fear.

Somebody's got to him, he thought.

CHAPTER FIVE

By the time they got to the station and put him in an interview room, Sonny had stopped panicking. During the journey in the patrol car he'd had time to think it through, and now he had it all straight in his head. Yes, the serial numbers tallied, but without the actual banknotes, and without Sonny giving them Murphy's name, that's all they had: a list of numbers.

Detective Chief Inspector Saunders joined Fuller and Reynolds to question him, really putting the pressure on, but Sonny stayed with his story: he had received a phone call from someone who refused to identify himself, the caller had given him the numbers and told him to contact the police. Sonny had agreed that if the numbers tallied with the underpass raid cash then they would split the £30,000 reward money fifty-fifty. That, Sonny insisted, was all he knew, and his partner, whoever he was, had not called him again.

The three policemen made him go over it all several times, trying to get him to contradict himself and trip himself up, but Sonny remained firm.

He knew they'd have got search warrants for his shop and his home while he was being questioned, hoping to find something that could help them break Sonny's story, but he also knew there was nothing.

'I'm a businessman,' he told them. 'Who'd turn their nose up at a bite of that reward money? But I run a legit business.'

It was 4:15 in the morning when they finally gave up. Sonny hadn't even bothered to call his solicitor. They didn't have enough to charge him, so he knew they'd have to let him go eventually.

'Last time I try an' help out the bleedin' law,' he muttered as he walked out of the interview room.

* * *

Fuller let himself into his flat. The place was in darkness; he tripped over something left in the hall.

'Fuck.'

The bedroom light went on, then was turned off again.

Fuller went into the kitchen and switched on the light. Cold steak and kidney pie, mashed potatoes and peas stared up at him from a plate on the table. He sat down and started eating without taking his coat off. Sellotaped to the HP Sauce bottle was a note: *Please don't wake me up. Use the spare bedroom.*

Fuller took his half-finished dinner to the sink and put the plate on the draining board. It was about the only thing out of place in the immaculate kitchen.

In the spare bedroom, Fuller made up the bed, tucking the ends of the sheets neatly under the mattress, just as he had been trained to do in the army. He loosened his tie and looked at his watch. It was now almost six in the morning, hardly worth even getting into bed. He got in anyway, without bothering to take off his clothes, and was asleep in seconds.

* * *

The following morning, Sadie Chizzel watched as the two officers went through the contents of the shop with a fine-toothed comb, examining items and checking the account books. She was sitting in a velvet chair, knitting contentedly. It didn't bother her; she'd been through it all before on numerous occasions. They wouldn't find anything out of place, anything not listed in the ledgers or the accounts. Sonny ran a good legitimate business; her father had taught him that.

Sadie saw the young red-haired officer glance over the books at her. She smiled and carried on knitting, thinking to herself that he didn't look old enough to be in uniform, let alone plain clothes.

Reynolds sighed. They'd found nothing; every item in the shop had been listed meticulously, each purchase tagged, sale prices, everything.

He was just about to call it quits when he saw one officer bending over the counter. He came up with a small object wrapped in news-paper. Carefully, he unwrapped an ormolu clock.

* * *

Fuller woke to hear his wife Maureen banging round in the kitchen. He had a thudding headache. He threw off the bedclothes and got up. He had overslept. It was after ten. He examined his face in the mirror. He looked shattered.

Maureen was sitting with a cup of coffee, reading the *Guardian*. She didn't even look up when Fuller walked in. He took a carton of fresh orange juice from the fridge and poured himself a glass.

'Sorry if I woke you last night.'

She shrugged and turned the page, then flattened the paper and began to do the crossword. 'There's eggs, bacon, whatever you want,' she said without taking her eyes off the puzzle.

Fuller ran the tap and rinsed out his fruit juice glass. 'No time, overslept, better get off.'

He saw her pursing her lips. He put his hand on her shoulder.

'Maybe tonight we could go out, eat some place nice.'

Maureen sighed, shrugged off his hand, then turned. She didn't seem angry, just resigned.

'Do you want me to book the table?'

He bent down and kissed her cheek. 'Leave it to me. I'll get home early. We can dress up, make a night of it.'

She could tell he was eager to go, so she got up and walked with him to the front door. She opened it as he got into his raincoat. He looked beat, worn out.

He fished in his pocket and took out his wallet. 'Why don't you buy yourself something new?'

Maureen sighed and took the money. She had a wardrobe full of dresses she never wore, but she'd go out and buy something anyway. She'd try her best to have a nice evening, too, but the truth was she couldn't take this much longer. It would be so much easier if they had kids; at least she would have something to occupy her time. She didn't want a job; she'd only ever worked at the local estate agent's as a receptionist and part-time secretary and she'd hated it. She was happy being a housewife; that was what she'd always wanted – a husband and kids. But how in the hell was she ever going to have any when she hardly saw him?

Fuller hovered a moment on the doorstep. She seemed to be deep in her own thoughts. Then she came back to herself.

'Is it still this Harry Rawlins business?'

Fuller nodded. He didn't want to go into details.

'But we're definitely going out, yes? I don't want to get all dressed up and then you not turn up until the restaurant's closed.'

'Don't you worry.' He kissed her and walked to his car. He turned before getting in, but the door had already closed behind her.

* * *

Shirley tried another turn under the watchful gaze of Mrs Hyde White. Along with ten other girls, she had enrolled in a two-week crash course at the Lucy Clayton model school. They were mostly debby types, who all seemed to know each other and giggled a lot. Mrs Hyde White, an ex-model herself, paid them scant attention. But she seemed to think Shirley had potential, even if that meant directing more criticism at her.

Shirley crossed the large gym floor, trying to walk in time with the music. She didn't mind being picked on and paid close attention to everything she was told. If she didn't make a good turn, she went back and tried again – and kept going until she got it right.

Mrs Hyde White took Shirley aside and made her walk alongside her, showing the spin turn on the base of the heel, making it look easy and natural. Shirley tried again, up and down, up and down.

'Better. Now keep your head up! Stop looking at your feet!'

Mrs Hyde White clapped her hands. 'Now pay attention, girls.' She began tossing out long drapes, and demonstrated how to tie them round their waists to act as trains. Then she switched tapes and heavy rock music started thundering through the studio. The girls huddled together and watched as Mrs Hyde White moved across the room at an angle, tossing the train, spinning on her heels with head held high and a haughty expression.

A few giggles accompanied the hopeless attempts of the girls as they tripped over their trains, but Shirley quickly got the hang of it, beginning to swing her body from side to side, the way the catwalk girls did.

After dismissing the class, Mrs Hyde White took Shirley to one side.

'I'm quite pleased with the way you're coming along. Have you thought very much about the future, what you want to do?'

'Well, I already have an agent – Marion Gordon,' Shirley replied rather self-consciously. 'I really want to be a professional model.'

Mrs Hyde White raised her carefully pencilled eyebrows. 'I see. Yes, well, Marion Gordon is certainly very . . . She has a very good eye for talent. I'm sure you'll do very well.'

Shirley beamed. 'Oh, thank you.' She skipped back to the changing rooms.

Mrs Hyde White watched her go. Marion Gordon. Well, you couldn't deny she was very successful . . . but one did hear such dreadful stories.

*   *   *

Bella was lolling in the bath. She loved Shirley's fancy bath oil. It almost smelt good enough to drink. She ducked her head under the soapy water, then came up to the surface, wondering if the oil was good for her hair. She heard the front door open and close below. If that was Dolly, she didn't want her to catch her getting too relaxed. She stepped out of the bath and grabbed Shirley's towel dressing gown.

Downstairs, Dolly was taking out her shopping and putting it on the kitchen table – rat poison, a torch and a loaf of bread. Bella popped her head round the door, her hair still dripping from the bath.

'You know, as soon as Shirley gets back from her class, she's off out again. She said as we hadn't told her . . . It's some fancy do; she's got out all her frocks.'

Dolly shook her head, banging down a tin of corned beef.

'Guess we'll have to do it on our own, then.'

* * *

As he sat outside Shirley Miller's house, his stomach rumbling, Vic Morgan could have kicked himself for not eating breakfast when he had the chance. The way things were going, he could be here for a while. He knew now that Shirley Miller was the widow of Terry Miller, killed in the underpass raid. And he had seen Dolly use her own key to enter the house – meaning the women were close friends. He sat up as a car pulled up outside the gate and an attractive blonde in a tracksuit got out.

Well, well, he thought. This had to be the one and only Shirley Miller.

* * *

Reynolds was beaming from ear to ear, his thin, freckled face aglow as he placed the ormolu clock on Fuller's desk. He then laid a report in front of him.

'Nicked three months ago from a house in Guildford, and valued at over £2000.'

Fuller looked at the clock and smiled. 'You little beauty! Now we can pull Sonny in and charge him with handling stolen property. We'll see if that loosens his tongue a little bit.'

* * *

Harry slipped into Arnie Fisher's club and up the stairs to the offices. If any of the waiters preparing for the party saw him, they knew not to ask questions. They all had instructions that tonight was a private party, invited guests only, with 'private' being the key word. As the trays of titbits were brought out and the bottles and glasses set up, it looked as though quite a crowd was expected.

Arnie had been buzzing round like a bluebottle, making sure the waiters knew what they were doing, and checking the wine.

'The good stuff when they arrive,' he reminded them. 'Then switch to the plonk. After a couple of glasses they won't know the difference.' With everything ready for the onslaught, he made his way up to his office.

Harry looked up from the desk and then back to studying a notebook. He didn't seem pleased to see him. Arnie hovered for a moment.

'All set, Harry. I'm going to go and get changed.'

'You do that, Arnie,' Harry said, still concentrating on the notebook.

Arnie waited for a 'thank you' or even just a 'see you later' but nothing more was forthcoming.

'Bastard,' he murmured as he turned to go.

* * *

Dolly and Bella had dressed up warm for the freezing lock-up. Dolly also had a flask, sandwiches, a torch and the rat poison. She wasn't bothered about the rats herself, but Bella clearly was, and they couldn't risk her screaming out. They were planning on staying all night if they had to, watching to see who came and went. Then – if the coast was clear – they would break into Harry's to find more details of the raid. To tip off the police they needed to know where and when. All they knew at the moment was how. Dolly took a deep breath. This time nothing must go wrong.

Shirley was still soaking in the bath when Dolly tapped on the door and went in. Shirley had her hair in rollers, lying back, eyes closed.

'We'll just have a cup of coffee, then go. You want one?'

Shirley pulled herself up and leant on the side of the tub.

'I feel bad not going with you and Bella. You sure it's OK? It's just that I promised him, and it's quite a big party – something to do with his work. I'll be meeting his boss.'

Dolly shrugged. They'd already had this conversation, and she'd told Shirley that she needed to start pulling her weight, but despite saying how bad she felt about it, Shirley's lack of interest was obvious. She hadn't even shown much surprise when they'd told her what they'd found at the lock-up. Dolly could feel Shirley drawing away. Any time now, she was sure, Shirley would come right out and say that she didn't want any part of it. But it wouldn't make any difference: she *was* part of it – and that was that.

Dolly just smiled and turned to go.

'Dolly . . .' Shirley was holding up her precious bath oil. 'Can you have a word with Bella? Just tell her if she wants some, then buy her own? It's not cheap, this stuff.'

Bath oil, Dolly thought, resisting the urge to slap Shirley there and then. With everything going on, she's worried about bleedin' bath oil.

* * *

Micky doused himself with cologne and checked himself in the full-length mirror. He wished he'd bought that long white silk scarf, but he hadn't had time; Harry had him running here, there and everywhere. He glanced at his watch. Harry was probably already at the club. Better get a move on and pick her up. He'd told Harry he was bringing the model girl for him to give her the once-over but all he'd got for his pains was a brief nod, before Harry had returned to his notepad. Always jotting down notes was Harry. It was like working with a bleeding reporter.

* * *

Dolly washed up the cups and placed them on the draining board. Time to go. Just as she picked up her bag, the doorbell rang. Bella was on her feet, but Dolly put a hand on her arm to stop her.

'Best if he doesn't see us,' she said quietly. They moved towards the kitchen as Shirley came down the stairs in a short evening dress, with a wrap and handbag.

'Don't ask him in, just go,' Dolly told her, as she shut the kitchen door.

Shirley frowned. Dolly and her damned orders! This was her house for God's sake! She'd been planning on sharing a cock-tail with Micky before they left. She made a face and opened the front door.

Through the kitchen door Bella and Dolly heard Shirley laughing, then the deeper tones of a man. As the front door closed, they raced out of the kitchen and into the lounge, leaving the lights off. They rushed to the window like two nosey old biddies. Bella flicked the curtains aside.

Micky was just closing Shirley's passenger door. He walked round to the driver's side and got in.

'I didn't get a proper look at his face,' Bella said. 'How about you?'

Dolly, leaning over Bella, shook her head.

'What sort of car's that?' Bella asked.

'Not sure, but it's very flash. Tell you one thing: Shirley seems to be doing all right for herself.' As Dolly made her way out of the darkened room, she banged into the coffee table and knocked over an ornament. She swore. Bella picked it up. The Balloon Seller was now minus a couple of balloons.

Bella laughed. 'Always said you were a ball-breaker, Dolly.'

* * *

Micky helped Shirley into her safety belt, kissed her on the neck and ran his hand down her thigh.

'I've missed you, darlin'.'

She giggled, feeling herself respond to him. She would have liked him to touch her some more, but he just gave her thigh one gentle squeeze then started the car. As they drove away, Shirley could smell his cologne, the scent even stronger than usual. Micky kept his eyes on the road; since Murphy had given him a ticking off, he'd taken more care with his driving. He could feel her looking at him and gave her a smile. When they stopped at traffic lights, he took his hand off the gear stick and stroked her leg again.

'So where are we going?' she asked, as the lights changed to green and they moved off again.

'Arnie Fisher's club. You know it?'

Shirley blinked. *Arnie Fisher?* She turned to look at Micky. He was still smiling; he clearly hadn't registered her shocked expression.

'You know the place? Little club up west?'

Shirley kept her voice calm and looked out of the window. 'Yeah, I've heard of it. Never been, though.' A warning bell was ringing in her head, and suddenly the smell of Micky's cologne made her feel sick.

* * *

Dolly and Bella shut the front door behind them and walked to Dolly's car.

Bella was shaking her head as Dolly put the car in gear and pulled out. 'I can't believe she said that about the bath oil!'

'If I was her, I'd be more worried about all my crockery getting smashed.' Dolly laughed.

'Not to mention her ornaments!' Bella added.

Neither woman noticed Vic Morgan's car pull out after them.

* * *

Sonny Chizzel's car, with Sadie driving, was just pulling out of their smart St John's Wood apartment block when Fuller and Reynolds arrived in the patrol car, blocking the exit. Fuller got out and peered through the driver's window. He was surprised to see Sonny was wearing an evening suit, with Sadie also done up to the nines.

'Going somewhere nice?' he asked, tapping the window.

'If you lot will get out of the way, yeah,' Sonny replied testily.

Fuller frowned. 'I'm sorry to spoil your evening, Sonny, but I'd like you to come down the station. I've got a few more questions for you.'

'I've said everything I'm going to say. Unless you've got an arrest warrant, you can whistle.'

Fuller pulled out the warrant with a flourish. 'This do, Sonny?'

Sonny paled visibly.

'Get out of the car, Sonny. There's a good lad.'

Chizzel bent over and kissed Sadie on the cheek, patting her shoulder. Fuller heard him say something about 'sorting out these wankers'. Fuller opened the door and yanked Sonny out of the car.

* * *

Colin Soal had been arguing with his wife all evening. First she'd complained that she hadn't had enough warning – she would have liked to have gone to the hairdressers at least. Then she had taken her moth-eaten old wrap out of the wardrobe and complained she had nothing to wear. Along with the moth-eaten fur came all the old nagging.

Ten years ago he had cheated on her with a cocktail waitress, a leggy blonde with big tits. He was only away for the weekend, and he had come home with his tail between his legs after the waitress's boyfriend had given him a thrashing. Muriel had bathed his cuts and bruises, swallowing his story about being mugged in Brighton on one of his business trips. Until someone had informed her otherwise, and then she went ballistic. Colin had never lived it down. Any argument always ended up revisiting that one miserable weekend in Brighton.

And now it was being thrown in his face yet again. If they ever had any money, she chided him that he would no doubt prefer to throw it at some cheap barmaid, rather than give his wife a decent thing to wear. The row continued all the way to Arnie's club, his wife driving and the Mini rattling along to the sound of her droning voice. As they pulled up, Colin got straight out and took a breath of air.

'Oh, thank you very much, yes, I can park it, no, I don't need your help,' she called out sarcastically.

Colin was about to get in again when she roared off in first gear.

Arnie stood at the club's entrance. He looked as if he was sweating.

'You seen Murphy? He hasn't shown. Not that havin' him on the door does me any favours. I've got my regular punters to think of. How're they going to feel coming out for a good knees-up, and they can't get into their own club? Some ape on the door telling you to piss off home?'

Colin thought what a wonderful couple his wife and Arnie would make, but then remembered Arnie's preferences were on the other side. Now his wife came marching round the corner, mouth in a thin, tight line. She whipped off her stole and tossed it to Arnie.

'Don't bother with a ticket. I hope someone does nick it; the only way I'm gonna get myself togged out in somethin' new is with the insurance money.'

Colin gave a sigh of resignation and followed his wife into the club, leaving Arnie holding what looked like a dead cat in his arms.

* * *

Taxis pulled up, dropped their passengers off and moved on. The club was filling up. Micky Tesco guided Shirley in by her elbow, a little too tightly for her liking. He seemed in a hurry to get into the club. Shirley stopped and pulled her arm away.

He looked at her. 'What's the matter now?'

'No need to push me. I've got high heels on.'

'Sorry. Big night, you know? Getting a bit edgy.'

They entered the club and joined a sea of people waiting at the coat check, men queuing one way, ladies the other. They pushed through into the main area, where waiters were waltzing round with trays of drinks and titbits while partygoers chatted animatedly. They were still trying to get their bearings when Micky was grabbed by an agitated-looking Arnie. Micky pushed Shirley gently in the direction of the ladies' cloakroom, then turned back to Arnie.

'Murphy's not bleedin' shown – I got no one at the door . . .'

Micky nodded, patted Arnie's sleeve and said he'd take care of it. He was looking round at the faces; some he knew, but a lot he didn't. He smiled greetings at everyone all the same.

'Where's the guv'nor?'

Arnie nodded to the stairs, then bustled back to the main entrance as yet more people entered. The club was becoming packed and there was a traffic jam building up round the cloakrooms.

* * *

One person who didn't want to be relieved of her coat was Audrey. The mink coat Dolly had given her was not only luxurious, it also hid her pregnancy. Audrey had thought about flogging it on more than one occasion, but something always held her back, and now she was enjoying it in all its glory. In fact, Audrey felt wonderful, happier than she could remember, and it wasn't just the coat. Ray was getting embarrassed, and was trying to shush her as she shouted and waved at old familiar faces, people she hadn't seen for years. She spotted Muriel Soal over by the ladies' room and yelled over.

Ray gave her a look. 'Keep it down, can't you? You're making a spectacle of yourself, girl.'

Audrey seemed not to hear him. She waved at Muriel and Muriel gave her a little wave back. Muriel gave her husband a dig in the ribs, and Audrey saw her mouth the word 'mink!' several times.

Audrey smiled to herself. She was sweating under the coat, but she wasn't going to take it off.

A nervous-looking Micky came up and pulled Ray aside.

'Any word on where Murphy is?'

Ray shook his head. 'Last time I spoke to him he was on his way home to get changed.' They looked over at the door, where Arnie was doing his best to cope with the influx of guests while keeping an eye on everything that was going on.

* * *

Muriel made her way over to Audrey and they fell into each other's arms, kissing each other's cheeks daintily. Muriel surreptitiously felt Audrey's coat. It definitely wasn't fake. Audrey then let out another yell as Shirley came out of the cloakroom, earning another warning tap on the elbow from Ray.

Shirley pushed her way towards her mother, surprised by how pleased she was to see her. Micky seemed to have disappeared, so Audrey did the introductions.

'Come on, mum, you must be boiling with that coat on!' Shirley exclaimed, helping her off with the mink. Muriel's mouth gaped open when she saw Audrey's bulging stomach.

'Oh my God! You having a baby, Audrey?'

Audrey flushed, then roared with laughter. 'I thought it was wind to begin with – until I realised it wasn't going away with just a burp!'

Shirley looked round again for Micky, while Ray made his way towards the cloakrooms carrying Audrey's coat.

'You be careful with that, Ray!' Audrey bellowed after him. 'That's ranch mink, that is.'

Muriel swallowed. God almighty, ranch mink! All she'd got was a bit of old moleskin her mother had left her.

'Don't you let any of the thieving so-and-sos in here swipe it!' Audrey added for good measure.

*   *   *

Upstairs, Micky was standing to attention while Harry leant back behind Arnie's desk.

'Right, Micky. You can start showing them up one at a time.'

'I'll try and make it quick,' Micky joked. 'The rate this crowd are knocking back the booze, we'll have run out pretty soon.'

Harry gave him a thin smile. 'And put in a call to Murphy while you're at it. It's unlike him to be late.'

Harry looked down the list of names again. There were a lot of old faces downstairs, enough to put a crack team together. He just had to let them know he was back, fighting fit, with cash in his wallet, and the promise of a big score.

The first man through the door was Geoffrey Barker: thin, cheap grey suit, crumpled tie – Barker had made no effort to dress for the occasion. But beneath the thin material of the suit you could tell that although Barker was well into his fifties, he still had the phys-ique of a heavyweight boxer. Barker had been used by Harry on a number of gigs. He was a hammer man, a good front man; when he went in shouting and waving his hammer round, you didn't want to mess with him. He was just what Harry needed.

Barker stared intently at Harry and walked over to the desk.

'Have a drink, Geoffrey.'

'All right. I'll have a scotch.'

Barker sat down, watching Harry pour him a generous double from the tray of bottles and glasses on the desk, his face expressionless. Harry handed him the glass.

Barker looked Harry in the eye and said coldly, 'To absent friends.' Then he knocked back his scotch in one.

Harry was prepared for Barker's attitude. He and Joe Pirelli had been like brothers. They'd even served time in the same cell. But he was confident he could talk him round. At the end of the day, money talks. And whatever happened . . . well, that was all in the past now.

Barker, however, didn't give him a chance. He put the empty glass down, then turned and walked to the door without another word. Harry didn't try to stop him.

Harry sat back in his chair, looked at his list and put a line through Barker's name. He sighed. Maybe Colin Soal had been right: some people didn't care how much money was on offer; they weren't going to work for Harry Rawlins, not after what happened with the security van heist.

He poured himself a large vodka and took a sip. This could turn out to be a long night.

* * *

'Receiving? Do me a favour, I run a legit business. I don't know what you're talking about.'

Sonny Chizzel then demanded the right to make a phone call, banging the desk, jabbing his finger at Fuller and telling him he'd have him for wrongful arrest.

Fuller just smiled, biding his time. He was actually quite enjoying seeing Sonny work himself up into a state. He looked up as Reynolds came in carrying a tray of tea.

'Tell you what, Sonny,' Fuller said pleasantly, 'while we're waiting for your brief, there's something I'd like to show you. An antique. Perhaps you could give me a valuation?'

Sonny looked at him as if he'd gone mad.

'Ah, here we are,' Fuller said, nodding to the Chief, who'd just appeared at the door, cradling an object wrapped in newspaper. The Chief put the object down on the desk and carefully unwrapped the newspaper, revealing the ormolu clock.

Sonny squinted at it. 'You want me to value this?'

'Oh, I know how much it's worth,' Fuller said. 'And so do you.'

'What are you talking about? I don't . . .' Sonny began. Then it hit him.

That bloody clock. His stomach churned as he silently called himself all the fucking idiots in the world. That bleeding, blasted clock – and that friggin' two-faced cunt that brought it in. He'd have her; he'd have the bitch. But deep down he knew the only person to blame was himself. They'd got him. They'd finally got him.

Then he threw up all over his evening suit.

* * *

Maureen sat by the phone, still wearing her new dress. She was done with waiting. And she was done with crying. Now she was just listening to the phone ringing at the other end and waiting for it to be picked up. She was surprisingly calm.

She thought it would be him, and was about to deliver the speech she had prepared, when she realised it was his sergeant, the little red-haired one.

'Would you ask him to come to the phone? It's important,' she told him, her voice even, her tone polite.

'He's rather tied up, I'm afraid. Interviewing a suspect. Can I help at all?'

*   *   *

Fuller wiped his jacket sleeve, where some of Sonny Chizzel's puke had splashed it, then rinsed out his handkerchief. His face in the washroom mirror looked drawn, but there was a glint of triumph in his eyes.

Reynolds pushed open the door, looking sheepish. 'I've got a message for you, guv. From your wife.'

Reynolds saw the colour drain from his boss's face. He held the piece of paper out awkwardly. Fuller finished drying his hands, then took the note.

'I don't think she can be serious, guv,' Reynolds said. 'I mean, you know, cutting up all your clothes and chucking them into the street just because you're missing dinner . . .'

Fuller read the note, then carefully tore it into pieces and dropped it in the bin. He pushed past Reynolds without looking at him.

'She's serious.'

*   *   *

Sonny took small sips from a glass of water. He no longer felt sick; just a terrible, hollow feeling inside.

At first, once the initial shock of seeing that damned clock had passed, he'd had a brief surge of hope. There was someone else who'd been in the shop when he'd bought it, who could testify that he hadn't known the piece was stolen.

Gordon Murphy.

Then his little ray of hope had been extinguished. Gordon Murphy was the one person he couldn't ask to help him. Not without revealing everything else. Sonny was caught in his own web. The problem was, he wasn't the spider; he was the fly.

And all the time, the ormolu clock had been ticking away.

He knew if they did him for receiving stolen goods, he'd do time, and the thought of it terrified him. It was his recurring nightmare; he could smell the dankness of the cells, taste the awful food.

So in the end he grassed.

*   *   *

Saunders joined Fuller and Reynolds at the coffee machine. 'So, Gordon Murphy. Never heard of him. You think Sonny's still playing games with us?'

Fuller shrugged. 'Could be.'

'Better pick him up anyway, though.'

Fuller nodded to Reynolds, then looked at his watch. 'On our way, sir.'

He wondered if Maureen would have started on his suits by the time he got home.

*   *   *

Gordon Murphy tried hard to remember the last time he had worn his evening suit. The problem was the bow tie, the clip-on velvet one. Always, always, when he took off his suit at the end of an evening, he'd slip the bow tie into the right-hand jacket pocket. Then he'd always know where it was.

Except that for some reason it wasn't there, and now here he was, over an hour late, every drawer in the house and every pocket of every suit searched and still he couldn't find it.

Murphy's mum had tried to help, knowing her son was getting his temper up, but in the end she'd decided the best thing was to sit it out in the kitchen. She heard the drawers banging, the swearing. Twice the club had called to find out where he was. And she could see him getting closer and closer to violence. She hated it when he got like this. Not that he'd ever lash out at her – he'd never given his mother so much as a slap – but wardrobe doors often got his fist through them and he'd been known to make a nasty dent in a wall.

Murphy stomped into the kitchen, now sporting a small red clip-on bow tie. 'I'll have to wear this. I can't find the other one. It must have been in the pocket when you had it cleaned. Those bastards have nicked it.'

'It looks just fine,' she soothed. She couldn't understand why he was in such a state. 'Plenty of people wear a coloured tie with an evening suit these days.' She saw his fist curl up in anger and busied herself looking at the *Radio Times*.

'I'm late now,' he grumbled. 'You know how I hate that.'

She watched him out of the corner of her eye as he squinted at himself in the mirror over the fireplace.

'You sure I look all right? It's a posh do and I have to look smart. What do you think?'

His mum just smiled up at him, nodding. 'You better get goin'. If they call again I'll tell 'em you're on your way.'

'Sorry for all the shouting an' that.' Murphy leant down and kissed her cheek, then turned on the TV for her. He always felt guilty about upsetting her. She'd suffered so much with his dad. And then there were all his stretches – and she'd always been there waiting when he came out, with never a harsh word, never a reproach. Murphy plumped up her cushions and kissed her again on the forehead.

'Love you, Ma. God bless.'

Murphy checked out his bow tie one more time before leaving. He was still angry, angry at himself. Harry had made a point of telling him to look smart, with all the faces coming to the club that night. He wanted to make a good impression, and now that was all up the spout.

Murphy fished in his pocket for his car keys, then bent down to open the driving door.

Fuller gave Reynolds the nod, and the two men got out of the patrol car. Reynolds moved behind Murphy and placed his hand on his shoulder before cautioning him. But he didn't even have the time to open his mouth. Murphy pivoted round and with one swing of his fist smashed Reynolds' nose. Reynolds collapsed, with his hands to his face, blood spurting through his fingers.

It was Fuller who got Murphy over the bonnet of the car, right arm twisted up behind him, pushing him forwards from the small of his back. Reynolds got to his feet and had the cuffs out in seconds and they managed to bundle Murphy into the patrol car before he could do any more damage.

Fuller was amazed how calm Murphy was, once the cuffs were on and they'd settled him in the back of the car.

'Thought I was being mugged, your pal coming at me from behind like that,' he said to Fuller. He leant over in the car and gave Reynolds a pat. 'No hard feelings, eh?'

After that, he didn't say another word, just sat staring impassively out of the window. He didn't even ask why he had been arrested.

* * *

Harry had now been given the thumbs-down by eight different men. He still had his temper under control, but only just. A nervous Micky was walking on eggshells as he ushered in Harvey Rintle, a six-foot-four Jamaican, with shoulders almost as wide as the door. Rintle was relaxed, his manner easy, but his eyes were like a cat's, sly and wary. Harry knew Rintle's history, knew he always worked solo, but right now he needed the big man. Fortunately, Harry also knew that Rintle wasn't particular about who he worked for, so long as he got paid.

Harry told him about the robbery, leaving out certain key details, but giving him the general idea. All the while he was speaking, Rintle just stared at his black suede shoes, not lifting his eyes until he was sure Harry had finished. When he spoke, his voice was quiet, a trace of accent softening the vowels.

'How much?'

* * *

Shirley was getting embarrassed about her mother. Every time a waiter passed, she grabbed what he had to offer, whether it was food or drink. She was eating and drinking for two, all right, Shirley thought wryly, and now she was at least three sheets to the wind. All her life Shirley had seen her mother behave like this at parties. She remembered as a kid hearing the taxis pulling up at three or four o'clock in the morning and watching out of her bedroom window as Audrey crawled out onto the pavement.

Audrey was getting ready for a singsong now, looking round for a piano.

Oh no, Shirley thought.

Audrey grabbed Micky's arm as he came past. 'Where's the old joanna, Micky?'

Micky smiled and whispered something in Audrey's ear that made her roar with laughter. Shirley noticed that Micky never touched a drink. He was still immaculate, still perfectly groomed, while some of the other partygoers had begun to look distinctly worse for wear. She watched him guiding Audrey across to a table, telling her that she should take the weight off her feet, a woman in her condition. Shirley lit a cigarette. Micky seemed to be ignoring her. He left Audrey and started circulating round the room, chatting away, a friendly word for everyone, his smile showing his perfect teeth.

Shirley wanted to hit him. She wanted to hit him even more when she saw Micky putting his arm round an attractive, dark-haired woman. The woman stiffened, made to push him away, but he just laughed. Shirley remembered her coming in with the huge black guy. She wondered what the hell Micky was playing at, and began to thread her way through the crowd towards him.

Micky copped Shirley on the move and eased away. She was getting on his nerves, following him round. He glanced up the stairs. It looked like Rintle was in; he'd certainly been up there longer than all the others.

* * *

Up in the office, Harry had his arm round Rintle's shoulders as he opened the office door for him.

Rintle turned. 'One thing you should know, Harry, before some prick tells you. I'm with Jackie, Jackie Rawlins. Eddie's old lady.'

For a moment Harry didn't know who he was talking about. Eddie? Then it hit him: his cousin.

He shrugged. 'That's your business. She's a lovely girl.'

Harry was smiling as he closed the door. But as soon as he was alone, it changed. His face became a mask of fury. He made a fist and was about to pound the desk with it when the door opened again. He looked up and Jackie Rawlins was standing there.

'Well, well, so the bastard's alive an' well, is he? Wondered how long it'd take for you to surface.'

Harry took a deep breath. 'Hello, Jackie. Long time no see.'

He poured Jackie a large vodka and tonic with ice and lemon, then handed it to her. Jackie's eyes were dark, her face was angular, her nose a little too big, but somehow it looked right on her. She was a sensual woman; even after two kids her body was still firm and strong. He'd always wondered what she saw in Eddie: big, soft, stupid Eddie.

Jackie sat down and sipped her drink. Then she placed the glass on the desk and lit a cigarette. After a couple of deep drags, she stubbed it out, took a breath, stood up and let him have it with both barrels.

'How could you fuckin' do it, Harry? Your own fuckin' cousin! You didn't just walk out on him – you let him rot in prison.'

Jackie picked up her drink and took a gulp. Her eyes were filling up, but she didn't want to cry; not until she'd said all she came to say.

'They got him in the hospital now. He's cracked up. He don't even know me half the time. I hate you! You must have known what prison'd do to him – an' he thought all along you'd see him right, but you never so much as sent him a tenner. He took the rap for you, Harry, an' never mentioned your name. You owe him, you owe his kids. You're his cousin, you bastard. Now he doesn't even know who he is.'

Harry watched her, the way her nostrils flared when she was angry, the way she held her head high, tossing her thick, black, glossy hair away from her face, the gold chain swinging on her neck.

He waited until she was finished, then opened up his wallet and took out a thick bundle of notes. He walked round and pushed the roll down the front of her dress. She breathed in hard. Her heavy breasts felt warm to the touch.

She smiled, all her rage gone. 'I know what all this is about, Harry. I've seen it all before: you putting a team together, are you?' Jackie stroked his thigh, moving her hand up towards his groin. 'Just leave Harvey out of it, for me, Harry. That's all I ask. He's a decent man. He's looking after me an' the kids.'

Harry pulled away.

'I love him, Harry. I really love him.'

Harry shook his head, then laughed, grabbed her wrist and pulled her to him. 'You leave that big lump alone and you'll get this every month.'

Jackie backed away from him. 'Please, Harry, don't get him involved in anything. He's straight.'

Harry let her prattle on, bleating about her precious man. Straight! She had no idea that her precious lover belonged to the highest bidder. Suddenly he wanted Jackie out; she was beginning to bore him.

He took her by the elbow. 'Whatever you say, darlin'. Just take care o' the kids. There's more coming your way, a lot more.'

Harry felt better about Eddie now. Not that his conscience had bothered him – but five grand should at least shut Jackie's mouth. He opened the door.

'Oh, one thing, Jackie. You've not heard or seen anything from Dolly?'

Jackie shook her head, then looked up into his face, his handsome, smiling, arrogant face. She'd often wondered why on earth he'd ever married Dolly. She had seemed so plain, so straight, compared to all the other women Harry had run round with. Jackie had never really thought about Dolly, what Harry must have put her through.

She looked up at him, touched him lightly on the cheek. 'She always knew about us, Harry. She knew, but never said.'

Harry shrugged. He didn't care about all that. 'You haven't seen her, then?'

'No one's seen her, Harry.' Jackie almost smiled. She'd heard Dolly had cleaned Harry out, and in a way she was pleased: good on her, bitch that she was. When Dolly had somehow found out about Jackie and Harry, she had never allowed Jackie to set foot in her house again. The reason was never mentioned, but the invites stopped, and the Christmas presents – even for the kids. Dolly had totally cut them out of her life – as if what happened outside her beloved home couldn't touch her.

Well, it had. In the end, Harry had cut her out of his life. He'd let her bury a stranger. Jackie shivered. For the first time, she felt truly sorry for Dolly – sorry because she was too damned stupid to see through the bastard she had lived with for twenty years. As Jackie was gently pushed out of the office, she wondered what Dolly Rawlins was feeling now.

If she were in Dolly's place, she would want revenge.

* * *

Fuller could get nothing out of Gordon Murphy. He still refused to admit to his own name. Sitting there, eyes half-closed, chain-smoking – maybe when his cigarettes ran out he'd be easier to break. Fuller felt exhausted. He looked at his watch. Maureen was probably busy on his jackets by now.

Reynolds, with a plaster across his nose, was standing outside the interview room. He jerked his head towards the Chief's office. Fuller sighed and walked down the corridor. He looked through the glass window and saw Saunders still talking to Sonny Chizzel. Chizzel now looked tired and deflated, a sad, pink-faced little man with all the air let out of him. Saunders saw Fuller through the window and joined him in the corridor.

'Sonny's chatting away like an old parrot,' Saunders told him with a grin. 'Not all of it of interest to us, of course, but one or two interesting things have come up. He had a call from a woman, for instance. He swears he doesn't know who it was, but she had mentioned Harry Rawlins, said she had something of his. Another interesting titbit: there is a big bash, a private party down at Arnie Fisher's place. Seems Sonny was on his way there. And now we've got Gordon Murphy wearing his DJ, so maybe he was on his way there, too.'

Fuller sighed. The last thing he fancied was a trip up west to a smoke-filled nightclub.

'Keep a low profile, just take a look round. Be interesting to see the faces at this so-called private party.' Saunders beamed, patted Fuller's arm and went back to Sonny Chizzel.

Fuller beckoned Reynolds over. 'Keep a low bleeding profile? What in Christ's name does he think we'd do, swing on the chandeliers?'

* * *

Dolly hovered at the entrance to Harry's lock-up, peeking from behind the door. The street was deserted, the rest of the lock-ups silent. Dolly closed the door and made her way to join Bella in the annexe. She was going over the plans, making notes in Dolly's black book. She looked up as Dolly joined her.

'OK, now we know for sure how he's gonna do it.'

'Come on then, let's get out of here.' Dolly swore this would be the last time just the two of them came; it had to be three so they had a proper look-out and early warning if anyone was on their way.

Bella folded the plans just as they had found them and put them back into the filing cabinet.

'Tell you one thing, Dolly: I wouldn't want to try it.'

'Good thing you're not, then, isn't it?' Dolly replied.

Bella turned with a slight smile. She spoke almost in a whisper. 'No, we're not, are we?'

* * *

Harry hadn't quite got over the finish line yet, but the list no longer had just crossed-out names. The team was slowly coming together. He yawned, stretched and rubbed his shoulders. He stood by the window, lifted the blinds and looked down to the street below. He stiffened as a patrol car pulled up and let the blind slip back into place.

Micky appeared at the door, muttering about Arnie drivin' everyone nuts down in the club. Harry gestured for him to join him at the window.

'Holy shit, it's the law.'

Two men in plain clothes were entering the club.

'That's DI Fuller,' Micky said. 'What the bloody hell's he doing here?'

Harry didn't seem bothered. He thought for a moment.

'Go down, treat him like a guest. Open a bottle of Arnie's best champagne. Let everyone down there know that prick's here by invitation.'

Harry began packing up his papers.

Micky stood, looking hesitant. 'I don't like it, Harry.'

Harry just laughed and shoved him out the door. 'Tell him the champagne is with my compliments.'

* * *

All eyes were on Fuller and Reynolds as they threaded their way towards the bar. Fuller was enjoying himself, making a mental note of the faces as they turned away from him, suddenly looking intently into their drinks. The party seemed to be suspended for a moment – then groups gathered and the talk grew louder again.

A burly bruiser called Kevin White, who'd clearly had quite a few drinks, watched Fuller as he went past, spat on the floor and returned to telling his dirty joke – but with one eye still on the policeman. He had just agreed to go in on the job; last thing he was hoping to see was the Old Bill showing their faces.

* * *

Colin Soal looked for Muriel. With that cop here, the one who had been shoving his nose in everywhere, it was definitely time to go.

On the other side of the room, Muriel was deep in conversation with Audrey, discussing wallpaper for the baby's room. Ray stood at the side of the table, looking bored – until he spotted Fuller and decided it was time to collect the mink and get out.

Shirley was still queuing for the ladies'. There had to be another one somewhere. As she turned to go into the main club, Micky went past her. She reached out to grab his arm, but he shrugged her off and pushed his way to the bar.

That was the last straw for Shirley; she was going. She'd see if Ray and Audrey could give her a lift, and then that was it: good-bye Micky. She wasn't going to be treated like some pick-up for the night.

Micky slipped behind the bar and grabbed a bottle of Bollinger just as Fuller and Reynolds arrived. He had a fixed smile on his face, keenly aware that everyone in the club was watching him.

'Glad you could make it.'

The cork popped and a little of the champagne splashed Fuller's sleeve. Micky leant over the bar and started dabbing Fuller's jacket with a dishcloth, all the while laughing and chatting as if they were the best of pals.

Colin Soal watched curiously. Maybe Rawlins had these cops in his pocket. It certainly looked like it. Micky was definitely very familiar with them. He saw him fill two glasses, smiling broadly. Then Fuller gave him a friendly pat on the arm.

In fact, Fuller was telling Micky to piss off and keep his champagne. He turned to Reynolds.

'Who is this prick, anyway?'

'Micky Tesco. Small-time crook,' Reynolds replied, eyeing the champagne greedily.

Fuller was about to give Micky another mouthful, when an attractive blonde shouldered her way to the bar. She looked familiar, but he couldn't put a name to the face, and again turned to Reynolds, who had a glass of champagne halfway to his lips.

'The blonde, you know her?'

Reynolds shook his head and turned to face the room. God almighty, half of London's underworld was here! Suddenly feeling acutely self-conscious, he put the champagne glass down and turned back to the bar.

Micky gave Shirley a scowl. 'Not now. Can't you see I'm busy?'

Shirley stepped back, as if slapped, and bumped into Fuller.

Seeing her up close as she turned to face him, Fuller remembered her. 'It's Shirley, isn't it? Shirley Miller?'

Shirley didn't answer, just gave him a tight smile before backing away. She turned and made her way quickly to Audrey's table, where Ray was trying to help Audrey into her coat. Just as Shirley joined them, Audrey fell back into her chair with a hoot of laughter, almost too pissed to stand. Ray hauled her up on to her feet and started guiding her towards the exit.

'Oi! A woman in my condition don't need to be pushed about,' Audrey protested. 'I need to go to the toilet.'

Fuller noticed the mass move towards the exit with a smile. Funny how everyone in the place suddenly needed to be somewhere else.

'Two beers,' he said to the barman.

Micky was still doing his act, repeating loud enough for anyone to hear how glad he was that Detective Inspector Fuller had granted them a visit.

Fuller gave him an icy stare, then caught Arnie Fisher's arm as he hurried past, pulling him to one side. Arnie was shaken; he'd been so busy making sure the booze didn't run out, he hadn't seen Fuller and Reynolds making their entrance.

What a night, he thought: the bastards had drunk him dry and now the Old Bill was hanging about. That was all he needed, especially Fuller: he'd had his fill with him trying to get his licence revoked a couple of months back.

'What's the party in aid of, Arnie?' Fuller pressed his face close.

Arnie swallowed. He looked at Micky, who was topping up the untouched champagne glasses.

'You deaf, Arnie? Who's throwing the bash?'

'Oh . . . you know . . . just a . . . a private party – nothing special,' he stammered.

* * *

Audrey, leaning heavily on Ray, had made it to the bottom of the stairs by the main entrance.

'Ooh, I'm desperate, Ray!' she moaned, slumping down onto the stairs. Shirley began moving up the stairs, looking for another ladies'.

'Just wait here, Mum.'

* * *

Harry had his coat on and was ready to move out. He'd already tidied up the desk and wiped it down. He let himself out of the office and walked towards the fire exit on the landing.

'Excuse me, is there a ladies' up here?'

Harry turned to see an attractive blonde at the top of the stairs. For a second there was a spark of recognition between them, but he didn't have time to think about it.

'Sorry, love.' He pushed open the fire exit and walked through.

For a moment Shirley couldn't move. She felt her mouth go dry and her knees almost gave way; then she turned and ran back down the stairs.

When she got to the bottom, Ray and Audrey had gone. Shirley didn't wait for them. She wasn't going to spend another second in this place.

* * *

Micky raised his glass and smiled over the rim. Fuller released Arnie's arm and picked up his beer.

'Don't fancy a glass of bubbly, Inspector? Compliments of Harry Rawlins.'

Kevin White, leaning against the bar, looked over with a smile, lifted his hands in the air and started singing: 'Why was he born so beautiful' at the top of his voice. Others nearby picked it up, and soon a raucous chorus was echoing through the club.

Fuller put his beer down and pushed his way through the crowd of laughing faces.

'Come on, Reynolds. It's time we took a look upstairs.'

* * *

Shirley tried hailing two cabs but they drove straight past her. She was about to try for another when saw a figure slip from the alley running alongside the club, collar turned up, carrying a briefcase.

She stared, trying to make out his features in the dim street lighting. Maybe she'd been wrong. Maybe it wasn't Harry after all.

The figure continued up the road and disappeared.

'You want a cab, darlin'?'

Shirley got into the taxi, gave her address and sat back with her eyes closed. What an awful evening. First Micky, and then literally bumping into that dreadful policeman, the one who had searched her house. It brought it all back again – Terry, the robbery. And then that man at the top of the stairs . . .

It was all too much. She hoped Bella was in bed when she got home. She wasn't sure she was up to talking to anyone. She just needed to be alone.

*　*　*

Dolly shone the torch round their lock-up. They had waited long enough; it didn't look as if Harry was going to show. They'd come back in the morning.

Bella followed the beam of Dolly's torch. Dolly had laid rat poison in every corner of the lock-up but there certainly wasn't a single one to be seen now. Then Bella felt it, crawling over her foot. She gasped and pulled her foot away. Instead of scuttling away, the creature just lay there, twitching. Bella took one look at it and let out a shriek.

'Let's get out of here, Dolly.'

*　*　*

Vic Morgan couldn't hold it any longer: he had to take a leak or he was going to wet himself. He was just doing up his zipper again when he heard the scream. It gave him such a shock he almost caught himself. He moved back into the shadows.

Dolly came out of the lock-up and followed Bella to her car. A few rats didn't bother Dolly. She unlocked the car.

'You got to control yourself, Bella,' she chided her. 'You could have brought half the neighbourhood out.'

Bella just shivered, thinking about the rat crawling over her foot.

'I'll bring a hammer next time. A quick knock'll finish them off,' Dolly assured her. She shook her head. 'Rats are nothing to be afraid of.'

Bella gave her a look. 'Yeah, well, I guess you should know – you married one!'

As they drove away, Vic Morgan pulled out to follow them. He'd stopped being so cautious, keeping well behind them with at least one other car in between. He'd been on their tail all night and it didn't look as if it had occurred to them that anyone would be on to them that fast.

'Where are you staying?' Bella asked.

Dolly reluctantly gave her the address. She felt safer with the girls not knowing her whereabouts.

'It's not much, just a rented place.' At least now she'd given it a good clean, she thought.

Bella nodded. 'Maybe I'll call round and take a look at it.'

Dolly dropped Bella off at Shirley's and drove home.

Vic Morgan followed her all the way, then took off to an all-night hamburger joint. He got his double-decker and crossed to a window seat, feeling conspicuous among all the punk kids. He sipped his chocolate milkshake and pondered his evening's work. It seemed he'd put in a lot of hours without being able to piece together what in the hell's name was going on. He hit the tomato ketchup hard. He'd better pay another visit to old Resnick, see if he could make any sense of it. One thing was sure, in all the time he had tailed Dolly, she had made no contact with her husband. Maybe she'd been telling the truth; maybe she didn't know where he was.

*   *   *

Dolly slept like a log and woke up feeling much better. She brewed herself a pot of coffee and was just sitting down to it when the doorbell rang. She moved quickly to the door.

'It's me, Bella,' came an urgent voice from the other side of the door.

Dolly sighed. She knew it had been a mistake to tell Bella where she was living, but there was nothing she could do about it now.

Dolly hadn't even closed the door behind Bella before she started slagging off Shirley.

'She wasn't even at home when I got back. I waited up for her, but I was so tired I passed out – then when I wake up she's already pissed off again.'

Bella chucked the note onto the table: *Gone to rehearsals*.

'It's all right for her, Dolly. She's out all the time, doing her bleedin' classes, going out with her fella – while I'm stuck here, just doing what you tell me. "Don't go out. Keep a low profile." It's driving me nuts.'

Dolly put a mug of coffee in front of her.

'I want my cash, Dolly. I reckon we've hung round long enough. All right, we'll shop Harry – but I want my cash now. Soon as that's done, I'm off.'

Dolly started to say something but Bella interrupted her.

'Different for you, though, isn't it? You already got more than enough. How much you got stashed away, then, Dolly? You don't even need the money from the drill hall.'

Dolly bristled. 'Whatever money I've got is my business.'

Bella wasn't going to stop, though. She was on a roll.

'It's not about the money for you, is it? It's just about getting Harry put away. You don't care what happens to me and Shirley.'

Dolly had had enough. First Shirley was driving Bella mad. Then it was all Dolly's fault. When would Bella ever take responsibility for her actions? She was about to give Bella what for when the doorbell rang.

They both froze. Then Bella got up.

'That'll be Shirley. I left her a note to meet us here.'

Vic Morgan was leaning against the doorframe with a cheeky grin. He quickly straightened up when Bella opened the door. Dolly pushed her out of the way.

Vic recovered himself. 'You forgotten our lunch date?'

Dolly had indeed forgotten.

'I'm double-parked so we ought to get a move on,' Vic said, trying to get a second look behind Dolly at Bella.

Dolly eased him out. 'Just give me a moment, will you?' She shut the door and leant against it. 'Shit.'

'What's that all about?'

Dolly filled Bella in about Vic Morgan while she dressed, flinging clothes out of the wardrobe.

'So what do I do all day then?'

'I won't be more than an hour. I'll see you back at Shirley's.'

Bella bit her lip. 'Maybe I'll go to the lock-up. See if anything's going on.'

Dolly spun round furiously. 'Don't you bloody dare go there on your own! It's too bloody dangerous. I thought you were supposed to be scared of the rats.'

'Come on, your fancy man's waiting,' Bella said by way of an answer, pushing Dolly out of the door.

*   *   *

DI Fuller walked into his office with a bunch of M&S shirts tucked under his arm. He shoved the shirts into a desk drawer, then yanked his coat off.

He fingered his collar and realised he had left the cardboard in. He was pulling it out when Saunders appeared at his desk.

'Gordon Murphy must have someone heavy behind him,' Saunders told him with a frown. 'He's got the best brief money can buy, swearing blue murder and telling us to charge him with something or release him.' He paused. 'Which room's Chizzel in?'

'Can't say, guv.'

Saunders placed a clock on the desk, similar to the one taken from Chizzel's shop. 'I just want him to take a look at this. An aunt left it to me. Never thought much about it, but that ormolu one was worth – what?'

Reynolds joined them, sporting a fresh plaster across his nose. 'Two grand, guv.'

Saunders held up his own clock and whistled. It looked almost identical. Fuller gave Reynolds a look.

Saunders caught it. 'Right, Fuller. You've got work to do. Looks like you had Rawlins right under your nose an' you let him walk away. You were made a right idiot of. 'Bout time you got it together on this one, Alex. It looks like you've taken your eye off the ball.'

Fuller was too tired to come up with a response. Which was probably just as well, he thought. He'd been on duty almost round the clock, and the last thing he needed was his Chief yelling at him.

Saunders strode off, clutching his aunt's clock.

'Jesus,' Fuller muttered. 'What does he think this place is, the *Antiques* bloody *Roadshow*?'

* * *

Shirley had expected Amanda's nightclub to be a lot more glamorous. After reading about it in *Vogue* and *Harper's* she'd been dying to actually see it. But now that she was here, an hour early for her rehearsal, it just smelt of stale cigarettes and booze, just like all the other clubs. In the harsh daylight, the dainty tables and chairs seemed rather scruffy, the plush carpet covered in cigarette burns.

Shirley asked where the models were supposed to go, but nobody seemed to know anything about it. So she sat watching the ramp being built up in the centre of the main club room, while lights, drapes and masses of floral displays were being carried in. The sound of hammering and banging almost deafened her.

Shirley watched a girl wearing a beautiful fox fur jacket and dark glasses walk into the club and knew immediately that she was a model. She chucked the coat over a chair. Underneath she was wearing a dirty old tracksuit and plimsolls. In her smart high heels and posh dress Shirley felt overdressed. The girl yelled out a few abusive remarks to the workmen, opened up a newspaper and began reading.

Two more models wandered in, shouting, 'Hi, Myra.' They were also casually dressed, wearing work clothes and no make-up, and they all seemed to know each other. But Myra was clearly the queen bee.

Two more models waltzed in, there was a lot of shrieking, and someone shouted for coffee. Shirley sat to one side, feeling very much an outsider. The girls nattered on about this job and that model, discussing agents. Shirley heard Marion Gordon's name being mentioned. Then an assistant brought in take-out coffee and handed it round. Shirley still made no move to join them, just sat there with her holdall, feeling embarrassed, her stomach churning. They all looked so confident, lounging round together. She just hoped she wasn't going to make a fool of herself.

A dapper little Japanese boy arrived wearing a bomber jacket and tight black leather trousers. He screamed excitedly at the girls, and they kissed and petted him. When the excitement had died down, he took a clipboard out and looked over.

'You Shirley?' he asked in a rasping Cockney accent.

She nodded and he waved her to come over. She was acutely aware of the girls watching her as she tried to walk with her head up, like a real model.

Jukko, the choreographer, pulled out a chair. He started introducing Shirley to everyone but halfway through someone started talking about a job they had been on and Shirley was forgotten. Jukko got up and kissed Myra on the forehead, making her promise to behave herself and not cause him any aggro. She gave him a kick with one long leg.

'Me? Aggro? Do me a favour.'

Jukko asked the sound man to play the music, and heavy metal started booming out.

The girls hooted at the lyrics, smoked and drank their coffee. Jukko went over to find out how long it would be before the ramp was finished so he could rehearse the girls. Meanwhile, the hammering and banging continued, the rock music belted out, and the floral sprays and the stacks of chairs were carried backwards and forwards. Shirley couldn't help a small, satisfied grin; she was loving it, doing something she had dreamt about. She couldn't believe she was here; it was really happening.

'You got a fag?'

Shirley couldn't open her cigarettes quick enough. Myra's catlike eyes looked her up and down.

'I've not seen you on the catwalk before. Where did you spring from?'

* * *

Dolly looked at the signpost as they went round the roundabout leading to Teddington Lock. She'd been getting more and more frustrated as they drove.

'Where the hell are you taking me, Vic?'

Morgan just grinned.

'For God's sake, just pull over and let me out! I'll get a taxi back.'

'We're almost there, Dolly. Just a few more minutes.'

'Almost *where*?'

His grin widened. 'My boat.'

Before Dolly could decide whether he really had gone nuts, Morgan pulled up alongside Teddington Lock.

At first she refused to get out.

'Come on, Dolly,' he coaxed. 'I was up first thing this morning refuelling her and making us a nice lunch. Champagne and smoked salmon sandwiches.'

Dolly followed him reluctantly along the wharf, feeling conspicuous in her high heels and tight skirt, until he stopped at a little ramp leading on to a tatty-looking cabin cruiser.

Dolly gripped her handbag tightly. 'Well, now I've seen it, wonderful. But I've got to go back – my dentist's appointment, you know.'

Morgan took no notice. He stood on the ramp and held out his hand. She hesitated, and he took her hand and guided her up the narrow plank. She teetered at one point, and he put his arm round her waist. She couldn't push him away or she would have fallen into the water.

'Come along into the cabin. Lunch is served.'

Dolly manoeuvred herself into the cramped cabin. The champagne looked cut-price and the sandwiches were already curling at the edges. She was thinking about turning round and getting off the boat when she felt the engines turning over and suddenly the boat was moving. The swell almost knocked Dolly over as she scrambled to the front of the boat, where Morgan was steering them out into the river.

'What the hell do you think you're doing?' she shrieked. 'Take me back, do you hear?'

Morgan just grinned and put a hand to his ear, pretending to be deaf.

This was turning into a complete nightmare. Dolly closed her eyes. If she really had gone to the dentist, it couldn't have been nearly as painful as this.

*　*　*

Jukko was shouting instructions: 'Three, two . . . now four, four . . .'

The girls grouped and regrouped as they moved down the ramp to the thudding rock music. They had been at it for nearly an hour and were showing signs of tiredness, but Jukko kept pushing them up and down the ramp, up and down. And they didn't glide along the way Shirley had been taught by Mrs Hyde White: they stormed it – rolling their shoulders, grinding their hips, pouting sexily like an army of Amazons. But Shirley quickly picked up how to do it, and soon she was swaggering aggressively to the beat like the best of them. Yukko never stopped yelling at them, but Shirley found it exciting, her adrenaline flowing so strongly she felt she could go on forever.

It was Myra who eventually yelled for a break. 'Fuckin' 'ell, Yukko – I'm knackered!'

As Yukko called a halt, he gave Shirley a little nod.

Yes! I've made it, she thought to herself.

*　*　*

Bella let herself into their lock-up. She'd had to travel by Tube, which she hated, and now she was here in this filthy hole, terrified of the dead or dying rats. She sat down on a box and wondered why the hell she'd come. The truth was, she just didn't want to be at Shirley's on her own. Plus, she quite liked the fact that Dolly had ordered her not to. And if she did find out something useful . . . well, that would teach Dolly not to be so high and mighty.

The noise of Harry's lock-up being opened startled her out of her thoughts. She stood up, listening to the heavy door being drawn across, then stepped up on the crate.

On the other side of the wall, Micky Tesco was filling the kettle, while Ray Bates dumped a pile of uniforms on the floor. Harry Rawlins followed Ray in, along with Kevin White. The men were relaxed and chatty, Harry standing immediately below Bella's peephole.

If only they knew, she thought.

'You sorted out a double-up Transit van for the getaway?' she heard Harry ask Ray.

'All sorted. Extra van plus driver.'

'Fine,' Harry said, nodding. 'Five hundred for the driver – that sound fair?'

'Sure, Harry.'

Standing on the crate, Bella could hear them as clearly as if they were all sitting together in Shirley's kitchen. She just hoped they couldn't hear the booming of her heart.

* * *

Dolly sat in the boat, trying her best not to have a good time. But it was hard, with the wind blowing in her hair, the sun glinting on the water and the gentle up and down motion of the boat rocking her. She felt herself beginning to doze off when a speedboat zipped past, towing a water-skier behind it. The man waved to Morgan as he weaved dangerously close to the boat, sending a plume of spray into the air. Dolly was transfixed – how graceful and effortless it looked! Until the wind blew the spray all over her. Morgan quickly put the boat on automatic, then took off his jacket and offered it to her. She swiped his hand away in a fury and his jacket sailed over the side and into the water.

Morgan gaped. 'That's my—'

Dolly tried not to laugh at the expression on his face. It was obviously an expensive jacket and he'd worn it to impress her. 'Sorry, I didn't mean to do that.'

Dolly had no idea why she thought it was so funny, but she just couldn't help herself. Maybe it was all the tension of the last few days suddenly coming out. He was leaning over the side, shouting for her to get hold of his belt, reaching over towards the jacket, which was gently floating away out of his reach.

'Get the boat hook!'

Dolly spotted it on the deck. She bent down to pick it up and then almost did a Buster Keaton as she turned round, nearly taking Morgan's head off as he reached for it.

'Oops, sorry!'

He yanked the pole out of her hand, and for some reason his furious expression started the laughter again.

'Come on! Grab hold of my belt again,' he shouted, leaning over the side of the boat and reaching out with the pole. Dolly grabbed hold and hung on for dear life as he finally managed to snag the coat and start dragging it towards him. But even with Dolly holding on to him, he was leaning too far over to keep his balance, and just as it seemed he was about to pull the coat out of the water, his head dipped under. Dolly pulled as hard as she could, thinking that the boat itself was about to tip over, and with an almighty heave he managed to raise himself out of the water, still clutching his precious jacket.

Dolly sat down on the deck and tried to get her breath while he rummaged in the pockets of the sodden jacket, eventually pulling out his wallet.

'Thank Christ for that,' he said, closing his eyes.

She looked at him, at his big, dopey face, with water dripping down it, and started to laugh again. She gave in to it, hysterical laughing, unable to stop.

He looked at her and shook his head. 'What a funny woman you are, Mrs Rawlins.' He came and sat beside her, and put his arms round her, holding her gently.

She turned to him and smiled, brushing a piece of weed from his forehead. 'Thank you, Vic. Thank you so much.'

He looked puzzled. 'For what?'

'For making me laugh,' Dolly said.

* * *

Bella was starting to shiver and she was getting cramp in her calves. But she didn't dare move. The men were trying on their uniforms and once each of them had found a uniform that fitted, and had taken them off again, Harry called them over and the men began to group round the orange boxes to listen to the guv'nor.

Harry was brisk and businesslike. The men were mostly silent, listening intently, no one interrupting. Harry assigned them their roles in the raid – who was to carry the shotguns or hammers – and carefully explained the timing. The men nodded in silence. Only when Harry had finished delegating their tasks did they ask any questions.

Bella noticed that the men didn't seem to like the only black man among them. He didn't say much, and nor did the small, younger-looking man. The handsome blond guy, on the other hand, was very much in evidence, laughing and joking confidently. Less confident was a white-haired, rather elegant man with horn-rimmed glasses, who seemed constantly to be looking to Harry for approval. She wondered about him.

One by one the men left. The white-haired man handed Harry a brand-new passport before going, saying something about DI Fuller that Bella couldn't quite follow, while Harry counted out his payment in cash.

'Tomorrow, then,' Harry said, shaking his hand.

Then Harry and the handsome blond boy were alone. They both seemed so relaxed it was hard to believe they'd just been going over the details of an £8 million jewel raid. She heard Harry call the other man Micky, and she made a mental note of the name.

'What about your model, then?' Harry asked.

Micky laughed. 'I got her in the palm of me hand, Harry.'

'Make sure you get all the info out of her, Micky. Everything, yeah?' Harry gave Micky a playful cuff round the ear.

Moments later the lights went off, leaving Bella blinking into the darkness. But she didn't relax until she heard Harry finally driving away. She gave it another couple of minutes before slipping out, then Bella opened Harry's lock-up and went in.

* * *

The girls were gliding up and down the ramp in formation, moving like tigers.

'In the midst of all this madness, let's dance, come on an' dance.'

Jukko screamed for the lights – now they were strobing, swirling round the girls' heads, then . . . *blackout.*

The next second the girls' heads and shoulders were picked out by spotlights, each girl lit to show off the final display of the jewels. At this precise moment they were wearing, in all, over eight million pounds' worth of gems.

The lights came back on and the girls fell down in exhausted heaps. Jukko clapped his hands and declared a break. Amid cheers they crawled down the ramp. Shirley jumped down, laughing, and Myra grabbed hold of her.

'Babe, why do we let them do this to us?'

Shirley loved the fact that the other girls included her naturally in the discussion about where to go to eat. But the truth was, she would have been happy eating a sandwich in the middle of a roundabout, she was so excited. As they all streamed out of the club, Shirley saw Micky standing on the corner, leaning against his E-type. Myra nudged her, making kissing sounds. Shirley would have preferred to go and eat with the girls, but Micky waved her over.

Myra walked off, yelling over her shoulder that Shirley had 'just an hour', and to be a good girl!

Shirley was feeling so good she'd almost forgotten how angry with Micky she'd been the previous night. He opened the door for her, tucked in her coat, and as he got in he took hold of her hand.

'First, I want you to tell me you're not angry about the other night. I've not been able to sleep. On my life, it was just one of those things, a heavy time all round.'

Shirley listened to him giving her the flannel, not really paying any attention. He was good with the chat, but that's all it was, and she'd realised that not only didn't she trust him, she didn't really like him much, either. For the moment, though, she was happy to go along for the ride.

The flannel finally stopped, and then he started up the car, gave her a quick kiss on the cheek and drove off.

'Nice little place, grab you a quick bite to eat, want to hear all about it . . .'

Shirley kept her eyes on his face as she asked him if he knew Harry Rawlins. She noticed a slight twitch at the side of his mouth, then he looked her directly in the eyes.

'Harry who?'

Shirley shrugged. 'It doesn't matter.'

Micky drove on, keeping up with the chatter, trying not to show she'd rattled him. He felt for her thigh, then hitched up her skirt. Her flesh was soft and warm. He looked at the clock on the dashboard. He fancied taking her back and giving her a good seeing-to, but he doubted they had the time.

They pulled up outside a small Italian restaurant. On the pavement, he cupped her face in his hands and kissed her, a long, deep kiss. He felt her respond, her arms tightening round him – then he released her.

Micky knew the proprietor and a table was quickly laid for them in a cosy alcove, even though it was way past lunchtime and the place was almost deserted. Micky tossed the menus aside and ordered two fettuccinis and a bottle of chilled Pinot Grigio. Then he tilted Shirley's chin and kissed her gently.

'Right, my little beauty, tell me everything. I want to know all about it.'

As Shirley started talking, the waiter came and opened the wine, while Micky was given a bottle of San Pellegrino without even asking. Shirley would have rather been telling someone else about her day – someone who she thought really cared about her – but right now there wasn't anyone else, and Micky was so attentive, and seemed so interested, that she soon forgot about it.

'You ended with a blackout?' he said incredulously. 'Like in the war?'

'No, silly,' she laughed. 'It's when the lights go out at the end of the show for the finale, when we walk down the ramp. We've got all the jewels on, and then the lights go out except for spotlights on your head and neck to show off the jewels.'

Micky smiled. 'Well, just shows you – you learn something new every day, don't you?'

*   *   *

Dolly lay in the bath and gently soaped her whole body. Funny, really, every morning she took a bath, and yet this one felt different. Special. She was suddenly aware of her body, not just something to wash, dry and put clothes on top of, but something that somebody else might want to touch.

Dolly studied her red toenails. She had nice feet, elegant. But then she'd always taken care of her feet, since shoes were one of her passions. Some women went for hats; Dolly went for shoes. Maybe it stemmed from her childhood, her feet being shoved into the cheapest ones available. Dolly remembered her mother's feet, with her bunions and corns, the heel worn into a bulge at the back. She looked at her own smooth, hairless legs and smiled. She began to think of Vic Morgan, saying his name to herself.

She sat up. This was getting stupid. But she couldn't get him out of her mind. She knew he felt the same way. But then, what way *was* that exactly? She shook her head. Why was she putting herself through this torture? For what?

Then a heavy cloud came sweeping over her . . . Harry. Morgan was dismissed from her mind – just a bungling, heavyweight man, who for one moment had made her laugh. But it had proved something: she was still capable of enjoying herself, and still capable of attracting someone else. Her mood shifted and Dolly got out of the bath. She caught her reflection in the mirror and decided she should have her hair cut.

*   *   *

Bella made herself a sandwich and ate it watching the telly. Where the hell was Dolly? She kicked herself for not having taken her phone number. She had so much to tell her.

She looked round Shirley's lounge. What was it she hated about it so much? There was nothing really ugly; nothing out of place. The sofa, the chairs, the carpet – they all matched.

That was it. Nothing stood out. There was nothing surprising. It was as if it had all been ordered from the same magazine. Bella began to think of Rio, the villa, José. It all seemed so far away, as if it had never happened. She wondered if this was her life now, watching stupid TV programmes in an empty house.

* * *

The lounge lights were still on as Shirley parked the car. She knew she'd be in for a grilling from Bella – and she probably had it coming. She'd been gone all day and hadn't even bothered to call in. Truth was, she hadn't really expected the rehearsal to go on for so long, but as Jukko pointed out, they rolled the following night – Sunday. They had to know exactly what they were doing.

* * *

Vic Morgan was standing shaving, with a towel wrapped round him, when the doorbell rang, almost making him nick himself. He wandered through to the hall and peered through the spyhole. Curious, he opened the door and the delivery boy shoved a parcel into his arms and asked him to sign for it. As he scribbled his name, Morgan noticed the boy had terrible BO.

He carried the parcel to the table and ripped off the outer layer of packaging. Inside was a box with Italian writing. What on earth . . . ? But as he opened the box it all fell into place. It was a jacket. Not exactly the same as his old one, but very similar.

He carefully took it out of the box and put it on. He looked a bit odd in the mirror, wearing a towel round his waist and a jacket on top, but the jacket looked so elegant, the material hung so perfectly, the colour was so rich and deep, that even wearing a towel, he looked decidedly elegant and stylish. He felt the soft material between his fingers. Must have cost a fortune, he thought. He turned this way and that in the mirror, grinning inanely. No one had ever, in his whole life, bought him a gift like this. He was touched. More than touched: he was so taken aback that he sat on his bed for a while wondering what his next move should be.

* * *

Shirley turned off the telly and Bella woke up with a start.

'Do you want a cup of tea? I'm just putting the kettle on.'

Bella stretched, then followed Shirley into the kitchen. 'You have a good time last night, then?'

Shirley filled the kettle. 'It was OK.' She hesitated. 'It's just there was . . .'

Bella came closer. 'What?'

Shirley put the kettle down. 'I saw someone. I mean, I *think* I saw someone.'

'What are you talking about?' Bella demanded, beginning to lose patience.

Shirley turned and faced her. 'Harry. I think I saw Harry.'

Bella couldn't believe it. 'Why didn't you tell me? Tell Dolly?'

'It might not have been him, Bella.'

'But you think it was.'

Shirley shrugged.

'So where've you been all day an' half the night?' Bella asked.

Shirley opened the fridge. It was empty, not even a bottle of milk left. She slammed the door shut. 'At the club, rehearsing.'

Bella perked up. 'What club?'

Shirley pushed past her. 'I've told you, it's this big charity show, tomorrow night.'

Bella grabbed her sleeve. '*What club?*' she repeated urgently.

Shirley looked at her. 'Amanda's.'

* * *

Dolly knew it was Morgan before she even picked up the phone. How he got her number she didn't ask; she was just pleased he'd called. Morgan thanked her for the jacket, saying she really shouldn't have given him such an expensive present. The conversation was easy, and Dolly was so enjoying their chat that she ignored the doorbell when it rang. But when it kept on and on, with no sign of stopping, she had to cut the phone call short, promising that, yes, she would see him again very soon.

When she finally opened the door, Dolly was almost flattened as Bella burst in, pushing Shirley in front of her. Bella marched Shirley into the front room, where she stood, red-eyed and sobbing, clutching a sodden tissue. Bella stood by the door, hands on hips, eyes blazing.

'Tell her, then. *Go on, tell her!*'

'I . . .' Shirley began.

Bella didn't give her a chance to finish. She turned to Dolly. 'We know exactly when they're going to pull that raid, Dolly, down to the last sodding minute!' She whirled on Shirley. '*Don't we?*'

'Oh, leave me alone!' Shirley wailed.

Dolly was losing patience. 'What are you talking about?'

'She's only one of the models, isn't she!' Bella shouted.

Dolly looked at Shirley incredulously.

Shirley swallowed. 'All right, yes! I'm one of the models, at the club. I'll be wearing the jewels.'

Dolly had to sit down. It wasn't true, it couldn't be true. But she knew by their faces that it was.

* * *

Harry made Micky repeat what Shirley had told him one more time: that at the end of the show, the finale when all the jewels would be worn, there would be a blackout. He shook his head wonderingly. It was almost as if they wanted to be robbed.

It was Colin Soal who added the next piece of the jigsaw. Unable to resist the money, Soal was now going to take part in the robbery. With his press card, he would have genuine access to the club. Along with all the other press photographers, he had been invited to take photographs during the dress rehearsal. And that's when the hit would take place. The models would be wearing the jewels, but the place wouldn't be full of punters getting in the way . . . All Soal had to do was give them the signal just before the blackout, and they could move in unobstructed.

Harry summoned the team and laid it out. Rintle wasn't convinced.

'It's one thing pulling a robbery at night. It's a different kettle of fish doing it in the middle of the afternoon. You ain't got the cover of darkness.'

Harry looked round at the rest of the men. 'Anyone else?'

There were no other dissenting voices.

'Daylight robbery it is, then,' Harry said with a chuckle.

'Just one question,' Colin Soal piped up. 'About the pay-off . . .'

Always the money, Harry thought sourly. Let's get the sodding jewels first.

'Just wondering where it was going to be,' Soal continued. 'Where you'll be.'

Without a flicker, Harry looked round at the men. 'I'll be there at the lock-up with fifty grand for each of you.' Except for Rintle, he thought with a trace of annoyance. The big man had insisted on being paid up front.

As the men filed out, Rintle hung back. Harry smiled and patted him on the shoulder. 'The money will all be taken care of,' he assured him.

'It better be,' Rintle answered, ''cos after the job, I'm not coming back here. I'm straight on my bike.'

Harry smiled again. 'Sure, sure. It's all in hand. How's Jackie, by the way?'

Rintle gave him a long look. 'Jackie's fine, just fine,' he said quietly.

As the outer door clanged shut behind Rintle, Micky and Harry were left alone. Micky rubbed his hands together.

'So, Harry, it's three-fifteen tomorrow, then?'

Harry was deep in thought, acutely aware of his shortage of cash. This cocky young so-and-so had no bloody idea what it took to pull off a big job like this, no idea how it was really going to go down.

Harry was the only one who knew, and that was the way he had always worked – well, up to a point. There'd been Dolly, of course. Harry sighed. He hadn't given much thought to Dolly of late. But in time he would take care of her. He sat down and rubbed his head.

Micky began picking up the used coffee mugs. It was hard talking to Harry when he was in one of his moods. Normally he couldn't stop – giving Micky orders, have you done this, do that. But when he was like this, just sitting, staring into space, you couldn't get a word out of him, unless it was 'piss off!'.

'Murphy sorted, is he?'

Micky didn't hear. Harry got up and walked into the kitchen. 'Murphy sorted, is he?' he repeated.

Micky turned the tap off. 'Sure, Harry. Got a top brief working on it.'

Harry nodded thoughtfully. 'You contacted his mother?'

'Er, not yet, Harry.' Micky tried to change the subject. 'We should do something about that fucking Sonny Chizzel – get someone to break his legs for him.'

Harry ignored Micky's outburst. 'I'll go talk to her then,' he said in a cold voice. 'I'll be round your place later.'

When he was gone, Micky threw one of the mugs in the sink, where it shattered noisily. Then another. Every time he thought he had got close to Harry, he just got slapped down. They were in this together, but the way he acted, it was as if Micky was of no more importance than the kid they had hired to ride the motorbike.

Micky walked over to the big motorbike and checked the saddlebag. This was where the jewels would end up. Micky got astride the bike and stroked the gleaming metalwork – it looked like Fisk had cleaned it. He kick-started the bike and it roared into life, the engine growling. Little Brian certainly knew his bikes. He'd even won a couple of track races. That was why he was on the raid: to bankroll his entrance on to the race circuit. Well, after tomorrow he'd have enough to buy a whole fleet of bikes. But he still wouldn't have as much as Micky. He felt a warm glow at the thought of eight million quids' worth of jewels. Him and Harry could live like kings . . .

* * *

From the outside, Gordon Murphy's council house looked like a tip. Graffiti defaced the walls, and the garden was littered with used beer bottles and empty Coke cans. The curtains were drawn. Harry rang the doorbell and waited, then rang again, before lifting up the letterbox flap. He was about to shout through when he heard someone shuffling to the door. It opened a crack, and he smiled through it.

'Hello, Ma, it's Harry, old friend of Gordon's.'

Mrs Murphy took an age to unlock the door, then without looking at Harry, she turned her walking aid round and began to shuffle back to the kitchen. Harry closed the door and watched her ease her body into the chair. She had aged a lot since he last saw her, but then it had been a long time.

She peered over at him as Harry placed a solid wad of twenties on the table. He got down on his haunches beside her, looking up into her face.

'Gordon won't be back for a while. Just a couple of days. Spot of trouble . . .'

'Yeah, I know. Filth's been in an' out all day. All right, is he?'

'Fine, Ma. We got a top brief working to get him out. He just needs a little while to sort it out, but they can't hold him.'

She smiled, chuckled, then gazed into the fire. 'They got nothin' on him. He wasn't even outside when them raids was done. They should check their bleedin' records – he was in the Scrubs.'

Harry patted her hand. She was still a game old bird. He straightened up, handed her the money and told her to tuck it away safe.

'Have to put it up me drawers, round here. The break-ins . . . If they know my Gordon's not here, they'll try it.'

Harry saw on the mantelshelf the faded picture of himself and Gordon, no more than sixteen, seventeen years of age. It had pride of place, the two boys clutching their cheap fishing rods and smiling into the camera.

'How's that wife o' yours?'

'Fine,' Harry muttered.

She sucked in her breath, looking at him. 'Wish my Gordon could find a good 'un, settle down. Never mind me, it's a wife he wants.'

Harry patted her hand, kissed the top of her head and told her not to bother showing him out. As he reached the door, he said, 'When you see him, tell him he'll be all right, understand? I'll send his wages on, right?'

'That's good of you, son. You've always been a good'un.'

Harry gave her a warm smile. 'Do you mind if I make a call from your phone in the hall before I go?'

'No, love, you go ahead.'

Harry closed the door quietly and crossed to an old beige coloured telephone on a small hall table. He scrunched his eyes. He had always had a phenomenal memory, ever since he was a boy. He could remember the number, but not the code. So he dialled the operator and asked what numbers he should call for Devon. The operator asked if he would like to be put through. Quick as a flash he was able to give Vera Stanley's phone number. He had to wait as it rang numerous times before it was picked up.

'Yes?'

'Is this Vera Stanley?' Harry asked.

'Yes, it is.' Vera didn't recognise the voice, she wondered if it was the landlord as they were behind on rent, but then it didn't sound like him.

'Who is this?' she asked

'I'm a close friend of your sister, Trudie,' Harry said.

'She's not here. I don't know where she is. Who's speaking?'

'Just an old friend wondering if she and the baby are all right.'

'She called not long ago.'

'Do you know where she is?'

'No, I don't. She woke us up in the middle of the night.'

Harry hesitated. 'Sorry to trouble you.' He hung up.

Late as it was, there were two little kids, no more than four or five years old, playing on the kerb when he got to his car.

One looked up. 'Eh, give us a fag, mister?'

Harry laughed at him, at his dirty little face, lips turned down, a scowling pug.

'Fuck you, then . . .'

* * *

Dolly had finally calmed Bella down. She sat with the now dry-eyed Shirley on the sofa. Shirley had seemed more upset by the fact that Micky Tesco had used her and she had been stupid enough to let him than by the fact that she was going to be smack bang in the middle of a robbery.

Dolly had grilled Shirley about the party at Arnie Fisher's club. It looked like Harry was still working in the same old way. She perked up when Shirley mentioned she'd seen Jackie Rawlins there: very interesting. She'd forgotten all about Jackie. Shirley couldn't really remember who else she'd met, so they moved from the party on to the raid, and the biggest question of all: whether Shirley should still take part in the fashion show.

'If I don't, it'll look suspicious. I've got to do it.'

They mulled it over. Dolly even wondered whether Marion Gordon had been paid off by Micky. Shirley could feel the tears coming again. Oh, God, was that all set up too? Had he even arranged that? She started to cry, mostly for her own foolishness. Well, if Marion had been paid by Micky then she didn't want anything to do with her. Her dreams of a professional modelling career were crumbling to dust in front of her eyes. Right from the beginning she had just been the girl on the inside. Even making love to her had been part of the scheme.

'You make damned sure you get the police on to them, Dolly. I hate him.' The tears had stopped and now anger had given her a harder edge. She seemed to gather strength as she went over all the information Micky had pumped out of her. 'The finale – that's the only point when we have all the gems on, every single one of them. And then there's a blackout.' She paused, remembering how Micky had made her go over the blackout sequence, apparently fascinated by exactly what they were doing.

She straightened. 'I reckon that's when they'll do it, Dolly, right at the end of the show, about 10:15.'

Dolly nodded. It all made sense. So now they began to formulate their own plan of action. If Harry and his team weren't going to pull the raid until 10 or 10:15, that gave them time to keep a watch on them at the lock-up, and as soon as they moved out, they could put in a call to the police.

Bella was now on her feet. 'We give them the names we've got so far, the registration numbers of the vans, the bike, everything. But they've got to be picked up when they're just about to do it. If we tip off the cops too soon, they might blow it. But we must give them enough time to stake out the club.' She turned to Shirley. 'Are you going to be able to cope? You know, rehearsing, dressing, acting normal, knowing what's about to happen?'

'Don't worry about me,' Shirley assured her, her face set. 'Just make sure you and Dolly do your bit. We can't make any mistakes this time.'

The three women sat at the table, and Dolly explained everything they'd gleaned from the plans in the lock-up. The most important thing was the bike rider, whose passenger would actually take the jewels from round the girls' necks, put them into the saddlebag, then return with the driver to the lock-up.

'What part is Harry playing? What's he doing?' Shirley asked.

Bella and Dolly looked at each other. That was the one thing they didn't know yet.

Shirley put her head in her hands, sighing. 'Once he's caught, though, then it'll be all over, won't it?'

'And then your money will get sorted,' Dolly assured her. 'Listen, I've got enough cash of my own to cover it. I'll be your fence. I give you my word, on Monday we'll be finished with Harry, you'll have straight money and you can do whatever you want.'

CHAPTER SIX

When Dolly arrived at Shirley's at 7:30 in the morning, she found her sitting in her dressing gown, sipping coffee and staring through the window at the drizzle outside.

'Couldn't sleep, Dolly,' she said, her face pale and drawn.

Bella joined them, dressed in trousers and a sweater, like Dolly. They were ready to take up their position at the lock-up.

'Come on, Dolly, we need to be there in good time. We can't risk being seen,' Bella said. She seemed agitated.

'You'll get the police there on time, won't you?' Shirley asked.

Dolly nodded. She patted Shirley's shoulder. She could feel her shaking beneath the thin dressing gown.

''Course we will,' Dolly answered. 'Now you take care, love. Just do everything like you rehearsed, then we'll see you back here. And don't worry!'

Shirley managed a wobbly smile. *Don't worry!* That was almost funny.

Bella and Dolly left, giving Shirley one final thumbs-up. As the front door closed behind them, Shirley raised the coffee cup to her lips. Her hand was shaking so much she was afraid she was going to drop it. She started to retch and ran to the sink, then stood there, heaving, waiting for the nausea to pass. She really didn't know if she was going to make it through the day.

* * *

Harry looked round Micky's kitchen. It was gleaming, neat, all wooden-fronted units, very modern. He touched it. Definitely real wood. He opened the fridge. It was well stocked. He took out eggs and bacon, some butter, then looked round for the pans. One of the cupboards was stacked with rows and rows of vitamins. Harry picked up a jar, read the label, then put it back. He'd never had time for that sort of crap. He moved to the stove and fiddled with a knob. It was one of those newfangled things, the hot plates just coloured circles. He couldn't work out which ring he'd turned on, so he held his hand out over all of them.

Bloody thing!

*   *   *

Micky was working out in his bedroom, sweating, grunting out press-ups. He could hear Harry moving round the kitchen. The rest of Micky's small flat was like the kitchen, neat and tasteful, devoid of any frills. All very masculine and clean-cut. He had done it on the cheap, by himself, and he was quite proud of the result. His dad had been a carpenter and he knew what he was doing.

Micky could smell bacon cooking. That was usually enough to get him salivating. But this morning his stomach was knotted, his nerves on edge. He didn't think he'd be able to face breakfast. He concentrated on his push-ups: forty-two ... forty-three. He'd hit fifty and call it quits.

Harry yelled from the kitchen that breakfast was up. Micky picked up a towel and wiped himself down. As he walked from the bedroom, he saw Harry's two cases all packed. Micky went back into the bedroom and picked up his own case, placing it beside Harry's, then grabbed a dirty ashtray and emptied it, replacing it with a new one. He hated the smell of stale cigarette smoke. Then he walked into the kitchen. Harry was sitting on a stool at the small table, his plate piled high with eggs, bacon and fried bread. He looked up with his mouth full and indicated with his fork a plate of eggs for Micky.

Micky went over to the cupboard and took down several jars of vitamins, then got himself some fruit juice. He shook a handful of pills into his palm and washed them down with the juice.

Harry raised an eyebrow. 'Don't want you rattling round this afternoon with that lot inside you.'

Micky replaced the jars, then took a cloth and wiped the grease spits from around the cooker. Then he saw the greasy frying pan and suddenly felt nauseous. He took a deep breath, got some honey from the cupboard and spooned it into his coffee, before sitting down opposite Harry.

Harry wiped his plate with his bread and pushed it away. He lit a cigarette.

Micky leant back and wafted the smoke away with his hand.

'Few last-minute details,' Harry began. 'You get the gear, move off on the bike with Brian, as arranged. Get a good distance away from the club, halfway to the lock-up, then give him some crap about having to pull up. You've got to dump him, fast, then turn tail and make it back here. I'll be waiting. We've only got an hour to make that plane. There's another one an hour after, but I'd like to get the first one.'

Micky didn't think he was hearing right. He couldn't make sense of what Harry was saying. He stared, open-mouthed.

Harry pushed Micky's plate of eggs closer to him. 'Something wrong with my cooking, Micky?'

'I'm not with you. Dump him? What d'you mean?'

Harry got up and walked into the lounge, looking for an ashtray. Micky watched him through the open door.

'Just get rid of him. You've got to get back here.'

Micky got up and went to the door. 'What about the lads back at the lock-up? If we're coming back here with the gear, who's paying them off? They're going back to the lock-up.'

Harry gave him a funny look. 'You got fifty grand for any of them? Well? They're coming steaming back to the lock-up, hands out for two hundred and fifty grand. You got it?'

Micky walked further into the room. Harry was now flicking through his passport, the forged one bought from Colin Soal. He seemed relaxed, businesslike. Micky felt the ground opening up under his feet.

'But you can't! You think they'll all just take it? Pull a caper like this and then get shafted? They'll come after us, every bleedin' one of them. Jesus Christ, I wouldn't blame them!'

Harry closed his briefcase and laughed. 'They'll have to find us first, won't they?'

Micky just looked stunned.

'Maybe we'll send them somethin' when we change the gems,' Harry said with a chuckle.

Micky began shaking his head. A few last-minute details. Holy shit.

'What about Jimmy, Jimmy Glazier back in Rio? I mean, he set the whole thing up, didn't he?'

Harry whipped round. '*I* set it up, Micky. Me and no one else. You better remember that.'

Micky followed Harry into the kitchen, watching as he poured himself another coffee. His hands were steady as he picked up the honey pot and stirred in a spoonful.

'I'll try this for a change.'

Micky sat down. The initial shock had worn off and he was starting to think it through.

It was true, they didn't have any cash left, if the sixty grand from the women was all there was. He'd assumed Harry had some more cash stashed away somewhere to bankroll the job. Micky could feel his heart pounding. And what about Rintle? Harry had agreed to give him cash up front, and there was no way they could pull off the job without him.

Then there was himself. Was he going to have to watch his own back now? How was it going to work between them once they'd got the gems?

Harry got up and patted him on the shoulder, as if he was reading his thoughts.

'I did the cooking, Micky. You do the washing up.'

* * *

Ray walked into the kitchen and found Greg leering at the Page Three girl in the paper.

'Right, put that away, son. You need to get cracking and pick up the Transit. You gotta be in position.'

Greg turned the page over. 'No panic, Ray. There's hours to go. I'm not even going to take the van 'til after two.'

Ray leant over the table, his voice a harsh whisper. 'You just get over to the garage and check the van's OK. You gotta get into position in plenty of time, so you need to leave *now*.'

Greg picked up the paper and shoved it under his arm. 'You gettin' the wind up, are ya, Ray?'

Ray clipped him one, then shoved him towards the door, as a sleepy-looking Audrey appeared.

'What you all doin'? You know the time? It's Sunday, for crying out loud.'

Ray gave a half-hearted laugh, flicking Greg a warning look to get going. Greg walked to the back door.

Audrey looked at him. 'Where you goin'?'

Ray patted Greg's shoulder. 'He's got some cars to clean down the garage.'

'See you later then, Ray,' Greg said cheerily.

I bloody well hope so, Ray thought to himself.

Audrey waddled to the fridge and took out eggs and bacon. 'You fancy a fry-up?'

Ray felt his stomach do a flip. 'I'm fine, love.'

'You all right, darlin'? You were up and down half the night, pacing round. You'd think you was having the kid, not me.'

The phone rang, and Ray almost jumped out of his skin. Audrey put her hand on his arm as he reached for it.

'It'll be the woman about the carrycot.'

Ray let out a breath, but his nerves were still jangling.

'Make us some toast, would you, love?' Audrey called, picking up the phone. Ray's hand shook so much he could cut nothing better than a huge doorstep.

'She wants fifty quid!' Audrey yelled to him. 'It's a pram and carrycot combined. In mulberry!' She came back into the kitchen. 'She wants an answer now; got another woman after it. Sounds nice, Ray. Mulberry . . . What shall I tell her?'

Ray pulled out a wad of notes, then took out two twenties and a ten. Audrey blew him a kiss and went back to the phone. Moments later she came back in, beaming.

'We can go over and pick it up this afternoon.'

Ray had to get out. 'Sorry, love, better get over to the garage. Tell her we'll pick it up tomorrow, all right?'

Audrey shrugged, went over to the toaster and looked at the slice of bread stuck halfway in. She shook her head. 'I dunno – men can't do a thing. Not even slice a bit of bread.'

Ray moved behind her, held her close and kissed her neck. She turned round in his arms.

'I can really feel him moving. Put your hand on him.'

Ray felt like crying. He touched her belly, could feel nothing but a big lump, but he said he felt him, felt his son. Then he kissed Audrey, gripping her tight.

'Gerroff, you soft bugger.'

He went to the door and gave her a little wave, before walking out.

Audrey stared after him. Funny feller. But one thing was for sure, he was going to make a great father, if the way he took care of her was anything to go by. She felt all warm and loving as she picked up the £50. At last she had a man that treated her right, who really loved her. She began singing, then had to sit down as she felt a sharp pain.

'Oh, you're a tough little bugger, aren't you? Just like your dad.'

* * *

Dolly had parked her car a safe distance away and they walked warily to their lock-up before slipping inside. She and Bella moved along the wall into position and listened. Next door was empty, dark and silent.

* * *

Amanda's nightclub, by contrast, was already a hive of activity. A Bronze Security wagon was parked at the main entrance and two guards were carrying a small box up the steps to the main entrance. Standing watching was the club's own chucker-out, Steve, wearing his smartest suit for the occasion. He eyed the guards as they passed him and headed across the reception area, then up the stairs towards the main club room and the offices. The club manager, Brian Shellskin, was also watching the proceedings. As the guards passed him he laid a hand on Steve's muscular arm.

'That's the last.'

'Yes, and those two will stay as added security.'

'Good. Now, remember, absolutely no one is allowed to enter the club without a pass. Only the names on the clipboard list are to be admitted, and you must double-check the names and passes before allowing anyone up the stairs.'

Steve nodded. 'I've got it. All the models are already checked in. They're upstairs.'

Shellskin seemed satisfied. He fussed over a huge floral display at the entrance, picked up a dried leaf carried in on the shoes of one of the security guards and handed it to Steve before going upstairs to the club. Steve looked at the leaf, tossed it back onto the carpet and sat down. One of the security guards came down the stairs. He picked up the clipboard and flipped through the names. It was going to be a long old day.

*   *   *

Dolly was up on the orange box, peering through the hole. Men crossed and recrossed her line of vision, getting into security guard uniforms.

'Aren't they getting ready a bit early?' Dolly whispered to Bella.

'You remember what they're like,' Bella whispered back. 'They'll be in and out of those uniforms ten times before they're ready.'

Dolly chewed her lip and went back to staring through the hole. She saw Harry pass across, holding a security helmet in his hand. So he *was* going to be on the raid himself. She tried hard to get him into focus.

Harry carried the helmet over to Harvey Rintle and took him to one side. With a look over his shoulder to see if they were being watched, he picked up a small holdall and opened it. It was full of cash.

'Just take it, put it where you want it, all right?'

Rintle took the holdall, had a look inside and zipped it up.

Harry let out a breath. If Rintle had dug down below the surface layer he would have found nothing but cut-up newspaper. Harry then walked over to Kevin White.

'Make sure you keep your visor down at all times, yeah?'

Kevin nodded, buckled his belt and picked up his helmet.

Micky was over by the shotguns, checking them out, cocking them, packing them with small capsules of rice. They wouldn't actually blow someone away, but they'd hear a bang and feel the impact – think they'd been hit.

Ray, wearing rubber gloves, was washing down the Transit van, cleaning all the prints off it.

Harry was now standing right under the wall by Dolly and Bella. They couldn't see if he was wearing a uniform or not, but Dolly was going on the assumption that he was, since she'd seen him with the security helmet. Then she heard his voice, almost as if he was speaking to her.

'We roll in fifteen minutes – everyone stand by.'

Dolly gasped. The men looked as if they were moving out. Shirley must have got it wrong; they were moving out *now*. She almost fell off the box, pushing Bella ahead of her.

'They're going. We need to get outta here fast!'

They made it out of the lock-up and sprinted across the road. As they ducked out of sight, the big door of Harry's lock-up slid back. The Transit van moved out, with Ray Bates at the wheel. Sitting in the back of the van were Johnny Summers, Micky Tesco and Kevin White.

Harvey Rintle then walked out, wheeling his bike. He crossed over the road and put it into the back of a small van, along with the holdall. Standing at the door, Harry saw Jackie in the driver's seat as the van drove off. Rintle then jumped into the Transit. Harry closed the doors behind him, banged once with his fist, and the van pulled away. Harry turned as Brian Fisk wheeled the motorbike out. Harry smiled, pulling the heavy door closed. Brian hopped onto the bike.

'See you later, Mr Rawlins.'

Harry looked at him. 'Yeah, remember the van's got to be in position before you take a look round the place.'

'Don't worry, Mr Rawlins, I'll be there in plenty of time on this baby.'

Harry patted him on the arm. 'Take it easy, eh, Brian? We don't want any aggro. Just take it nice and slow.'

Brian turned in the saddle, his boyish young face beaming. 'You can trust me, Mr Rawlins.'

Harry was already back in the lock-up by the time the bike sped off. He had to clear everything away, burn the plans and make sure there was not a scrap of evidence to lead anyone back to him.

* * *

Dolly made it to the car first, with Bella close on her heels. The car was already moving as Bella slammed her door closed, and Dolly put her foot down as they headed for the nearest phone booth. As they pulled up, Bella was already out, yanking open the booth door.

'It's dead! The bloody phone's dead!'

* * *

Trudie was running out of money. She had paid the hotel bill, afraid that if she stayed any longer she would not be able to afford a ticket home. Her depression and her loneliness were making her drink too much, and she had started to find caring for the baby emotionally draining. Uppermost, though, was the fear that something terrible had happened to Harry and he wasn't coming for her. She had even detected suspicious glances at the hotel reception as she continued asking if someone had tried to reach her. She called her sister, again not considering the time. Vera answered, having been woken.

'Vera, it's me, Trudie.'

'Jesus Christ, do you know what time it is?'

Trudie started to cry. 'I'm sorry, I'm sorry, I just needed to tell you I'm coming home. But has anyone tried to call me?'

Vera had a coughing fit as she stood in the hallway in her night-dress, reaching for cigarettes. 'Yeah, we did have someone bloody call here. Never left his name, but he was asking after you and where you were.'

'What did you tell him?'

'What could I tell him? I don't know where you are.'

'It's very important, Vera, that if he calls again you tell him I'm coming home and I'll be at your place.'

'He asked after the baby,' Vera said, 'but he wouldn't give his name. Are you with Jimmy? That no good bloody husband of yours?'

Trudie hesitated and then lied, 'Yeah, I'm with Jimmy, but I'm coming home, all right?'

She hung up. Vera lit a cigarette. She suspected Trudie was in trouble, she usually was. And that so-called failure of a racing driver that was her husband would probably be part of her problems. Vera was sick to death of always having to pick up the pieces for Trudie. It sounded like she'd have to put up with her living in her flat. She was not going to enjoy telling her partner when he came off night duty.

*   *   *

The main office was now the girls' dressing room. Extra lights had been placed round the makeshift make-up tables and racks of dresses lined up. The dresser was carefully checking that the accessories to go with each garment were tagged and listed: belts, scarves, shoes – everything ready for the quick changes.

It was organised chaos. The girls were at various stages of dressing and undressing, while hairdressers teased and set hair, Carmen rollers everywhere, hairdryers blowing. Make-up artists were equally busy painting faces and bodies. From down in the club, music could be heard, the hubbub of voices, people rushing in and out.

Shirley had been made up and her hair was being backcombed into a high punk style, sprayed with golden highlights. Myra was having a fit over a dress that she screamed had been designed for a stuffed elephant.

Standing at the door with her clipboard was Mrs Harper, the petite but fearsome-looking woman in charge of the jewel collection. She had to shout at the top of her voice to be heard over the babble as she began calling the order of the girls to accompany her to the main office for the jewels to be matched with the outfits.

Myra and Shirley were first.

'Please get a move on, girls!' she shouted. 'The press have already started to arrive.'

All the noise had given Shirley a stabbing pain in one eye, while the girl was pulling at her hair mercilessly, moulding it into shape.

Jukko screamed her name. She still wasn't in her dress, and the dresser bustled over and started to shake out a delicate, shiny silk and chiffon gown.

Myra was now dressed and moving towards the door, yelling that she had asked to wear the chiffon, but they'd stuck her in a ghastly-looking old sack! She stormed out.

Inside the club it was a different kind of bedlam: the final drapes were being hammered round the catwalk, floral displays had been plonked on every available table, as the tables had not been dressed yet, and the rows and rows of gilt chairs sat tiered, ready to be placed round the catwalk. All the while the music belted out, while the constant comings and goings of dressers and models made the room seem like a bus station during rush hour.

A group of pressmen sat round a table drinking coffee, cigarette smoke creating a haze above their heads. They were checking cameras, complaining about being kept hanging round, while keeping a professional eye on all the half-naked women running in and out. Among them was Colin Soal, unshaven, relaxed, wearing a raincoat, and sporting his press card and pass. Twice he looked over to the fire exit doors, then got up and stretched.

'Just going to see what's the best angle to get the girls, eh?' he said with a dirty laugh, before going on a casual wander round the club.

On instinct, the pressmen all looked up. One of the models, wearing only a long skirt, was yelling for Jukko. One of them managed to aim his camera, but the model had already run back into the dressing room.

Colin Soal held his camera to his eye while backing carefully towards the fire exit door. He quietly released the crossbar, all the time making out that he was just trying to get a good shot of the catwalk. Then he moved off to fire exit number two. He needn't have worried about the two security guards standing on duty outside the manager's office; their eyes were out on stalks as one half-naked woman after another rushed past. He released the bar on fire exit number two just as one of the guards was holding the office door open for Shirley.

* * *

At King's Cross Station, Dolly was running from one phone booth to another, but they were all out of order. The only one that seemed to be working was occupied – a big man in a raincoat talking loudly on it. Bella stood outside and glared at him, but he just turned his back.

'Emergency!' Dolly shouted desperately, banging her fist on the side of the booth.

The man took one look at the wild-eyed woman outside and quickly put the phone in its cradle. Bella pushed past him into the booth and started dialling.

* * *

Shirley stood at the manager's desk, which was draped with a large piece of black velvet on which the jewels were laid out, some tagged, matching earrings, necklaces and bracelets grouped together. Myra, adorned in emeralds, was moodily complaining about the weight pulling on her earlobes.

'Emeralds, diamonds and gold cluster,' noted Mrs Harper.

'I don't give a fuck – they're killing me!' she moaned, but Mrs Harper just shooed her away and motioned for Shirley to move closer. She studied her for a moment, then spoke to a small, immaculately dressed man seated at the desk.

'The diamonds, I think, with this dress.'

The small man nodded, replying to Mrs Harper in French. She laughed and placed the diamonds round Shirley's neck.

Shirley could see what Myra was complaining about: they *were* heavy. Mrs Harper added earrings, then slipped a bracelet on to Shirley's wrist and stood back. Speaking in French to the dapper little man, she looked her up and down, gesturing for her to turn. Satisfied, she made a note on her board and sent Shirley to the catwalk.

As she reached the door, Mrs Harper stopped her. 'Oh, Shirley . . .'

Shirley felt her heart miss a beat.

'As soon as they've photographed that set, come straight back – just security. Thank you, dear.' She beckoned the next model in, a Chinese girl.

Shirley walked out and took her place at the far end of the catwalk. Myra was up ahead of her, posing for single shots, muttering all the time about the wankers clicking away below her. Shirley reckoned she must be wearing over a million pounds' worth of diamonds and she could feel the watchful eyes of the two security guards behind her. The Chinese model was moving up behind her, covered in pearls.

As Myra finished her session and slouched back up the ramp, she goosed Shirley, snorting at the Chinese girl as she passed.

'You dive down for all those pearls, darling? Your hair looks as if you did.'

The girl turned to give Myra a mouthful, but Myra was already being whisked into the office, her dresser standing by with her change of dress.

Shirley stood at the end of the ramp, turning, smiling, holding poses the way Myra did it. The cameras clicked away, while Mrs Harper started giving detailed descriptions of the gems to the photographers.

* * *

Bella had almost reached screaming point. The police had put her through to various different stations, each one asking the caller's name and what department she wanted.

Dolly snatched the phone. They were now through to Kensington Police Station. Dolly didn't care which bloody department they were talking to, she just barked out names – Harry Rawlins being number one – and the details of the raid.

'Never mind my name, just bloody listen! There's a raid, understand me, an armed raid on Amanda's nightclub, *and it's happening right now!*'

Dolly slammed down the phone and ran across the train station.

'Come on! We've got to get to the club and warn Shirley to get out of there.'

* * *

Kevin White took only a few moments to spring open the local telephone control box and find what he was looking for. He knew exactly what he was doing, and started slicing through the wires that served the club and its surrounding area.

The men waiting inside the Transit van watched nervously. He was taking too long. Ray looked round, the sweat pouring down his face. He had the van moving as Kevin jumped aboard. Next stop: Amanda's nightclub.

'You sure it's all cut?' Rintle asked.

'I know what I'm doing. You just take care of your own side of things,' White snapped back.

Micky Tesco patted White's knee to calm him down, and gave a warning look to Rintle to shut it. Johnny Summers, shotgun resting across his knee, stared calmly out of the window. At least the rain had eased off; that was something in their favour, making the fire escape run less hazardous.

* * *

Brian Fisk was the first to arrive at the club. He parked his bike on the street and walked casually into the club's forecourt through the 'In' gate, where a few parked cars were scattered round the horseshoe pathway. He knew the guard at the front entrance was watching him but continued looking over the cars.

'Know where the kitchens are, mate?'

The guard pointed round the back, watching as Brian, walking unhurriedly, moved round the horseshoe, past the 'Out' gate and down the small alley into the wide access area by the kitchens.

The building work was still only half-completed, but there was no one around. He looked at the closed-up garages, then wandered over to the trees, giving the whole area a careful once-over. Then he froze.

'Oi, you! What you want?'

A guard was leaning on the basement stairs at the rear entrance of the kitchens.

'Just looking for a toilet,' Brian shouted.

'Well, look somewhere else,' the guard told him, waving him away.

Brian shrugged and walked off, back down the alley, into the forecourt and through the 'Out' area on to the street where the Transit van was in position, waiting. Fisk wandered back to his bike, giving a little 'All clear' signal as he passed the van. He sat astride his bike and waited, turning to watch a green Fiesta slowly driving past.

* * *

Dolly was hunched over the wheel as Bella scanned the front of the club.

'Shit, Dolly, we're too late. They're already here!'

Dolly could feel the sweat running from her armpits as she gripped the steering wheel tightly. In the rear view mirror she could see the Transit van and the motorbike.

Dolly drove on, then took a left, aiming to go round the block and come back on to the road behind them.

'Where in Christ's name are the police?' she cursed.

* * *

Jukko was standing on the stage, shouting down to the photographers and press below.

'OK, now for the finale! Get ready for the spectacular lighting effects!'

The girls were grouped at the end of the ramp. Mrs Harper was explaining to the press that the girls were now wearing all the gems, more than eight million pounds' worth of diamonds, rubies and emeralds. Her voice droned on, explaining each piece's history, which jewellers had loaned what . . .

It was time for Colin Soal to make a move. He began shaking his camera.

'Shit!' He shrugged. 'Bleedin' shutter's frozen,' he muttered and wandered off towards the exit, giving a couple of waves to his colleagues, who were more intent on getting into position for the big final display.

Colin passed the two watching guards standing by the manager's office and out, past Steve, who stood up and stretched.

'All over, is it?'

'Not quite.' Colin smiled. 'But my camera's packed in. It's all right, though – I've got enough.'

He went down the front steps, even stopping to exchange a few words with a security guard, then he walked casually out of the 'In' gate and crossed the road.

The men waiting in the Transit were following his every move intently. They knew they were close now, very close.

'Why doesn't he get a bloody move on?' Kevin White muttered nervously as they began pulling up their visors, checking their guns, their hands already beginning to sweat inside their gloves.

Colin jumped up into the van without a word and began pulling off his raincoat, revealing his security uniform underneath. Micky held out his helmet. Now it was Harvey Rintle's turn . . .

Micky checked the radio one more time and gave him the signal. Rintle tapped his radio, the doors opened and he stepped down.

All the men now watched Rintle, with his visor up, move into the forecourt via the 'Out' gate, out of sight of the guard on duty at the main entrance, who was busy proferring a cigarette to Steve, the two men chatting easily as if their day was almost done.

* * *

Kensington Police Station was by now a hive of furious activity, with DI Frinton at the centre of it, barking out orders left, right and centre. The details of the raid were still sketchy, but all the names they'd been given by the anonymous caller had checked out. This was looking more and more like the real thing, and Frinton was urgently calling for backup from Notting Hill, Cromwell Road – anywhere that had spare bodies they could use. Lurking at the back of his mind was the fear that the whole thing was a hoax, and he was going to end up with egg on his face, but when they were unable to contact the club on the phone, the conviction hardened that they really were dealing with an armed robbery in progress. As every available car sped to the scene, Frinton gave strict orders that no one was to go in and try and be a hero – just seal off the area and await instructions.

As he left the station and got into his own waiting patrol car, Frinton's gut tightened and he felt his heart racing. He knew full well if he messed this one up, his career would be over. On the other hand, if he was responsible for foiling an £8 million jewel heist, his name would be up in lights: no more soddin' Kensington nick for him – he'd be playing with the big boys from now on.

As the car accelerated towards the club, he told himself to focus on the job in hand, not get ahead of himself. He quickly got on the radio.

'Keep the pandas back. Let the unmarked cars go in first. Remember, we have every reason to believe this lot are armed and dangerous!'

A fresh-faced young officer in the back seat asked about the Chief – had anyone been able to contact him?

Frinton turned in the front seat. 'If you fancy scouring the golf course you might find him, but right now we've got better things to do.'

*　*　*

Vic Morgan arrived at Shirley's wearing his new jacket and carrying a big bunch of roses. He'd already tried Dolly's flat, but she wasn't there. As he pressed and held the doorbell for the fourth time with no response, he had to acknowledge she wasn't here either. He turned back to the street, wondering what to do. Talk about being all dressed up with nowhere to go.

Then he had a thought: perhaps he'd go and pay a visit to old Resnick. He'd had so much else on his mind, he'd almost forgotten about him. He looked down at the roses. At least they'd make a change from sodding grapes.

*　*　*

'What's he bloody doing? Why doesn't he get on with it?' Kevin White muttered from inside the van as they watched Rintle, his visor down now, taking his time to move round to the side of the building, then along to the front steps of the club. The security guard stubbed out his cigarette, before returning to his position.

Rintle stepped out in front of him. 'Got a problem with this,' he said, holding the radio out.

The guard might not have seen Rintle before, but he was wearing the same uniform. He reached for his own radio, and Rintle brought his right knee up sharply between the guard's legs, then as he doubled over with a grunt, swung an elbow into his temple. It connected with a sickening crack, and the guard slumped to the ground. Rintle quickly lifted the body up and heaved it over the side of the stairs. He turned, glancing quickly back at the van, and entered the club.

Steve was facing the stairs, listening to the rock music belting out. Rintle tapped him on the shoulder, and as the guard turned round, he dealt him such a flurry of fierce blows to the head and neck that he quickly collapsed in an unmoving heap. Rintle got his arms under Steve's shoulders and heaved him up into a sitting position, so it looked as if he was just taking a break, then picked up his radio.

'Time to roll, fellas.'

* * *

Dolly saw the van move through the 'In' gate into the forecourt. They were too late to warn Shirley. All they could do now was watch.

* * *

The Transit moved into the side alley. Micky was first out, followed by Kevin White with the shotgun. Micky strolled towards the kitchen. He looked through the railings, and there was the guard, standing in the basement by the door.

Micky called down. 'I think we've got a problem out front.'

'What are you on about?' the guard grumbled, climbing the steps. As soon as he was within reach, Micky's right hand shot out, grabbing the man's windpipe and squeezing for all he was worth. The guard grabbed on to Micky's arm and Micky could feel his grip weakening – then Kevin White slipped behind him and smashed the guard on the back of the neck with the shotgun barrel. Micky grabbed the guard's radio and stomped it under his heel. Then, with the unconscious man held between them, they moved down the steps to the kitchens.

Micky got on the radio to Rintle. 'Hold your position.' Then to the waiting van: 'Go!'

The Transit van, with Ray behind the wheel, hurtled into the yard behind the club, and Terry Summers and Colin Soal leapt out. They legged it up the fire escape, each stopping to wait at his allotted door.

The kitchen staff turned to look as the body of the guard was pushed into the room. He fell heavily, his helmet crashing against a table leg. Micky swung the shotgun round.

'On the floor – *now!*'

The four men and two girls didn't need telling twice, throwing themselves to the ground.

The guard was coming round. Kevin White hauled him up, flung him across the table and pointed his shotgun between the man's spreadeagled legs.

Micky kicked one of the kitchen staff in the ribs. 'You lot stay down!' he shouted. 'Now put your hands out in front of you!'

'I've got this lot covered. Go!' White shouted, and Micky darted out through the door.

* * *

The girls were sashaying down the catwalk, most of the dressers and staff crowded round the ramp to watch the show. This was the climax, and the volume of the music went up a notch, helping to build the excitement as the lights blinked on and off, the spotlights picking out the pouting faces festooned with sparkling gems. Press cameras flashed crazily, the men yelling for the girls to come down the ramp again together. They moved back, then walked forward again, the music pounding all the while.

Rintle watched the two guards outside the office door, their attention focused on the catwalk. Where the hell was the rest of the team? Any minute now all the goddamn lights were going to come back on.

Then he heard the crash as Johnny Summers kicked open the doors, screaming at the top of his voice. At the same time Colin Soal barged through the second fire exit. Still yelling, Johnny fired two shots into the ceiling.

The whole place went mad.

Rintle caught the security guards on the blind side as they ran towards the ramp, hitting the first one with a vicious punch to the neck that sent him to the floor. The second guard checked his run and managed to grab Rintle from behind. Rintle dropped a knee, pivoted and swung him round, just as the first guard got to his feet. Rintle kicked out viciously, connecting with his groin, then put his hands round the second guard's neck and twisted hard. As he flopped, doll-like, to the floor, he lashed out at the first guard's head with a boot, making contact with a sickening crunch. He dragged the inert bodies towards the office door, just as it opened, revealing the open-jawed stare of a terrified little man. Rintle shoved the guards inside and locked the door.

Down below, the women were screaming like alley cats and most of the pressmen were instinctively lying face down. Colin Soal was pushing and shoving those still on their feet, shouting out orders, kicking the men's legs from underneath them. Rintle joined him. They now had the room more or less covered.

The models were darting this way and that like a flock of crazed birds, their brightly coloured feathers flapping, jewels sparkling in the flashing strobe lights. Most of them huddled together in the centre of the ramp, where they were confronted by Micky Tesco. He wore a bag at his side, already open for him to drop the jewels in. A hysterical Mrs Harper made a lunge for him. He grabbed her by the hair and swung her over the side of the ramp. She fell badly, her head hitting the side of one of the gilt chairs. The floral displays were falling like ninepins, showering petals on the people scrambling round on the floor. Pressmen tried to save their cameras, as tables, flowers and chairs crashed around them.

Above it all, standing there calmly, Johnny Summers surveyed the room, then pointed up to the boy on the lights.

'Get down here now!' he screamed, barely audible above the blaring music, the vocalist bellowing out: *'Let's dance with the moonlight in our eyes . . .'*

Then the tape ran out, and the music was replaced by a whining, crunching noise, as if the band were being put through a mincer.

Micky was snatching necklaces and bracelets off the models. They tried desperately to help, ridding themselves of the cursed gems with fumbling fingers. He had already torn one of the girls' lobes as he ripped off the earrings. They were crying, desperate to save themselves, terrified of being hurt – all except Myra. With a scream she went straight for Micky, and just as it looked as if she was going to claw his eyes, he brought his hand up hard and punched her in the jaw, before viciously tearing at her earrings. Despite the pain, she tried to fight him off, screaming at him to let her take them out. But Micky didn't have the time to mess around and continued pulling.

Shirley grabbed hold of Myra. 'Don't fight him!' she pleaded, terrified that Micky was going to do her real harm.

Micky finally got what he was after, leaving Myra sobbing, with her hands to her ears.

Then it was Shirley's turn. His eyes were glazed and he showed no sign that he recognised her; all he could think of was what was round her throat. Her skin was slashed by the diamonds as he tore them away and she screamed in pain. She already had her hands full with the ring, the bracelet and earrings, just wanting him to take them and leave her alone.

He grabbed the jewels, but instead of letting her go, he pulled her wrist as he started walking backwards, using her as a shield. She fell over the side of the ramp and he hauled her back. She was sobbing now, stumbling over the long frock. He grabbed her hair and, like a caveman, dragged her back towards the kitchens.

Harvey Rintle did a slow move backwards, ready to take off for the front exit. Now Johnny Summers did likewise, knocking over a chair as he backed towards his exit route. He turned to Colin Soal, who was also making slow, steady progress to the fire exit.

Micky half dragged, half pushed Shirley into the kitchens, his pouch bulging with jewels.

Kevin White turned. 'Drop the fucking girl, Micky, and get the hell out!' he shouted.

As the shotgun aimed away from him, the guard on the table saw his chance, slid off the table and made a grab for it. Still holding Shirley, Micky tried to pull a .38 revolver from his waistband. As Kevin swung back in front of him, with the guard desperately hanging on to the shotgun, Micky lost his balance, fell against Shirley, and the gun went off. Screams came from the kitchen staff, still face down on the floor. His head spinning, Micky just ran, almost knocking Kevin over in his desperation to get out and save his skin.

* * *

Outside, Ray Bates had done a slow U-turn round the big yard and was now waiting near the alley for the men to get into the van. The last one to be picked up would be Harvey Rintle, round at the front door.

Brian Fisk was in position right outside the kitchen exit, engine ticking over. All Micky had to do was jump aboard, then they'd be away.

* * *

Shirley slid in slow motion down the cold, tiled wall to the floor. As the two men ran from the kitchen, the chef raised his head from the floor, then gasped in horror. The front of Shirley's dress was a deep red, the stain spreading slowly across the chiffon as he watched. He looked at the girl; from her expression she seemed to be asking him if it had really happened. She looked down at her blood-soaked dress, then back to him.

'Dear God, he's shot her!'

He got to his knees and crawled across to her. The girl put her hand out to him, tears rolling down her cheeks. 'Dolly . . .'

As soon as she said the word, he knew he would never forget it. Was she pathetically asking for a child's dolly in her last moments? He crawled nearer. She was like a doll herself, he thought, her head on one side, leaning against the white-tiled wall, her beautiful face calm, eyes wide open, the heavy make-up accentuating the toy-like appearance. The terrible red stain continued to spread, now on to the white kitchen floor.

* * *

Johnny Summers made it to the fire escape. He could see Colin Soal below him, already on the move, and way below him there was Kevin White, running from the kitchen. The bike roared as Micky Tesco shovelled the jewels into the saddlebag, then jumped on. The bike tilted for a moment, then slowly moved towards the Transit, still standing with its back doors open.

Dolly was standing by the side of the car when the first police car screeched through the 'In' gate of the club. Ray crashed through the gears, starting to move the van towards the 'Out' gate, but he was cut off by the patrol car just as Kevin White, Johnny Summers and Colin Soal threw themselves into the back of the Transit.

Seeing the hold-up in the alley, Rintle turned and made a run for it, but Frinton was quickly out of the car and right behind him, bringing him down in a crunching rugby tackle. But he couldn't hold him. Rintle scrambled up, desperately looking for a way out, but before he could decide which way to go, another squad car pulled up and three policemen spilt out. He braced himself, but even he couldn't beat those odds, and he was soon on his knees, the three coppers hanging on for dear life.

The men in the van saw what happened to Rintle and could hear the squeal of brakes as more police cars arrived. They knew they were done.

Micky was luckier. Brian squeezed the bike through the gap between the van and the wall, Micky's leg scraping painfully against it, and then they were bouncing over the grass verge. They hit the kerb hard, Brian made a sharp turn, almost losing his passenger before righting the bike, then opened the throttle and let rip.

Dolly and Bella watched helplessly as the bike screamed past them. Then they turned their attention to the scene of chaos outside the club. Frinton, holding a handkerchief to his bloody nose, was shouting instructions to the second group of officers, whose car was blocking the 'Out' gate, to move the Transit. The captured men were lying on their stomachs, with their arms and legs apart as they were searched and handcuffed, along with Rintle, who was still snorting and snarling like a raging bull.

Bella grabbed Dolly's arm.

'Get back in the car! We need to follow the bike!'

'Harry, I can't see Harry . . .' Dolly was desperate, breathing in short, sharp gasps.

Bella grabbed her and shoved her into the car. 'For Christ's sake, they're getting away!'

Hardly knowing what she was doing, Dolly started the car and took off after the bike.

As the patrol car was also turning to follow the bike, the chef ran into the alley, hysterically pleading for an ambulance. Seeing the men being led into the patrol cars, he suddenly made a grab for the handcuffed Kevin White and tried to land a punch, his face distorted with anger. A policeman held him off, but White ducked instinctively, hitting his head on the bonnet of the car.

Frinton approached the kitchens with two plain-clothed officers, picking their way through the discarded shotguns and helmets, the debris of a failed heist. They ran down into the basement. Immediately surrounded by hysterical kitchen staff and the traumatised security guard, it was a few moments before Frinton saw the crumpled figure, lying on the floor in a spreading pool of blood. Shoving the people away from around Shirley, Frinton got down on his knees. Even before he touched her, he knew the girl was dead, but he still felt for the pulse at the side of her neck, his hand shaking. At his touch, as if brought back to life, she started to slide sideways and he instinctively reached out to cradle her in his arms. He had seen his fair share of dead bodies, but it never got any easier; there was still that sudden twist inside him. She seemed weightless in his arms, almost childlike. He could hear the siren of the approaching ambulance, but there was nothing anyone could do.

Frinton turned away from the body as two ambulance men ran down the basement steps with a stretcher. As they approached Frinton, he shook his head.

'She's dead.'

* * *

Bella craned forward in the seat, eyes glued to the road. 'I can't see them!'

Dolly couldn't see the bike either, but she crossed Park Lane, followed the traffic round and drove into the park from Marble

Arch. Then she spotted them, already turning through the big curve, moving fast, weaving in and out of the traffic.

Bella grabbed her arm. 'Come on, Dolly!'

Dolly put her foot down. They were already doing seventy and as the needle flicked upwards, they began to overtake the rest of the traffic, almost overshooting the left-hand turn into the park before Lancaster Gate, as an oncoming car shot across in front of them and skidded into the roundabout. Dolly instinctively slowed but Bella practically shoved her foot back to the floor, and they carried on, picking up more speed, Dolly gripping the wheel, her knuckles white, beads of sweat appearing on her forehead as she tried to keep control of the car – just managing to avoid a head-on collision with a car coming the other way, horns blaring as people stopped and stared.

The bike raced through the park, across the Serpentine, and jumped the lights at Exhibition Road before racing away – with Dolly and Bella close behind. Dolly started slowing for the lights, then changed her mind before Bella could do it for her, narrowly missing a bus coming from their right as they veered after the bike.

'I can still see it!' Bella screamed.

Dolly was driving like a mad thing, all sense of danger gone. Eighty-five, ninety, tyres screeching as they shot between two parking meters and back on to Exhibition Road.

* * *

Hearing the noise behind them, Micky looked back over his shoulder.

'Turn right – into Cromwell Road!' he shouted.

The bike had to pull to the left as roadworks forced the traffic into a single line.

'Do a U-turn!' Micky bellowed.

Brian manoeuvred the bike alongside the kerb, shot across the path of an oncoming car, then made a wide U-turn. He saw the coach out of the corner of his eye and opened up the throttle to weave past it, but skidded on the new gravel from the roadworks and, hampered by Micky not leaning into the turn, slid sideways. Brian kicked out with his leg to try and right the bike, Micky leant over, and the next thing the bike was skidding directly towards the oncoming front wheels of the coach.

The coach driver slammed his brakes on hard, throwing his passengers forwards in their seats, but the bike kept on coming, and he braced himself for the inevitable crunch of metal on metal.

Brian took the full weight of the impact, his upper body smashed against the huge wheels of the coach, while the bike buckled beneath him. Micky was thrown on to the side of the road, his helmet crashing into the raised kerb. He felt the visor splintering, cutting into his face, while his left arm twisted out of its socket with a sickening snapping sound.

The coach driver jumped down, shaking, his face ashen, saying over and over that there was nothing he could do.

'The boy drove right at me!'

Traffic began to build up as people ran from their cars to see if they could help. A driver ran to Micky Tesco, who lay moaning, one hand clutched to his helmet, the blood running down onto his chest.

Bella was out of the car and running towards the coach. As she pulled up she could see, between the legs of the onlookers, the open carrier on the side of the crushed bike. She began pushing her way through.

Micky was now sitting up, the helmet being eased off his head. He could hear voices desperately shouting: 'Ambulance! For Chrissake get an ambulance!'

He wiped the blood out of his eyes, his head beginning to clear. The pain in his shoulder was like a red-hot vice squeezing him. Then he saw the black girl – watched her reach down under the coach to where the bike had gone. No one seemed to see her do it – their eyes were riveted to the twisted metal and the crushed, lifeless body of Brian Fisk, everyone talking and gesticulating wildly.

A police siren wailed as a motorbike patrol rider arrived at the scene and began moving the traffic on, the jam now stretching almost to the park. Micky was up on his feet, shoving away the helping hands of the driver. He pushed through the pain as he staggered towards the girl.

Dolly was being waved on by the police officer. She could hear the siren of an approaching police car. Bella was now running back and Dolly inched the car forward. Bella jumped in and they slowly passed the policeman, the traffic ahead still moving at a snail's pace.

'I got 'em, I got 'em!'

Bella held out the jewel bag for Dolly to see, then felt the car door open beside her. Micky Tesco was jogging alongside her, hanging on to the door, his face covered in blood, eyes crazed. The traffic suddenly opened up and they were able to move faster. Tesco still ran alongside, screaming incoherently as the car picked up speed. He hung on for a moment, then fell, dragged along the ground for a few seconds before eventually releasing his hold.

Dolly and Bella were past Harrods now. Twisting round in her seat, Bella couldn't make out what had happened to Micky through the cars crawling along behind them. All she could see was the flashing lights of an ambulance.

Bella held up a diamond necklace. She laughed, dangling it in front of Dolly's face. 'Look! We got them! We got them!'

Dolly's voice was flat, expressionless. 'Harry . . . they didn't get him, I know it.'

* * *

The police motorbike was parked outside Harry's lock-up, radio crackling. The doors opened and the officer walked out. He picked up the radio.

'The place is empty.'

* * *

Greg was starting to get nervous. He'd started up the engine, even though there was no sight of the men. He had a feeling they weren't coming and wondered what to do. Ray must have got it wrong. He had a moment of panic that he was in the wrong place, and although he'd checked it already five or six times, he took out the A-Z and checked yet again. While Greg was flicking through the pages, the unmarked police car pulled up directly behind him. The officer was at the driver's door before Greg knew what was happening. He didn't look much older than Greg.

'Your friends aren't coming, son. You might as well come on out. You're nicked.'

* * *

Trudie caught a flight home from Sydney. This time was very different from her experience in first class. She was in economy with the baby on her knee and a very overweight man sitting next to her who had become intolerant as the child kicked and cried until Trudie was able to get a stewardess to heat up a bottle for him. Just the thought of the long flight ahead and the train journey to Devon filled her with trepidation. She had only £1,500 left.

* * *

It was a job no one liked to do – telling a parent or a relative about the death of a loved one. But why did they always have to give it to the female officer?

Janet Adam straightened her cap, walked up the path of Shirley Miller's house and rang the bell. Behind her the officer in the car gave her a look of encouragement.

Thanks a lot, mate, she thought.

Dolly and Bella were about to pull up when they saw the car. Dolly took her foot off the brake and kept going, resisting the urge to watch the policewoman ringing Shirley's doorbell. Dolly took the first left and stopped the car. For a moment neither woman could speak. Dolly was the first, her voice tight.

'Maybe they're just questioning her.'

Bella started panicking. 'She'll talk, Dolly, you know it. She couldn't hold out, not Shirley.'

Dolly was clenching and unclenching her hands, trying desperately to think what their next move should be.

Bella was getting more and more hysterical by the second. 'My clothes – everything – it's all in the house. My bloody passport!'

Dolly went pale. 'Is there anything there about me, where I'm staying, Bella? Bella, listen to me!'

Bella was crying now. 'I can't remember, Dolly.'

'A bit of paper with my address?'

'I don't remember!' A wrenching sob escaped her. 'We've had it, Dolly. It's over . . .'

Dolly took a deep breath, somehow finding the self-control to calm Bella down.

'It's going to be all right. We'll go back to my flat and keep on calling Shirley until we get some kind of news – even call the police if we have to.'

'They'll pick us up, I know it, I know it.'

Dolly was exhausted. She couldn't take any more. 'Just shut up! We haven't been caught yet and if you bloody pull yourself together we won't be.'

She made a three-point turn and drove out of the side turning. The policewoman was standing by the patrol car now, leaning in. It looked ominously as if they were waiting for Bella and Dolly to return.

*　*　*

Micky Tesco had given the cab driver twenty-five quid – all he had on him.

'I've been in a bike crash. Gotta get back to my place, call a doctor.'

The cabbie was worried about the blood still streaming from the cuts on Micky's face.

'You sure you don't want to go to a hospital, mate? Looks like you need stitches on them cuts.'

Micky didn't have the energy to argue. 'Just take me home.'

He lay back in his seat, trying to fight off the waves of pain threatening to overwhelm him. He suddenly realised it would be crazy to let this cab driver take him to his own door; much better to get out before the flat. As he leant forward, he could feel the dried blood sticking to his neck. He rapped on the glass.

'Just drop me at the next corner, OK?'

The cab driver was just relieved to get the boy out of his cab. With the twenty-five quid in his hand, he inspected the back seat. It was covered in blood.

'Shit.'

Micky limped off, keeping to the back streets as he threaded his way towards his flat. He didn't think he was going to make it past the porter and up in the lift. His head was throbbing and his vision began to blur. The white-hot pain in his left arm was making him feel sick. He kept on seeing the girl, the black girl. He knew her, he was sure of it. His mind churned as he staggered down into the underground car park – then it came to him: it was the girl from the airport when he'd first met Harry Rawlins, the black girl at the airport. Harry Rawlins, Harry Rawlins – the name banged like a hammer in his brain. If the car was gone, he would know that Harry had cheated him, just like he had cheated everyone else.

Micky began sobbing. 'Bastard, bastard, son of a bitch, *bastard.*'

But the Jaguar was still in the parking bay. Micky leant against it and tried to get his breathing under control.

There was still time.

* * *

Harry couldn't wait any longer. If Micky wasn't here by now, he wasn't coming. Something must have gone wrong. Time to cut his losses. He checked he had his passport, then picked up his suitcases, and with one look at Micky's solitary case, he walked out.

* * *

Bella had the jewels laid out on the coffee table. She couldn't stop touching them, and it was getting on Dolly's nerves. She put in yet another call to Shirley's, the ringing echoing on and on like a dirge. Where the hell was she? Surely if she'd been picked up, they'd have let her go by now?

Bella held up a diamond necklace. 'At least we got these.'

Dolly ripped it out of her hand and threw it onto the table. 'I never wanted those fucking things in the first place!'

If she thought that was going to shut Bella up, it had the opposite effect. One moment she was sitting looking at the diamonds, the next she was screaming at the top of her voice, jabbing a finger at Dolly.

'If anything's happened to Shirley, it's your fault . . . it's *all your fault!*'

Dolly slapped her hard across the face, and Bella instantly collapsed into a sobbing heap, like a puppet with its strings cut. At least Dolly knew now that if they were ever questioned by the police, Bella wouldn't be able to hold out; she actually had more faith in Shirley.

She suddenly had a thought. 'That girl, the one you rented your flat to?'

Bella couldn't understand where Dolly's mind was going. 'What girl?'

Dolly walked into the bedroom, explaining it all to her as Bella followed her into the room. 'You get her passport, then you get on a plane, get out of the country.'

'Oh yeah? How am I gonna do that? What about my money? What about all your promises, Dolly?'

Dolly opened the case on the bed and began taking out bundles of banknotes. Bella stared at the cash in disbelief.

'I'll stick to my part of the bargain. It's all legitimate cash, Bella. I'm paying you with my own money, you just get out of the country.'

Seeing the money, hearing Dolly's voice, calm and in control, brought Bella round. She knew Dolly was right. Soon she was stacking the money in a holdall. All she wanted now was to be gone.

* * *

Frinton was still buzzing, despite his exhaustion. The statements at the club had taken up most of the afternoon, and now he was questioning each man in turn. He'd got little joy out of Colin Soal, Harvey Rintle or Johnny Summers – all old lags, all prepared to keep shtum. But with Kevin White he had an added lever: the girl, the dead girl, Shirley Miller.

Kevin White had asked for aspirins for his head; he'd almost knocked himself out when that crazy chef had gone for him. He was out of cigarettes and hadn't been given the phone call he knew he had a right to. He was beginning to get bolshie, giving the officer on duty an earful. The officer stood impassively at the door, without looking at him, letting the stream of abuse flow over him.

'And what about these bleedin' handcuffs?' White said finally, holding up his hands, showing the red weals round his wrists.

The officer looked through the small observation window. Standing outside were Detective Inspector Frinton and a CID officer.

Frinton gave the officer a wink and gestured for him to move away from the door. Then he walked into the interview room and before White could open his mouth, he was leaning over him, eyes glinting. White shrank back in the chair.

'I'm going to say one fucking word to you, Kevin: *murder*.'

Frinton was so close, White could smell the cigarettes on his breath. 'What do you—'

'The girl's dead, Kevin, an' I got a witness who says you shot her. You're goin' down this time, and you're never coming up again.'

Kevin started to panic. 'I never shot anyone. It wasn't me, honest!'

That was all Frinton needed. 'So who was it, Kevin?'

* * *

Harry entered the underground garage and walked smartly over to the Jaguar. He opened up the boot, put his cases inside and slammed the lid down. Then he saw the blood. He stepped back from the car. The trail of blood led to the driver's side door.

Micky Tesco, his face swollen and bloody, stared back at Harry. He held the revolver in his right hand, and it was shaking as he pointed it at Harry. His eyes were mad, staring, and when he spoke, his lips were so swollen that his voice was distorted.

'Get in the car, Harry.'

Harry wavered. Then he saw Micky lean forward, the gun shaking. He put up his hands in a gesture of compliance, opened the passenger door and sat down.

'Son of a bitch, you set me up.'

'What are you talking about?'

'She's got the jewels.'

Harry saw the arm hanging limply at Tesco's side. He inched his hands along the seat.

'*Don't move!*'

Harry lifted his hands away from the seat and held them in the air. 'What happened?'

Micky didn't seem able to focus. The gun wavered and he closed his eyes for a moment.

'You need a doctor. Your face . . . What you done to your arm?'

Micky started crying like a little boy. 'My arm . . .'

Harry waited, his hands at the ready.

'I trusted you . . . You were with her.'

Harry had difficulty making out what Micky was saying. Micky coughed, the hand holding the gun dropped onto the seat, and Harry quickly grabbed hold of Micky's wrist.

Micky started wailing, a high-pitched screech. 'I'm gonna *kill* you!'

Harry put his left hand over Micky's mouth to shut him up, and Micky sank his teeth into the flesh between Harry's thumb and first finger. Harry felt a searing flash of pain. He tried to rip his hand away, but Micky just sank his teeth in deeper. And now he was pulling his gun hand away . . .

The first shot cracked open the windscreen – then there was another, a dull, thudding boom inside the car. Harry's body twisted and slumped against the seat.

*   *   *

Fuller was driving home from a squash match. He'd lost, but that was the least of his worries. Maureen had packed up and gone. In her note, she said that when he had the time to talk to her – really talk – she would see him.

Fuller hadn't had the time. Well, maybe he had; it was just that he couldn't bring himself to drive round to his mother-in-law's for a scene. It would be too painful.

The newsflash on the radio interrupted his thoughts, making him almost drive into the back of an ice cream van.

*   *   *

Reynolds was waiting for him when he arrived at the office, still in his tracksuit. Reynolds had got a few details – as much as he could get from Kensington – but the gist of it seemed to be that DI Frinton had made the coup of all time, and his nick was bursting at the seams. Fuller slumped in his chair, head in hands.

'Tip-off came from a woman – said that Harry Rawlins was on the raid. She had all the details – was right about most things. Except one.'

Fuller looked up. 'Have they got him?'

Reynolds shook his head. 'Two men escaped on a motorbike with £8 million in gems.'

Fuller was on his feet. Maybe it wasn't too late to get in on the act.

* * *

At first Bella had tried to persuade Dolly to come with her. 'If Shirley spills the beans, you're better off out of it, too.'

Dolly had shaken her head. 'She'll need a lawyer if they've got her. She'll need money. I'm staying.'

Dolly could have added that she had more faith in Shirley than Bella did, but there was no point getting into that.

'You go, Bella. At least one of us will be safe. Take the twenty-five grand. I'll get more to you as soon as I can.'

Now here they were at Victoria. Bella got out of the car, gave Dolly a wan smile, then walked into the station. From there she would catch a train to Gatwick, and then ... Dolly didn't know where she was going to go; the important thing was she was gone.

Dolly heaved a sigh of relief as she got back into the car. As she started the engine, she saw the jewel pouch, sticking out from under the passenger seat. She tucked it away and drove off.

* * *

Kevin White had finally broken. It had taken a lot longer than Frinton had anticipated, but now he finally had two more names: Brian Fisk and Micky Tesco. Harry Rawlins was still missing, but he'd have to wait. Kevin White had told him who had shot the girl. The first thing was to get a warrant for the arrest of Micky Tesco on a murder charge.

Frinton was feeling buoyant, even when he spotted DI Fuller lurking.

'Sorry.' Frinton smiled. 'I'm a bit busy right now. Perhaps you could talk to a junior officer?'

'Of course,' Fuller replied stiffly.

It was a slap in the face, but Fuller took it, desperate for so much as a crumb. Frinton almost felt sorry for him, but he knew if things had been the other way round, Fuller wouldn't have given him the time of day. This was Frinton's baby now, and he didn't want anyone else getting in on the act. It was still Sunday; come Monday he'd have the Chief all over it, with the possibility of the Yard taking over. He knew he had to move fast. He could almost see the headlines: *Detective Inspector Frinton single-handedly nets the biggest team of villains since the Great Train Robbery . . .*

He just needed to pick up Tesco and hit him with a murder charge. Then it would only be a matter of time before they picked up Rawlins, the elusive dead man, himself.

* * *

Vic Morgan sat by Resnick's bedside, beginning to wish he hadn't come. He'd thought, on first seeing the pathetic scarecrow in the bed, that Resnick wouldn't have the strength to talk to him. What little hair Resnick had left after the chemotherapy stuck to his skull in pathetic wisps. His face was gaunt, and his pyjamas seemed four or five sizes too big. To put it simply, he looked as if he was dying.

But now here he was, fighting to push himself up in the bed, his face almost puce with anger, as he jabbed a bony finger at Morgan's chest.

'So she bought you a bleedin' jacket, and you think she's God's gift? I'm telling you, she's been with him all along, you stupid son of a bitch. I told you, warned you to keep your eye on 'er. Any chance we had of that reward money's gone out of the bloody window now.'

Moans of 'shut up' came from some of the other beds in the ward.

Morgan sighed, still desperately hanging on to the small thread of hope that Dolly wasn't involved.

The night nurse appeared beside the bed.

'You're really going to have to go, I'm afraid. If Matron finds out you were here, I'll more than likely get the sack.'

Morgan nodded. 'I'll come back soon,' he assured Resnick. 'As soon as I have anything.'

He wasn't looking forward to it. He'd turned up feeling quite pleased with himself, but now he was leaving with his tail between his legs.

'You stick to her like I told you to,' Resnick added. 'Don't for a minute think she's straight. She's as bent as my crippled hand.'

Morgan stood to go.

'And take your soddin' roses with you. They give me hay fever.'

*   *   *

As Reynolds drove them to Tesco's place, Fuller tried to piece it together. Micky Tesco had last been seen at Arnie Fisher's club with Shirley Miller. And Rawlins had been there, too. Then, when Shirley was shot, she apparently called out 'Dolly'.

Fuller sat back and closed his eyes. Dolly was Harry Rawlins' wife. Could she have been working with Rawlins all along? Fuller remembered Dolly's face when she asked for the watch, the gold watch that had identified her husband. If she had been acting then, she was National Theatre material. Had she also been acting when they told her her husband was dead? He shook his head, seeing her face again, the eyes wide, staring, her body taut. She had been unable to speak. If Dolly Rawlins was in cahoots with her husband, then by God they were one hell of a team.

* * *

Audrey had wheeled her new pram and carrycot combined into the tower block. She pressed the button for the lift. Nothing happened. She waited, then tried the second one. The graffiti was hacked into the chrome: 'FUCK off cunts'.

Audrey muttered that they all were, then pushed the pram towards the stairs, hauling it up awkwardly, knowing she had three floors to go and wishing she had waited for Ray. She managed the pram up the first flight, and was wheeling it round to begin the next flight when a female police officer appeared.

Audrey was glad of the assistance. The WPC called for her male colleague, and together they carried the pram up to Audrey's flat.

'It's the first time I've needed you lot.' Audrey caught the look between the two and felt a moment of panic. 'You're not coming to see me, are you?'

They helped her wheel her pram into the hallway, then both stood by the door.

'It's Greg, isn't it? What's he done this time? I've told 'im and told 'im. He's not been thieving again, 'as he?'

The WPC followed Audrey into the kitchen. Audrey was wheeling the pram through to put it out on the fire escape.

'You'd better sit down, love. I'm afraid I've got some bad news for you.'

Audrey looked at her, her hands tightening on the handle of the pram. The male officer pulled out a chair and Audrey sat, still holding on to the pram.

'Is it Greg? An accident . . . ? Has there been an accident?'

'No, it's not Greg. It's your daughter, Shirley.'

* * *

Fuller pulled up at the block of flats, behind the patrol car stationed outside. An officer was standing on duty outside the entrance to the underground car park and walked over. Fuller showed his badge and the officer stepped aside.

Blue and white tape had been hung round the Jaguar, and DI Frinton was in the middle of politely but firmly explaining to a tenant that no he could *not* remove his car, and that, yes, he needed to leave the car park now.

Frinton turned to see Fuller's car heading down the ramp. 'What's he bloody doing here?' he muttered.

Fuller got out of the car and walked towards the Jag. Face down on the concrete, with one leg still in the car, was a body.

Frinton stormed over. 'What do you think you're doing? This is a crime scene.'

Fuller looked at the sprawled body, then back to Frinton. 'I can see that.'

'*My* crime scene,' Frinton added.

Fuller ignored him. 'Who is it?'

An ambulance came down the ramp and stopped behind Fuller's car.

Fuller looked up. 'Bit late for that, isn't it?' He stepped over the red tape and bent over the body. One arm was bent upwards, partially obscuring the face, but Fuller knew it was Tesco. It was the hair, even matted with dried blood – that blond hair.

Frinton had had it. 'All right, you've seen enough. Now get the fuck out of it.'

Fuller stood to one side as a pair of medics approached.

'Don't worry, Frinton,' he said with a sour smile. 'He's all yours.'

*　　*　　*

Dozing in the TV room, Resnick almost fell out of his wheelchair when he heard the newsflash. He'd missed half of it, and it was over before he got the facts straight. He felt trapped, helpless, with no one to scream at. As if on cue, the nurse opened the door, carrying a beaker of tepid tea. Vic Morgan followed in behind her.

'You can have ten minutes, but, really, that's all.' The nurse wheeled out one of the sleeping wheelchair patients.

Morgan sat down. 'Don't know where to begin – all hell's been let loose.'

Resnick pointed to the TV. 'What the hell 'ave you been soddin' doin'? I told you, what did I tell you—'

Morgan held up a hand. 'Let me give you what I know, all right?'

Resnick's face was bursting with fury. He swore that Morgan didn't know anything, hadn't from the beginning – that's why he was out of the force. He was wet, more occupied with getting his leg over with that bitch Dolly Rawlins.

Morgan let him have his tirade, then quietly began to tell him what he had gathered so far from his contacts about the raid on Amanda's nightclub, the bottom line being that they were still looking for Micky Tesco and Harry Rawlins. Also missing was £8 million pounds' worth of gems.

Resnick looked at him with barely concealed contempt. 'You bloody idiot.'

Morgan sighed. 'Wait. There's something else. The only reason the police were able to prevent the raid from succeeding was because they got a tip-off – one hell of a tip-off, as it happened, giving all the names, the details of the getaway, the lot. And the tipster had been a woman; a woman who seemed desperate to have the raiders caught, but one in particular – the one name she repeated over and over again: Harry Rawlins.'

Resnick was quietened. He thought for a moment, then looked at Morgan. 'But was he on the raid? And where are the jewels?'

* * *

Dolly finished cleaning her flat, then started on the packing. That done, she took out a packet of envelopes. She remembered the way

Vic had laughed at her, always paying his account in cash placed neatly inside an envelope with his name printed on it. Had she bought a job lot, he asked? But she didn't have time to think about him, not now. She began placing the jewels, neatly wrapped in tissue, into the stack of envelopes, and then Sellotaped them all into a toiletry bag, securing them with yet more tape.

* * *

Reynolds and Fuller sat in a quiet corner of the cafe, going over everything they knew. The conclusion was obvious: if they could find Dolly Rawlins, then they would have her husband.

The night nurse almost hit the roof when they arrived, but Fuller was insistent, saying it was a police matter.

'That's what they all say,' she muttered to herself, leading Fuller and Reynolds to the TV room.

Fuller was surprised to see Resnick and Vic Morgan sitting and chatting together at almost ten o'clock at night. He was even more taken aback by Resnick's shrunken body and wasted features.

'Evening, gents.' Fuller brought out a bottle of malt whisky from under his coat, along with a packet of plastic cups.

'Don't mind if I do, Alex.'

Resnick took in Fuller's appearance as he poured a generous measure into three cups. He was unshaven and wearing a tracksuit under his coat. Gone was the cockiness: he looked as if he had had the stuffing knocked out of him. Resnick also noted that for a so-called non-drinker, Fuller knocked back his scotch remarkably quickly.

Resnick felt the whisky hit him hard, making him flush. He held out his cup for a refill with his left hand, his right hand curled in his lap. He felt better than he had felt for weeks. He liked them coming to him; it made him feel needed, made him believe he would be back with the lads as soon as he got himself fixed up.

'Shirley Miller, Terry Miller's widow, was shot in the raid – died almost instantly. The last word she uttered was "Dolly".'

Resnick glanced at Morgan, who looked stunned.

'They got Tesco,' Fuller added. 'Hell of a mess. Found him shot dead in his car park.'

Fuller poured another round of drinks. They sipped in silence, then Fuller placed his cup carefully on the table.

'Rawlins is still on the loose. I've tried to track down his wife, but it looks like wherever he is, she is too. I need anything you've got, and I swear if you have anything that can help me, help me in any way at all, I'll see you clear to getting a slice of that reward.'

Morgan stayed silent, his head bowed, looking into his drink. Resnick looked at him. Now was his chance. He couldn't do it on his own. He was a fool to keep shtum.

'You'd better cough up, Vic.' He looked at Fuller. 'He knows where she is.'

Morgan picked up his jacket, the one Dolly had given him, and walked to the door. As he opened it, his voice was heavy with emotion.

'I'll take you to her.' Then he walked out.

Fuller couldn't keep the look of surprise off his face. Reynolds just grinned, as if Christmas had come early. Fuller patted Resnick's shoulder.

'Thanks, George. I won't forget this – that's a promise.'

Resnick knew Morgan was hurting. 'Take care of him. He's a great soft bastard, but he's a good man.'

Fuller nodded, then followed Morgan out, with Reynolds at his heels.

Resnick drained his cup and reached for the bottle. Shame to let good whisky go to waste. He leant forward, stretching, then felt a terrible pain in his bad arm and fell forwards, crashing into the table, before sliding, helpless, to the floor. He lay there, unable to move, watching the bottle rolling slowly across the floor.

He knew in that moment that he was never going to be back with the lads. He wasn't going anywhere. This was his life now – what was left of it. And it was all Rawlins' fault. He was to blame for everything.

'You bastard, Rawlins!' he cried in agony. 'You filthy bastard!'

* * *

It was now 11:15, and Audrey was sitting in the kitchen. She wouldn't take her coat off, and she wouldn't drink the tea they'd made her. In one afternoon she had lost her daughter, the father of her unborn son, and even her Greg had been picked up. She stared ahead, gently rocking the pram backwards and forwards.

'You're sure you don't want a doctor?'

Audrey shook her head.

It was unnerving the way she kept on slowly rocking the pram, backwards and forwards.

Suddenly Audrey turned and smiled, a sweet, innocent smile.

'I'm going to have a boy. I know it's a boy 'cos of my age, you see, and he's all right. They said he's all right.'

The door opened and the WPC stood up. Her heart went out to Audrey, but there was nothing more she could do.

Greg was led into the kitchen by a uniformed officer. At least they'd let her son out on bail so she had someone to look after her. He looked sheepish, still in shock about Shirley, the arrest, all of it. He hadn't been able to take it all in, and seeing his mother sitting there, her hands gripping an empty pram, made him want to run to her and cry like a baby himself. Like he'd done when he was told his dad had run off. Like he'd done whenever he'd needed her.

But now he knew she needed him.

'Ray not with you?'

He shook his head. Ray wouldn't be coming home for a long time. But he couldn't tell her that; he couldn't find the words to tell her anything. He walked to her side and sat down. He laid his hand on top of Audrey's, let it rock with the motion of the pram. He could feel the tears trickle down his cheeks, but still he could say nothing. He looked to the WPC for help and she mimed a hug. Greg had to ease Audrey's hands from the pram bar, then he put them round his neck. He could feel Audrey's belly with her unborn baby pressing against his stomach. He stopped crying, feeling more of a man than he had ever felt before. Gently, he wrapped his arms round his mother, rocking her as if she was a baby, and at long last Audrey began to weep, deep, heartbreaking sobs, her head buried in her young son's neck.

The WPC could feel tears welling up, while the male officer looked away. Now they could go.

As they let themselves out, the WPC couldn't help but notice the large black and white photograph of Shirley Miller, standing with Miss Paddington, and wearing a 'runner-up' sash on her white swimsuit. The girl was blonde, beautiful and, with her smiling face, she looked as if she knew she had the whole world in front of her. The photo had scrawled across it: *To the best mum in the world, love Shirley.*

* * *

Dolly was sitting in her car, numb. She had heard the news about the diamond robbery on the radio, reporting that a model, identified as Shirley Miller, had been shot dead. Dolly had the jewels in a carrier bag and was contemplating what she should do.

She saw Greg leaving his mother's house and although she was shocked to the core, time was against her and there was nobody else she could trust. She waited a further fifteen minutes before she picked up the carrier bag and walked into the estate towards Audrey's front door. She was still unsure about what she should do, but in reality she had run out of options. Her hand shook as she rang the doorbell.

* * *

As soon as Greg had left the house to go to the pub, Audrey got out of bed. She needed a drink as much as her son, and had already had half a tumbler of gin when the doorbell rang. She was certain it was Greg coming back to check up on her, and he certainly wouldn't approve of her inebriated state. The last person she expected it to be, or ever believed she would see again, was Dolly Rawlins.

Audrey stepped back from the open door to let Dolly in.

'I had no one else to turn to, Audrey . . . I need to talk to you.'

Audrey could not even bring herself to speak.

Dolly continued. 'Can we go into the kitchen? I don't have long . . .'

Audrey was dumbfounded at the audaciousness of this woman who she so despised, but she led the way to the kitchen.

Dolly put the carrier bag down on the kitchen table, not looking at Audrey. Her voice was hoarse.

'I've just heard about Shirley . . .'

Again Audrey remained speechless.

Dolly bowed her head and, barely audible, whispered, 'I am so sorry . . . I am so sorry . . .'

It was so unexpected when Dolly reached out with both arms and drew Audrey close to her, hugging her tightly.

'I didn't know where else to go.'

Audrey was tight-lipped, her hands clenched into fists as Dolly stepped away from her.

'I need you to do something, Audrey . . . But it's up to you. I want you to take this bag to a man I know I can trust, Jimmy Donaldson.' Dolly pulled out a note from her coat pocket. 'This is his address. You want to instruct him to keep this bag safe for me. He is not to open it, and must find a good hiding place. He'll do whatever you ask because Harry controlled him, and he still does – so he'll be too afraid not to go along with it. I could get him put away for life.'

Dolly looked at Audrey.

'Are you all right?' she asked softly.

Audrey spat her reply. 'Am I all right, you two-faced bitch! How dare you show your face here! I've got a good mind to call the cops! I'd like to take a carving knife to you myself . . .'

Dolly took her by the shoulders and gripped her tightly. 'Listen to me, Audrey: I don't know the facts about what happened.'

Audrey pushed her away. 'What happened is you got my daughter killed, you two-faced bitch!' she shrieked.

Dolly took a few deep breaths before she replied. 'Audrey, I can walk out of here now if you want me to. But if you do what I ask you to, I'll get you a cut of the diamonds and you'll be secure for the rest of your life.'

It was only then that Audrey realised the carrier bag contained the stolen diamonds.

Years later, she would be unable to recall the rest of their conversation. In the space of one night she had lost her daughter and the father of her unborn child was going to prison, probably for the rest of his life. She hadn't agreed to Dolly's request straight away, and would never forget the fact that Dolly's icy blue eyes were brimming with tears.

After Dolly left, Audrey had another half tumbler of gin and opened the carrier bag. She put the note with Jimmy Donaldson's address in her handbag, and then carried the bag up to her bedroom and hid it under her mattress.

Mixed emotions flooded through her, but the words 'you'll be secure for the rest of your life' made her wonder just how great that security would be.

*　*　*

Vera had made up the sofa bed in their lounge. Trudie had arrived exhausted and had done nothing but cry and was refusing to tell Vera what on earth was going on. She just asked Vera if she would look after the baby as she needed to get some sleep and she would explain everything once she had had a rest. Vera sat in her kitchen with a cup of tea and a cigarette, pushing the baby in a stroller up and down with her foot. She had seen the luggage tag on Trudie's suitcase. Bloody Australia, that's where she's been. Vera was determined that she was going to interrogate Trudie when she woke up. She had become quite hysterical when told the man had called again but had left no number. It definitely wasn't her husband, and whoever it was made Trudie repeat, 'Thank God, thank God.'

Vera would be thanking God when Trudie left as she had two children of her own and her husband was not happy with this arrangement. It was only a small, overcrowded council flat, after all.

* * *

Morgan watched as Fuller and Reynolds went over Dolly's flat. A few clothes still hung in the closet, some sweaters and under-wear in the chest of drawers. There was also a suitcase on top of the wardrobe. It didn't look as if she had gone, but there was no sign of Rawlins, no men's clothes, nothing. If she had been working with him, he hadn't been living with her.

A withered bunch of flowers, dead, their petals stiff and dried, were in a small cracked vase. He remembered when he'd given them to her.

'Maybe we'll hang around for a while, see what turns up,' Fuller said.

Morgan wanted to get out. He watched Fuller sifting through the waste bin. He felt uneasy, as if he had betrayed a confidence. Still he refused to believe that Dolly would have lied to him.

'You mind if I push off?'

Fuller shrugged. 'Just be sure you call me if she gets in contact.'

* * *

Dolly had driven away from the house, unsure if she had been right to rely on Audrey. She still couldn't believe that Shirley was really dead and wondered whether perhaps the news report she had heard on the radio was inaccurate. Now she was making her way to the only other person she needed.

Dolly rang and rang Morgan's doorbell, then peered through the letterbox. Where could he be? She rang again, and was just about to turn and go back down the stairs when she heard footsteps, slow and heavy. He rounded the bend in the stairway and stopped.

'You said if I ever needed you . . .' Dolly began.

Morgan smiled. He took out his keys, noticing that she had no luggage, just her handbag. He pushed the door open.

'You'd better come in then, hadn't you?'

Dolly followed him into his flat.

'You hungry?'

Dolly hadn't realised it until now. She hadn't eaten all day.

'Yes.'

Morgan slipped off his jacket, walked ahead of her into the kitchen and opened the fridge.

'Omelette OK?'

Dolly nodded. She felt a real warmth towards him, but she still didn't really know how far she could trust him. How far she could go. She made an effort to relax, following him round the kitchen as he busied himself whisking the eggs.

'I do need you to do something for me, actually,' she said finally. She took a deep breath. 'There was a robbery this afternoon. It was me that gave the tip-off, and . . . there was a girl. Shirley, Shirley Miller. I need to know if she's been arrested. She had nothing to do with it, she just happened to be there, and . . .'

Morgan listened to her talk as he heated butter in the pan, trying not to show any reaction.

'Would you know where she is? Could you find out for me?'

Morgan stood over the stove, the omelette mixture in a bowl.

'I know where they've taken her, yes.'

Dolly moved closer. Her hands were twitching, and it was obvious to him she was trying desperately not to show how tense she really was.

'Where?'

Morgan wanted to shock her, to see her reaction. He poured the omelette mixture into the pan, where it started sizzling. Then, shaking the pan, he said just one word: 'Morgue'.

Dolly said nothing. Then she began to retch, heaving uncontrollably, her whole body shaking.

* * *

Jackie Rawlins was still waiting for Harvey Rintle to call her. She had put his bike and holdall in his apartment as instructed, and he'd promised to ring her at five. Now it was gone midnight. The kids had really been giving her a hard time. She had let them watch a video of *Werewolf of London,* then they wanted to see another. Her youngest had cheekily said that as the werewolf had been so frightening, he had to watch something funny or he wouldn't be able to sleep. They'd sat through some weird comedy about a talking VW car that Jackie couldn't make head nor tail of. Then, at long last, they had gone to bed. She was just about to follow when the back door opened. She guessed it was Harvey – he often slipped in that way. She turned, smiling.

Harry Rawlins closed the door behind him, locked it, then turned to her with a smile.

'Didn't have the change to ring, sweetheart, so thought I'd come in person.'

Jackie, hands on hips, looked at him coldly. 'Thought you might appear eventually.'

He gave her a puzzled look.

'Dolly's called here twice asking for you. Said she'd keep on trying, but I told her you . . .' Jackie stopped mid-sentence when she caught sight of Harry's right hand. It was wrapped in a bloody handkerchief.

'Called here? Dolly?'

Jackie realised he hadn't been expecting a call from Dolly, and almost chuckled. Harry began to unwrap his hand.

'What you done?'

He held it out. She could see the deep teeth marks.

'Mad dog went for me. You got some Dettol?'

Jackie noticed there was more blood on Harry's jacket. He was taking it off, making himself at home.

'I don't want you here, Harry. I got kids. I don't want any trouble.'

Harry ignored her and began to take off his shirt. He took a passport and wallet out of his jacket pocket and put them on the table.

'Just need to get cleaned up, Jackie, then I'm off. You got any cash about?'

Jackie laughed. 'If you're after what you gave Harvey, you've got another think coming.' She found a bowl, and then fetched some Dettol and a bandage.

Harry now had his shirt off. He put his hand in the water. 'Christ almighty!' He winced.

'You've been bleedin' like a pig. It's all over you.'

Harry said nothing. He wasn't about to tell her whose blood it was.

'I won't be staying long. I just need a change of clothes. And I need your car. Then I'm going to catch a plane.'

'I don't believe it! She's going with you, is she? Dolly? After what you done to her, I don't believe it.'

Harry studied his hand, the blood still flowing from the punctures. They would stay with him for life, in memory of Micky Tesco. Harry remembered something that Micky had said. Could Dolly and the black girl somehow have got their hands on the jewels? Surely not. But what Dolly did have was money, and a lot of it. Perhaps Jackie's idea wasn't completely mad. If Dolly called again . . . The more he thought about it, the more he liked the idea.

Jackie went upstairs to get some of Harry's cousin Eddie's clothes. She knew they'd fit. Most of poor Eddie's stuff had been Harry's cast-offs in the first place.

'You got Eddie's shavin' gear handy?'

Jackie threw the clothes at him and walked out. She wasn't about to let him upstairs. As Jackie passed the boys' bedroom on the way to the bathroom, she looked in. They were sprawled on the bunk bed, the duvets hanging off. She gently covered them. The youngest, cheeky as he was during the day, looked like an innocent little cherub at night, clutching an old toy submarine. She eased it out of his hands and tucked them under the duvet. She wouldn't let Harry anywhere near her kids, especially this one, Jason. She'd often wondered if Eddie had spotted it, but he hadn't. But then Eddie couldn't see anything right under his nose. But as Jason grew older, it became more obvious to her: he was Harry's double, right down to his dark, brooding eyes. It almost amused her, gave her at least something over the bastard; she'd got the thing he'd most wanted. Poor old Dolly had tried to give him a son and lost four, all boys – lost them at four months. Perhaps that was why she'd loved that wretched little dog so much – a child substitute. It was Jackie's secret, but there, sleeping, was Harry Rawlins' son, ten years old now, and one hell of a handful.

Jackie went downstairs and handed over Eddie's shaving gear. The brush looked as if it had been used to clean the floor; it more than likely had, by that little bugger Jason.

'Bit peckish,' he said. 'You think you could fix me somethin' to eat?'

Jackie sighed. 'You go right after, yeah? I'll feed you and clothe you, but that's it.'

As she went into the kitchen, she glanced back. He was staring at his face in the mirror. He caught her watching him and gave her a wink. Shivers went up and down her. His expression at that moment was identical to her son's.

She opened the fridge. 'I've got a quiche Lorraine and some salad. You want some quiche?'

*   *   *

Morgan had listened without interrupting as Dolly had told him everything, right from the moment they had begun watching Harry's lock-up. She left out any mention of their part in the aftermath, and made no mention of the jewels. But she didn't lie.

Morgan sighed. He wanted more than anything to believe her, and she did sound as if she was telling the truth. When he asked why she hadn't gone to the police, she smiled sarcastically.

'I gave them the times and the name of every man I knew on it, and they still didn't catch him. That's why.'

'Do you know where he is?' he asked.

She bit her lip. 'I'm not sure, but there's one place he might go, one place . . .'

Then somehow it all came tumbling out. How Jackie and her husband had had an affair eleven years ago. She'd known about it but ignored it, like she'd ignored a lot of things, lots of 'bits' he'd had on the side. Although she'd never said anything, Jackie and Eddie had never been invited to her home after that, and everybody except poor old Eddie had sussed out why; Eddie just thought that Dolly didn't like him. Harry had never mentioned Jackie's name in front of Dolly again. But maybe if he needed a place to lie low . . . just maybe he would go to Jackie.

'I've tried calling her,' she said.

Morgan got up and handed her the phone. 'Why not try again?'

Dolly stalled for time. She hadn't worked it all out yet. What she didn't want was the police brought in – not yet. He could slip through the net again.

'My husband's very clever. How many men do you know, living like he did, who've never been sent down – not once. Only for six weeks when he was a kid. Harry is careful and he'd smell a set-up. The thing is . . . I have the money, and right now he must need it.' She looked at him. 'He'll come to me.'

* * *

Harry finished the quiche and pushed his plate aside. He had shaved, but was still wearing only his boxers. He got up and began to put on one of Eddie's shirts. The phone rang. It was now 2:15 in the morning. Jackie looked to him for instructions. He gave her a nod and she picked up the phone.

Harry kept his eyes on her. She didn't even speak, just listened and then covered the mouthpiece.

'She's asking for you.'

Harry took the phone. He glanced at the closed door.

'Kid's crying.'

Jackie gave him a look and left the kitchen.

Harry spoke in his gentlest voice, almost caressing. 'Hello, Doll. So . . . you got the jewels, then?'

* * *

Morgan was standing right behind her. Dolly nodded to him, whispered, 'He's there,' then, turning her back, she spoke.

'Hello, Harry . . .'

After she hung up, Dolly was still shaking like a leaf. Morgan put his big hands on her shoulders and gave her some time to compose herself.

'So?'

Dolly let out a breath. 'I said let's meet up west somewhere, but he wasn't having any of it.'

'Where then?'

'Kenwood House, on Hampstead Heath, by the old footbridge.'

Morgan nodded to himself. 'Smart. Plenty of cover. Hard for anyone to run him to ground. OK, what time?'

'Four o'clock,' Dolly said.

Morgan smiled. 'Well, at least that gives us plenty of time to set something up. What we'll—'

'No,' Dolly interrupted. 'Four in the morning. Today. *Now*.'

'Crikey. Right. I'd better get on it then. Dolly, you stay here in the flat and don't move until I've arranged things. My God, they'll have to move fast. And don't worry, I'll cover for you – do a deal if I can. After all, you gave them the tip-off in the first place. Call me at the Yard.' He paused and held her face in his hands. 'I can trust you, can't I? Because it's me on the line too.'

In answer, Dolly kissed him, a gentle kiss on his lips.

'We'll go on, Dolly, you and me – that's a promise.'

Dolly touched the big man's cheek and smiled up into his face. 'We can only go on with Harry caught.'

She brushed the shoulders of Morgan's jacket, just like his wife used to do before he went off for an important meeting. Then, at long last, the door closed behind him, and Dolly leant against it, her eyes closed.

She knew that Harry had chosen that specific place because it was where he had proposed marriage to her, all those years ago. He'd taken her there on a picnic and they had walked round the house together. She'd been surprised, not thinking that tearaway Harry Rawlins would even know about such a place. There had been a concert playing in the outdoor theatre – classical music. She had liked it, and from then on they'd begun to listen to classical music together.

She pulled herself together. It was now 3:15. She didn't have very long to get to Kenwood House.

* * *

Harry knew Jackie was upstairs and made sure the door was closed. This was the last time he was going to attempt to talk to her. He dialled the number and waited. Vera snatched up the phone and snapped 'Yes'. This was getting to be ridiculous. It was three o'clock in the morning.

'I'm sorry to disturb you,' he said softly. 'Is Trudie there?'

Vera told him to hang on. She went into the sitting room and roughly pushed Trudie to wake her. 'That bloody man is on the phone again. I don't know if either him or you can't tell the time, but it's 3 a.m.'

Trudie pushed Vera away and ran from the room to pick up the phone in the hall. Harry was about to hang up. 'Is that you?' Trudie said. 'Is it really you? Dear God, I've been waiting for you to contact me for so long.'

He interrupted very quietly. 'I haven't got long, Trudie, but make sure you never mention my name to anyone. The police are very close, but everything is going to be fine. I'm going to be a rich man. I will call you first thing and we'll go and you, me and my son will start a new life. Is that what you want?'

'What I want?' she screeched. 'Yes! Yes! Yes!'

'I'll call you tomorrow.'

Trudie could hardly catch her breath. She felt hysterical, but before she could say anything the phone went dead. She turned to her sister and said, 'Everything is going to be all right now, Vera. I'll be leaving.'

Vera couldn't believe it. Trudie was like a kid, spinning around the hall laughing and crying at the same time.

Harry rested his hand on the phone. Just hearing the way she reacted made him doubt very much that he could keep his promise. In reality, if she did not have his son, he wouldn't want anything to do with her. He knew he could easily get rid of her if he needed to and take the child.

He went back to check his appearance in the mirror and straightened his tie. Standing behind him, Jackie watched. She couldn't believe Dolly was meeting him, after all he had put her through. And what's more, Harry seemed to be dressing himself up for it like a date he had waited for, longed for. He had changed his shirt twice, even put on cologne.

'Do you still love her, Harry?'

He was whistling. Even at this hour in the morning he was fresh, bursting with energy. But he didn't reply to her question.

He took her car keys. She'd tried to persuade him not to, but he had made her a promise that she would have the car back, and a lot more besides. She knew he was probably lying; he had said he was going abroad, and he would have to stay away for a long time. In a way, it was a relief; she could live with Harvey in peace, without having to worry about Harry ever coming back, ever having contact with Jason, the son he didn't know he had. Jackie just wanted him gone, and when the door finally closed behind him, she almost collapsed with relief.

Now all she wanted was for Harvey to come home. She had no idea that at that moment he was sitting in a cell, charged not only with robbery but with the murder of a security guard.

Harvey Rintle would not be seeing Jackie for a very long time.

* * *

Dolly let herself out of Morgan's flat. She'd remembered that when he had taken the gun from her – the one Linda had gone to the lock-up for – he had put it into one of the little drawers on the top of the dresser. And there it was, nestled between his handkerchiefs and socks.

She picked it up and put it in her bag.

* * *

Reynolds had been having an uncomfortable kip in one of the interview rooms, his head resting on his coat, when Fuller started barking from the doorway.

'Get your arse up to the office! Things are moving.'

Morgan was sitting smoking. He had laid out the deal. Dolly had arranged to meet Harry Rawlins on the footbridge at Kenwood House, Hampstead, at four o'clock. She wanted the police there, and she wanted Rawlins picked up. It had been Dolly who had given the tip-off, and Morgan was able to give Fuller the exact time Kensington had received the call to verify her story.

Morgan took another drag of his cigarette. Time was running out. Fuller was still sceptical. He couldn't just go on a story from Morgan; he wanted Dolly Rawlins brought in to the Yard. What if he got half the police force surrounding the place and nobody turned up?

'I'm giving you my word that she's straight.'

'Then why won't she come in?'

Morgan rubbed his eyes, exasperated. 'Don't you want him? She won't come in. She's willing to tell you where the bulk of the under-pass raid cash is. She's willing to set her husband up. Don't ask her to come in, because she won't do it.'

Fuller sucked his teeth. 'So what's in it for you, then?'

Morgan shrugged wearily. 'There's still the thirty grand reward money up for grabs, isn't there? A piece of that would do nicely.'

'You got something on with this woman?' Fuller asked. 'Resnick insinuated that you had.'

Morgan stood up. He'd had enough. He looked at his watch and his heart missed a beat. It was 3:55. He grabbed Fuller's phone and dialled, standing there, ashen-faced, as it rang and rang.

* * *

Harry drove carefully, unused to Jackie's old Morris Traveller. He switched on the radio.

'And now, still climbing up the charts at number four, "Widows' Tears".' Harry turned the volume up.

He chuckled. Well, the night was almost over, and he and Doll were going to meet again.

He parked on the edge of the heath. He would walk across it towards the house and the footbridge; walk the pathways like he had when he was a kid, on the day trips his mother had brought him on. Walking over the fields in the darkness, he thought about his old lady, the way she had taken him round Kenwood House, showing him the paintings, her favourite Gainsborough, even the cases with the old household bills and accounts. He had been bored to tears, but it must have meant something to him, because this is where he'd brought Dolly.

Doll – she'd been such a shy one, unlike the rest of them. But there had been something about her that he'd gone for: her class, her style. He reckoned you could never teach that; style was something you either had or you didn't, and Doll had always had it. She liked the best, whatever it was – clothes, furniture. She'd been the one the whole street talked about, who'd got in to university with more 'O' and 'A' levels than anyone else had ever had from round their way. But she'd given it all up for him. He remembered the rumpus it had caused in her family. Her mother cried, her father threatened to have him done in; his girl was going to make something of herself, not marry the local bad boy doted on by his mother. Well, he'd shown them. It was a shame they were no longer alive when they'd got the house in Totteridge; he'd have liked to shove the cut-glass decanter down her father's throat. Harry had always borne a grudge against him; Dolly had simply never seen him again after the marriage. She was like that, Doll – stood by him through thick and thin.

As Harry picked his way through the bushes, he gave no thought to what he had done to her; it was in the past, as if it had never happened. He wasn't thinking about the way he betrayed her, the child he'd had with Trudie Nunn; he was actually thinking about what a good woman Dolly had been and that with all the cash she'd got, maybe they should try again. She'd proved she was one in a million. He never allowed himself to imagine she wouldn't want him. He was Harry Rawlins, the guv'nor, and he was a rich man again. Not only would he have the money from the underpass raid, but the cash from the sale of his house, his businesses . . .

It was a pleasant walk and even the nagging pain in his hand had stopped bothering him. It was a fine, clear night and the air felt cool and fresh.

He stopped suddenly and wondered if he'd made a wrong turning – maybe things had changed on the heath. Then he got his bearings and went on, vaulted over the small wire fence and was finally in the grounds of Kenwood House.

* * *

Dolly felt like kicking herself when she found the gates leading to the house were locked. Of course they were – it was four in the morning! Actually, it was after four and she was late.

How long would he wait for her?

She turned the car round and headed back towards the heath, then remembered a short cut from close to Whitestone Pond, just past the Spaniard's Inn. Dolly parked the car at the side of the road and began running, afraid that he wouldn't be there. The gun felt heavy in her pocket.

* * *

Harry stood on the footbridge and looked at his watch. He was late and suddenly felt a moment of panic that he had missed her. He found the emotion interesting. Had she come and gone? No, not Dolly. Then he saw her, some distance away, the moonlight shining almost ghostlike on her cream-coloured coat. She seemed younger, her face flushed as she came nearer. She wasn't carrying a bag or holdall, but then of course she wouldn't: the jewels would be in the car. She was walking quickly now, pushing aside the bushes. One caught in her sleeve and she stopped and unhooked it. She was only twenty-five yards away. He lit a cigarette, his face illuminated for a brief moment in the reddish flame, and she saw him.

Harry flicked the match into the water. Seeing her now had churned him up somehow. It wasn't like seeing her on the heath that night, and he was reluctant to turn towards her in case she could read his feelings on his face. The truth was he needed her, he needed this woman. And she belonged to him. She was his.

Now he turned. It was as if everything had fallen into place for him. *He needed her.* He almost thrust his arms out towards her, but held himself in check. What if she didn't want him back, was still afraid of him, wanted another deal?

* * *

Dolly knew that she had been right to come alone, knew it the moment the match flickered and she saw his face. It wasn't the same feeling this time, not like the night Linda had died. She had felt her whole body lurch when she'd seen him then, standing, smiling, fooling round at the Jag as he showed her that there was no gun up his sleeve, no gun in his pocket, nothing in the car.

She instinctively removed her hand from the cold gun in her pocket. There was no lurch now, no searing pain. At long last the pain had gone.

She walked towards him, this time unafraid. He had hurt her, almost destroyed her, but he couldn't any more: it was over.

Harry hitched himself up to sit on the bridge, one leg resting on the ground, the other swinging. He took a heavy pull on the cigarette and tossed it into the water behind him. She was just yards away.

'Hello, Doll. You're looking good. Come here.'

His voice sounded coarse, with a sexual edge. He patted his knee, held a hand out to her.

Oh God, no . . . Please, no, she thought.

It was the coarseness that repelled her. She could smell him, the stink of cheap cologne, and now it was as if he was drawing her towards him by a thin, transparent cord.

'Money safe, is it? Ah, my girl's clever. Come here, Doll.'

She moved closer. Money: she knew that was all he had ever loved. The knowledge helped her keep moving towards him.

Then he surprised her.

'I love you, Doll. I need you. It won't work without you. Go for it again with me, one more time. I'll get down on my knees, just like the first time.'

Dolly knew he might be acting, being flippant, but there was something in his eyes that she hadn't seen for a long, long time, and she knew what it was – love. He'd always tried so hard to act like the 'guv'nor' with her, but at this moment she was stronger than him, she knew it – stronger because of the undying love she had held on to during all the years she had devoted to him, guided him, cared for him, tried to bear his children. For him, those years had meant nothing. He had only now, right now, realised he needed her.

He said it again, and this time the sound was as raw as the helpless look on his face. 'I love you, Doll.'

She was so close, she could put out her hand and touch him.

'It's what you want, isn't it?' he said.

He was what she had wanted, from the age of seventeen. She had never loved anyone else. The tears began to trickle down her cheeks. She couldn't speak; just one more step and she would be in his arms.

* * *

Vic Morgan drove his Rover straight at the heavy white gates at the main entrance to Kenwood House. The impact sent shock waves up his spine, but the gates remained closed.

Fuller and Reynolds ran from their patrol car. Morgan was now slamming his shoulder into the gates – and one finally gave way and swung open. Morgan ran back to his car and drove through.

'Crazy son of a bitch.'

Fuller ran back to the patrol car and followed Morgan through, up the driveway to the house, which was suddenly lit up starkly by their headlamps. Morgan was already running to the back of the house, Fuller and Reynolds close behind.

Morgan stopped at the top of the hill and looked. He could see Dolly, alone on the footbridge, looking into the water.

Fuller took a hold of his arm. 'I'll take it from here, Vic.'

Morgan threw him off and started running down the hill towards Dolly. As he reached the flatter ground, Fuller caught him up.

Morgan kept his voice low. 'I think she's got a gun. Go round to the right. Come from behind her.'

Fuller knew it was pointless to argue. He waited for Reynolds to join him, then they split up, moving round the lake to approach the bridge from the opposite side.

Where the hell was Rawlins?

Morgan stepped onto the bridge. Dolly turned to face him. She didn't seem surprised.

'Hand over the gun, Dolly. Please, just give me the gun.'

She lifted her arm, holding the gun out. Then she dropped it, her arm remaining stretched out to him for a moment.

Morgan stared at her. His mouth twitched.

'Why?'

Dolly turned away, facing the water.

Morgan moved in closer. He couldn't bring himself to look at her. He picked up the gun and put it in the pocket of his overcoat.

Again he asked her, 'Why? Just tell me why?'

Her voice sounded as if it belonged to someone else, a stranger, distant, expressionless. 'We didn't stand a chance. It was the only way.'

She was shivering. He thought he heard her whisper she was sorry. He was sorry too. He felt such a fool; she had made him look such a bloody fool, but then that's what he was.

He looked down and saw the body floating in the filthy water. Harry Rawlins lay face down, arms outstretched, as if reaching for the safety of the bank.

Morgan looked up. Fuller was standing at the opposite end of the bridge. Morgan walked over and handed him the gun. He spoke quietly, almost in a whisper.

'Take it. She's killed him – he's in the water under the bridge. *Wait.*'

Fuller stepped back, as if frozen by Morgan's command.

Morgan took off his overcoat, wrapped it round Dolly's shoulders, and gently guided her away from the bridge. She was shivering, her hands icy cold to the touch.

Glancing back, Morgan nodded to Fuller, said he would take her to the car. Reynolds now appeared at the side of the bridge. Fuller pointed beneath the bridge. Reynolds stepped down the side and saw the floating body.

As Morgan and Dolly moved away from the bridge, he felt her ease away from him slightly, as if she wanted to walk alone, without his help. She held her head up proudly.

Reynolds was now knee-deep in the stagnant water. He reached for the body and grabbed hold of the left leg, pulling it towards the bank. Fuller stepped down into the water to help him. Together they dragged the body closer to the bank and turned it over.

Harry Rawlins was dead. On his face was a peaceful, almost serene smile.

Fuller was shocked. He straightened up, as if the body was contagious.

Dolly turned midway up the hill and gripped Morgan's coat tightly round her for warmth. She looked back to Fuller, their eyes briefly met, and she gave him a small nod, like a tiny salute. That, too, unnerved him. He watched her continue her walk to the waiting patrol car, head held high.

Fuller sighed. It was finally over. He looked back down to the body as the water lapped round it. Then it started to rain, small drops at first, then the sky opened up and it was coming down in torrents. The wind seemed to shift the water, and the body moved slowly with it. It was as if, even in death, Rawlins was still trying to get away.

Leabharlanna Poiblí Chathair Baile Átha Cliath
Dublin City Public Libraries

AFTERWORD

Detective Inspector George Resnick died the day after he learnt that Rawlins had finally been buried. The only mourners at Resnick's funeral were DI Alex Fuller and Victor Morgan.

Morgan received a large share of the reward money from the underpass raid, and donated it to charity. He closed the investigation bureau and retired. He never made any further contact with Dolly Rawlins.

All the men involved in the jewel raid received lengthy sentences.

Bella O'Reilly caught a plane to Mexico. She never made any further contact with Dolly Rawlins either.

Shirley Miller was buried alongside her husband, Terry Miller.

Dolly Rawlins was arrested and charged with the murder of her husband. This was later dropped to manslaughter. She was sentenced to nine years' imprisonment and taken to Holloway.

The bulk of the money stolen from Samson's Security Company in the underpass raid was recovered with the help of Dolly Rawlins. The cash was stashed under the stage at a drill hall.

There was never any acknowledgment that the women had been involved in the raid. The widows took their secret to the grave – or to prison.

Audrey did as Dolly requested but she would have a long wait for her promised security.

The police have never recovered the £8 million worth of gems stolen from Amanda's nightclub.

Lynda La Plante
Readers' Club

If you enjoyed Widows' Revenge, why not join the
LYNDA LA PLANTE READERS' CLUB
by visiting www.lyndalaplante.com?

Dear Reader,

Thank you very much for reading *Widows' Revenge*. *Widows*, as many of you may know, was my first ever TV show, commissioned by Verity Lambert of Euston Films for Thames Television and it remains a special favourite of mine. In the wake of the phenomenal TV success – it became one of the highest rating series of the early 1980s – I turned the screenplay and script into a tie-in novel, which was first published in 1983. The original *Widows* ran to two series on ITV and went on to have a sequel set ten years later – *She's Out*.

Since then I have produced many TV series, films and novels. However, I was particularly delighted when award-winning film director Steve McQueen chose to use *Widows* for a major movie that was released in November 2018. Following Steve McQueen's decision to make the film, I decided to edit and reshape my original novel of *Widows* for a new audience. I loved doing it and both the reworked novel and the film were a huge success, so I have gone on to write this second book, following directly on from the events of the first book when Dolly, Linda, Shirley and Bella had successfully carried out the raid and fled to Rio after hiding the money. It's been brilliant to revisit these characters.

Dolly Rawlins was the first of my heroines to emerge into the limelight on screen and on the page. She was followed by, among others, Anna Travis and, most famously, Jane Tennison. I particularly enjoy writing about strong, independent women making their way in this tough male world. My series about the young Jane Tennison, who goes on to become the heroine of *Prime Suspect*, follows Jane as she starts out as a police detective on the streets of London. The first four books in the series – *Tennison*, *Hidden Killers*, *Good Friday* and *Murder Mile* – are all available in paperback and ebook now. There will also be a new book in the series following in Autumn 2019 – *The Dirty Dozen* – which is set in 1980 and sees Jane as the first female detective posted to the Met's renowned Flying Squad, commonly known as the 'Sweeney'. If you enjoyed *Widows' Revenge*, do look out for the Jane Tennison series.

If you would like to hear more about the next *Widows* book, or about the new book in the Tennison series, you can visit www.lyndalaplante.com, where you can join the LYNDA LA PLANTE READERS' CLUB. It only takes a few moments to sign up, there are no catches or costs and new members will automatically receive a message from me with some exclusive insight into what I am writing presently.

We promise to keep your data private and confidential, and it will never be passed on to a third party. We won't spam you with loads of emails, just get in touch now and again with news about my books, and you can unsubscribe any time you want.

And if you would like to get involved in a wider conversation about my novels, please do review *Widows' Revenge* on Amazon, on GoodReads, on any other e-store, on your own blog and social media accounts, or talk about it with friends, family or reader groups! Sharing your thoughts helps other readers, and I always enjoy hearing about what people experience from my writing.

Thanks again for your interest in *Widows' Revenge*, and I hope you'll return for *The Dirty Dozen*, the fifth in the Jane Tennison series. And you can read the first chapter of *The Dirty Dozen* following this letter.

With my very best wishes,

Lynda La Plante

THE DIRTY DOZEN

**The fifth book in the Sunday Times bestselling
Jane Tennison series.**

April 1980 and Jane is the first female detective to be posted
to the Met's renowned Flying Squad, commonly known as
the 'Sweeney'. Based at Rigg Approach in East London,
they investigate armed robberies on banks, cash in
transit and other business premises.

Jane thinks her transfer is on merit and is surprised to discover
she is actually part of a short term internal experiment,
intended to have a calming influence on a team that
likes to dub themselves as the 'Dirty Dozen'.

The men on the squad don't think a woman is up to the dangers
they face when dealing with some of London's most ruthless
armed criminals, who think the only 'good cop' is a dead cop.
Determined to prove she's as good as the men, Jane discovers
from a reliable witness that a gang is going to carry out
a massive robbery involving millions of pounds.

But she doesn't know who they are, or where and
when they will strike . . .

Coming 2019

CHAPTER ONE

It was a rainy and overcast April morning as the brown 1976 Mark 4 Ford Cortina saloon parked up on the offside of Aylmer Road, a few meters down from the junction with Leytonstone High Road. The four men in the vehicle sat in silence as the engine slowly ticked over, and the windscreen wipers swept away the rain. The men were dressed in blue boiler suits, heavy black donkey jackets and leather driving gloves. The heating was on to stop the windows misting up, but it made the men sweat profusely and a musty odour filled the car. The two men in the front used their jacket sleeves to wipe the condensation off the windscreen, so they could get a better view of Barclays Bank on the far side of the High Road. The bank manager was holding an umbrella as he opened the large wooden front doors for business at 9:30 a.m. Smartly dressed in a three-piece grey pinstripe suit, white shirt and tie, he stood to one side to let two customers in, and looked up the High Road, which was quieter than usual for a Thursday morning, due to the bad weather.

As the manager turned and walked back inside, the driver of the Cortina put a cap on and opened the car door. He hadn't seen the elderly lady pulling a canvas shopping trolley along the pavement, and narrowly missed hitting her with the door. The lady swore at him, but the driver ignored her and pulled the peak of his cap down, before walking towards the bank.

As the old lady moved off, one of the men in the back of the Cortina reached under the driver's seat and pulled out a twelve bore, double-barrel, sawn-off shotgun. He pushed the unlocking lever to one side to 'break' the gun, then placed a cartridge in each chamber. Holding the wooden stock of the gun with one hand, he snapped the barrel closed with a well-practiced upward flick of his wrist, then slid the shotgun into a self-made pocket inside his jacket.

* * *

Jane drove up and down Rigg Approach twice, but couldn't see a police station or blue lamp anywhere. She was becoming frustrated and beginning to wonder if she'd got the right place, as she appeared to be in an industrial site with a variety of different businesses. She parked her yellow Volkswagen Golf near a mobile burger van, and got out to speak with the owner. Pulling her coat up over her head, to protect her hair from the rain, she ran across the road.

'Excuse me, is there a police station near here?' she asked.

'There's no nick around here, love ... the nearest are Stoke Newington or Hackney – a couple of miles away, but in opposite directions.'

'I know where they are, but I'm looking for the Flying Squad offices, which I was told were in Rigg Approach.'

'The Sweeney work out of that place over there, not a nick,' he said, pointing to a two storey, grey brick office building with a flat roof. 'I know most of the lads, as they're regulars at my van. Anyone in particular you're looking for?'

'The DCI. I've got an appointment with him.'

'Bill Murphy? That's his office on the top floor – far right. I don't think he's in yet, as he hasn't been down for his usual bacon and egg roll.'

'Thanks for your help.'

Jane crossed the road and on closer inspection thought the building looked run down. Although there were large windows on both floors, the ground floor ones all had faded white metal Venetian blinds, which were closed. The metal front door had a push button entry number pad above the handle, and an intercom on the wall beside it. As Jane pressed the button on the intercom, she wondered what the building would be like on the inside.

'How can I help you?' a female voice asked over the intercom.

'I'm WDS Tennison. I'm here to see DCI Murphy.'

'Is he expecting you?' the woman asked, in a haughty manner.

'Yes, he is. I start on the Flying Squad today and was told to report to his office for 10 a.m.'

'It's only 9.30, and he didn't mention you to me . . . new officers generally start on Mondays.'

'I've been in court all week and . . . Look, I'm getting soaked out here; can you please open the door or tell me the number for the entry pad?'

The woman sighed. 'I suppose so . . . the Squad office is on the first floor.'

Jane thought the woman was rude and wondered if she was a detective on the squad or clerical staff. As she waited for the electronic lock to be released, she flapped her coat to remove some of the rain. As it was her first day on the Flying Squad, Jane wanted to look good and had worn a blue two-piece skirt suit, white blouse, stockings and black high-heeled shoes. She heard the electric lock on the door buzz, and leaned forward to open it. Her hand was on the round knob when the door was pulled open with force from the inside, causing Jane to stumble forward. She felt a hand grab her arm tightly, stopping her from falling over.

'You all right, luv?' a deep male voice asked, as the man helped her straighten up.

Jane was dwarfed by the man. She noticed he had a pickaxe handle in his left hand. He was about six foot seven, with wide shoulders and a muscular frame. He had blonde hair, blue eyes and boyish looks. He was dressed in a white England rugby shirt with the red rose emblem on the left breast.

'Come on, Bax, I need to get the motor fired up,' the man behind him said, in a broad Scottish accent, as he used a pickaxe handle to usher Jane and Bax to one side. He was in his late thirties, and although slightly smaller, at about six foot two, he had a large beer belly.

Bax frowned, 'All right, Cam, less haste more speed.'

Jane heard footsteps running down the metal stairs and a male voice called out, 'Right, I'm tooled up, so we're good to go, Bax. The Guv and the Colonel are booking out their guns and will go in Cam's car. Teflon is on his way round the front with Dabs in the Triumph for us.'

Jane instantly recognised the voice of Detective Sergeant Stanley, whom she had worked with on the 'dip squad' a few years ago. They had also been involved in the hunt for an active IRA unit that had bombed Covent Garden Tube station. Stanley had helped to disarm a car bomb and been awarded the Queens Police Medal for his bravery.

Jane looked up and saw the short, slim frame of Stanley tucking a police issue .38 revolver into a shoulder holster under his brown leather jacket. He still had his long, dark straggly hair, but had grown a 'Jason King' style moustache, which on first sight didn't suit him.

'Hi, Stanley.' Jane waved. She still didn't know what his Christian name was, as everyone just called him 'Stanley'.

'Tennison, what you doing here?'

'I've been transferred to the Flying Squad.'

'Have you? That's news to me.'

'And me,' Bax said.

Jane thought it strange that no one seemed to know about her transfer, and began to wonder if she'd got the right starting day.

'Are you off on a shout?' she asked.

'Yeah, we just got a call from I.R. There might be a blagging about to go down in Leytonstone. Gotta go, so I'll catch up with you later,' Stanley said, and hurried out of the building with Bax.

Jane started to walk up the stairs when two more men appeared armed with .38 revolvers carried in belt holsters around their waists. The man in front was wearing a blue baseball cap and tight white T-shirt, which accentuated his muscular frame and large biceps. As he hurried down the stairs two at a time, Jane moved quickly to one side to let him pass.

The man behind wasn't rushing and stopped in front of Jane. He had a healthy-looking complexion and misshapen nose, which looked like it had been broken in a fight. He wasn't dressed casually like the others, and wore a tailored slim-fit grey suit and white open-neck shirt. He sniffed and stared at Jane with narrow eyes.

'You Tennison?'

'Yes, Sir,' she replied, sensing his air of authority.

'I'm DI Kingston. We're short on the ground today as some of the team are out with the surveillance squad on another job, so you may as well come with us.'

'What, to Leytonstone?'

'No, to a tea party,' he replied, drily.

'DCI Murphy was expecting . . .'

'He's not back from Scotland Yard yet, so come on, shift your backside.'

Kingston had the swagger of a confident man and Jane followed him out to the street where she saw Stanley sitting in the front of a dark green four door Triumph 2500S, which had a blue magnetic flashing light on top of it. A black man was driving and Bax was in the back, with a diminutive looking man wearing dark glasses next to him.

Behind the Triumph, Cam was in the driver's seat of a four door black BMW 525i, again with a flashing light on the roof and its engine running.

'We're in the beamer,' Kingston told her.

'Come on, Guv!' the man in the white T-shirt shouted from the back seat of the BMW.

Kingston got in the front passenger seat as Jane ran around the back of the car and got in behind Cam, but there was little room for her legs as the driver's seat was almost as far back as it would go. No sooner was she in the car than Cam pulled the automatic gear stick to drive, and pushed the accelerator pedal to the floor. The car took off at high speed, causing Jane to jolt backwards, and it felt like someone had pushed her hard in the chest as her back slammed against the seat. As Cam braked at the T-junction, Jane felt her body lurch forward, but just managed to get her hands on the back of his seat to brace herself before her head hit it. The Colonel had his feet firmly propped up against the front passenger seat and a large London *A–Z* open on his lap.

'Fastest route is left on to Lea Bridge Road, then right . . .'

'I've worked this manor for years, so I know how to get there, Colonel,' Cam said calmly, and turned the siren on.

Kingston opened the glove box and picked up the radio mike. 'M.P, from Central 888 receiving, over . . .'

'Yes, go ahead, Central 888, M.P. over,' a male voice replied.

'We are en route with Central 887 to Aylmer Road and the men acting suspiciously near Barclays bank. Any updates?'

'The vehicle is still in situ. It's a brown Mark 4 Ford Cortina, 1.6L saloon, index Sierra Lima Mike 273 Romeo. The vehicle is not reported stolen and may have false plates as the PNC shows a blue Mark 4, 1.6 GL saloon with a registered keeper in Sussex.'

'Can you give me the informant's details, please?' Kingston got out his notebook and pen.

'Fiona Simpson. She's the landlady of the Crown public house on the High Road and corner of Aylmer. She lives on the premises and noticed the suspect vehicle parked up with its engine running and wipers on. The driver has left the vehicle and turned right into the High Road, out of sight of the informant. He's wearing a grey cap, black donkey jacket and blue overalls.'

'Number of other occupants in the Cortina?' Kingston asked.

'The informant can only see the nearside of the vehicle and states two people, believed male, and wearing dark clothing, but there may be three including the driver.'

Kingston ran his hand through his hair. 'There could be a robbery about to take place, M.P. We and Central 887 are armed gunships. Our ETA is about four minutes, so tell uniform to hold back until we get there.'.

'Received and understood . . . we will advise you of any developments . . . M.P. over.'

Jane felt uneasy. As it was her first day on the infamous 'Sweeney', she wasn't sure what was expected of her, especially if DI Kingston was right in thinking an armed robbery was about to take place.

* * *

The driver of the Cortina returned to the car. 'She's coming,' he said, as he got in the car and put on a full-face balaclava, which had a mouth and eye holes cut out. The two men in the back also put on balaclavas, but the man in the front passenger seat pulled a light brown stocking over his head, which distorted the features of his face. Having adjusted the stocking so it was comfortable, he reached into his jacket pocket and took out a Second World War 9mm German Luger, then pulled back the toggle, which loaded a bullet from the magazine into the chamber.

The four men sat and watched as the blue Ford transit Securicor van pulled up outside the bank. The driver remained in the van while his colleague went to the rear and looked up and down the High Road, before knocking three times, pausing and then knocking twice.

The passenger from the front of the Cortina and the two men from the back got out of the car and strode with purpose towards the bank. The men knew exactly what they had to do, as everything had been well planned thanks to the information they had received about the cash in transit delivery. They knew from experience that robbing the Securicor van should take no more than a minute. As the cash box appeared in the chute at the rear of the van, the three men pounced with military style precision.

* * *

Jane was beginning to feel nauseous due to the speed Cam was driving and the way he was skidding the car around corners and roundabouts in the rain. She'd been in police pursuits before, but never encountered high-speed driving as dangerous as this.

'This is our new WDS, Jane Tennison,' Kingston told the others, as he lit a cigarette and handed one to the Colonel.

'Hello,' Jane said.

'You really been posted to the squad?' the Colonel asked as he lit his cigarette.

'Yes, Sir.' She put her hand out to shake his.

He didn't reciprocate. 'Well, you've got a bit more essence than most plonks.'

Jane didn't have a clue what he meant by essence and wasn't sure she should ask.

Kingston laughed, 'Gorman's not an officer; he's an ex-military Corporal and a DC, who thinks you're better looking than most female officers.'

Jane blushed, feeling embarrassed that the Colonel thought she was 'essence'. The rim of his cap cast a shadow over his steely eyes and accentuated his high cheek bones and a dimpled chin. She noticed part of a tattoo, below his t-shirt sleeve, on his right upper arm. There was a globe with a laurel wreath either side and an anchor at the bottom with the Latin words *Per Mare, Per Terram* underneath.

'Is that an army tattoo on your arm?' she asked.

The Colonel looked offended. 'No, it is not! I was a Marine Commando in the Royal Navy before I joined the Met. My name's Ken, but this bunch of nob heads decided to call me the Colonel. The tattoo is the Marines insignia and the Latin means 'By Sea, By Land'.

'Ironic really as he can't swim,' Cam laughed.

'Shut up, O.F.D,' the Colonel said, and looked at Jane. 'In case you're wondering, O.F.D means 'only the fucking driver', as he's a lowly PC.'

'I like to think of myself as a shit hot taxi driver without whom they'd get nowhere,' Cam replied, as he went the wrong way around a roundabout to turn right.

Kingston smiled. 'As much as we all hate to admit it, Constable Cameron Murray is the best Class 1 driver in the Met. He even souped-up this car's engine himself so it outperforms every other Flying Squad vehicle.'

Jane could sense the mutual bond of respect and comradery amongst the officers and felt a bit of an outsider. She instinctively knew that she would have to prove herself a capable detective if she wanted to become part of the team.

'What should I do when we get there?' she asked, wanting to show her enthusiasm.

'Stay in the car with Cam,' Kingston and the Colonel said in unison.

'Central 888 from M.P., receiving, over.' The same male voice from the Met's control room asked over the radio.

'888 receiving,' Kingston replied.

'A Securicor van has pulled up at the bank and three men dressed in blue boiler suits, donkey jackets and head masks have just left the vehicle.

'They're going to rob the van, not the bank,' Kingston said calmly. 'We're about two minutes away and approaching silent,' he replied, as Cam switched off the car's siren.

* * *

The man with the sawn-off shotgun tapped the Securicor driver's window with the barrel and rotated his finger, indicating to him to wind it down, which the driver quickly did. The man leant in to the van and pulled the key from the ignition, then spoke in a deep tone to disguise his natural voice.

'Keep your hands on the steering wheel. You so much as twitch towards the horn or alarm and I'll blow your fucking head off.'

The Securicor driver shook with fear as he nodded and gripped the steering wheel so hard his knuckles turned white.

The man with the Luger was at the back of the van, pushing the barrel of the gun in to the neck of the other Securicor Guard, who was frozen to the spot. The unarmed robber grabbed the metal case with the money in it from the guard's hand and pushed him down on to his knees. He leant forward and whispered, so as not to alert the security guard in the back of the van.

'Tell him to put the other case in the chute.'

The guard's voice trembled as he said, 'there's only the one.'

The robber shook his head. 'Don't lie, son . . . I don't want to hurt you, but I will if . . . t

'Frank, George . . . What's happening out there? Is everything all right?' The third guard shouted from inside the van.

The man with the Luger moved round and put the gun to the forehead of the kneeling guard. 'Last chance, son . . . tell him to put the fucking case in the chute.' The guard was unable to stop shaking and the fear in his voice was evident. 'Everything's fine. You can send out the other case.'

Suddenly the van's alarm went off, closely followed by the sound of a shotgun being fired once. The two robbers at the back of the van ran to the front and saw their colleague standing over a young man lying on the ground clutching his stomach and crying out in pain.

The robber with the shotgun was breathing heavily, causing a white foam of spittle to build up around the mouth hole of his balaclava. 'The fucking idiot tried to get the shotgun off me.' The unarmed man raised his hand to shut his colleague up. The man with the Luger turned and headed back to the rear of the van, intent on getting the second cash box. The unarmed robber grabbed him by the arm, shook his head and pulled him towards the Cortina, which skidded to a halt beside the Securicor van.

* * *

'Central 888 from M.P., receiving over.'

'Go ahead 888, over,' Kingston replied.

'Sounds of gunshots heard outside the bank. Local uniform units requesting permission to move in.'

'ETA, Cam?' a concerned looking Kingston asked.

Cam hit the accelerator. 'A minute, tops, Guv.'

'M.P. from 888 local units can move in. Is India 99 in the air?' Kingston asked, referring to the police helicopters call sign.

'No, at present 99 is refuelling, but should be airborne shortly.'

Kingston threw the radio mike against the dashboard. 'Fuck it. They'll be well on their toes before we get there!'

'Central 888, update from M.P. Call received for an ambulance to Barclay's bank, Leytonstone . . . one man shot in stomach by an armed suspect.'

The Colonel punched the roof of the car. 'Bastards. If I get my hands on em I'll fuckin kill em!'

* * *

As the three robbers jumped into the Cortina, they could hear the police sirens getting closer. The unarmed man put the Securicor cash box in a travel bag on the back of the vehicle and got in. The driver knew from experience the 'Old Bill' would use the main streets, so he decided to take the back roads and drive within the speed limit. As he indicated right, to turn into Grove Road from the High Road, two uniform officers in a marked Rover 3500 V8 police car came flying past in the opposite direction, sirens blaring and blue lights flashing. The unarmed man looked over his shoulder, out of the rear window, and saw the brake lights of the police car come on as it skidded to a sudden halt and started to do a U-turn.

'They've seen us . . . put your foot down and get us out of here,' he said calmly to the driver, who pressed the accelerator hard and turned right across the path of an oncoming car, which swerved across the road and hit another vehicle head on in the inside lane.

'This car's not as powerful as theirs. Maybe we should take a side street down here and bail out while they can't see us,' the man with the shotgun suggested.

As the driver approached the junction with Mornington Road he looked in his rear-view mirror and saw the police car in the distance.

'That ain't an option, they're closing on us.' He drove straight across the junction into Woodville Road without stopping.

An oncoming car clipped the rear of the Cortina, knocking the bumper off and causing the car to judder and swerve erratically. The driver gripped the steering wheel hard to maintain control, but the Cortina side-swiped a parked car and careered across the road. Left with no alternative, the driver hit the brakes hard and skidded across the road, towards a parked car. The four men lurched forward as the car came to an abrupt halt inches from another vehicle. The man with the Luger smashed his head on the front windscreen, causing a deep cut to his forehead, which began to bleed heavily through his stocking mask.

'Fuck dis for a game of soldiers,' he said, in a broad Irish accent, and got out of the car.

'Get back in or I'll go without you,' the driver shouted, but was ignored, so he leaned over and pulled the front passenger door closed, then reversed to straighten the car up and drive off.

'Stop!' the unarmed man snarled, then grabbed the shotgun from his colleague's lap and opened the car door.

* * *

'Central 888 from M.P. receiving, over.'

Kingston picked up the radio mike. 'We're a mile away at the Langthorne Park end of the High Road and nearly on scene, M.P.'

'Received . . . I'm linking you up with Juliet 1, who are in pursuit of suspect vehicle Sierra Lima Mike 273 Romeo,' the radio operator replied.

'Listen up for their location, Colonel, and find it in the *A–Z*,' said Cam.

The calm voice of the PC in Juliet 1 came over the radio. 'Suspect vehicle has turned right into Grove Road . . . heading towards junction with Mornington Road.'

'Got it. Cam, Grove Road is the next right after Aylmer Road. Your best bet to catch up is a right into Lister Road, which leads into Mornington Road. I'll tell you when Lister is coming up,' the Colonel said.

Thanks, mate.' Cam was now swerving in and out of the inside lane to the offside lane to overtake other vehicles.

Jane was clutching the back of the driver's seat with one hand, and the door pull with the other, to stop herself from being flung about the back seat. Although the speed and manner of Cam's driving scared her, the adrenalin rush to her body was strangely stimulating. She felt excited to be involved in the apprehension of four armed robbers on her first day with the Flying Squad.

The radio operator on Juliet 1 came back on the radio, the pitch of his voice becoming slightly higher as the pursuit progressed.

'Suspect vehicle accelerating. Forty . . . forty-five . . . fifty miles per hour. Jesus Christ he's gone straight across the junction without stopping.' There was a brief pause before the officer continued, 'Suspect vehicle has been hit by another car and now stopped in Woodville Road.'

'We're gonna get the bastards. Next right, Cam,' the Colonel said, and Cam turned into Lister Road.

'They're probably about to bail out and do a runner,' Kingston surmised.

'They won't get far if Teflon's after them . . . he's quicker than Allan Wells,' Cam replied, referring to the British and Commonwealth sprint champion.

'All units from Juliet 1 . . . a suspect is decamping from the front passenger seat towards the rear of the vehicle.'

The man with the Luger stood in the road as the police car approached, then raised the gun to eye level and started firing. As a bullet penetrated the windscreen, the radio operator continued his commentary.

'Lima one under attack, suspect armed and firing at us!' he shouted, and the distress in his voice was obvious to everyone listening in.

The sound of gun fire could be heard over the radio, as well as the impact thud of the bullet as it penetrated the windscreen. Ducking to avoid the shots, the police driver was finding it hard to see where he was going, but his intention was to run the armed robber over.

'I've been hit . . . I've been hit!' the radio operator cried out.

Next there was the sound of a loud bang, followed by screeching tyres, then a sickening crunch of metal and breaking glass before the radio went dead. It was clear the police vehicle had come to an abrupt halt after a serious crash.

'That sounded like a shotgun going off,' Cam remarked, and the Colonel nodded.

'Let's hope they're both alive.' Kingston replied, but feared the worst.

Want to read
NEW BOOKS
before anyone else?

Like getting
FREE BOOKS?

Enjoy sharing your
OPINIONS?

Discover

READERS FIRST
Read. Love. Share.

Sign up today to win your first free book:
readersfirst.co.uk

For Terms and Conditions see readersfirst.co.uk/pages/terms-of-service